Praise for Gail Gaymer Martin and her novels

"*Upon A Midnight Clear*, by Gail Gaymer Martin, is an emotional, skillfully written story about mature subject matter."
—*Romantic Times BOOKclub*

"*Upon a Midnight Clear* is a special story of rediscovery and healing. I cried through the entire read and couldn't put it down. Refreshing, giving fresh hope to those who experienced hurt and loss in their past, *Upon A Midnight Clear* is a tender journey of healing and renewal you don't want to miss."
—Cheryl Wolverton, RITA® Award finalist

"Gail Gaymer Martin writes with compassion and understanding in *Secrets of the Heart*. Don't miss this happily ever after story!"
—*Romantic Times BOOKclub*

"Martin...writes a gentle story about two devout people who are a perfect match. The gentle development of the love between them is heartwarming."
—*Oakland Press* on *Secrets of the Heart*

GAIL GAYMER MARTIN

Upon a Midnight Clear

Secrets of the Heart

Published by Steeple Hill Books™

STEEPLE HILL BOOKS

ISBN-13: 978-0-373-65269-3
ISBN-10: 0-373-65269-0

UPON A MIDNIGHT CLEAR AND SECRETS OF THE HEART

This edition published by arrangement with Steeple Hill Books.

www.SteepleHill.com

Printed in U.S.A.

CONTENTS

Books by Gail Gaymer Martin

Love Inspired

Upon a Midnight Clear #117
Secrets of the Heart #147
A Love for Safekeeping #161
**Loving Treasures* #177
**Loving Hearts* #199
Easter Blessings #202
"The Butterfly Garden"
The Harvest #223
"All Good Gifts"
**Loving Ways* #231
**Loving Care* #239
Adam's Promise #259
**Loving Promises* #291
**Loving Feelings* #303
**Loving Tenderness* #323
†*In His Eyes* #361

*Loving
†Michigan Islands

Steeple Hill Books

The Christmas Kite
That Christmas Feeling
"Christmas Moon"

GAIL GAYMER MARTIN

is still amazed that she's an author, When friends share experiences, they often stop short and ask, "Will this be in your next novel?" Sometimes it is. Gail lives in Michigan with her husband, Bob, her dearest friend and greatest support. She loves the privilege of writing stories that touch people's hearts and share God's promises.

Gail is multipublished in nonfiction and has written over thirty works of fiction. There are over one million copies of her books in print. Her novels have received numerous awards: a 2005 Booksellers Best, a Holt Medallion in 2001 and 2003, the Texas Winter Rose 2003, the American Christian Fiction Writers 2002 Book of the Year Award and the *Romantic Times BOOKclub* best Love Inspired Novel in 2002.

When not behind her computer, Gail enjoys a busy life—traveling, presenting workshops at conferences, as well as speaking at churches, business groups and civic events, She is a soloist and member of the choir at her church, as well as a handbell and hand-chimes ringer. She sings with the Detroit Lutheran Singers.

She enjoys hearing from her readers. Writer to her at P.O. Box 760063, Lathrup Village, MI, 48076 or at gail@gailmartin.com. Visit her Web site at www.gailmartin.com.

UPON A MIDNIGHT CLEAR

Then you will call upon me and come and pray to me, and I will listen to you. And you will seek me and find me, when you seek me with all your heart.

—*Jeremiah* 29:12–13

Dedicated to my sister, Jan,
who knows the sorrow of losing a child.
And in living memory of her infant daughters,
Lisa Marie and Beth Ann, who live with Jesus.

Thanks to my husband, Bob, for his devotion,
support and hours of proofreading. To Flo Stano
for her nursing expertise, and to the
Bedford Chamber of Commerce for their
invaluable information.

Chapter One

Callie Randolph scanned the employment ads of thc *Indianapolis News.* Her eyes lit upon a Help Wanted entry: *Special child, aged five, needs professional caregiver. Live-in. Good wage. Contact David Hamilton. 812 area code.* Southern Indiana, she assumed. "Live-in," she wanted. But a child?

She raised her head from the ad and caught her mother, eyeing her.

"You've been quiet since you got home," Grace Randolph said, resting back in the kitchen chair. "Tell me about the funeral."

"It was nice, as funerals go. But sad, so close to the holidays." Ethel's death, coming as it did on the footsteps of Christmas, jolted Callie with the memories of a birth six Christmases earlier. Pushing away the invading thoughts, Callie shifted in her chair and focused on her mother. "More people than I would expect at the funeral for someone in her nineties, but I suppose most of the mourners were friends and business acquaintances of Ethel's children. The family has a name in the community."

"Ah yes, when we're old, people forget."

"No, it's not that they forget. When we're *that* old, many of our own friends and acquaintances have already died. Makes coming to a funeral difficult." Callie hoped to lighten Grace's negative mood. "It'll feel strange not taking care of Ethel. She had the faith of a saint and a smile right to the end. Always had a kind word." She raised her eyes, hoping her mother had heard her last statement.

Grace stared across the room as if lost in thought, and Callie's mind drifted to the funeral and the preacher's comforting words. *"Ethel lived a full and glorious life, loving her Lord and her family."* Callie pictured the wrinkled, loving face of her dying patient. Ethel's earthly years had definitely been full and glorious.

In contrast, Callie's nearly twenty-six years had been empty and dull. Her dreams had died that horrible March day that she tried to block from her memory. Her life seemed buried in its own tomb of guilt and sorrow.

"So, about the funeral—?"

Callie slammed the door on her thoughts and focused on her mother.

"Tell me about the music? Any hymns?" Grace asked.

Callie eyed her, sensing an ulterior motive in her question. "Real nice, Mom. Organ music and hymns."

"Which hymns?"

Callie pulled her shoulders back, feeling the muscles tightening along the cords of her neck. "'Amazing Grace,' 'Softly and Tenderly.'"

"I can hear you singing that one. So beautiful."

Callie fought the desire to bolt from the room. She sensed an argument heading her way. Instead, she aimed her eyes at the newspaper clutched in her hands.

Grace leaned on an elbow. "So what will you do now?"

"Find a new job, I suppose." She hesitated, wondering what comment she'd receive about her newest resolve. "But I've made a decision." Callie met her mother's eyes. "I'm not going to give elderly care anymore. I'll find something else."

"Praise the Lord, you've come to your senses. Callie, you have a nursing degree, but you continue to waste your time with the deathwatch. You need to live and use the talent God gave you."

Deep creases furrowed Callie's forehead. "Please don't call it the deathwatch. Caring for older people has been a blessing. And I *do* use my talents." She shook her head, amazed at her mother's attitude. "Do you think it's easy to nurse someone who's dying? I use as many skills as I would in a regular hospital."

Grace fell back against the chair. "I'm sorry. I don't mean to belittle your work, but it's not a life for a young woman. Look at you. You're beautiful and intelligent, yet you spend your life sitting in silent rooms, listening to old people muttering away about nothing but useless memories. What about a husband...and children? Don't you want a life for yourself?"

She flinched at her mother's words. "Please, don't get on that topic, Mom. You know how I feel about that."

"I wish I knew when you got these odd ideas. They helped put your father in his grave. He had such hopes for you."

Callie stiffened as icy tendrils slithered through her. How many times was she reminded of how she had helped kill her father? After his death three years earlier, the doctor had said her dad had been a walking time bomb from fatty foods, cigarettes and a type-A personality. Though guilt poked at her, she knew she hadn't caused his death. Yet, she let her mother rile her.

Grace scowled with a piercing squint. "I think it began when you stopped singing," she said, releasing a lengthy, audible sigh. "Such a beautiful voice. Like a meadowlark."

"Stop. Stop, Mother." Callie slammed her hand on the tabletop. "Please, don't call me that."

Grace looked taken aback. "Well, I'm sorry. What's gotten into you?" She gaped at Callie. "You're as white as a sheet. I only called you a—"

"Please, don't say it again, Mother." Callie pressed her forehead into her hand.

"I don't know what's wrong with you." Grace sat for a moment before she began her litany. "I don't know, Callie. I could cry when I think of it. Everyone said you sang like an angel."

Callie stared at the newspaper, the black letters blurring. Her mother wouldn't stop until she'd made her point. Callie ached inside when she thought about the music she'd always loved. She struggled to keep her voice calm and controlled. "I lost my interest in music, that's all." Her fingernails dug into the flesh of her fisted hand.

"Your father had such hopes for you. He dreamed you'd pass your audition with the Jim McKee Singers. But his hopes were buried along with him in his grave."

Callie modulated her pitch, and her words came out in a monotone. "I didn't pass the audition. I told you."

"I can't believe that, Callie. You've said it, but everyone knew you could pass the audition. Either you didn't try or…I don't know. Being part of Paul Ivory's ministry would be any girl's dream. And the Jim McKee Singers traveled with him in the summer all over the country, so it wouldn't have interfered with your college studies. And then you just quit singing. I can't understand you."

"Mother, let's not argue about something that happened years ago."

"But it's not just that, Callie. I hate to bring it up, but since the baby, you've never been the same."

Unexpected tears welled in Callie's eyes, tears she usually fought. But today they sneaked in behind the emotions elicited by Ethel's death, and the memory of the baby's Christmas birth dragged them out of hiding.

Callie had never seen the daughter she bore six years earlier. The hospital had their unbending policy, and her parents had given her the same ultimatum. A girl placing a child for adoption should not see her baby.

She begged and pleaded with her parents to allow her to keep her daughter. But they would have no part of it. She struggled in her thoughts—longing to finish an argument that held weight. In the end, her parents were correct. A child needed a secure and loving home. Adoption was best for her baby daughter. But not for Callie. Against her wishes, Callie signed the papers releasing her baby for adoption.

Grace breathed a ragged sigh. "Maybe your father and I made a mistake. You were so young, a whole lifetime ahead of you. We thought you could get on with your life. If you'd only told us who the young man was—but you protected him. Any decent young man would have stood up and accepted his responsibilities. For all we knew, you never told him, either."

"We've gone over this before. It's in the past. It's over. It's too late." She clutched the newspaper, crumpling the paper beneath her fingers.

"We meant well. Even your brother and sister begged you to tell us who the fellow was. You could have been married, at least. Given the baby a name, so we could hold our head up in public. But, no."

Callie folded the paper and clasped it in her trembling hand. She rose without comment. What could she say that she hadn't said a million times already? "I'm going to my room. I have a headache." As she passed through the doorway, she glanced over her shoulder and saw her mother's strained expression.

Before Grace could call after her, Callie rushed up the staircase to her second-floor bedroom and locked the door. She could no longer bear to hear her mother's sad-voiced recollections. No one but Callie knew the true story. She prayed that the vivid picture, too much like a horror movie, would leave her. Yet so many nights the ugly dream tore into her sleep, and again and again she relived the life-changing moments.

She plopped on the corner of the bed, massaging her neck. The newspaper ad appeared in her mind. *David Hamilton.* She grabbed a pen from her desk, reread the words, and jotted his name and telephone number on a scratch pad. She'd check with Christian Care Services tomorrow and see what they had available. At least she'd have the number handy if she wanted to give Mr. Hamilton a call later.

She tossed the pad on her dressing table and stretched out on the bed. A child? The thoughts of caring for a child frightened her. Would a child, especially a sick child, stir her longing?

She'd resolved to make a change in her life. Images of caring for adults marched through her head—the thought no longer appealed to her. Nursing in a doctor's office or hospital held no interest for her: patients coming and going, a nurse with no involvement in their lives. She wanted to be part of a life, to make a difference.

She rolled on her side, dragging her fingers through the old-fashioned chenille spread. The room looked so much the way it had when she was a teenager. How long had her mother owned the antiquated bedspread?

Since college, her parents' home had been only a stop-off place between jobs. Live-in care was her preference—away from her parents' guarded eyes, as they tried to cover their sorrow and shame over all that had happened.

When she'd graduated from college, she had weighed all the issues. Geriatric care seemed to encompass all her aspirations. At that time, she could never have considered child care. Her wounds were too fresh.

Her gaze drifted to the telephone. The name *David Hamilton* entered her mind again. Looking at her wrist-watch, she wondered if it was too late to call him. Eight in the evening seemed early enough. Curiosity galloped through her mind. What did the ad mean—a "special" child? Was the little one mentally or physically challenged? A boy or girl? Where did the family live? Questions spun in her head. What would calling hurt? She'd at least have her questions answered.

She swung her legs over the edge of the bed, rose, and grabbed the notepad. What specific information would she like to know? She organized her thoughts, then punched in the long-distance number.

A rich baritone voice filled the line, and when Callie heard his commanding tone, she caught her breath. Job interviews and query telephone calls had never bothered her. Tonight her wavering emotions addled her. She drew in a lengthy, relaxing breath, then introduced herself and stated her business.

Hamilton's self-assured manner caught her off guard. "I'm looking for a professional, Ms. Randolph. What is your background?"

His tone intimidated her, and her responses to his questions sounded reticent in her ears. "It's *Miss* Randolph, and I'm a professional, licensed nurse." She paused to steady her nerves. "But I've preferred to work as a home caregiver rather than in a hospital.

The past four years, I've had elderly patients, but I'm looking for a change."

"Change?"

His abruptness struck her as arrogant, and Callie could almost sense his arched eyebrow.

"Yes. I've been blessed working with the older patients, but I'd like to work with…a child."

"I see." A thoughtful silence hung in the air. "You're a religious woman, Miss Randolph?"

His question confounded her. Then she remembered she'd used the word *blessed*. Not sure what he expected, she answered honestly. "I'm a Christian, if that's what you're asking."

She waited for a response. Yet only silence filled the line. With no response forthcoming, she asked, "What do you mean by 'special,' Mr. Hamilton? In the ad, you mentioned you needed a caregiver for a 'special child.'"

He hesitated only a moment. "Natalie...Nattie's a bright child. She was always active, delightful—but since her mother's death two years ago, she's become...withdrawn." His voice faded.

"Withdrawn?"

"Difficult to explain in words. I'd rather the prospective caregiver meet her and see for herself what I mean. Nattie no longer speaks. She barely relates to anyone. She lives in her own world."

Callie's heart lurched at the thought of a child bearing such grief. "I see. I understand why you're worried." Still, panic crept over her like cold fingers inching along her spine. Her heart already ached for the child. Could she control her own feelings? Her mind spun with flashing red warning lights.

"I've scared you off, Miss Randolph." Apprehension resounded in his statement.

She cringed, then lied a little. "No, no. I was thinking."

"Thinking?" His tone softened. "I've been looking for someone for some time now, and I seem to scare people off with the facts...the details of Nattie's problem."

The image of a lonely, motherless child tugged at her compassion. What grief he had to bear. "I'm not frightened of the facts," Callie said, but in her heart, she was frightened of herself. "I have some personal concerns that came to mind." She fumbled for what to say next. "For example, I don't know where you live. Where are you located, sir?"

"We live in Bedford, not too far from Bloomington."

Bedford. The town was only a couple of hours from her mother's house. She paused a moment. "I have some personal matters I need to consider. I'll call you as soon as I know whether I'd like to be interviewed for the position. I hope that's okay with you."

"Certainly. That's fine. I understand." Discouragement sounded in his voice.

She bit the corner of her lip. "Thank you for your time."

After she hung up the telephone, Callie sat for a while without moving. She should have been honest. She'd already made her decision. A position like that wouldn't be wise at all. She was too vulnerable.

Besides, she wasn't sure she wanted to work for David Hamilton. His tone seemed stiff and arrogant. A child needed a warm, loving father, not one who was bitter and inflexible. She would have no patience with a man like that.

David Hamilton leaned back in his chair, his hand still clasping the telephone. *Useless.* In two months, his ad had resulted in only three telephone calls. One courageous soul came for an interview, but with her first look at Nattie, David saw the answer in the woman's eyes.

He supposed, as well, the "live-in" situation might be an obstacle for some. With no response locally, he'd extended his ad further away, as far as Indianapolis. But this Miss Randolph had been the only call so far.

He longed for another housekeeper like Miriam. Her overdue retirement left a hole nearly as big, though not as horrendous, as Sara's death. No one could replace Miriam.

A shudder filtered through him. *No one could replace Sara.*

Nothing seemed worse than a wife's death, but when it happened, he had learned the truth. Worse was a child losing her mother. Yet the elderly housekeeper had stepped in with all her love and wisdom and taken charge of the household, wrapping each of them in her motherly arms.

Remembering Miriam's expert care, David preferred to hire a more mature woman as a nanny. The voice he heard on the telephone tonight sounded too young, perhaps nearly a child herself. He mentally calculated her age. She'd mentioned working for four years. If she'd graduated from college when she was twenty-one, she'd be only twenty-five. What would a twenty-five-year-old know about healing his child? Despite his despair, he felt a pitying grin flicker on his lips. He was only thirty-two. What did he know about healing his child? Nothing.

David rose from the floral-print sofa and wandered to the fireplace. He stared into the dying embers. Photographs lined the mantel, memories of happier times—Sara smiling warmly with sprinkles of sunlight and shadow in her golden hair; Nattie with her heavenly blue eyes and bright smile posed in the gnarled peach tree on the hill; and then, the photograph of Sara and him on his parents' yacht.

He turned from the photographs, now like a sad monument conjuring sorrowful memories. David's gaze traversed the room, admiring the furnishings and decor. Sara's hand had left its mark everywhere in the house, but particularly in this room. Wandering to the bay window, he stood over the mahogany grand piano, his fingers caressing the rich, dark wood. How much longer would this magnificent instrument lie silent? Even at the sound of a single note, longing knifed through him.

This room was their family's favorite spot, where they had spent quiet evenings talking about their plans and dreams. He could picture Sara and Nattie stretched out on the floor piecing together one of her thick cardboard puzzles.

An empty sigh rattled through him, and he shivered with loneliness. He pulled himself from his reveries and marched back to the fireplace, grabbing the poker and jamming it into the glowing ashes. Why should he even think, let alone worry, about the young woman's phone call? He'd never hear from her again, no matter what she promised. Her voice gave the telltale evidence. She had no intention of calling again.

Thinking of Nattie drew him to the hallway. He followed the wide, curved staircase to the floor above. In the lengthy hallway, he stepped quietly along the thick Persian carpet. Two doors from the end, he paused and listened. The room was silent, and he pushed the door open gently, stepping inside.

A soft night-light glowed a warm pink. Natalie's slender frame lay curled under a quilt, and the rise and fall of the delicate blanket marked her deep sleep. He moved lightly across the pink carpeting and stood, looking at her buttercup hair and her flushed, rosy cheeks. His heart lurched at the sight of his child—their child, fulfilling their hopes and completing their lives.

Or what had become their incomplete and short life together.

After the telephone call, Callie's mind filled with thoughts of David Hamilton and his young daughter. Her headache pounded worse than before, and she undressed and pulled down the blankets. Though the evening was still young, she tucked her legs beneath the warm covers.

The light shone brightly, and as thoughts drifted through her head, she nodded to herself, resolute she would not consider the job in Bedford. After turning off the light, she closed her eyes, waiting for sleep.

Her subconsciousness opened, drawing her into the darkness. The images rolled into her mind like thick fog along an inky ocean. *She was in a sparse waiting room. Her pale pink blouse, buttoned to the neck, matched the flush of excitement in her cheeks. The murky shadows swirled past her eyes: images, voices, the reverberating* click *of a door. Fear rose within her. She tried to scream, to yell, but nothing came except black silence—*

Callie forced herself awake, her heart thundering. Perspiration ran from her hairline. She threw back the blankets and snapped on the light. Pulling her trembling legs from beneath the covers, she sat on the edge of the bed and gasped until her breathing returned to normal.

She rose on shaking legs and tiptoed into the hall to the bathroom. Though ice traveled through her veins, a clammy heat beaded on her body. Running cold tap water onto a washcloth, she covered her face and breathed in the icy dampness. *Please, Lord, release me from that terrible dream.*

She wet the cloth again and washed her face and neck, then hurried quietly back to her room, praying for a dreamless sleep.

Chapter Two

Christian Care Services filled the two-story office building on Woodward. Callie entered the lobby and took the elevator to the second floor. Usually she walked the stairs, but today she felt drained of energy.

Twenty-five minutes later, she left more discouraged than when she'd arrived. Not one live-in care situation. How could she tell the young woman she couldn't live at home, not because she didn't love her mother, but because she loved herself as much? The explanation seemed too personal and complicated.

Feeling discouraged, she trudged to her car. Live-in positions weren't very common, and she wondered how long she'd have to wait. If need be, she'd look on her own, praying that God would lead her to a position somewhere.

Standing beside her car, she searched through her shoulder bag for her keys and, with them, pulled out the slip of paper with David Hamilton's phone number. She didn't recall putting the number in her bag, and finding it gave her an uneasy feeling. She tossed the number back into her purse.

The winter air penetrated her heavy woolen coat, and she unlocked the car door and slid in. As thoughts butted through her head, she turned on the ignition and waited for the heat.

Money wasn't an immediate problem; residing with others, she'd been able to save a tidy sum. But she needed a place to live. If she stayed home, would she and her mother survive? God commanded children to honor their parents, but had God meant Callie's mother? A faint smile crossed her lips at the foolish thought. Callie knew her parents had always meant well, but meaning and reality didn't necessarily go hand in hand.

Indianapolis had a variety of hospitals. She could probably have her pick of positions in the metropolitan area, then get her own apartment or condo. But again the feeling of emptiness consumed her. She wasn't cut out for hospital nursing.

Warmth drifted from the car heater, and Callie moved the button to high. She felt chilled deep in her bones. Though the heat rose around her, icy sensations nipped at her heart. Her memory turned back to her telephone call the previous evening and to a little child who needed love and care.

She shook the thought from her head and pulled out of the parking lot. She'd give the agency a couple of weeks. If nothing became available, then she'd know Bedford was God's decision. By that time, the position might already be taken, and her dilemma would be resolved.

* * *

Callie glanced at David Hamilton's address again. Bedford was no metropolis, and she'd found the street easily.

Two weeks had passed and no live-in positions had become available, not even for an elderly patient. Her twenty-sixth birthday had plodded by a week earlier, and she felt like an old, jobless woman, staring at the girlish daisy wallpaper in her bedroom. Life had come to a standstill, going nowhere. Tired of sitting by the telephone waiting for a job call, she had called David Hamilton. Despite his lack of warmth, he had a child who needed someone to love her.

Keeping her eyes on the winding road lined with sprawling houses, she glanced at the slip of paper and reread the address. A mailbox caught her eye. The name *Hamilton* jumped from the shiny black receptacle in white letters. She looked between the fence pillars, and her gaze traveled up the winding driveway to the large home of oatmeal-colored limestone.

She aimed her car and followed the curved pathway to the house. Wide steps led to a deep, covered porch, and on one side of the home, a circular tower rose above the house topped by a conical roof.

Callie pulled in front, awed by the elegance and charm of the turn-of-the-century building. Sitting for a moment to collect her thoughts, she pressed her tired back against the seat cushion. Though an easy trip in the summer, the two-hour drive on winter roads was less than pleasant. She thanked God the highway was basically clear.

Closing her eyes, she prayed. Even thinking of Mr. Hamilton sent a shudder down her spine. His voice presented a formidable image in her mind, and now she would see him face-to-face.

She climbed from the car and made her way up the impressive steps to the wide porch. Standing on the expanse of cement, she had a closer view of the large tower rising along the side. *Like a castle,* she thought. She located the bell and pushed. Inside, a chime sounded, and she waited.

When the door swung open, she faced a plump, middle-aged woman who stared at her through the storm door. The housekeeper, Callie assumed. The woman pushed the door open slightly, giving a flicker of a smile. "Miss Randolph?"

"Yes," Callie answered.

The opening widened, and the woman stepped aside. "Mr. Hamilton is waiting for you in the family parlor. May I take your coat?"

Callie regarded her surroundings as she slid the coat from her shoulders. She stood in a wide hallway graced by a broad, curved staircase and a sparkling crystal chandelier. An oriental carpet covered the floor, stretching the length of the entry.

Two sets of double doors stood closed on the right, and on the left, three more sets of French doors hid the rooms' interiors, leaving Callie with a sense of foreboding. Were the doors holding something in? Or keeping something out? Only the door at the end of the hallway stood open, probably leading to the servants' quarters.

The woman disposed of Callie's coat and gestured for her

to follow. The housekeeper moved to the left, rapped lightly on the first set of doors, and, when a muffled voice spoke, pushed the door open and stepped aside.

Callie moved forward and paused in the doorway. The room was lovely, filled with floral-print furnishings and a broad mantel displaying family photographs. Winter sunlight beamed through a wide bay window, casting French-pane patterns on the elegant mahogany grand piano. But what caught her off guard the most was the man.

David Hamilton stood before the fireplace, watching her. Their eyes met and locked in unspoken curiosity. A pair of gray woolen slacks and a burgundy sweater covered his tall, athletic frame. His broad shoulders looked like a swimmer's, and tapered to a trim waist.

He stepped toward her, extending his hand without a smile. "Miss Randolph."

She moved forward to meet him halfway. "Mr. Hamilton. You have a lovely home. Very gracious and charming."

"Thank you. Have a seat by the fire. Big, old homes sometimes hold a chill. The fireplace makes it more tolerable."

After glancing around, she made her way toward a chair near the hearth, then straightened her skirt as she eased into it. The man sat across from her, stretching his long legs toward the warmth of the fire. He was far more handsome than she had imagined, and she chided herself for creating an ogre, rather than this attractive tawny-haired man whose hazel eyes glinted sparks of green and brown as he observed her.

"So," he said. His deep, resonant voice filled the silence.

She pulled herself up straighter in the chair and acknowledged him. "I suppose you'd like to see my references?"

He sat unmoving. "Not really."

His abrupt comment threw her off balance a moment. "Oh? Then you'd like to know my qualifications?"

"No, I'd rather get to know *you.*" His gaze penetrated hers, and she felt a prickling of nerves tingle up her arms and catch in her chest.

"You mean my life story? Why I became a nurse? Why I'd rather do home care?"

"Tell me about your interests. What amuses you?"

She looked directly into his eyes. "My interests? I love to read. In fact, I brought a small gift for Natalie, some children's books. I thought she might like them. I've always favored children's literature."

He stared at her with an amused grin on his lips.

"I guess I'm rattling. I'm nervous. I've cared for the elderly, but this is my first interview for a child."

David nodded. "You're not much beyond a child yourself."

Callie sat bolt upright. "I'm twenty-six, Mr. Hamilton. I believe I qualify as an adult. And I'm a registered nurse. I'm licensed to care for people of all ages."

He raised his hand, flexing his palm like a policeman halting traffic. "Whoa. I'm sorry, Miss Randolph. I didn't mean to insult you. You have a very youthful appearance. You told me your qualifications on the telephone. I know you're a nurse. If I didn't think you might be suited for this position, I wouldn't have wasted my time. Nor yours."

Callie's cheeks burned. "I'm sorry. I thought, you—"

"Don't apologize. I was abrupt. Please continue. How else do you spend your time?"

She thought for a moment. "As I said before, I love to read. I enjoy the theater. And the outdoors. I'm not interested in sports, but I enjoy a long walk on a spring morning or a hike through the woods in autumn— Do I sound boring?"

"No, not at all."

"And then I love..." She hesitated. *Music.* How could she tell him her feelings about music and singing? So much time had passed.

His eyes searched hers, and he waited.

The grandfather clock sitting across the room broke the heavy silence. *One. Two. Three.*

He glanced at his wristwatch. "And then you love..."

She glanced across the room at the silent piano. "Music."

Chapter Three

Callie waited for a comment, but David Hamilton only shifted his focus to the piano, then back to her face.

She didn't mention her singing. "I play the piano a little." She gestured toward the impressive instrument. "Do you play?"

David's face tightened, and a frown flickered on his brow. "Not really. Not anymore. Sara, my wife, played. She was the musician in the family."

Callie nodded. "I see." His eyes flooded with sorrow, and she understood. The thought of singing filled her with longing, too. They shared a similar ache, but hers was too personal, too horrible to even talk about. Her thought returned to the child. "And Natalie? Is your daughter musical?"

Grief shadowed his face again, and she was sorry she'd asked.

"I believe she is. She showed promise before her mother

died. Nattie was four then and used to sing songs with us. Now she doesn't sing a note."

"I'm sorry. It must be difficult, losing a wife and in a sense your daughter." Callie drew in a deep breath. "Someday, she'll sing again. I'm sure she will. When you love music, it has to come out. You can't keep it buried inside of..."

The truth of her words hit her. Music pushed against her heart daily. Would she ever be able to think of music without the awful memories surging through her? Her throat ached to sing, but then the black dreams rose like demons, just as Nattie's singing probably aroused sad thoughts of her mother.

David stared at her curiously, his head tilting to one side as he searched her face. She swallowed, feeling the heat of discomfort rise in her again.

"You have strong feelings about music." His words were not a question.

"Yes, I do. She'll sing. After her pain goes away." Callie's thoughts turned to a prayer. *Help me to sing again, Lord, when my hurt is gone.*

"Excuse me." David Hamilton rose. "I want to see if Agnes is bringing our tea." He stepped toward the door, then stopped. "Do you like tea?"

Callie nodded. "Yes, very much."

He turned and strode through the doorway. Callie drew in a calming breath. Why did she feel as if he were sitting in judgment of her, rather than interviewing her? She raised her eyebrows. Maybe he was.

In only a moment, David spoke to her from the parlor doorway. "Agnes is on her way." He left the door open, and before he had crossed the room, the woman she'd seen earlier entered with a tray.

"Right here, Agnes. On the coffee table is fine." He gestured to the low table that stretched between them. "Miss Randolph, this is Agnes, my housekeeper. She's caring for Nattie until I find someone."

"We met at the door. It's nice to know you, Agnes." The woman nodded and set the tray on the highly polished table.

"Agnes has been a godsend for us since we lost Miriam."

"Thank you, Mr. Hamilton," she said, glancing at him. "Would you like me to pour?"

"No, I'll get it. You have plenty to do." With a flicker of emotion, his eyes rose to meet the woman's. "By the way, have you checked on Nattie lately?"

"Yes, sir, she's coloring in her room."

"Coloring? That's good. I'll take Miss Randolph up to meet her a bit later."

Agnes nodded and left the room, closing the door behind her. David poured tea into the two china cups. "I'll let you add your own cream and sugar, if you take it," he said, indicating toward the pitcher and sugar bowl on the tray. "And please have a piece of Agnes's cake. It's lemon. And wonderful."

Callie glanced at him, astounded at the sudden congeniality in his voice. The interview had felt so ponderous, but now he sounded human. "Thanks. I take my tea black. And the cake looks wonderful." She sipped the strong tea, and then placed the cup on the tray and picked up a dessert plate of cake.

David eyed her as she slivered off a bite and forked it into her mouth. The tangy lemon burst with flavor on her tongue. "It's delicious."

He looked pleased. "I will say, Agnes is an excellent cook."

"Has she been with you long?"

He stared into the red glow of the firelight. "No—a half year, perhaps. Miriam, my past housekeeper, took Nattie—took all of us—under her wing when Sara died. She had been with my parents before their deaths. A longtime employee of the family. She retired. Illness and age finally caught up with her. Her loss has been difficult for us."

He raised his eyes from the mesmerizing flames. "I'm sorry, Miss Randolph. I'm sure you aren't interested in my family tree, nor my family's problems."

"Don't apologize, please. And call me Callie." She felt her face brighten to a shy grin. "Miss Randolph sounds like my maiden aunt."

For the first time, his tense lips relaxed and curved to a pleasant smile. "All right. It's Callie," he said, leaning back in the chair. "Is that short for something?"

"No, just plain Callie."

He nodded. "So, Callie, tell me how a young woman like you decided to care for the elderly. Why not a position in a hospital, regular hours so you could have fun with your friends?"

She raised her eyes to his and fought the frown that pulled at her forehead. Never had an interview caused her such stress. The man seemed to be probing at every nerve ending—searching for what, she didn't know. She grasped for the story she had lived with for so long.

"When I graduated from college, I had romantic dreams. Like Florence Nightingale, I suppose. A hospital didn't interest me. I wanted something more…absorbing. So I thought I'd try my hand at home care. The first job I had was a cancer patient, an elderly woman who needed constant attention. Because of that, I was asked to live in their home, which suited me nicely."

"You have no family, then?"

She swallowed. How could she explain her relationship with her mother. "Yes, my mother is living. My father died about three years ago. But my mother's in good health and active. She doesn't need me around. My siblings are older. My brother lives right outside Indianapolis. My sister and her husband live in California."

"No apartment or home of your own?"

"My mother's house is the most permanent residence I have. No, I have no other financial responsibilities, if that's what you're asking."

David grimaced. "I wasn't trying to pry. I wondered if a live-in situation meets your needs."

"Yes, but most important, I like the involvement, not only with the patient, but with the family. You know—dedication, commitment."

A sound between a snicker and harrumph escaped him. "A job here would certainly take dedication and commitment."

"That's what I want. I believe God has a purpose for everybody. I want to do something that has meaning. I want to know that I'm paying God back for—"

"Paying God back?" His brows lifted. "Like an atonement? What kind of atonement does a young woman like you have to make?"

Irritation flooded through her, and her pitch raised along with her volume. "I didn't say *atonement,* Mr. Hamilton. I said *purpose.* And you've mentioned my *young* age often since I've arrived. I assume my age bothers you."

The sensation that shot through Callie surprised even her. Why was she fighting for a job she wasn't sure she wanted? A job she wasn't sure she could handle? A sigh escaped her. Working with the child wasn't a problem. She had the skills.

But *Callie* was the problem. Already, she found herself emotionally caught in the child's plight, her own buried feelings struggling to rise from within. Her focus settled upon David Hamilton's startled face. How could she have raised her voice to this man? Even if she wanted the position, any hopes of a job here were now lost forever.

David was startled by the words of the irate young woman who stood before him. He dropped against the back of his chair, peering at her and flinching against her sudden anger. He reviewed what he'd said. Had he made a point of her age?

A flush rose to her face, and for some reason, she ruffled his curiosity. He sensed a depth in her, something that aroused him, something that dragged his own empathy from its hiding place. He'd felt sorry for himself and for Nattie for such a long time. Feeling grief for someone else seemed alien.

"To be honest, Miss Rand—Callie, I had thought to hire an older woman. Someone with experience who could nurture Nattie and bring her back to the sweet, happy child she was before her mother's death."

Callie's chin jutted upward. Obviously his words had riled her again.

"Was your wife an old woman, Mr. Hamilton?"

A rush of heat dashed to his cheeks. "What do you mean?"

"I mean, did your wife understand your child? Did she love her? Could she relate to her? Play with her? Sing with her? Give her love and care?"

David stared at her. "Wh-why, yes. Obviously." His pulse raced and pounded in his temples, not from anger but from astonishment. She seemed to be interviewing him, and he wasn't sure he liked it, at all.

"Then why does a nanny—a caregiver—have to be an elderly woman? Can't a woman my age—perhaps your wife's age when she died—love and care for your child? I don't understand."

Neither did he understand. He stared at her and closed his gaping mouth. Her words struck him like icy water. What she said was utterly true. Who was he protecting? Nattie? Or himself? He peered into her snapping eyes. *Spunky? Nervy?* No, *spirited* was the word.

He gazed at the glowing, animated face of the woman sitting across from him. Her trim body looked rigid, and she stared at him with eyes the color of the sky or flowers. Yes, delphiniums. Her honey-colored hair framed an oval face graced with sculptured cheekbones and full lips. She had fire, soul and vigor. Isn't that what Nattie needed?

Callie's voice softened. "I'm sorry, Mr. Hamilton.

You're angry with me. I did speak to you disrespectfully, and I'm sorry. But I—"

"No. No, I'm not angry. You've made me think. I see no reason why Nattie should have an elderly nanny. A young woman might tempt her out of her shell. She's needs to be around activity and laughter. She needs to play." He felt tears push against the back of his eyes, and he struggled. He refused to sit in front of this stranger and sob, bearing his soul like a blithering idiot. "She needs to have fun. Yes?"

"Yes." She shifted in her chair, seemingly embarrassed. "I'm glad you agree." Callie stared into her lap a moment. "How does she spend her day now?"

"Sitting. Staring into space. Sometimes she colors, like today. But often her pictures are covered in dark brown or purple. Or black."

"No school?"

David shook his head. "No. We registered her for kindergarten, but I couldn't follow through. I took her there and forced her from the car, rigid and silent. I couldn't do that to her. But next September is first grade. She must begin school then. I could get a tutor, but…" The memories of the first school day tore at his heart.

"But that won't solve the problem."

He lifted his eyes to hers. "Yes. A tutor won't solve a single problem."

"Well, you have seven or eight months before school begins. Was she examined by doctors? I assume she has nothing physically wrong with her."

"She's healthy. She eats well. But she's lethargic, prefers to be alone, sits for hours staring outside, sometimes at a book. Occasionally, she says something to me—a word, perhaps. That's all."

Callie was silent, then asked, "Psychological? Have you seen a therapist?"

"Yes, the physician brought in a psychiatrist as a consultant." He recalled that day vividly. "Since the problem was caused by a trauma, and given her age, they both felt her problem is temporary. Time will heal her. She can speak. She talked a blue streak before Sara's death. But now the problem is, she's unwilling to speak. Without talking, therapy probably couldn't help her."

Callie stared into the dying flames. "Something will bring her out. Sometimes people form habits they can't seem to break. They almost forget how it is to live without the behavior. Maybe Nattie's silence has become just that.

Something has to happen to stimulate her, to make her want to speak and live like a normal child again."

"I pray you're right."

"Me, too."

He rose and wandered to the fireplace. Peering at the embers, he lifted the poker and thrust at the red glow. Nattie needed to be prodded. She needed stimulus to wake her from her sadness. The flames stirred and sparks sprinkled from the burned wood. Could this spirited woman be the one to do that?

"You mentioned you'd like me to meet your daughter," Callie said.

He swung around to face her, realizing he had been lost in reverie. "Certainly," he said, embarrassed by his distraction.

"I'd like that, when you're ready."

He glanced at the cup in her hand. "Are you finished with the tea?"

She took a final sip. "Yes, thanks. I have a two-hour drive home, and I'd like to get there before dark, if I can."

"I don't blame you. The winter roads can be treacherous."

He stood, and she rose and waited next to the chair, bathed in the warm glow of the fire. David studied her again. Her frame, though thin, rounded in an appealing manner and tugged at his memory. The straight skirt of her deep blue suit hit her modestly just below the knee. Covering a white blouse, the boxy jacket rested at the top of her hips. Her only jewelry was a gold lapel pin and earrings. She stepped to his side, and he calculated her height. Probably five foot five or six, he determined. He stood a head above her.

He stepped toward the doors, and she followed. In the foyer, he gestured to the staircase, and she moved ahead of him, gliding lightly up the steps, her skirt clinging momentarily to her shape as she took each step.

Awareness filled him. No wonder he'd wanted to hire an elderly woman. Ashamed of his own stirrings, he asked God for forgiveness. Instead of thinking of Nattie's needs, he'd struggled to protect his own vulnerability. He would learn to handle his emotions for his daughter's sake.

At the top of the stairs, he guided her down the hallway and paused outside a door. "Please don't expect much. She's not like the child God gave us."

His fingers grasped the knob, and Callie's soft, warm hand lowered and pressed against his.

"Please, don't worry," she said. "I understand hurt."

She raised her eyes to his, and a sense of fellowship like electricity charged through him, racing down to the extremity of his limbs. She lifted her hand, and he turned the knob.

He pushed the door open, and across the room, Nattie shifted her soft blue eyes toward them, then stared again at her knees.

Callie gaped, wide-eyed, at his child. Pulled into a tight knot, Nattie sat with her back braced against the bay enclosure, her feet resting on the window seat. The sun poured in through the pane and made flickering patterns on her pale skin. The same light filtered through her bright yellow hair.

Standing at Callie's side, David felt a shiver ripple through her body. He glimpsed at his child and then looked into the eyes of the virtual stranger, named Callie Randolph, whose face now flooded with compassion and love.

Chapter Four

Callie stared ahead of her at the frail vision on the window seat. She and David stood in Nattie's bedroom doorway for a moment, neither speaking. Finally he entered the room, approaching her like a father would a normal, happy child. "Nattie, this is Miss Randolph. She wants to meet you."

Callie moved as close to the silent child as she felt comfortable doing. "Hi, Nattie. I've heard nice things about you from your daddy. I brought you a present."

She detected a slight movement in the child's body at the word *present.* Hoping she'd piqued Nattie's interest, she opened her large shoulder bag and pulled out the books wrapped in colorful tissue and tied with a ribbon. "Here." She extended her hand holding the books.

Nattie didn't move, but sat with her arms bound to her knees.

Stepping forward, Callie placed the package by the

child's feet and backed away. She glanced at David. His gaze was riveted to his daughter.

He took a step forward and rested his hand on his daughter's shoulder. "Nattie, how about if you open the present?"

The child glanced at him, but made no move to respond.

David squeezed his large frame into the end of the window seat. He lifted the gift from the bench and raised it toward her.

She eyed the package momentarily, but then lowered her lids again, staring through the window as if they weren't there.

Frustration rose in Callie. The child's behavior startled her. A list of childhood illnesses raced through her mind. Then other thoughts took their place. How did Sara die? Was the child present at her death? Questions swirled in her thoughts. What might have happened in the past to trouble this silent child sitting rigidly on the window seat?

David relaxed and placed the package on his knees. "I'll open the gift for you, then, if you'd like." Tearing the paper from the gift, he lifted the books one by one, turning the colorful covers toward her. "'The Lost Lamb,'" he read, showing her the book.

Callie looked at the forlorn child and the book cover. If ever there were a lost lamb, it was Nattie. The next book he showed her was a child's New Testament in story form, and the last, children's poems. Nattie glanced at the book covers, a short-lived spark of interest on her face.

David placed the books again by her feet and rose, his

face tormented. Callie glanced at him and gestured to the window seat. "Do you mind?"

He shook his head, and she wandered slowly to the vacated spot and nestled comfortably in the corner. "I think I'd like to read this one," Callie said, selecting "The Lost Lamb," "if you don't mind." The child made no response. Callie searched David's face, but he seemed lost in thought.

Leaning back, Callie braced herself against the wall next to the window and opened the book. She glanced at Nattie, who eyed her without moving, and began to read. "'Oh my,' said Rebecca to her father, 'where is the new lamb?' Father looked into the pasture. The baby lamb was not in sight."

Callie directed the bright picture toward Nattie, who scanned the page, then returned her attention to her shoes. Callie continued. Nattie glimpsed at each picture without reaction. But, the child's minimal interest gave Callie hope. Patience, perseverance, attention, love—Callie would need all of those attributes if she were to work with this lost lamb.

Glancing from the book, she caught David easing quietly through the doorway. The story gained momentum, as Rebecca and her father searched the barnyard and the wooded hills for the stray. When they found the lamb, who had stumbled into a deep hole, Nattie's eyes finally stayed attentive to the page. When the lamb was again in Rebecca's arms, Callie heard a soft breath escape the child at her side. Nattie had, at least, listened to the story. A first success.

"That was a wonderful story, wasn't it? Sometimes when

we feel so alone or afraid, we can remember that Jesus is always by our side to protect us, just like Rebecca protected the lamb. I love stories like that one, don't you?" Callie rose. "Well, I have to go now, Nattie. But I hope to be back soon to read more stories with you."

She lay the book next to Nattie and gently caressed the child's jonquil-colored hair. Nattie's gaze lifted for a heartbeat, but this time when she lowered her eyes, she fastened her attention on the book.

Callie swallowed her building emotions and hurried from the room. She made her way down the stairs, and at the bottom, filled her lungs with refreshing air. When she released the healing breath, her body trembled.

"Thank you."

Callie's hand flew to her chest, she gasped and swung to her left. "Oh, you scared me."

David stood in the doorway across from the parlor where they had met. "You did a beautiful thing."

"She's a beautiful child, Mr. Hamilton. She breaks my heart, so I can only imagine how she breaks yours."

"Call me David, please. If we're going to live in the same house, 'Callie' and 'David' will sound less formal."

She faltered, her hand still knotted at her chest. *If we're going to live in the same house.* The meaning of his words registered, and she closed her eyes. He was asking her to stay. Could she? Would the experience break her heart once more? But suddenly, her own pain didn't matter. Her only thought was for the child sitting alone in an upstairs room.

Callie stepped toward him. "Yes, if we're going to live in the same house, I suppose you're right...

David. The 'David' will take some doing," she admitted with a faint grin.

He extended his hand. "I pray you'll make a difference in Nattie's life. In our lives, really. I see already you're a compassionate woman. I can ask for no more."

Callie accepted his hand in a firm clasp. "I hope you'll continue to feel like that." She eyed him, a knowing expression creeping on her face. "You've already seen me with my dander up, as they say." Her hand remained in his.

"Then we have nothing to worry about. I survived."

"Yes, you did. And quite admirably. Thank you for trusting in my...*youthful* abilities."

His hazel eyes captured hers and held her suspended until his words broke the spell. "It's my pleasure."

Callie gazed around her childhood bedroom, facing a new and frightening chapter in her life. Five times she had packed, heading for a patient's home. But tomorrow was different.

Nattie appeared in her mind, the child's face as empty of feeling as Callie's would be when she stepped into David Hamilton's home in Bedford. He was the last person she wanted to have know the fear that writhed inside her. She would step through the doorway with a charade of confidence. She had announced with no uncertainty that she could provide professional, compassionate care for Nattie. And she would.

The sound of Grace's unhappy voice echoed in Callie's head. *"Bedford is too far away. Why must you be a live-in nurse? What if I need you? Dr. Swanson, right here in town, still needs an office nurse."*

She'd heard the same questions and comments since she chose home-care. Tomorrow, another day—a new beginning.

Though she hadn't finished packing, Callie's thoughts dragged through her, sapping her energy. A good night's sleep would refresh her, she thought. With that notion, she crawled into bed.

But Callie couldn't escape her dream. It soon rose in her slumber, shrouded in darkness and mist.

In a foggy blur, his stare toyed with her, sweeping her body from head to toe, and her flush of excitement deepened to embarrassment. His smooth voice like a distant whisper echoed in her head. "Callie. That's a lovely, lovely name. Nearly pretty as you are, sweetheart."

An uneasy sensation rose in her, unexpected and unnatural. Why was he teasing her with his eyes? She felt self-conscious.

In the swirling darkness, he flashed his broad, charming smile, and his hushed voice touched her ear again. "You're nervous. No need to be nervous." He turned the bolt on the door.

The *click* of the lock cut through her sleep. Callie wrested herself from the blackness of her dream to the darkness of her room.

"Bedford's only a couple hours away, Mom. I told you

already, I can get back here if you need me." Packing the last suitcase the next morning, Callie glanced over her shoulder at Grace. "I don't understand why you're worried. You've never needed me yet."

Grace leaned against the door frame. "Well, I get older every year. You never know." Grace's pinched expression gave witness to her unhappiness.

Callie bit back the words that could easily have sailed from her lips: *Only the good die young.* Her mother was well-meaning, she knew that, but Callie found a chip growing on her shoulder when she spent too much time with Grace. She needed to keep that situation in her prayers—only God could work a miracle.

Callie chuckled out loud. "We have the same problem, Mom. I seem to get older every year myself. Any idea how we can fix that?"

Grace's compressed features gave way to a grin. "Can't do much, I suppose. I just worry. Your sister lives thousands of miles away. Kenneth is useless. Sons don't care much about their mothers."

"If you need Ken, he can be here in a minute. But you have to call him and let him know. Men just aren't as attentive as women." Guilt swept over her. She hadn't been very attentive, either. And Grace was right—though she wasn't ready for the grave, they had celebrated her sixty-fifth birthday. And no one was getting any younger.

A sudden feeling of tenderness swept over her. She was her parents' "surprise" baby. At the age of forty, Grace had her "babies" raised. Patricia was fourteen, and Ken, eleven. Then came Callie, who was soon deemed the "little princess." All her parents' unfulfilled hopes and dreams were bundled into her. She had let them down with a bang.

A heavy silence hung in the room as Callie placed the last few items in her luggage. When she snapped the locks, she turned and faced her mother. "Well, I guess that's it. I may need a few other things, but I'm not that far away. And at this point, I'm not sure how long I'll be needed."

The words caught in her throat. Already, the face of Nattie loomed in her mind. Her greatest fear was beginning to take shape. This child would continue to linger in her thoughts when her job was completed in Bedford. And could she walk away from another child? She prayed she could handle it.

Grace stood at the doorway, her hands knotted in front of her. "You'll be coming back occasionally? So I'll see you once in a while, then?"

"Well, sure. I'm not chained to the house. At least, I don't think so." She grinned at Grace, trying to keep her parting light. Most of her previous patients had lived in the area. Living in Bedford would make trips home a bit more complicated.

Grace heaved a sigh and lifted her smaller bag. Callie grabbed the larger piece of luggage and followed her mother down the stairs and out the door.

As Callie loaded her car, she shuddered, thinking of her dream the night before. She drew the chilled, winter air through her lungs, clearing her thoughts. She stood for a moment, staring at the house where her parents had lived for most of her life, remembering…

When she returned inside, Grace had lunch waiting on the table. Seeing the food as another attempt to delay her, Callie wanted to say "no, thank you," but she had to eat somewhere. Noting her mother's forlorn expression, she sat at the table.

"Thanks, this will save time. I should arrive in Bedford in the mid-afternoon, if the weather cooperates. I'll have a chance to get settled before dinner." She bit into her sandwich.

Grace raised the tuna salad to her lips, then lowered it. "Are you sure you're safe with this man, Callie? He saw your references, but did you see his?"

Callie understood her mother's concern. "I think seeing his daughter is reference enough. He's not an outgoing, friendly man. I saw so much sadness in his eyes. Anyway, he has a full-time housekeeper who lives in. She looked comfortable enough. Though once I'm there, I imagine she'll enjoy having the opportunity to go home." Callie sipped her tea.

"You mean you have to keep house, too?"

Callie choked on her sip of tea. She quickly grabbed up her napkin to cover her mouth. "No, Mother. Agnes is from the community. She'll be able to go home and visit her family. Since I'm there, she won't have the responsibility to be the nanny. That's all. He says I'll have my own suite of bedrooms—room, private bath and a little sitting room. And

I'll have dinner with the family. Now, don't worry. I'll be fine."

Grace raised an eyebrow. "What kind of business is this man in to afford such a big home and all this help?"

"Limestone quarries and mills. They've been in the family for generations. His grandfather opened a quarry in the middle eighteen-hundreds, I think. Eventually his father took over."

"Family business, hmm? Must be a good one to keep generations at it."

"It is. I was really amazed. I picked up some brochures at the Chamber of Commerce office on my way out of town. So many famous buildings were made with Indiana limestone—the Pentagon, the Empire State Building, lots of buildings in Washington, D.C. So I'd say the family has enough money to get by."

Grace grinned. "To get by? I'd say. One of those aristocratic families…with money to throw away."

"Not really. It's a beautiful house, but David seems down to earth."

"David? What's this 'David' business?"

"Mother." Callie rolled her eyes, yet heat rose up her neck at her mother's scrutiny. "Since we're living in the same house, I suppose he thought 'Miss Randolph' and 'Mr. Hamilton' sounded too formal."

"A little formality never hurt anybody."

"I'm an employee, Mom. And he has no interest in me. The man's not over the death of his wife."

"Accident?"

Callie's brows knitted. "I don't know. He didn't say, and I didn't ask. I'd already asked too many questions for someone who was supposed to be the person interviewed."

"Never hurts to ask questions."

"I'm sure I'll find out one of these days. And I don't expect to be with him much. Mainly dinner. He'll be gone some of the time, traveling for his business. I'm there to be with Natalie. Nattie, they call her. She's a beautiful child."

"Just keep your eyes focused on the child, hear me?"

Callie shook her head. "Yes, Mother. I think I've learned to take care of myself."

She caught a flicker of reminiscence in Grace's expression, and froze, praying she wouldn't stir up the past. Grace bit her tongue, and Callie changed the subject.

"The area is lovely there, all covered with snow. And imagine spring. The trees and wildflowers. And autumn. The colored leaves—elms, maples, birches."

An uneasy feeling rippled down her back. Would she see the autumn colors? Nattie needed to be ready for school. If the child was back to normal by then, her job would be finished.

"It's snowing," Grace said, pulling Callie from her thoughts. "And hard."

"Then, I'd better get moving." Callie gulped down her last bite and drained the teacup.

Without fanfare, she slipped on her coat and said goodbye. She needed to be on her way before she was snowbound. Time was fleeting, and so was her sanity.

Chapter Five

David sat with his face in his hands, his elbows resting on his large cherry wood desk. The day pressed in from all sides. Callie should arrive any time now. He'd expected her earlier, yet the uncooperative weather had apparently slowed her travel.

The day of her interview lingered in his memory. Though Nattie had responded minimally to Callie's ministrations, David was grateful for the most insignificant flicker of interest from his daughter these days. Callie had brought about that infinitesimal moment.

The major concern that lodged in his gut was himself. He feared Callie. She stirred in him remembrances he didn't want to face and emotions he had avoided for two years. His only solution was to avoid her—keep his distance.

Though often quiet, Sara had had her moments of liveliness and laughter. He recalled their spring walks on the hill and a warm, sunny day filled with play when she dubbed him "Sir Knight" with a daisy chain she'd made. Wonderful moments rose in his mind of Sara playing pat-a-cake with Nattie or singing children's songs.

If he let Callie's smiles and exuberance get under his skin, he might find himself emotionally tangled. Until Nattie was well, and he dealt with his personal sorrow, he had no interest in any kind of relationship—and he would live with that decision. But he wished wisdom had been his gatekeeper when he'd extended her the job with such enthusiasm.

On top of it all, today they would celebrate Nattie's sixth birthday. Tension caught between his shoulder blades when he pictured the occasion: a cake with candles she wouldn't blow out, gifts she wouldn't open, and joy she wouldn't feel.

David was reminded of the day Sara had surprised him for his birthday with tickets to see Shakespeare's darkest, direst play, *King Lear*. Yet, he'd accompanied her, looking pleased and interested so as not to hurt the woman he loved so deeply.

But Nattie would not look interested to please him. She wouldn't say "thank you" or force a smile. The lack of response for the gift was not what hurt. She appeared to feel nothing, and that tore at his very fiber.

His wife's death had been no surprise; Nattie's living death was.

Rising from his chair, David wandered to the window and pulled back the draperies. The snow piled against the hedges and mounded against the edge of the driveway. Lovely, pure white at this moment, the snow would soon become drab and monotonous like his life.

A flash of headlights caught the mounds of crystal flakes and glowed with diamond-like sparkles. David's heart surged, and for a heartbeat, he held his breath. Dropping the edge of the drapery, he spun toward the doorway. She would need help bringing in her luggage. He could, at least, do that.

Callie climbed the snow-covered stairs with care and rang the bell. When the door opened, her stomach somersaulted. Her focus fell upon David Hamilton, rather than Agnes. "Oh," she said, knowing her face registered surprise, "I expected Agnes." Her amazement was not so much at seeing him at the door as feeling her stomach's unexpected acrobatics.

"I was keeping an eye out for you, concerned about the weather." His face appeared drawn and serious.

"Thank you. The drive was a bit tense."

He stepped back and held the door open for her.

She glanced at his darkened face. "I hope nothing is wrong. You look..." Immediately she was sorry she had spoken. Perhaps his stressed appearance had to do with *her*—hiring someone "so young," as he had continually reminded her.

"I'm fine," he said, looking past her toward the automobile. "Let me get my jacket, and we can bring in your luggage."

He darted to the entrance closet, and in a brief moment, joined her.

Heading down the slippery porch stairs, Callie's eyes filled with his Titan stature. In her preoccupation, her foot missed the center of the step and skidded out from under her. She crumpled backward, reaching out to break her fall.

David flung his hand behind her and caught her in the crook of his arm, while the other hand swung around to hold her secure. "Careful," he cautioned.

Captured in his arms, his gaze locked with hers, she wavered at the sensation that charged through her. She marveled at his vibrant hazel eyes in the dusky light.

"Be careful. You could get hurt," he repeated, setting her on her feet.

She found her voice and mumbled a "thank you."

Capturing her elbow, he helped her down the next two steps. When she opened the trunk, he scanned its contents.

"I'll help you in with the luggage," he said, "and I'll come back for the rest."

She nodded. Hearing his commanding voice, she couldn't disagree. He handed her the smallest case, taking the larger himself, and they climbed the steps with care.

Once inside, David set down the larger case and addressed Agnes, who was waiting in the foyer. "Show Callie her rooms, please. I'll carry in the boxes and bring them up."

Agnes nodded and grabbed the larger case. But when David stepped outside, Callie took the case from her. "Please, let me carry this one. It's terribly heavy."

Agnes didn't argue and grasped the smaller case, then headed up the stairs. At the top, the housekeeper walked down the hallway and stopped at a door to the left, across from Nattie's room. She turned the knob and stepped aside.

As Callie entered, her heart skipped a beat. She stood in the tower she had admired from outside. The sitting room was fitted with a floral chintz love seat and matching chair of vibrant pinks and soft greens, with a lamp table separating the grouping. A small oak desk sat along one curved wall, and oak bookshelves rose nearby. A woman's touch was evident in the lovely decor.

Callie dropped her luggage and darted to the center window, pulling back the sheer white curtains framed by moss-colored draperies. She gazed outside at the scene. A light snow floated past the window, and below, David pulled the last carton from the trunk and closed the lid. He hefted the box into the air, then disappeared beneath the porch roof.

Agnes remained by the door, and when Callie turned back and faced the room, the housekeeper gestured through the doorway to the bedroom. Callie lifted her luggage and followed her inside. The modest bedroom, too, illustrated a feminine hand. Delicate pastel flowers sprinkled the wallpaper that ended at the chair-molding. Below, the color of palest blue met a deeper blue carpet.

"Agnes, this is beautiful." She wanted to ply the woman with questions about Sara and how she used the charming rooms.

"Mr. Hamilton hoped you'd like it."

"How could I not? It's lovely. So dainty and feminine."

Agnes nodded and directed her to a door that opened to a walk-in closet; across the room, another door led to a pristine private bathroom, graced by a claw-foot bathtub.

As she spun around to take in the room once again, David came through the doorway with the box.

"Bricks?" he asked.

"Nearly. Books and things."

"Ah, I should have guessed. Then you'd like this in the sitting room."

"Please." Callie followed him through the doorway.

David placed the box between the desk and the book-shelves. "I'll be right back with the other. Much lighter, I'm happy to say."

Callie grinned. "No books."

He left the room, and she returned to Agnes, who hovered in the doorway.

"Miss Randolph, did you want me to help unpack your things?"

"Oh, no, Agnes, I can get it. And please call me Callie. The 'Miss' stuff makes me nervous." She gave the woman a pleasant look, but received only a nod in return.

"Then I'll get back to the kitchen," Agnes said as she edged her way to the door.

"Yes, thank you."

Agnes missed David by a hairbreadth as he came through the doorway with the last box. He held it and glanced at Callie.

"Bedroom," Callie said, before he asked, and she gestured to the adjoining room.

David turned with his burden and vanished through the doorway. Before she could follow, he returned.

"So, I hope you'll be comfortable here. I still want to get a television for you. But you do have a radio."

Callie's focus followed the direction of his hand. A small

clock radio sat on the desk. "The rooms are lovely. Just beautiful. Did your wif—Sara decorate them? They have a woman's touch."

"Yes," he said, nodding his head at the sitting room. "She used this as her reading room, and she slept here if she worried about Nattie's health. The bedroom was the baby's nursery then."

"I couldn't ask for a nicer place to stay. Thank you."

He glanced around him, edging backward toward the door, his hands moving nervously at his sides. "Then I'll let you get unpacked and settled. Dinner will be at six. We're celebrating this evening. We have a couple of guests for Nattie's birthday."

"Really? I'm glad I'm here for the celebration. And pleased I brought along a couple of small presents. I'd be embarrassed to attend her birthday party empty-handed." She kept her voice level and free of the irritation that prickled her. Why hadn't he thought to tell her about the birthday?

"I'm sorry. I should have mentioned it." A frown flashed over his face, yet faded as if another thought crossed his mind. He stepped toward the door. "I'll see you at dinner."

He vanished through the doorway before Callie could respond. She stared into the empty space, wondering what had driven him so quickly from the room.

Glancing at her wristwatch, the time read four-thirty. She had an hour-and-a-half before dinner. She needed time to dress appropriately if they were celebrating Nattie's birthday.

The word *birthday* took her back. Nattie was six today, so close in age to her own child, who had turned six on Christmas Day. Her chest tightened as the fingers of memory squeezed her heart. Could she protect herself from loving this child too deeply? And why did Natalie have to be six? Eight, four…any other age might not have bothered her as much.

She dropped on the edge of the bed and stared at the carpet. With an inner ache, she asked God to give her compassion and patience. Compassion for Nattie, and patience with herself.

As he waited for Callie's entrance, David prepared his guests for her introduction. Reverend John Spier listened attentively, and his sister Mary Beth bobbed her head, as if eager to meet someone new in the small town of Bedford.

"How nice," Mary Beth said, lowering her eyelids shyly at David. "Since I've come to help John in the parsonage, I've not met too many young unmarried women. Most people my age have already settled down. I look forward to our meeting."

"Yes, I hoped Callie might enjoy meeting you, too."

"Although once John finds a proper bride, I assume I'll go back to Cleveland…unless God has other plans."

David cringed inwardly, noticing the young woman's hopeful look, and wondered if he'd made a mistake inviting the pastor and his younger sister to the birthday dinner. The evening could prove to be difficult enough, depending on Nattie's disposition.

Looking toward the doorway, David saw Callie descending the staircase. "Here's Callie, now. Excuse me." David made for the doorway.

By the time Callie had reached the first floor, he was at the foot of the staircase. Caught off guard by her attractiveness, David gazed at her burgundy wool dress adorned with a simple string of pearls at her neck. The deep red of her gown emphasized the flush in her cheeks and highlighted the golden tinges of her honey-colored hair. As he focused his gaze, their eyes met, and her blush heightened.

"I see the party has already begun," she said. "I heard your voices as I came down the stairs."

"Now that you've joined us, everyone's here but the guest of honor." A sigh escaped him before he could harness it. "I invited our new pastor and his sister. I thought you might like to meet some of the younger people in town." He motioned for her to precede him. "We're in the living room."

She stepped around him, and he followed, watching the fullness of the skirt swish around her legs as she walked. The movement entranced him. Passing through the doorway at her side, he pulled his attention from her shapely legs to his guests.

As she entered the room, John's face brightened, and he rose, meeting her with his outstretched hand. "You're Callie."

"Yes, and you're David's pastor."

"John Spier," he said, then turned with a flourish. "And this is my sister, Mary Beth Spier."

"It's nice to meet you," Callie said, glancing at them both.

The young woman shot Callie an effusive grin. "And I'm certainly pleased to meet you. Being new in town myself, I've been eager to meet some young woman who—"

"Have a seat, Callie." David gestured to the love seat. Interrupting Mary Beth was rude, but he couldn't bear to hear her announce again that she was one of the few single women in town. David chided himself. He should have used more sense than to invite a young woman to dinner who apparently saw him as a possible husband.

When he joined Callie on the love seat, she shifted closer to the arm and gracefully crossed her legs. His attention shifted to her slim ankles, then to her fashionable gray-and-burgundy brushed-leather pumps.

John leaned back in his chair and beamed. "I hope we'll see you at church on Sundays. We're a small congregation, but loaded with spirit. Although we could use a benefactor to help us with some much-needed repairs." His glance shot toward David.

David struggled with the grimace that crept to his face, resulting, he was sure, in a pained smile. "Agnes will announce dinner shortly. Then I'll go up and see if I can convince Nattie to join us. I never know how she'll respond." He eyed them, wondering if they understood. "I've had a difficult time here since Sara... Well, let's not get into that."

He wished he would learn to tuck his sorrow somewhere other than his shirtsleeve. He turned his attention to Callie. "Would you care for some mulled cider?"

She agreed, and he poured a mug of the warm brew. He regarded her full, rosy lips as she took a sip. She pulled away from the rim and nodded her approval.

His mind raced, inventing conversation. Tonight he felt tired, and wished he could retire to his study and spend the evening alone.

When Pastor John spoke, David felt himself relax.

"So where do you hail from, Callie?"

Without hesitation, she related a short personal history. Soon, Mary Beth joined in. David listened, pressing himself against the cushions rather than participating.

To his relief, Agnes announced dinner.

"Well, finally," David said, embarrassed at his obvious relief. David climbed the stairs to find Nattie, as Callie and the guests proceeded toward the dining room.

Callie held back and followed David's ascent with her eyes. He was clearly uncomfortable. She wondered if it was his concern for Nattie or the obvious flirtations of Mary Beth.

In the dining room, Agnes indicated David's seating arrangement. Mary Beth's focus darted from Callie to Agnes; she was apparently wondering if the housekeeper had made an error. She was not seated next to David.

When he arrived back with Nattie clinging to his side, he surveyed the table without comment. Except for a glance at Callie, the child kept her eyes downcast. David pulled out her chair, and Nattie slid onto it, focusing on the folded napkin on her plate, her hands below the table. David sat and asked Pastor John to offer the blessing.

Callie lowered her eyes, but in her peripheral vision she studied Nattie's reaction to the scene around her. Until David said "Amen," Nattie's eyes remained closed, but when she raised her lids, she glimpsed around the table almost without moving her head.

When her focus settled on Callie, their gazes locked.

In that moment, something special happened. Would she call the fleeting glimmer—hope, premonition or fact? Callie wasn't sure. But a sweet tingle rose from the base of her spine to the tips of her fingers. Never before had she felt such a sensation.

Chapter Six

After dinner, Nattie withdrew, staring into space and mentally recoiling from those who addressed her. David blew the lit candles on her cake as they sang "Happy Birthday" and excused her before the gifts were opened, saying she needed to rest. The wrapped packages stood ignored like eager young ladies dressed in their finery for the cotillion, but never asked to dance.

Callie longed to go with the child to the second floor, but refrained from suggesting it. Tonight was her first evening in the house, so she was still a stranger. And Nattie needed her father.

After they left the room, Callie sat uneasily with the Spiers, lost in her own thoughts.

"Such a shame about the little girl," John said, looking toward the doorway. "Has she always been so withdrawn?"

With effort, Callie returned to the conversation.

"Since her mother died a couple of years ago. I'm sure she'll be herself in time."

Mary Beth sighed and murmured. "Such a shame. And poor David having to carry the burden all alone."

John turned sharply to his sister, his words a reprimand. "Mary Beth, we're never alone. God is always with us."

"Oh, John, I know the Lord is with us. I meant, he has no wife." Her look pleaded for forgiveness, and she lowered her eyes.

Callie didn't miss Mary Beth's less-than-subtle meaning. "I don't think you need to worry about David. He'll come through this a stronger person, I'm sure. And don't forget, Mary Beth…"

The young woman looked curiously at Callie. "Don't forget…?"

"David's not alone anymore. I'm here to help him."

Mary Beth paled, and a flush rose to Callie's cheeks. Callie raised her hand nonchalantly to her face, feeling the heat. Her comment astounded her. She sounded like a woman fighting for her man.

When David returned to the parlor, the guests rose to leave, and Callie took advantage of their departure to say goodnight and head for her room. Confusion drove her up the stairs. She felt protective and possessive of this family—not only of Nattie, but of David. In less than a day, the situation already tangled in her heart.

* * *

Callie woke with the morning light dancing on the flowered wallpaper. She looked around the room, confused for a moment, and wondered where she was. Then she remembered. She slid her legs over the edge of the bed and sat, collecting her thoughts. How should she begin? What could she do to help this child, now bound in a cocoon, to blossom like a lovely butterfly?

One thing she knew. The process would take time. She stepped down to the soft, lush carpet and padded to the bathroom. A shower would awaken her body and her mind, she hoped.

When she finished dressing, she steadied herself, knowing what she had to do wouldn't be easy. She bowed her head, asking for God's wisdom and guidance, then left her room to face her first day.

Across the hall, Nattie's door stood open. Callie glimpsed inside. The child again sat on the window seat, but this time was looking at one of the books Callie had given her. Suddenly, she lifted her head and connected with Callie's gaze.

With her eyes focused on Nattie, Callie breathed deeply and strode purposefully to the doorway. "Well, good morning. Look at the wonderful sunshine."

Nattie followed her movement, but her face registered no response.

"When I woke, I saw the sun dance on my walls. I bet you did, too."

Nattie's attention darted to her wallpaper and back again

to Callie. Was it tension or curiosity Callie saw settling there? She longed for a cup of coffee, but she'd made her move, and she'd stick it out. When she ambled toward the window seat, Nattie recoiled slightly. Callie only leaned over and glanced out the window. Nattie calmed.

"Did you look outside? The sun has turned the snow into a world of sparkling diamonds. And I've been told 'diamonds are a girl's best friend.'" She giggled lightheartedly, hoping Nattie would relax. "That's pretty silly, isn't it. I think the *snow* is a girl's best friend. Maybe we could take a walk outside today. We might even make a snowman."

Callie saw Nattie turn toward the window and scan the fresh, glistening snow. She had piqued the child's interest.

"Nattie, I imagine you had breakfast already." She looked for some kind of response. None. "I'll go down and have a bite to eat. If you'd like to go outside, you can put on some warm stockings before I return. How's that?" Callie swung through the doorway with a wave and headed toward the stairs.

Would the child have the stockings on when she returned? If Nattie didn't want to talk, Callie would find another way to communicate until the child trusted her. Callie's thoughts thundered with questions. But mainly, she wanted to learn about Sara's death.

Silence filled the lower level of the house. She followed the aroma of breakfast and entered the dining room, where a lone table setting waited for her. She filled a plate with scrambled eggs and bacon from a small chafing dish, and poured a cup of coffee. This morning she didn't feel like eating alone. Looking for company, she carried the plate and cup through the door leading to the kitchen.

She found herself inside a butler's pantry, but through an arch, she spotted a stove and counter. Sounds emanated from that direction, and she headed through the doorway.

Agnes spun around, flinging her hand to her heart.

"Sorry, Agnes. I scared you."

The housekeeper's wide eyes returned to normal. "I didn't expect anyone, that's all. Can I get you something? I left your breakfast in the—" Her gaze lowered. "Oh, I see you have your plate."

Callie placed her dish and cup on the broad oak table. "Do you mind if I eat in here with you, Agnes? I don't feel like eating alone this morning."

Agnes appeared flustered. She rushed forward with a damp cloth to wipe the already spotless table.

"I'm not trying to make work for you. The table's fine. I just thought you and I could get to know each other a little better. We're both employees here, and I'm sure familiarity can make our days more pleasant."

Agnes eyed her for a moment, then her face relaxed. "I sort of keep my place around here. Behind the scenes. You're more involved with Mr. Hamilton and Natalie. Except recently, while Mr. Hamilton looked for someone. But I'm at a loss. I never quite knew what to do for the child." She took a deep breath.

"Do you have a moment to join me in a cup of coffee?" Callie motioned to the empty chair across from her.

Agnes glanced at the chair, then at Callie. "Why, I don't mind if I do." She poured herself a mug of coffee from the warming pot and slipped onto the chair. "Black," she said, raising the mug. "I drink it black."

"Never could drink coffee black, myself. I like a little milk. I say 'cream,' but I prefer milk really." Callie smiled, and for the first time received a sincere smile in return. "So you've been here only a half year, if I remember correctly."

"Yes, about seven months now."

"I suppose following in Miriam's shadow was difficult."

Agnes nodded vigorously. "Oh yes, very hard. Miriam was part of this family forever. She's a wonderful woman. I knew her from church—Mr. Hamilton's church. That's how he knew me. When Miriam had to retire, he asked if I might be interested in the job. I'd been working for a family that had recently moved. Sort of destined, I suppose."

"Do you like working here?" In Callie's view, Agnes seemed to tiptoe around the house. The image didn't imply comfortable working conditions.

"Mr. Hamilton pays me well, and I'm always treated with respect."

Callie eyed her. "But you don't like working here."

Agnes fidgeted for a moment. "It's not that I don't like it here. The place isn't really homey, if you know what I mean. Mr. Hamilton has his moods. He's quiet and so is the child. Like the house is filled with shadows. He travels a lot, and

I struggle to relate to the poor little thing upstairs. Yet whether he's here or not, she doesn't seem to notice one way or the other." She paused, drawing in a deep breath. "Now I don't mean Mr. Hamilton doesn't love his child. I'm sure he does."

"Don't apologize, Agnes. I know what you mean. Sometimes he seems as withdrawn as Nattie. Once in a while, I sense a chink in his wall, but he mends it as quickly as it appears."

Agnes's head bobbed again. "You do understand."

Callie nibbled on a piece of bacon. She was filled with curiosity. "Did you know Mrs. Hamilton?"

"So lovely. Yes, she played the church organ."

"The church organ? Well, that explains some things." Callie recalled David's comment about music.

"Such a sad thing, when she died."

Callie's pulse skipped through her veins. "You know how she died, then? I wasn't told."

"She was sick for a time. Cancer. They weren't married very long…maybe six or seven years. Such a shame."

Callie shook her head at the thought of someone dying so young. "I wonder what caused Nattie to withdraw so badly. All children are close to their mothers, but her behavior seems so unusual. Odd, really."

"Wondered that myself. I didn't know the family real well. Just Sundays, that's all, and being a small town, you hear about troubles. They were a happy family until the missus got sick."

"I'll ask Mr. Hamilton sometime, but I don't want to sound nosy. If I had a clue to Nattie's problem, I'd have someplace to begin with her."

Callie rose and placed her empty plate and cup in the sink. "Mr. Hamilton is at work, I suppose."

"Yes, he left early this morning. Probably relieved you were here."

"I'm hoping to coax Nattie outside. She's in her room too much. She needs fresh air."

"That'd be nice. I hope she goes out with you."

"Me, too," Callie said, wondering what to do if her plan didn't work.

When she returned to the second floor, she found Nattie on the floor with a puzzle. Her feet were tucked beneath her, so Callie couldn't see her stockings. She scanned the room and saw a pair lying discarded on the floor. Her stomach flip-flopped. Had the child put on the thick ones?

"I'm back," Callie called as she made her entrance.

Nattie glanced at her, then turned her attention to the odd-shaped puzzle pieces spread out on the floor. Callie wandered in and sat next to her on the carpet. The child withdrew her hand for a moment, glancing at Callie with a slight frown, then changed her mind and continued to locate the pieces.

Callie didn't speak, but searched until she found a piece, then placed it in the correct spot. They continued until the last piece remained. Callie waited, letting Nattie fit in the last of the puzzle.

"That's wonderful, Nattie, and you got to put in the last piece. I love to find the last piece." She tittered, hoping to gain some reaction from the child.

Instead, Nattie slid the puzzle aside and pulled her feet out in front of her.

Relief spilled over Callie. The child had donned thicker stockings. "Good. I see you want to go outside. Now, it's my turn to get ready. Would you like to come with me to my room?" Callie rose, but Nattie remained where she was. "Okay, then, you wait here, and I'll be back in a minute. You'll need a sweater, too, to wear under your coat."

She slipped quickly from the room to collect her warm coat and gloves, and hoped she could find Nattie's coat, boots and gloves somewhere. She'd ask Agnes.

David pulled down the driveway as dusk settled. Once again, he'd put in a long workday. The sky had faded to a grayish purple, and the ripples of glistening snow he had admired early in the morning now looked dull and shadowed. As he neared the house, he felt a twinge at his nerve endings, and he applied the brake and peered at the snow-covered lawn.

Sets of footprints had trampled through the snow. He shifted into park and opened his door, intrigued by the sight of the boot marks. The woman's print would have meant little, but beside the larger indentions, he saw the smaller footprint of his daughter.

In a trance-like state, he followed the prints that wove

through the evergreens and around the elms. In an open area, he paused. On the ground, he stared at imprints of angels. Heads, wings and bodies pressed into the snow. But, sadly, all adult angels. No seraphim or cherubim. No Nattie. Only the impression of the household's newest employee stamped a design into the fresh snow.

Yet a bright thought pierced his disappointment. Though Nattie had not made an angel, she had been outside and had walked in the snow—more progress in one day than he had seen in months. He should be grateful for each small gift.

He looked again at the fanned angel impressions at his feet. He counted three, four. He pictured the young woman, flinging herself to the ground, flailing her arms and legs to amuse his silent child. Callie's laughter rang in his mind. Angel? Yes, perhaps God had sent a human angel to watch over his daughter.

He dashed to the car and drove the short distance to the house. His eager feet carried him up the steps, and when he opened the front door, the house had come alive. In place of the usual silence, music played softly from a radio or television program in the parlor, and with anticipation he glanced into the room before hanging his coat. Callie sat curled on the sofa with her feet tucked beneath her, a book in her hand.

She heard him, for she raised her eye from the book, and a playful look covered her face. "Hello. You're home late this evening."

From the doorway, he stared at her in the firelight, his coat still clutched in his hand. "Too often, I'm afraid."

"Let me take your coat, Mr. Hamilton."

David jumped slightly and turned apologetically to Agnes. "Oh, thanks." After he released his coat to her care, he strode into the parlor, his eyes riveted to the firelight glinting on Callie's golden-brown hair.

He fell into the chair across from her. "I noticed a slight miracle outside when I came up the driveway."

Her lips parted in an easy smile. "The angels?"

Watching the animation on her face, he nodded.

"Only mine, I'm afraid. I tried." She lifted a bookmark, slid it between the pages and closed the volume.

"Oh, don't feel discouraged. Nattie went outside with you. We haven't been able to move her beyond these doors. In one day, you've worked wonders. I'm amazed."

Her eyes brightened. "I'm pleased then. I thought I was a minimal failure."

"Not at all." A scent of beef and onions drifted through the doorway and his stomach growled. "You've eaten?"

"No." She shook her head, and her hair glistened in the light. "I waited for you."

"That's nice."

"But Nattie ate, I'm afraid."

"Let me run up and see her, and I'll hurry right down." He rose and dashed up the stairway.

Callie watched him hurry away and filled with sadness, thinking of his excitement over something as simple as his child's walk in the snow. Her attention fell to her lap and the book that lay there.

Then his words rang in her head, and she raised her hand to her chest to calm the fluttering from within. "That's nice," he'd said, when she told him she'd waited for supper. Callie closed her eyes. Why did she care what he said? She was an employee doing her job. That was all.

His footsteps left the oriental carpet and hit the shiny wood floor at the entrance to the parlor, and she looked toward the doorway.

"Agnes says dinner is ready," he said.

She rose, and as they neared the dining room, the aroma stirred her hunger. A low rumble from her stomach echoed in the hallway. She glanced at him apologetically.

"Don't feel bad. My stomach isn't complaining loudly, but I'm starving. You shouldn't have waited, but I'm glad you did."

A flush of excitement rose in her, until she heard his next sentence.

"I'm anxious to hear about your day with Nattie."

I'm being foolish. Lord, keep my mind focused on my purpose in this home. Not on silly thoughts. Her flush deepened in her embarrassment, and she hoped he might not notice in the softened light of the dining room doorway.

As they stepped into the room, Agnes came through the kitchen entrance with a steaming platter. She placed it on the table, then hit the switch as she exited, brightening the lights above the table.

David pulled out a chair for Callie, and she sat, waiting for him to be seated. The platter, sitting before them, aroused her senses. A mound of dark roasted beef was surrounded by sauteed onions, browned potatoes and carrots. She bowed her head to murmur a silent prayer, but before she asked God's blessing, David's warm voice split the silence.

He offered thanks for the food and the day, then he thanked God for Callie's presence in the house. A heated blush rose again to her cheeks. Now in the brightened room, when David looked up from his prayer, she knew her pink cheeks glowed.

"Sorry," Callie said, touching her cheeks, "I'm not used to being blessed along with a roast."

An unexpected burst of laughter rolled from David's chest. Agnes halted in the doorway, balancing a gravy boat and a salad bowl in apparent surprise. She looked from David to Callie, then added a smile to her face as she approached the table.

"This roast looks and smells wonderful, Agnes," David said, the merriment still lingering in his tone.

"Why, thank you, Mr. Hamilton." She placed the items on the table and scurried from the room with a final wide-eyed glance over her shoulder.

"Poor Agnes hasn't heard much laughter in the house since she came. I think I've surprised her." His hazel eyes crinkled at the edges as he looked at Callie.

"Then it's about time," Callie said lightly, trying to ignore the beating pulse in her temples. "'Laughter is good for all that ails you,' my father used to say."

"He was right. Laughter is music everyone can sing."

The word *music* seemed to catch them both off guard, and they each bent over their plates, concentrating on filling their stomachs. They ate quietly, keeping their eyes directed at the meat and potatoes. Callie scarched her mind for something to draw him out again and distract her own thoughts.

"I borrowed a book from the library. What a lovely room. And so many wonderful books." She pictured the room next to the library. She'd turned the knob, but the door had been locked. Though curious what the room was, she didn't ask. "I hope you don't mind about the book."

"No, not at all. You're welcome to read every one."

"I'd have to live here forever to do that."

He lifted his eyes to hers. "Yes, I suppose you would."

Silence lingered again, until David asked about Nattie. The rest of the meal was filled with tales of Callie's day with the child. They both were comfortable with the topic, and the conversation flowed easily until the meal ended.

When they reentered the foyer, she said goodnight and climbed the stairs. But the *click* of a door lock startled her, and she spun around. David slipped quietly into the room at the bottom of the stairs. Another faint *click* told her he had locked himself in. The sound bolted her to the floor, as her dreams rose up to haunt her. She stood a moment until she gained composure, then continued up the stairs.

Chapter Seven

After breakfast, Callie knocked on Nattie's door. Since the day in the snow, two weeks had passed with no new breakthrough.

Today, Nattie sat staring out the window with a doll in her lap. Pieces of doll clothing lay at her side, and Callie sensed she had stopped in mid-play. The doll wore a diaper and dress, with the shoes and bonnet waiting in a pile.

Nattie glanced at Callie, but turned her attention to the doll. Callie ambled to the window seat and sat for a moment before she spoke. "What a pretty baby you have there. But the poor child is only half dressed. What about her shoes and bonnet?"

Nattie ignored Callie, though occasionally she looked curiously at her and then lowered her eyes again.

Callie wondered what would make a difference. How could she get through to the lonely little girl. "Would you like to color? Or maybe we could draw some pictures?"

Nothing. Whatever she encouraged Nattie to do, Callie would first do it alone. That much she had learned. She shifted to the floor and pulled out one of Nattie's puzzles. Tumbling the pieces onto the floor, she turned them so all the picture pieces were facing up.

Nattie glanced at her, swiveling so her legs dangled over the window seat. She lay the doll to the side and watched.

Callie began forming the outer rim of the puzzle. When the frame was nearly complete, Nattie slid from the bench and joined her. She peered at the pieces to see if the fit matched, and often they did. Each time the child joined her, Callie felt they had made some progress.

Callie hummed a tune as she worked the puzzle. The sound surprised her. Humming, like singing, had vanished from her life. Today she felt like murmuring the simple melody, and best of all, Nattie eyed her more than usual. The child seemed comforted by the droning sound. Certainly her mother had hummed to her, too. Perhaps the memory soothed her.

Eventually, Callie rose and stared outside. The past days had seemed lonely. David had gone to Atlanta on a business trip, and except for an occasional conversation with Agnes, her world was as silent as Nattie's.

March would be along shortly, and she longed for warmer weather when she and Nattie could go for walks and run in the fresh air. Maybe then the child would warm the same way the summer sun would heat the soil, encouraging new shoots to sprout. Nattie, too, might come alive again.

* * *

As David finished his breakfast, Callie entered the dining room. Each time she appeared, a deep longing filled him.

"Good morning," she said brightly, and turned to the buffet.

David returned her greeting and watched as she took a plate and scooped up a serving spoonful of scrambled eggs. With toast and sausage on her plate, she sat on David's left. "How was your trip?"

"Fine. Too long actually, but that's business."

They hadn't talked much recently. All he'd learned was that nothing dramatic had occurred as yet with regard to Nattie. Though his hopes remained high, the process seemed to be taking forever.

"I wouldn't know much about business. I've always been a nurse. Whole different career. Though, we notice how quiet it is when you're away." She lowered her eyes, focusing on her plate and scooping egg onto her fork.

David knew exactly what she meant. Before she had come, the house had seemed a tomb. He sipped his coffee, hating to tell her he would be gone again that evening.

"I have a dinner invitation this evening, so I won't be home. I suppose you can endure one more night without my tantalizing conversation."

As he spoke, her face faded to disappointment. "One more night, huh? When I took the job I didn't have any guarantees of dinner entertainment, so I suppose I can handle it." She put a smile on her face, but David had learned enough about Callie to know the smile was to appease him.

He folded his napkin and laid it next to his plate. "To be honest, I'd rather stay home."

"Business dinner?"

"Probably, but on the pretense of a social evening at the parsonage."

Callie's face gave way to a wry grin. "Ah, an invitation from Mary Beth, no doubt."

A sigh escaped him before he could control it. "No doubt." He eyed his wristwatch and rose, longing to stay and talk. He had forgotten how comfortable it was to sit after a meal and chat. He and Sara had often lingered at the table long after the meal was finished. He could easily do the same with Callie. But his business waited him. "I'd better be on my way."

"I'm sure you'll have fun." Callie tilted her face toward him, and her words sounded to David as if they wavered between sarcasm and wit.

"How about a wager?"

"Sorry, kind sir, I don't make bets. It's sinful, you know." Her smile sent a tingle through him, and he glanced at his face as he passed a mirror in the entry to see if the unexpected sensation showed.

"I suppose we should have been polite and invited Callie to join us," Mary Beth gushed, after they settled into the cozy living room after dinner. "I don't know where my mind was."

I do, David thought as he gallantly tried to smile at her comment. "I'm sure she understands." Thinking of Callie's wry smile, he realized she understood Mary Beth Spier was looking for a husband—but in the wrong direction.

"Perhaps next time," John said. "We should enjoy each other's company more often. Other than Sundays, I might add."

David enjoyed his private joke. If John were to be perfectly honest, he might also add that he didn't see David on many Sundays, either. David waited, wondering where John was going from there.

"Speaking of Sundays," John said, "we certainly miss having an organ for worship. Looking back at the records, I see your wife was the organist for a couple of years."

David gathered his wits, keeping his face unemotional. "Yes, she was. I believe a lady named Ruta Dryer filled in for my wife while she was ill…and after Sara died."

"Yes, I noticed that, too. But then the organ needed some work, and I'm afraid financially we haven't been able to make those repairs."

"I see," David said, waiting for the pitch.

"I wonder if you'd considered helping out with that little project. I imagine we could find an organist—but first, we need the instrument."

David bit his lip, struggling to control his emotions. "Sara's death was a tremendous loss for my daughter and me, as you can imagine. I haven't given much thought to the organ since then. I've been concerned about my child, and to be honest, thoughts of the organ music fill me with some raw spots yet. You'll have to let me think about it."

"Oh, certainly, I wasn't suggesting that—"

"I may seem self-indulgent, but the congregation has adjusted to the piano. And I need to deal with my own problems—and my daughter's—before I deal with someone else's."

"Yes. Do take your time. I suppose I should have been more considerate in my request."

"Don't worry about it. How would you know what goes on in my head?"

Mary Beth leaned across the table and latched onto David's arm. "I wish I could help. I'm sure life isn't complete without…well, being alone and with your daughter, too. Hiring a woman to fill in for Nattie's mother is all right, but—"

"Callie is far more than a fill-in. She's a professional nurse, well-trained. I'm very hopeful that her influence with Nattie will bring her out of her cocoon. Callie's full of spirit and a delightful…" He looked at their astounded faces and realized he had gone overboard in Callie's defense.

Mary Beth stared at him wide-eyed. "Oh, I didn't mean she isn't capable. I'm sure she is. I mean your daughter has needs, but so do—"

"David knows what you meant, Mary Beth," John sputtered. "We shouldn't dwell on the subject. Would you care to play a game of Chinese checkers, David?"

Better than the Chinese water torture you're putting me through. David nearly laughed aloud at his thought.

* * *

On the first Sunday in March, late in the afternoon, Callie sat curled on the sofa in the library, reading Jane Austen's *Mansfield Park.* She'd read the author's other novels, enjoying the wit and social commentary on the lives of women in the early eighteen-hundreds.

Sometimes, she felt her own life was tangled in social principles.

Today for the first time since her arrival, Callie had gone to church. She had chosen to worship at a new, larger church on Washington Avenue, one with a large vibrant pipe organ. She longed to hear something uplifting, something to take the ache from her heart and give her patience and courage.

Even in church, for the past few years, she had avoided singing. But today she raised her voice, and her spirit lifted with the music. *Sweet hour of prayer, sweet hour of prayer.* Prayer? Had she prayed as she ought to have done? Or had she leaned on her own humble abilities, forgetting God's miracles?

The pastor's voice shot through her mind, like an answer to her question, with the Scripture reading. *"Then you will call upon Me and go and pray to Me, and I will listen to you. And you will seek Me and find Me, when you search for Me, with all your heart."* The morning's message settled into her thoughts. Pray, she must.

Now, as the sun lowered in the sky, Callie snapped on the light. Doing so, a shadow fell across her page. She glanced up to see David standing a distance from her, observing her silently.

He slid into a chair across from her. "Disappointed?"

"Disappointed?"

"With Nattie. I suppose you imagined by now she'd be playing like any six-year-old?" His face told his own story.

"I'm optimistic again. But you're disappointed, I think."

He lowered his head, studying his entwined fingers laying in his lap. "Oh, a little, I suppose. I don't know what to expect, really."

"You can't expect more from her than you do from yourself."

His head shot upward, and Callie swallowed, wondering why she had been so blunt.

"What do you mean?" His brows knit tightly, and his eyes squinted in the artificial light.

Well, here goes. Callie took a deep breath. "You can't hide behind these walls, totally. Not with your business. But look at you. You aren't living, either. Just marking days off the calendar."

"That's what you think, huh?"

"I suppose I'm too forward."

"I expect nothing less."

His eyes, despite the abrupt comment, crinkled in amusement.

"I should be angry at you, but I imagine you're telling the truth."

"That's what I see. Maybe you have another side, but here, everything is shut off. The doors are closed as if you want nothing to escape. Or is it, nothing to enter? You build walls around yourself…or lock yourself in your secret room."

His face pinched again. "Secret room?"

Callie tilted her head forward. "Yes, the room next door. The locked door."

He released a quiet chuckle. "That's my study. I suppose I've gotten into the habit of keeping it locked. All my business secrets are in that room." He rose. "Come. I'll show you."

Callie felt her cheeks grow hot. "No, I didn't mean—"

"Up, up." He reached down and took her hand, pulling her to her feet. "I don't want you to think I have bodies locked away in there or skeletons hiding in the closets."

"I'm sorry. Really."

But her pleading did no good. David wrapped his arm around her shoulder and marched her to the hallway. He turned the handle, and the door opened without a key. He glanced at her with a playful, smug look and pushed open the door.

Though she felt foolish being led in as if she were a naughty child, she savored the warmth of his arm embracing her. She longed to be in his sturdy arms, feeling safe and secure. But as she stepped into the room, he raised his hands to her shoulders and pivoted her in one direction, then the other, showing her the room.

"See. Not one body."

His voice rippled through her. She turned toward him, her eyes begging forgiveness. "I wasn't suggesting you had something bad in here. I meant, you lock yourself away. There's a difference."

He looked deeply into her eyes, and her heart stopped

momentarily, dragging her breath from her. When the beat returned, its rhythm galloped through her like a horse and rider traversing rocky ground. Faster. Slower. Faltering. She struggled for control.

"You're right, I suppose," he said.

His words unlocked their gaze. But in the lengthy silence, Callie became flustered. "I'm right?"

"Yes, about locking myself away from the world."

He moved into the room. "Since you're here, come in. As you see, your sitting room is directly above this one. It's the tower room."

The tower intrigued her, and she moved voluntarily into the depth of the uniquely shaped room. The heavy wooden paneling darkened his study in comparison to her sunny room. Centered on one wall, his vast desk faced the outer hall. Tall shelves and a row of file cabinets stood nearby. A leather sofa and chair sat in the center of the room on an elegant Persian carpet.

"All man. No woman's touch here," she said.

A fleeting grin dashed across his face. "This room is mine, remember." His right hand gestured toward the tower room, and she wandered through the archway. Only two windows lit the circular room, smaller then hers above. As she turned, her eyes were drawn to another piano, a console, against an inner wall.

She stepped forward, noticing manuscript paper spread along the stand. She turned to him in surprise. "You write music?"

"Not really."

She felt him withdraw, swiftly rebuilding the wall he had opened when he let her enter his sanctuary. "But this is an unfinished manuscript." Her eyes sought his.

"I used to write music. I haven't touched that in a long time. I haven't played in a long time."

She nodded. Neither had she. She'd let the music in her life die the way part of her had died that terrible day. Yet, today, truth rose from the solemn moment. David would never live again until he lived fully. And neither would she.

A sound caused them to turn toward the foyer. Agnes stood in the doorway of the study.

"Dinner's ready when you are, Mr. Hamilton."

"Fine, we're coming now."

Callie pulled herself from the room. "I'll get Nattie," she said, hurrying into the hallway. She climbed the stairs, trembling over her second revelation of the day. Earlier, she'd considered the importance of prayer. Now, she knew she could ask no one else to join the living unless she lived herself.

After breakfast two weeks later, Callie and Nattie lay together, coloring on the parlor floor. David stepped into the room wearing his overcoat, his briefcase in his hand. He leaned down and kissed Nattie's head. "Goodbye, Nat."

Callie tilted her head and looked at him standing above her. "We'll see you later."

"Yes, I shouldn't be too late. By the way, this Friday I have a meeting in Indianapolis. I don't know if you need to make a trip home, but you're welcome to ride along. The meeting should run only a couple of hours. Perhaps you'd like to visit with your mother."

Callie rose from the floor, surprised at his offer. "Yes, I'd like that. I know my mother would enjoy the visit, and I have a few things I can pick up while I'm there." Retrieving her light-weight clothing excited her more than did visiting with her mother, but she kept that to herself. Most of all she'd enjoy the private time with David. "I'd love to go, if you don't mind."

"Not at all, I'd enjoy the company. And Agnes said she'd be happy to keep an eye on Nattie."

Their gazes connected, and Callie sought the flashing green specks that glinted in his eyes. A flush rose to her neck, and she looked away from him. "I'll call my mother then, so she'll be expecting me."

He nodded and took a step backward toward the door. "Good." He spun around, and she heard the front door close.

Nattie paused momentarily, almost as if she would speak, but instead, she lowered her head and concentrated on her picture. Recently, her dark-toned coloring had given way to brighter shades, one success Callie had noticed. Nattie used a yellow crayon to color the sun, then traded for a medium green to fill in the grass. Big progress in Callie's view.

She stretched out on the floor again next to the child and turned back to her picture: red tulips, green leaves, yellow daffodils. It reminded her that spring lay on their doorstep.

Then, without direction, her thoughts jumped to the changing colors in David's eyes. In the morning light that streamed through the window, the colors had shifted and altered, creating earthy, vibrant hues. Her heart skipped at the vision, and the image hummed within her.

Humming. Callie eased back on her elbows and held her breath. She hadn't been humming, but a sweet lilting melody rose to her ears. Without moving, she listened. Softly, Nattie hummed as she concentrated on the coloring book, her silence finally broken.

Callie's pulse raced, and her joy lifted as high as the prayer of thanks she whispered in her mind for the wondrous gift.

Chapter Eight

With David at the wheel, Callie leaned back and enjoyed the passing scenery. Though spring was yet a few days away, a fresh green hue brightened the landscape, and a new warmth promised things to come.

David, too, seemed to sense Nattie's own promise of things to come. Since hearing of her latest progress, David smiled more often. He referred to Callie as another miracle worker, though she reminded him more than once that God worked miracles, she didn't.

David glanced at the dashboard clock. "I figure we'll arrive about eleven. I'll drop you off and still have time to get to the meeting." He shot her a glance. "I should only be a couple of hours."

"Just come when you're finished. I'll be ready I'm sure." She'd probably be ready sooner. Yet she had to admit, she and her mother had plenty to talk about. She had spoken to Grace only briefly since arriving in Bedford.

"Are you sure? Maybe I should call."

Callie opened her shoulder bag and jotted down the telephone number. "Here you go."

"Slip it in my pocket so I remember to take it with me."

She leaned across the space between them, slipping the note into his nearest suit coat pocket. Her fingers tingled at the touch of the soft cashmere wool, and she warmed at his nearness. *Don't get carried away,* she chided herself.

Romantic fantasies had long disappeared from her dreams. She had never known a man before or after the experience of her child's conception. The thought of intimacy with any man frightened her.

As a teen, she had dreamed of the special day when she would dress in a white gown and float down the aisle as a bride, giving herself to a loving man, exploring and learning about love and passion. The dream had vanished as quickly as her virginity, and in its place, shame and guilt festered like an infected wound.

"You're so quiet," David said.

"Sorry. Just thinking."

"I hope they're nice thoughts."

She closed her eyes and avoided the truth. "Yes, they're very nice." She couldn't tell him the private things that filled her mind. No one would ever hear those thoughts. Another reason she could never fall in love.

After a short distance, the outskirts of Indianapolis spread along the horizon, and David soon left her at Grace's front door. She raised her hand as he pulled away, then she entered the house. She expected her mother to be hanging out the window, waiting for her, but instead the rooms were silent.

"Mom," she called. She wandered to the kitchen, where dishes lay piled on the countertop. Very unlike her mother.

"Mother." She listened and heard a noise above her.

"Callie?"

"You're upstairs, I take it." Callie climbed the steps, and saw her mother standing in the hallway, still in her bathrobe. Concern prickled her. Grace never slept late. "What's up with you?"

"I don't know," Grace answered, seeming confused. "I didn't feel well this morning."

"Or last night," Callie added.

"What do you mean?" Grace shuffled down the hallway.

Callie stood by the stairs, transfixed. "The dishes. You didn't clean up after dinner last night. That's not like you at all. Something's wrong. You need to see a doctor."

Grace swished the air with her hand as if erasing her words. "I don't need a doctor. Probably just a little spring cold. You know how they can be."

She studied her mother's face. Grace's mouth was pulled to the side in a faint grimace. Dark circles ringed her eyes, raccoonlike against her pale skin. "I don't know, Mom."

"You go down and make us some coffee, and I'll get dressed. I'll look much better when I wash my face and comb my hair."

Callie moved to her mother's side, giving her a brief hug. "Okay, but we'll talk about this when you come down."

When she returned to the kitchen, she put on a pot of coffee and rinsed last night's dishes, then loaded the dishwasher. It hadn't been run for a couple of days. Callie's concern was not the untouched dishes or her mother's appearance. Grace loved to play the martyr. Yet today, she denied valiantly that something was wrong. Callie knew something was *very* wrong.

She started the dishwasher, then looked into the refrigerator. "Old Mother Hubbard's cupboard," she said aloud to herself. Inside, she found three eggs and the end of a bread loaf. When the eggs were scrambled and in the frying pan, Callie popped the bread into the toaster. Her mind worked over the problem. No question. Grace wasn't herself. Living two hours away, she'd have to depend on Ken to keep an eye on their mother. She'd call him after breakfast.

Grace entered the kitchen as the toast popped.

"Perfect timing, Mom. I made us some breakfast." Though Callie had eaten, she joined her mother at the table. She heaped the egg on Grace's plate, giving herself only a tablespoon full.

"Now, I'm not going to leave you without knowing what happened. When did you get sick?"

"Please, Callie, I'm fine. Wait until you're an old woman. Then you'll understand about being tired…and confused once in a while." She nibbled the toast.

"I'm tired and confused now, Mom. Age has nothing to do with it. I think you need to see a doctor. You're not ninety. You're only in your mid-sixties. I'll call Ken before I go."

"I felt fine until yesterday afternoon. I got a terrible headache. Sort of achy in my left arm. I think it scared me. I laid down for a while, and it seemed to pass."

Callie pictured the dishes piled on the counter. The problem hadn't passed as fast as Grace wanted her to believe. Rather than press her mother, she allowed Grace to change the subject, and filled her in on Bedford, her progress with Nattie, and a description of the lovely house.

As the time approached to leave, Callie made a doctor's appointment for Grace and phoned Ken. "I know you're busy, but could you please see Mom gets to the doctor?"

"Are you that worried?" Ken asked, sounding as if he thought she was being foolish.

"Look, Ken, she said her arm ached, and she had a bad headache. We can't play around with symptoms. Let's let a doctor tell her it's nothing."

"I suppose you're right."

"And you really should check with her every day or so, at least until she's feeling better."

"Easy for you. You go off and let me do the work, huh?"

"For a change, it won't hurt you. The thought of leaving her here alone bothers me."

"Where's our dear sister Patricia, when we need her?"

Callie sighed at her brother's complaining. "In California, where she's always been. Quit trying to wheedle out of this. Just check on her once in a while. Can you do that?"

"Okay, I give."

Though his voice was teasing, Ken left Callie less than

confident, but there was little else she could do. Before she walked away from the telephone, David called to say he'd be later than expected.

When he finally arrived, Callie hurried out to his car. "Would you mind coming in a minute? Mom insists upon meeting you."

David turned off the ignition and stepped out into the afternoon sunshine, a knowing look etching his face. "We have to make mothers happy."

Callie led him up the porch steps. "I'm worried about her, actually." She glanced at him over her shoulder and grasped the doorknob.

He paused. "Something wrong?"

"Yes, but I'm not sure what. She seems ill, but she denies it."

David's brows furrowed as Callie led him inside. As they came into the living room, Grace eyed him.

"Mother," Callie said, "this is my employer, David Hamilton. David, my mother, Grace Randolph."

David reached forward as if to shake hands, but Grace's arms remained folded against her chest. Unabashed, he retraced his hand and tucked it into his pocket. "I'm sorry to hear you're not feeling well, Mrs. Randolph."

"I'm fine. My daughter lives so far away she's forgotten what I look like."

"Mother," Callie said, controlling her irritation, "you are not fine. I've called Ken, and I want you to promise to call me after you see the doctor."

"It's nothing. You're making a mountain out of nothing."

Callie rested her hand on her mother's shoulder. "Let the doctor tell me that, okay?"

Grace snorted her protest.

"Promise you'll call," Callie said.

After a lengthy pause, Grace nodded her head.

Callie bent and brushed a kiss on her cheek. "We have to go, Mom. Please do as I say."

Callie gave David a desperate look and stepped backward. David proceeded ahead of her and held the door open while Callie gave her mother a final wave, then stepped outside.

When they had settled in the car, Callie rubbed her temples. "She won't call. I'll have to call Ken. I pray he knows something. Sometimes brothers are useless when it comes to asking questions."

David glanced at her. "Do you want to drive up and take her yourself?"

Callie sighed. "I don't know. Ken should be able to handle it. I'll call him when we get home. Maybe I'll feel better."

"That's fine, but if you need to come here, Agnes can keep an eye on Nattie for the day."

"Thanks." She caught his image in the rearview mirror. His concern touched her.

Callie leaned her head against the headrest, and they drove in silence until they passed the city limits of Indianapolis. A few miles beyond the Franklin exit, she straightened in her seat. "Sorry. I'm not good company."

"No problem. Did you get a little rest?"

"Yes, I think I drifted off for a minute. I've spent my life in silent battles with my mother, and now that something's wrong, I'm dealing with some guilt. And a lot of worry."

"That's part of life." David drew his shoulders upward in a deep sigh. "I think we all do that, Callie. It's so easy to take things for granted. Complain and grumble. Then when we're gripped by worry, we have all the 'I wishes' and 'I should haves' thrashing around inside us."

"I want to resolve some of those things with my mom before anything happens. I guess this scare reminded me of that."

"Good. Look at the positive side. And speaking of positive thoughts, how's your stomach? Mine's empty. They only gave us coffee and pastries at the meeting. No good wholesome food. Did you eat at your mother's?"

"I made her breakfast, but I only nibbled."

"Then we'll stop for dinner. We should reach Columbus about five o'clock. I think Weinantz opens about then. The food is excellent. I called Agnes and warned her not to cook for us."

A strange shyness filled her. David had planned ahead for their dinner together. She'd chased such thoughts from her foolish dreams, and now he was making her hopes come true. She could deal with fantasy, but reality made her vulnerable. *The boss is taking his employee to dinner. Nothing more.* She repeated the words over and over in her mind until they reached Columbus.

The town proved to be a surprise. In the middle of small, turn-of-the-century communities, Columbus rose like a contemporary misfit. Buildings of modern design filled the city center; buses carried tourists through the streets to view the renowned architecture. The restaurant lived up to David's praise, and after their meal, Callie relaxed over coffee, the worries of the day softening.

David studied her concerned face, as she sipped from the steaming cup. For the first time since they had left her mother's, a slight smile touched her rosy lips. "You look more relaxed."

"I feel better. The meal was wonderful," Callie said.

Her smile warmed him. "I'm glad. I know what worry can do. And I've had the same guilty thoughts myself. I look at Nattie's situation and blame myself. After Sara's death, I wasn't there for her. Such a little girl, and I crept away like a wounded animal. I feel terrible about that."

"I think it's more than that, David. Something happened. Something more than Sara's death. I don't know exactly what I mean, but her silence seems deeper than normal grief. You know, children are usually known for bouncing back."

"They do." Her comment pushed him deeper into thought. "I don't know. I've always blamed myself." Was she right? What could have happened? Sara's death was no surprise. And still, it hit him harder than he would ever have imagined. Then, what about Nattie? Could something else have happened?

He gazed into Callie's perplexed-looking eyes, and felt his chest tighten. Bluer than the sky. Rich, deep and filled with her own secrets. What dark moments hid behind those lovely eyes?

"What you've been able to do for Nattie makes me so grateful," he said. "You've already made a difference in her life." In *my* life, he thought, feeling his pulse waver as he regarded her. "Nattie leaves her room now…and the humming. Something more will happen. I sense it."

Callie's face tensed. She lowered her eyes, then raised them shyly. "Could we talk a little? About things that might bother you?"

A knot of foreboding formed in his stomach. "Like what?"

"Tell me about Sara's death. You've never said anything, and like I said, I suspect something more happened to Nattie than losing a mother. Was Nattie with Sara when it happened? Would she feel to blame for some reason?"

"To blame? No, how could she?" He closed his eyes for a moment, the awful memories rippling through him. "Sara had cancer. Leukemia. Nattie couldn't feel responsible for that. Anyway, she was only four."

"I know, but children overhear things that they don't understand. They fill in the blanks, make up their own stories, and things get out of context. I just wondered if that might be possible."

"No, I'm sure that didn't happen." Though he said no, thoughts galloped through his mind as he wondered if something had been said to make Nattie feel Sara's death was her fault.

"If she misunderstood something, anything, it might explain her silence," Callie repeated. "I suppose I'm grasping for it all to make sense."

"I've done the same. Wondered. Worried."

"When did you learn your wife had cancer?"

An overwhelming sorrow washed over him, and the answer stuck in his throat. Callie's question disturbed thoughts he'd tucked away. Now they came crashing into his memory. Without knowing, she was treading on raw nerve endings and deep painful wounds that had yet to heal.

Her drawn face overflowed with tenderness. "I'm sorry," she said. "I guess I'm dredging up hurtful memories. I just thought, the more I understand, the more I'll know what to look for."

He reached across the table and touched her hand clasped in a tense fist. At first, she flinched at his touch, but in a heartbeat her hand relaxed.

"You're right. On both counts." He drew his hand away, balling it, too, into a fist. "Sara had leukemia before we married…but we were hopeful. Like all young, idealistic couples, we thought love could solve every problem—even cancer."

"Oh, David, I'm so sorry. I had no idea. And then when she got pregnant…" Callie tossed herself back against the cushion with a lengthy sigh. "Never mind, I understand."

He grimaced. "Thanks." But she didn't really understand. Not everything. He was not ready to open all the wounds. He hid behind her misconceptions in safety. What would she think of him if she knew the whole story? He leaned against the seat and folded his arms across his chest. He had told her enough.

Chapter Nine

The following week Callie stayed in the parlor after dinner, trying to concentrate on her book. Concern dogged her as she assessed Ken's surprise telephone call.

"Dr. Sanders thinks Mom may have had a minor stroke."

"Minor stroke? How bad is that? Major. Minor. The thought scares me, Ken."

"He'll know more after he gets the results of the MRI test. It's scheduled for next week. Apparently, it takes some kind of picture of the brain."

"MRI. Yes, it's magnetic resonance imaging."

"Thank you, Florence."

"Florence? Oh, Nightingale." She snickered. "Poor Florence wouldn't know anything about an MRI. Anyway, how's Mom doing? Do you think I should come up there?"

"She's good. I don't notice a difference."

Callie rolled her eyes. "Do you really think you'd notice?"

"Thanks, sister dear."

"You're welcome. You'll call me as soon as you hear something."

"Don't worry. She's okay…really."

When Callie hung up the receiver, she had a tremendous urge to get in her car and go to Indianapolis. At dinner, she told David. Again, he encouraged her to go if she would feel better, but wisdom stepped in. She'd wait to hear the test results.

After the meal, David went to his study to work, and she relaxed on the sofa, her legs stretched on the cushion and her feet over the edge. Staring at the book propped in her hand, she saw only a blur, as her thoughts twisted and turned. Nattie had carried storybooks down with her before dinner, and she lay on the floor nearby, flipping through the pages.

When David stepped into the room, she and Nattie glanced up.

"Hmm? All the ladies have their noses buried in a book, I see." He walked to Nattie and stroked her hair with his fingers.

Callie watched her raise the book toward her father, and her heart stood still when she heard the child's soft, sweet voice.

"Read to me, Daddy."

"Nattie," David gasped. His eyes widened and his face paled momentarily, then brightened with happiness. "I sure will, sweetheart." He scooped her up in his arms and carried her to the chair.

Callie's heart skipped and hammered in wild rhythm. She fixed on Nattie's face, witnessing the special moment of her first full sentence since her mother's death. Where one sentence lived, there were two. Then three. It was only a matter of time.

Glowing with rapture, David read two storybooks without stopping, holding the child in his arms. She hugged him tightly when he finished, and for the first time, Callie witnessed Nattie showing affection. Callie and David shared the special moment with quiet looks of elation, not wanting to break the spell.

After Nattie had gone to bed, David returned, bounding into the room like a man saved from a firing squad. Callie rose at his exuberant entrance, feeling her own joy. In a flash, he closed the distance between them, grasping her in his arms and pulling her to his chest.

"Thank you. Thank you," he whispered into her hair.

His warmth surrounded her, and the heat of surprise rose to her face.

"What you've brought into our lives has been like a miracle. Two years I've waited and longed for a single sentence, and tonight—" he looked into her eyes "—my prayer was answered."

A gasp escaped her, and David stepped back abruptly as if embarrassed.

"I'm sorry," he said. "I didn't mean to frighten you."

"Surprised me was all. Not frightened." Though she said the words, the truth was that she was shaken by his actions. She hadn't been that close to a man since… She remembered her father's arms comforting her, but that had been so long ago.

"No, I scared you. I saw the look in your face. I'm sorry. But I didn't think. Tonight's been so wonderful."

"Oh, David, it is wonderful." Though thrilled with the moment, her reaction concerned her. Had she truly been frightened? In her daydreams, she imagined herself in his arms. She had never expected the fantasy to come true. "I guess I didn't expect—"

"Don't apologize. Any apology should come from me."

But she didn't hear one. And she didn't want one. Looking into his eyes, she saw a hint of mischief. "Perhaps," Callie teased, "but I don't hear you apologizing."

A wry grin lightened his face. "And you probably won't. It was my way of saying thank you."

She grinned. "And much less expensive than a raise."

While Callie lay in bed that night, thoughts of the evening filtered over her like warm sunshine. Nattie's words, *"Read to me, Daddy,"* sang in Callie's mind like a melody. David's smile and his joy rushed through her, jostling her pulse to a maddening pace. *Stop. I'll never go to sleep.*

Though Callie cautioned herself, she didn't heed her own warning. Again, her thoughts stirred, and she remembered his strong, eager arms embracing her. But with that image, her dreams ended, and her nightmare began.

She stiffened at the thought. What could she do with herself? Frustration dampened her lovely memories, and she threw the pillow over her head, fumbling in her self-inflicted darkness to turn off the lamp.

Her black dreams had lain dormant for weeks. Tonight, like a rolling mist, the nightmare crept silently into her sleep. *As she moved through a fog, a* click *resounded in her ears. Then, she saw the lock. He flashed his broad, charming smile. "You're nervous enough, I'm sure. We don't want anyone popping in and making things worse, do we?"*

Her chest tightened, anxiety growing inside her. She nodded, afraid to speak.

His fingers ran over the keys in flourished arpeggios, *and she lifted her voice, following his fingers, up and down the scales. Her tone sounded pinched in her ears. She wished she could relax so he could hear her natural quality. Suddenly her singing turned to a silent scream.*

In the pulsing silence, Callie's eyes opened to blackness. She raised her hand and wiped the perspiration from her hairline. Again she fumbled in the deep darkness for the light switch. The flash of brightness hurt her eyes, and she squinted.

"I can't bear this anymore," she said aloud. "Please, go away and let me live." Her shoulders lifted in a shivered sigh. She pulled her flannel robe over her trembling body and slid her feet into her slippers. Milk? Tea? Something to wash away the dreams.

She dragged herself into the bathroom and rinsed her face. Her image in the mirror frightened her, her skin pale as a gray shroud. She turned from the glass and wandered through her rooms to the hallway. Quietly she edged her way down the stairs. The whole house slept, and falling down a dark staircase would add not only grief to her terrible night, but also chaos to everyone else's rest.

At the bottom of the stairs, the moon shining through the fanlight above the door guided her path around the newel post toward the kitchen. Deeper in the wide foyer, darkness closed in, but she kept the carpet beneath her feet, knowing the door would be straight ahead at the end.

With her hand in front of her, she touched the knob and swung open the door. A light coming from the kitchen surprised her. She hesitated. Having a middle-of-the-night conversation with Agnes didn't appeal to her, but despite the thought, the choice seemed better than turning back.

As she stepped into the kitchen, she halted. It wasn't Agnes, but David, who sat at the table, sipping from a thick mug. When their eyes met, he looked as surprised as she must have. "Well," she said. "I thought I'd be the only nightwalker wandering the house. Am I intruding on your solace?"

"No, to be honest, you're a pleasant sight."

She thought of her ashen face and disheveled hair and grinned. "I beg to differ, but beauty is in the 'beholder's eye,' they say."

His gaze swept hers, and warm tenderness brushed her heart.

"Beauty is," he agreed, and took another drink. He held the cup poised in the air. "How about some hot chocolate?"

The aroma reached her senses. "Sounds wonderful."

"I made more than I wanted. Sit, and I'll get it for you."

He rose and pulled a mug from the cabinet. Callie slid into a chair, running her fingers through her hair and thinking how perfectly terrible she must look.

He poured the cocoa and placed the hot beverage in front of her. "There." He sat again, then regarded her. "So what brings you out of a warm bed in the depths of the night?"

"A mind that won't stop, it seems." She avoided the truth.

"I know what that means. Nattie's in my mind…among other things."

"Business?" she asked, looking into the milk-chocolate liquid. Rays from the overhead light glinted in splayed patterns on the surface of her drink. When she experienced his silence, she looked up. His eyes met hers.

"No, not business. I was thinking about you, to be honest."

Protectively, her hand clutched her robe. "Me? Why?"

He shook his head. "You'll never know how much you mean to me, Callie. All you've done for us here. You're like a breath of spring after a long winter." A grin tugged at the corners of his mouth. "Pretty poetic for the middle of the night, huh?"

She couldn't speak. She struggled to keep her eyes from widening any more than they already had. "But that's why you hired me. To help Nattie."

"But you've done more than that." He reached across the table and laid his hand on hers. "You've helped me, too. I feel alive again, like a man released from prison, his life restored."

Callie looked at his hand pressing against the back of hers. Though her initial thought was to recoil, she joyed in feeling the warm pressure against her skin.

His gaze traced the line of her face. "I wish you'd tell me what troubles you. You know so much about me. I know so little about your life."

She drew her hand from under his and tucked it in her

lap. "What troubles me? Nothing really. Old problems crop up once in a while. Nothing you can do about them."

"But…sometimes you seem frightened. Is it me? Are you afraid of me? Callie, I'd never hurt you. If you think—"

Lifting her hand, she pressed her finger on his lips to quiet him. "Please, it's me. Not you."

He raised his hand, capturing her finger against his lips. A kiss as gentle as a fluttering breeze brushed across her skin. Her heart stopped, and she drew in a quick breath. He wrapped her fingers in his and lowered his hand. "I pray someday you can tell me. Whatever it is."

She withdrew her hand a second time. He tilted his head, his face filled with emotion. She wanted to touch his unshaven cheeks with her palms and kiss the worry from his eyes. A worry that she knew was for her, not for himself. Everything in her cried out to tell him, but she pushed the urge deep inside her, praying this time the pangs would stay there.

Patches of sunlight glinted through the sprouting foliage. Callie glanced over her shoulder at Nattie running behind her, looking like any happy child. A rosy glow lit her cheeks, and her eyes sparkled in the brightness of the afternoon.

"Can't keep up with me, can you?" Callie called as she neared the crest of the hill.

Nattie stumbled along, her young, inactive legs not used to the rigors of dashing up a hillside. When Callie reached the top, she fell to the grass, laughing and breathless. Nattie reached her, puffing, and plopped down near her.

Though the hillside was sprinkled with trees, the landscape offered a view of a smattering of houses and distant barns. The new grass and tree leaves, sporting their pale green colors, sent a charge of rebirth and excitement through Callie.

Like spring bursting on the scene, so Nattie's blossoming was another new gift. Nattie had opened her silent world a little more, and brief sentences popped from her like the unexpected surprise of a new Jack-in-the-box. Neither David nor Callie knew at what moment the child might add another sentence to those they had already tallied with joy.

With her heart full of the abounding changes around her, she began with a hum, and before she realized she had risen, as if the trees were her audience, and had opened her mouth in song—*"Beautiful Savior, King of Creation."* She began timidly as a lilting murmur. She hadn't sung in such a long time. But by the third verse, her voice soared into the sky.

Nattie blinked, then widened her curious eyes. A glimmer of awareness covered her face. Callie studied her. Had her mother sung to her in this spot? Or was it the song? Something in the child's look gave Callie a sense of connection. Could music be a catalyst to help the child heal from her terrible hurt?

The sunlight shimmered through Nattie's hair, creating a golden halo around her face. Callie's heart tugged at the lovely picture. Lost forever was the sight of her own child. Since arriving in Bedford, she had locked her own sorrow in her heart's prison. How could she help Nattie if she spent all her energies grieving over something that could never be?

But today, the sorrow gushed from her like a geyser pent up in the earth. Did her child have dark hair like her father, or honey-toned tresses like hers? Were her eyes blue or brown? Was she happy? Or was she sad the way Nattie had been? All the questions that she had stuffed away rose, pouring over her.

She let the questions flow, then, with new conviction, forced them away. In her silence, the only sounds were the chirping birds and a distant mooing cow. Then Nattie tilted her head, and a grin pulled at the corners of her bowed mouth. "Sing more."

Hearing the child's voice, Callie's heart skipped a beat. Her voice little more than a whisper, she asked, "Do you have a favorite?"

Nattie shook her head.

"No favorite?" With a chuckle, Callie leaned down and tickled her neck. "I won't know what to sing for you, then." She sank to the ground as near to Nattie as she dared. "Maybe someday you'll want to sing with me."

Callie began humming softly. A favorite hymn tangled in her memory. As the words unscrambled in her mind, her heart lifted like the melody of the song. *"What wondrous love is this, oh my soul."* The years that her voice had been silenced by her battered memories seemed forgotten. *"That caused the Lord of life to bear the heavy cross."* The child only listened, staring at the ground with an occasional glimpse toward Callie's face. She too bore some secret "heavy cross."

A deep sorrow filled the child's eyes, and when the line of the verse had ended, Callie stopped her song. Music had definitely touched the child's heart. But with *sadness.* Callie longed to tell David her discovery.

Chapter Ten

David was out of town again, and Callie felt antsy for adult conversation. With a short grocery list tucked in her shoulder bag, she drove into town. Agnes usually shopped, but today Callie needed fresh air and a distraction, and the housekeeper had graciously agreed to keep an eye on Nattie.

Outside, spring worked its magic on her spirit. She wanted to run and play in the bright, new grass, not be bound to the quiet, closed-in house. She longed to leave her worries and sadness behind.

Through the trees, she caught a glimpse of the steeple of John Spier's church, and an unexplained urge tugged at her. She pulled the car into the empty parking lot, stepped out onto the gravel and looked around. The young pastor's car was parked in the parsonage driveway. She headed for the door, wondering if Pastor John might be working inside.

At the entrance, she pushed the handle on one of the big

double doors, and it opened. The bright sun shine spread inside along the worn carpet in the small foyer.

She stepped inside, pulling the weighty door closed. Standing still, she waited for her eyes to adjust to the gloom. She listened for a sound, but heard nothing. With hesitant steps, she wandered down the aisle, which was lit by the daylight shining through the deep-toned stained glass. Above the dark walnut altar hung a large wooden cross. But the image that caught in her eye was the piano.

She moved as if drawn to the fruitwood console, which was flanked by chairs for a small choir. A trembling melancholy clung to her as she edged forward. Her gaze caressed the keys, and she slid onto the bench, an old desire surging within her.

A hymn book lay open on the music stand, and her hands trembled as she placed them on the keyboard. As she followed the music, her fingers felt stiff and uncertain on the keys. Though the grand piano sat in silence at the house, she hadn't been moved to play, perhaps knowing the piano was Sara's.

When the hymn ended, she turned the pages to another, then another. Before she realized it, her voice was lifted in song. *"There's a quiet understanding when we're gathered in the spirit."* She had often sung that song in her church in Indianapolis. Longing tugged at her heart. She had not sung in church for the past seven years, and today, with no congregation, she sang for God alone. When the song ended, she bowed her head.

"That was wonderful."

Callie jumped, her head pivoting at the sound of a familiar voice. "Oh, you scared me."

Pastor John halted. "I'm sorry. I didn't mean to."

"How long were you there?"

Smiling, he shrugged. "About two hymns, I'd say. I didn't want to stop you. You play and sing beautifully."

Her hands slid from the keyboard to her lap. "Thanks. I, um, don't sing much anymore."

"But you should." He leaned toward her, his elbows resting on top of the piano. "You have a real gift. It's a shame not to use it."

Callie's shoulders tensed; she felt cornered. "I…I did years ago."

"We could use a soloist in church some Sundays." He raised his eyebrows in question.

Callie lowered her lids, then raised them. "Yes, well, I've been giving thought to singing again."

"And?"

"And I guess I'm not quite ready."

"Not stage fright? You seem so confidant, I can't imagine your being intimidated by an audience."

His tone pushed her for an explanation. "I don't have stage fright. I had a bad experience a few years ago."

"I'm sorry."

She shifted uncomfortably. "Wounds heal eventually."

"Well, I'll keep your…wound in my prayers."

Callie whispered her thanks, relieved to end the conversation.

John lifted a chair from the choir area and swung it next to the piano. He sat, and a need to escape gripped her. Not wanting to be rude, she struggled against the urge.

He leaned toward her. "Have you ever thought about directing a choir?"

She sputtered a laugh. "Direct? No. Never in my life. I take it you need a choir director."

"Pam Ingram, our pianist, is doing her best, but playing and directing is difficult, especially for someone with limited training."

"Yes, it is." Callie's heart thudded, as she wondered how to escape without being utterly rude. "I really should get going. Agnes is waiting for the groceries." A nervous titter broke from her lips. "Today wasn't the best day to stop, but I've never been here, and…I was curious."

"You're a member somewhere else?"

"No, I've been going to, um, New Hope over on Washington."

John nodded. "Ah, the new church. We have a terrible time keeping members here. They have so much. Including an organ."

Callie's attention was drawn to the small balcony and the line of pipes. "The organ needs work, you mentioned."

"Yes, a few thousand dollars. We don't have it. I'd sort of hoped since Sara Hamilton had been the organist—and David directed the choir—he might make a donation."

Callie's stomach somersaulted. "David was the choir director here?"

His eyebrows shot upward. "Yes, I've been reading all kinds of things to learn the church's history. I was surprised. And so are you, I see."

Callie felt defensive. "He's never mentioned it, but why would he? He's still healing."

"That's what he said."

"So you asked him?"

John rose, stepped to the console, then spun around. "Yes, I mentioned it."

Wounds heal. She prayed they would. Music was the way to reach Nattie. Might David refuse to let her try? Time and patience, that's what they both needed. "Give him time. Things will get better, I'm sure."

A grin curled his lips. "And you? Should I give you time, too, to consider my offer?"

"Your offer?"

"To sing for us? Or help with a choir?"

"Yes, time. It's something we all need." She rose abruptly and stepped to the center aisle before turning around. "I'd better be on my way."

She surveyed the surroundings again as she headed for the door, then stopped halfway down the aisle. "Your church has charm, you know," she said, turning toward him. "New Hope doesn't have charm at all. You should stress that. A lot of people still enjoy the 'old-time religion.'" She waved and rushed up the aisle before he asked her any more questions—or favors.

* * *

Though David had returned from his trip, he kept himself closed up in his study. Callie was disappointed. She missed him and hoped to talk to him about the questions that filled her mind regarding Nattie. Sitting in the parlor, she looked through the foyer to the closed door across the way.

Since Nattie had already gone to bed for the night, Callie's responsibilities for the day were over. She rose and marched across the hall, but when she reached the door, she halted. Filling her lungs with air, she released a stream of anxiety from her body, then knocked.

Seconds ticked by. A near-eternity passed before she heard David's response.

"Yes?"

She closed her eyes, prayed, and turned the knob.

David sat at his desk across from the door. "Callie, come in," he said.

She stood shyly near the door. "I'm sorry to disturb you."

"Is something wrong?"

"No, I...I wondered if you have a minute to talk."

"Sure, have a seat." After shuffling the papers in front of him, he rose, motioning for her to sit. "I'm sorry to be hidden away again. I've been preoccupied with a ton of paperwork and some big decisions since I came back from the trip."

"I understand, but I've had a lot on my mind, too." She sank into an overstuffed chair. "And...and I wanted to get your opinion."

David joined her, choosing one of the comfortable chairs across from her. He leaned over with his elbows on his knees, his hands folded in front of him, as he listened to her story of Nattie's day on the hillside. His eyes brightened when he heard about the child's interest in Callie's singing. Yet, as always, sadness followed when he learned of her retreat into silence again.

"But I know music is the key," Callie said. "I believe if I encourage that interest, we'll get somewhere. But since it's a sensitive issue, I wanted to check first. I don't want to do anything that might hurt either of you."

David stared at his shoe, moving the toe along the pattern in the oriental carpet. "I appreciate your concern."

She waited.

In time, he lifted his gaze to hers. "I've been selfish in many ways, protecting myself more than thinking of Nattie." Stress tugged at the corners of his mouth. "I'd like to think I've made some progress. So as they say, you're the nurse. I'll trust your judgment to do what's needed. Anything that will make Nattie a happy child again is fine with me."

Callie relaxed. "Thanks for your confidence."

"You're welcome."

His eyes connected with hers again, and a twinge shot through her chest. The connection sparked liked wires charged with unbound electricity. Finally, she found her voice. "What are you thinking?"

He lowered his gaze. "Nothing. I'm sorry."

She longed to know his thoughts. But she had more to ask, and struggled to organize her musings. "Did Nattie have a particular song she liked to sing with you and Sara?"

David leaned his head back for a moment and then tilted it forward. "Oh, some of the children's songs, I suppose. 'Jesus Loves Me,' for one. Something else about 'two little eyes.'"

"Yes, I know them both. I'll see if she'll sing them with me. I'm grasping for anything."

"Yes, even the slightest progress."

Callie knew she should say goodnight, but she longed to be with him, to talk…about anything.

He drifted away in thought. She sensed she should go and leave him with his own reveries, but a playful look glinted in his eyes. "Have you gotten into mischief since I've been gone?"

"Just a little." She grinned. "On the way to town the other day, I stopped by the church. *Your* church, I should say. I talked a bit with Pastor Spier."

"I suppose he's asking you to join the coalition to pry a donation from me."

"No, but he did mention that he'd asked you." She glanced down at her fingers and realized they were tapping the edge of the chair. "He told me you were once the choir director at First Community Church. Is that right?"

David closed his eyes, and lifted his shoulders in a heavy sigh. "Wish I could get my hands on those church records." He peered at her. "Yes, I'm guilty as charged. I did it to help

Sara. Playing and directing is difficult. She could do it, but having a director made things easier."

"I just wondered. Was surprised, naturally. But I suppose you have a lot of surprises hidden away that I don't know about."

He flinched. "Only a few. And you seem to pry them out of me daily."

"Good for me." She shifted in her chair. "So, are you thinking about helping with the organ repairs?"

"Should I throw you out on your ear now? Or later?"

A pleasant expression hovered on his face, so she continued. "He paid me good money to pry this information out of you." She rose with a grin. "I'd better leave before you follow through on your threat." She headed for the door. "Good night."

David rose and stepped toward her. "How's your mother?"

She spun around, meeting his questioning eyes. "Mom seems to be fine, but she did have a minor stroke, according to the MRI test. The doctor has her on some new medication. Now all I can do is pray she takes care of herself."

"I'm glad to hear it was minor. God gives us warnings sometimes, a little reminder to take care of ourselves. Problem is, we have to listen."

Callie grinned as she turned the doorknob. "And listening is definitely one of Mom's serious problems." She glided through the door and closed it before he could respond.

Climbing the stairs, she hummed a simple children's hymn. The tune brought back old questions. Did her own child, living somewhere in the world, know the song? Had Christian parents adopted her tiny little girl? A heavy ache weighted her heart. Drawn by her emotions, or perhaps more by her loneliness, Callie opened Nattie's bedroom door and tiptoed inside.

The child lay curled in a tiny ball on the edge of her bed. The rosy night-light sent a wash of pink over her face, her cheeks glowing with the warm hue. Callie had fought her instincts so often to lavish her affection on Nattie, knowing it might not be good for the child when she had to leave, and positive it would not be good for her own throbbing hurt.

But tonight, she leaned over, brushed the child's hair from her cheek with her finger, and lay her lips against Nattie's warm, soft skin. Tears filled her eyes as she backed away and turned to the door. Taking one more glimpse, she stepped into the hallway—and into David's arms.

Chapter Eleven

Callie gasped as David held her in his arms outside Nattie's room. Her body trembled in fear as she pulled away from his grasp and closed the bedroom door.

"I didn't mean to frighten you," he said. Pausing, he searched her face, then raised his fingers to capture her chin. "Why do you have tears in your eyes? Is something wrong?"

"Nothing. Nothing's wrong with Nattie, if that's what you mean." Callie released a trembling sigh and pulled herself together.

"But why are you crying?" he whispered, sounding concerned.

"I'm not crying." She kept her eyes lowered, praying the evidence of her tears would vanish. When she raised her eyes to his, he held her riveted.

David lifted his hand and brushed his fingers across her lashes. "Your eyes are still wet. Please tell me what's wrong."

Callie grasped for something to tell him. "I'm worried about my mother, I suppose. Looking down at Nattie reminds me how my mother hovered over me when I was a child. I keep praying for my mother, but fears still creep into my thoughts."

He drew a clean handkerchief from his back pocket and daubed her eyes. "You know, Callie, if you need to go home for a few days, I can manage without you. Not that I want to—but Agnes will take care of Nattie. Please, go home. You'll feel better."

Callie's lie had gotten out of control. She remembered her mother's words that a lie spoken becomes a web of deceit that grows bigger and bigger. "No, really. A good night's sleep is all I need. But thanks for the offer. Maybe one of these days I'll visit her for a weekend."

He rested one hand on her shoulder and tilted her face with the other. "If you're sure?"

His eyes again bound her, and her breath quivered through her body. "I'm sure," she whispered.

His fingers touched her cheek in a tender caress before he pulled his hand away and turned toward his own room.

Callie darted into her bedroom across the hall. Overwhelmed, she shut the door and leaned against the jamb. Her cheek tingled where his fingers had touched, and she raised her own hand and pressed her burning skin.

Her mind raced. Was she a fool? Was his touch only kindness, or had his feelings grown? If he cared about her, she should leave now while she still could. She leaned her head back, pressing her eyelids closed. She could offer him nothing. But how could she walk away from Nattie now that the child had begun to leave her shell.

Foolish. Foolish. Her thoughts were nothing but nonsense. She rushed to the bathroom and turned the shower on to a full, heavy stream, stripping her clothes from her shaking body. She stepped into the tub and let the water rush over her, feeling its calming warmth. She scrubbed herself until her thoughts, like the soapy bubbles, washed down the drain.

No man would love her once he knew the truth. She could offer a man like David nothing but her less-than-perfect self. He deserved a lovely, unsullied woman. She dried herself, rubbing the nubby towel over her body until she glowed bright pink. As she brushed her hair with heavy strokes, she stared at herself in the mirror. No one wanted a used, sinful wife.

Callie tossed the hairbrush on her vanity table and crawled into bed, praying sleep would come quickly. In the darkness, her mind drifted, and, as on so many nights, the mist rolled in. His voice came from the shadows.

"Why, Callie, that's a lovely, lovely name. Nearly pretty as you are, sweetheart."

A flush of excitement deepened to embarrassment. He pulled the door closed behind her, and she stepped inside the room, moving toward the black, gleaming grand piano.

He flashed his broad, charming smile. "You're nervous enough, I'm sure. We don't want anyone popping in and making things worse, do we?" The lock clicked.

Her chest tightened, anxiety growing inside her as his fingers touched the keys. She wished she could relax, so he could hear her natural quality.

He winked, then eyed her hand resting on the piano edge. He stopped playing and placed his hot, sweaty fingers on hers. "You just relax there. I can hear you have a pretty voice."

Callie filled her diaphragm with air, and her voice soared from her, natural and strong.

He looked at her with admiration, swaying and moving on the bench as she sang. "Why you're a little meadowlark, aren't you."

Callie's eyes shot open in the darkness, as the name pierced the night like a knife, *Meadowlark, Meadowlark.*

A gentle breeze drifted through the open parlor windows. Callie leaned her head against the sofa back, her attention drawn to Nattie. With an array of crayons and a coloring book, Nattie concentrated on her artwork, her golden curls hiding her face. The afternoon sun glinted through the windows, and rays danced on the child's hair like a sprinkle of fairy dust.

Each time Callie allowed herself to think about the little girl, her heart ached. No matter how hard she tried to avoid the inevitable, her heartstrings tangled more and more around Nattie.

Daily, she prayed for Nattie's healing, yet the reality sent a sad shiver through her. Nattie, healthy and happy, would start school in September, and Callie would have completed her task. She would have to leave Bedford. How could she ever say goodbye?

As if the child knew she filled Callie's thoughts, she sat up, tearing the picture carefully from the book.

She rose, glancing with lowered lids toward Callie, then carried the picture to her side.

"How beautiful," Callie said, holding the paper in front of her. "You color so well, Nattie. Everything's inside the lines. And such pretty colors, too. I love it."

Nattie's timid grin brightened her face. "It's for you."

Her pulse skipped a beat, and she clutched the paper to her chest. "Thank you. This is one of the nicest presents I've ever had."

Nattie slid onto the sofa and nestled by her side. Callie pulled herself together, reviewing the event as if it occurred in slow motion. With caution, she slid her arm around the child's shoulders. Nattie leaned into her arm without hesitation. Longing, delight, amazement swirled through her in one rolling surge.

"Oh, Nattie, you are a gem," Callie said.

Nattie tilted her face upward, her brows knit together.

"You don't know what a gem is?"

Nattie shook her head.

"I didn't say a 'germ,' did I?" The moisture in her eyes belied her mirth. "I said a gem. Like a diamond. You know what a diamond is?"

"Uh-huh," Nattie said, her face glowing.

"You're *my* diamond, Nattie."

Nattie snuggled more closely to her side. Callie savored the moment, wishing and longing for miracles, thoughts she couldn't speak for fear of losing them.

The magic moment evaporated when Agnes called them to lunch, but Callie's mind replayed the scene over and over. Nattie had already made a giant stride forward, though Callie had yet to put her plan into effect to use music to draw her out more completely.

The thought filled her mind, and she decided to begin after lunch. When they had settled back in the parlor, Callie wandered to the piano and lifted the bench lid. Inside, she found music books of all kinds. She ruffled through them, pulling out a bound selection of well-known classics. She lowered the lid and adjusted the bench. Nattie watched her with curiosity.

Sliding onto the bench, Callie propped the music on the stand, and glanced through the pages and found a favorite. Her hands rested on the keys covered with the dust of disuse. She made a mental note to clean the ivory with witch hazel. But for now, she allowed her fingers to arch and press the first notes of the sonata.

The rich, vibrant tone of the piano filled the room. Like a tonal magnet, Nattie rose, drawn to the instrument. She stood at Callie's side, her sight riveted to Callie's experienced fingers moving over the keys. The music held the child transfixed, and Callie continued, her emotions caught in the rhythm and tones of the masterpiece.

When she finished the selection, she sought Nattie's eyes. The child's face seemed awed by the experience.

"Would you like to sit next to me?" Callie held her breath.

Nattie tried to scoot onto the bench, and Callie put her arm around the girl's slender shoulders, giving her a boost.

"There, now you can see much better. How about another song?"

Nattie nodded, and Callie selected a shorter piece, hoping to keep the child's interest. The Bach etude resounded in a bright lilting melody, and when she finished, she turned to Nattie. "Okay, now it's your turn. Would you like to play?"

Nattie's eyes widened, and a small grin curved her lips.

"Good. I'll show you a simple song. And later, I'll pick up a beginner's book for you. We can surprise your daddy."

Again, Nattie's quiet voice broke her silence. "Okay."

Though her word was a near whisper, to Callie the sound was a magnificent symphony.

Callie slid the beginner's book into the piano bench when she brought it home from the music store. In her excitement, she wanted to share the moments with David, but she wondered if the fact would stir up sad memories. And she'd only asked him about singing, not piano lessons. Waiting seemed to be the better option. Yet already, Nattie's natural talent blossomed.

She and Nattie had made a pact to keep her lessons a secret. When Nattie felt ready to play for her father, they would hold a surprise concert. Like true comrades, their secret bonded them.

With the music book stowed in its hiding place, Callie returned to her room. Tonight she wanted to give Nattie and David time alone. Each day the child's progress seemed more evident. With more than three months before the beginning of school, Nattie would be ready for first grade.

Bored with television, she turned the clock-radio dial on her desk. A familiar hymn drifted from the speakers, and the music wrapped around her like a loving arm. She settled into her favorite recliner and leaned back, closing her eyes.

John Spier's request glided into her thoughts. Years had passed since she'd sung in church. But like Nattie, she'd begun to heal. For so long, her throat had knotted when she opened her mouth to sing. Now her voice lifted often in praise to God and in her love of music. Music completed her and made her whole again. At least, almost whole.

Maybe she should consider Pastor John's request. She could praise God all she wanted on the hillside and in private, but singing in church was a loving testimony. Hymns drifted through her mind, favorites she had not sung forever, it seemed.

Woven into the radio's musical offering, Callie heard a rhythmic sound. She lowered the radio's volume. The tap came again. She grinned to herself. The door—someone had knocked. She strode across the room and pulled it open.

David stood outside, a sheepish expression on his face. "We missed you."

Callie stepped backward. "Missed me?"

He scanned her face, then his eyes focused behind her.

Callie turned around and glanced into her sitting room, trying to figure out what he wanted. "Did you want to come in?"

He shifted from one foot to the other. "If you don't mind—I just tucked Nattie in for the night, and I felt lonely."

Callie teetered backward, opening the door for him to enter. He had never come to visit, and the situation caused her a strange uneasiness. "Have a seat." She motioned to the recliner, but instead, he pulled out a smaller chair from the desk and straddled the seat, resting his hands on the back.

"You're welcome to sit here," she repeated, but he ignored her offer and remained seated. "So." She glanced around her. "I don't have anything to offer you, except tap water." Her nervous titter sounded ridiculous in her ears.

David shook his head. "I didn't come for refreshments. I just wondered why you made yourself so scarce this evening."

"Oh." Callie relaxed. Now she understood. "Well, I thought since Nattie and I spend a lot of quality time together, you and she deserved a night alone. Sometimes, it's nice for the two of you to be together…without me. I'm a distraction."

Again his gaze traced her face. "But a pleasant one," he finally said.

She felt a rush of heat rise to her face, a blush she couldn't hide. "You embarrass me. I don't know how to handle comments like that."

"I suppose that's one of the reasons I find you so lovely."

Her blush deepened. "See, you're doing it again." She covered her face with her hands, feeling like an utter fool.

"You're beautiful when you blush, Callie. You remind me of a butterfly locked in its chamber, then suddenly released." He rested his chin on his arms. "Sorry, my poetry's running wild again."

Her gaze sought his. "But it sounded lovely. Really."

"I can never pay you for the joy you've brought back to my life. Every day I see Nattie grow more open, like the little child she was before her mother died. If it was Sara's death alone or something else that made her so withdrawn, I don't know. But whatever it was, you're bringing her out of it. And I...love you for it. I'm sorry if I've embarrassed you again, but I have to tell you."

Callie's feelings tumbled into words. "I see the same progress. Each day I watch her open up a little more, and I'm happier than I can tell you. But I have to be honest with you. It makes me sad, too."

He studied her. "Sad?"

"When she's herself again, I'm out of a job. Joyful for her. Sad for me. Do you see the paradox? I long to see her bubbling with happiness like children her age—but then I have to say goodbye. And...she's stolen a piece of my heart." Callie lowered her lids, the tears building along her lashes.

David rose, moving to her side in one giant stride. In a flash, he knelt before her and grasped her hand. "No, not goodbye. Nattie needs you…and *will* need you. You're the one who's making her strong again. You can't just up and leave her. Even when she begins school, she'll need support and someone who loves her…a woman who loves her. Little girls need a mother's nurturing, not a father who bungles his way along. Don't even think of leaving us. Please."

Callie heard his words, but what he said knotted in her thoughts. *A mother's nurturing.* By delaying her departure, she would only hurt herself more. Could she bear it? "I appreciate the nice things you're saying. But, David, I have to look after my own wellbeing, too. Time will tell what I can handle emotionally. I can't make any promises."

"I'm not asking for promises, just understanding that we need you."

Words left her mouth that she didn't bite back fast enough. "What you need, David, is a wife. That's who should be nurturing Nattie, not me. You need to live again, too. I'm sure somewhere in the community is a fine, single woman just waiting to be someone's wife."

To Callie's astonishment, David laughed.

"Please don't laugh at me, David. I'm speaking from my heart."

Again, he touched her hand. "I'm not laughing at you, Callie. Please, don't even think such a thing. I forgot to tell you about our invitation."

"Our invitation?" Her forehead wrinkled to a frown.

"Pastor John called earlier this evening. He asked to

speak to you about accompanying him to the church picnic. I told him you had already retired for the evening. Then, Mary Beth latched onto the telephone and invited me."

Callie's stomach flip-flopped with his words. "Pastor John asked me to the picnic?" What she really wanted to say was *"Mary Beth asked* you *to the picnic?"*

David nodded his head. "Yes, I told him to call you tomorrow. But I couldn't come up with an excuse quick enough, so I had to accept Mary Beth's offer. Please accept John's invitation. At least we can be a buffer for each other. You'll save me from a fate worse than…well, from a trying experience."

Though an unexpected jealousy raged inside her, she contemplated his poignant pleading. A protective camaraderie bound them together. "But accepting the invitation isn't kind, David—not if we're making fun of them."

"I don't mean to make fun. I suppose both of them would be a good—how should I put it—catch. But I'm not ready to be caught, and Mary Beth's efforts are so obvious. I'll have to be honest with her. Somehow."

"Honesty is the best thing."

"Then let me be honest. Make my day worthwhile and accept John's invitation. I can bear it if you're there. And Nattie will want to be with you, too. Please."

She lowered her eyes, and when she raised them, her heart fluttered like the wings of the butterfly David had just compared her to. She nodded.

"Thank you from the bottom of my heart." He rose and

stepped back. “I suppose I should let you get back to… whatever you were doing.” He turned toward the door.

“David,” she said, stopping him in mid-stride. “Could you stay a minute? I’d like to talk.”

Chapter Twelve

David faltered when Callie spoke his name. Turning, he faced her, his heart galloping at the sound of her voice. His eyes feasted on her tonight, sitting near him as if she belonged in the house forever. Not an employee, but a woman. A woman who loved his child and who, he prayed, could learn to love him. Startled by his own longings, he shivered.

"I hope I didn't startle you. This has been on my mind for some time now."

He tensed, considering the serious expression on her face. "Is something wrong?"

"No. When I visited the church a while back, Pastor John asked me if I would sing for a Sunday service." She grinned. "He also asked me to direct the choir, but I'll leave that talent to you."

David halted her with a gesture. "Forget that." He wondered if Pastor John had put her up to the comment.

"Well, anyway, I'm thinking about singing, and I wanted to warn you."

"Warn me? You have a lovely voice, Callie. You should sing."

She halted and searched his face. When she spoke, her voice sounded controlled and thoughtful. "How do you know I have a lovely voice?" Her eyes lit with a questioning brightness, as if she'd learned the answer to a secret.

He'd spoken without thinking. "I've heard you sing with Nattie. The children's songs. I have ears."

"And you? Do you sing, David?"

"I sang long ago. Nothing like you."

She squinted as if weighing his response, then continued. "I just wanted to tell you that I'm accepting your pastor's invitation to sing."

"If you're singing—" He faltered over the words. "I'd like to hear you. I'll attend worship that Sunday."

Her eyes widened. "You don't attend worship?"

"I've felt very lonely at First Community. Too many memories." He thought of his promise to Sara. "Since Nattie's doing better, I'm taking her to Sunday School, but I usually drop her off and wait."

"You wait for her." Her eyes widened even more. "David, you'll never get *less* lonely unless you work at it."

But it was more than lonely. Much more. "I'm angry, too, I suppose…at God." The words escaped his control.

"Angry? At God?" Her face bent to a scowl. "Because of Sara's death? But you said you knew she had cancer."

"You've asked a whole parcel of questions. Which do you want me to answer?" Despite the tension edging inside him, a quirky grin flickered on his mouth.

Callie eyed him. "It's wrong, you know, to be angry at God."

"I know." He wandered back to the chair he had left a few minutes earlier and again straddled the seat, leaning on the back. "But as I said before, I had tremendous faith that our love would heal Sara's cancer. A young lover's error. But I had faith. When Sara died, I felt betrayed."

The scowl retreated, and her face overflowed with empathy.

Surprised, he felt his eyes mist at his admission. "And when Nattie reacted like she did, I felt devastated. God took my wife, and then my daughter. I couldn't accept that."

"Oh, David, I understand. We shouldn't, I know, but I've been angry at God, myself. When I stopped singing, I wasn't only punishing my parents, but I probably thought I was hurting God, too."

Her own vulnerability wrapped around his thoughts. Questions that he'd tucked back in his mind surged forward. "And why were you punishing your parents, Callie? What secret hides behind your lovely face?"

She paled, squeezing her saddened eyes closed for a heartbeat. When she opened them, fear clouded her face. "Please don't ask. Don't we all have things in our lives we don't want to talk about to anyone?" She lowered her eyes to her hands knotted in her lap, then raised them and focused on him. "At least, not yet."

David nodded, yet his heart tugged inside; he wanted to know what caused her such pain. What stopped her from sharing her grief with him? What scared her when he touched her? Who had hurt her so badly?

"Thanks for understanding," she added. Her eyes softened as she gazed at him. "I'm pleased Nattie's going to Sunday School."

If he were honest, he couldn't even take credit for that. "I promised Sara I'd raise Nattie to know Jesus. I'm keeping that promise. I take her to Sunday School. But church…my heart hasn't been in it."

"I know you pray, David. Maybe at dinner it's for Nattie, but you do say prayers." Her gaze searched his. "Let's pray for each other, David. Prayers can work miracles. We both need help."

Her eyes glowed with her request as she looked at him. *Prayer.* Such a simple gift he could give her…and himself. "A deal," he said, and rose. "I'll pray for you, and you pray for me. How's that?"

She peered into his eyes. "Not quite what meant."

Her look penetrated his soul. The guilt he'd hidden under layers of self-pity peeled away, one by one.

"I said, let's pray for each other. 'Where *two* or *three* are gathered,' the Bible says. We need to pray for our *own* needs, too. Still a deal?" Her hand jutted toward him.

He stepped forward and clasped her tiny fingers in his. Their eyes locked as firmly as their handshake, and heat radiated through him like a match flame touched to gasoline, searing his frayed emotions.

He needed her—wanted her in his arms nestled against him. Yet her fear permeated his thoughts. Moving with caution and tenderness, he drew her to his chest. Her body trembled against him. His voice caught in his throat, and his "thank you" was only a murmur. When he'd corralled his emotions, he gently released her and left the room, feeling as if he had left a piece of his heart behind.

David woke in the morning and looked out the window. The weather couldn't have been better for the church picnic. The sky shone a bright blue, with no hint of rain.

If he hadn't accepted Mary Beth's invitation, he might have looked forward to the occasion, but instead, he glowered as he drove to the parsonage with Callie and Nattie belted in the back seat. He wanted, with all his heart, to seat Callie in the front, but protocol determined the spot belonged to Mary Beth.

When their tedious journey to the park ended, John helped tote their gear, and they found a table beneath a large elm tree.

Nattie clung to Callie's side, her timidity obvious in the crowd of gathering church members. Though distressed at Nattie's discomfort, David found pleasure in watching her relationship with Callie. As soon as she opened a folding chair and sat, Nattie slid onto her lap. The love, evident between them, warmed his heart.

Mary Beth unfolded a chair. "Nattie, aren't you too big to be sitting on your nanny's lap?" Mary Beth asked as she eyed the child. "I think it would be nice if you sat on your own chair here by me." She opened another chair. "I'd like to get to know you better."

Nattie shook her head and Mary Beth's mouth dropped in an awkward gape.

"My, my, aren't we a temperamental child." She plopped into a chair and glowered at Callie, whose protective hand cupped Nattie's shoulder.

"Nattie's shy, Mary Beth," David countered. "Give her time to adjust." He wanted to shake the woman for her comment.

Mary Beth beamed at him with a smile as false as her long, well-polished fingernails. "You're right, David. I wasn't thinking. Let's go for a little walk. What do you say?" She rose without waiting for his response.

David glanced at Callie in desperation, hoping she would intervene. But she only looked at him with an arched eyebrow, and he slumped off, not knowing how to avoid Mary Beth without being rude.

"What did you have in mind?" he asked her, as they moved away from the safe circle of chairs. He realized too late that his question might be misconstrued.

"I'm sorry?" Her pitch elevated.

"I meant, where did you want to walk?"

She let out a minute sigh, her fingers playing with the collar of her blouse. "Nowhere in particular. I thought we might enjoy some privacy."

She had thought wrong, but he allowed her to lead him

through the trees and up a grassy knoll. His mind wandered, envisioning Callie and Nattie sitting back under the elm tree.

Mary Beth squeezed his arm. "My, you are quiet today."

Her comment amused him. "Obviously, you don't know me very well. I'm not a live wire, I'm afraid."

His words didn't ruffle her confidence. "You see, then, our little walk is important. We'll get to know each other better."

He shrugged off her statement and uttered a thought of his own. "When are you returning home, Mary Beth?" His blatant question dropped in the air like a cement brick.

His weighted words seemed to squelch her enthusiasm. "I haven't made plans yet. I've considered staying in Bedford for a while. I had hoped to…develop some lasting friendships here."

"I see." *Coward*, David yelled inside his head. How could he tell her with finesse that he didn't want to be one of her lasting friendships. The only friendship he wanted at the moment was Callie. But in her case, he wanted more than friendship.

He tried with discretion to uncurl her fingers from his arm and step away. "I'm sure your brother enjoys your company. And if I recall, the congregation has a number of young women…and men eager for a new friendship. You have a particular young man in mind?"

Her look sought his, sadly pleading, and he wished he could retract his foolish statement, throwing in the white flag. Obviously, she had a man in mind—not a young man, perhaps, but a man. *Him.* "I'm sorry, Mary Beth, my question was much too personal."

She averted her eyes, staring back toward the groups of parishioners gathering under the trees near the pavilion. "I had hoped you already knew the young man I find so attractive."

He pressed his lips together, wondering how to worm his way out of the pitiful situation he'd created. "Sometimes, I'm thick-headed, Mary Beth. My wife's death was two years ago, but I haven't quite thought of myself as single. I've been preoccupied with my daughter's problems. But thanks for your compliment."

Glowing red splotches appeared on her cheeks, and she turned toward their picnic spot beneath the trees off in the distance. "I doubt if anyone will attract your attention until the nanny leaves your employ. You seem to have eyes only for her."

"I beg your pardon?" David might have been less surprised by a kick in the shin. "I don't have a relationship with Callie." *But I want one.* His own realization brought a rush of heat to his neck.

"Your heart does, I think." She turned and headed back toward the picnic tables.

Flustered by her reaction, he followed her. Was his heart that obvious? He could no longer deny his feelings to himself—nor, apparently, to the rest of the world. Perhaps he needed to let Callie in on the news. Or did she know already?

* * *

When David walked away with Mary Beth, Callie wished she were the woman on his arm. He had squeezed into her thoughts and into her heart, and she had no way of protecting herself.

A romantic relationship frightened her, even one with David. His innocent touch excited her, yet a prickling of fear crept through her at the thought of intimacy. She had prayed, but had she really given her fear to God?

Callie observed Nattie. The child's gaze, too, followed her father and Mary Beth across the grass. Callie's hand rested lovingly on Nattie's arm, and she brushed the girl's cool, soft skin with her fingers. Her heart swelled, feeling Nattie's body nestled against hers. As David had said, the young girl needed a mother's love, and Callie had so much love to give.

When Callie looked away from Nattie, Pastor John was studying her. Did he see how much she loved the child snuggled in her arm?

"Are you enjoying your life here in Bedford?" he asked. His query sounded innocent, but Callie sensed more behind it.

"Yes, very much."

He nodded with a subtle reflex toward Nattie. "I notice you have other things holding you here, too."

Callie glanced down at the quiet child and back at him. "Pretty obvious, huh?"

"I worry about you. You need to take care of yourself. One day things will change, and you'll be the one left empty-handed. And empty-hearted."

His words washed over her like ice water. "Yes, I know."

"I didn't mean to offend you. I just wish your days could be a little more pleasant for *you*...personally. I'd like to see you if you're willing."

She gave him a blank stare. Obviously, he wasn't referring to church services. Why hadn't she seen this coming? "Well, I've decided to take you up on your Sunday morning offer. I'll be happy to sing occasionally for the worship service."

"Great. I'm pleased to hear that. But...that's not exactly what I had in mind."

"I know, and I'm sorry. For now, let's begin there. I'm not sure how settled I want to get in Bedford. I have family in Indianapolis, and...well, I suppose you understand."

He fixed his eyes to the ground. "For now, then, I'll just enjoy having you sing with us." He lifted his gaze and a half-hearted smile rose to his lips.

"Daddy."

Callie glanced at Nattie, her word a whisper. She looked up to see Mary Beth charging toward them, David following her with a look of helplessness.

Mary Beth shot Callie a glance and plopped into the folding chair. It lurched, giving a precarious bounce to one side. If it hadn't been for John, she might have ended up sitting on the ground.

"Careful," John said, eyeing her and then David. "You could have fallen flat on your face."

She raised her eyes, scanning her audience. "I already have," she sputtered.

Chapter Thirteen

Callie awakened early, knowing this morning she was singing in church. Feeling jittery, she rushed through breakfast and dashed to church before service for a final rehearsal.

Waiting for her solo, she sat in the front row. When the sermon ended, Pastor John gave a faint nod, and she rose and joined the pianist. As the musical introduction to "The Gift of Love" rippled from the keys, Callie faced the congregation.

Already the words of I Corinthians 13 filled her thoughts, *"Faith, hope, and love abide, these three; and the greatest of these is love."* Awareness jolted her. Much of her life had been loveless. Not her childhood, perhaps, but her later years—empty, punishing years of feeling unloved by others, by herself and by God.

As she sang, lifting the words in song, her gaze swept over the congregation. Her stomach tightened. David and Nattie sat conspicuously among them. Two pairs of eyes met hers, and like strands of a fragile cord, woven and bound together, she felt strengthened by their presence. The song touched her heart. What was life without love—both human and divine?

When the service ended, Callie rose and turned to where David and Nattie had been seated, but they were gone. Her pleasure turned to disappointment, and she edged her way to the exit.

As Pastor John greeted the worshipers, he caught Callie's hand before she slipped away and asked her to stay until he was free. She hung in the background, waiting. When the last parishioner had left, he joined her.

"Thanks so much for sharing your wonderful voice with us. And I see you persuaded David to worship with us this morning." He eyed her with a wry smile.

"No, I was as surprised as you."

"Then you've been a good influence without trying."

He made her uneasy. "Perhaps," she said, avoiding his eyes.

"I hope you'll sing again soon."

"Sure. I'll be happy to sing once in a while."

He offered a pleasant nod and rocked back on his heels. "And, by the way," he said, his hand sweeping the breadth of the sanctuary, "we had a few more people here today. Your idea seems to have worked."

She sent her mind back, but came up empty. "My idea?"

"The church with charm, remember? You suggested we advertise we're an old-fashioned church. We hung a few posters in the local supermarkets, and I put an ad in *The Bedford Bulletin.* I've already noticed a difference."

"That's great. I'm glad." She sensed he was stalling.

"Well, thanks for the idea." He dug his hands into his navy blue suit pockets. "And have you given any thought to *my* idea?"

She felt her brows knit again. "Your idea?"

"That you have dinner with me."

The floor sank beneath her. She kept her eyes connected to his and swallowed. What could she say? *I'm falling in love with my employer.*

He shuffled his feet and pulled his hands from his pockets. His eyes never wavered.

"You know I can't get away easily. Nattie still needs a lot of—"

"You have a day off? An evening when David's home?"

She bit the corner of her lip and released it immediately. *Trapped.* "Why don't you call, and I'll check my schedule."

He contemplated her words for a moment. "All right, I'll do that." He touched her arm. "Thanks for singing today."

"You're welcome, John...Pastor John."

"Call me John, Callie."

Callie stepped backward toward the door. "John, then." She lifted her hand in a wave and hurried through the door.

When Callie arrived home, David was nowhere in sight. She climbed the stairs to slip out of her Sunday clothes. As she approached her room, she noticed Nattie's door ajar. Listening outside, she heard Nattie singing softly to herself. *"Jesus loves me; this I know."* Her murmured tone was sweet and wispy.

Callie stood still. What might Nattie do if she stepped inside the room? Her heart soared with each note of the song, perfectly in tune. When the melody ceased, she pushed open the door and stood at the threshold.

"Did I hear you singing?" she asked.

Nattie's face sprouted a tiny grin, and she nodded.

"You sing very pretty." Callie took a step forward. "Just like your mom, I would guess."

"Like you," Nattie said.

The child's words danced in her heart. "Thank you." She eyed the scene for a moment. "What are you doing?"

Nattie tilted her head the way David often did. "Playing."

"Playing, huh?" She moved into the room and slid onto the window seat. "I saw you in church. Did you see me?"

Nattie giggled and nodded.

"What's this head nodding? Cat got your tongue?"

Nattie gave another titter, but this time she opened her mouth wide and wiggled her tongue. When she closed her mouth, she added, "You're silly."

"Well, I guess I am."

In one motion, Nattie scurried up from the floor into Callie's arms. Her heart pounding, Callie hugged the child. "Well, what do I owe such a wonderful greeting?"

The child lifted her soft blue eyes to meet hers. "You sang pretty in church."

Air escaped Callie in a fluttered breath. "Thank you, sweetheart. You sounded pretty, too, just now."

The child wrapped her arms around Callie's neck, and Callie drew her to the window seat, keeping her arm around the girl's shoulders. Nattie cuddled to her and laid her head against Callie's side.

"I have an idea. Sometime we can sing together. Maybe on our next walk on the hillside." She glimpsed down at the bright eyes looking up at her. "Okay?"

Nattie nodded, her eyes drooping sleepily.

Callie swung Nattie's legs up on the window seat, and the child rested her head in Callie's lap. With pure joy, Callie caressed the child's cheek and arm as she hummed a lullaby she remembered from her childhood. As the words rose in her mind, she sang them gently, and Nattie's breathing grew deep and steady as she sank into a restful sleep.

She smiled down at the little girl, and when she raised her eyes, David stood in the doorway watching her. Her pulse galloped like a frisky colt in a spring meadow. She longed to rush to his arms.

But then he vanished, and, not wanting to disturb Nattie, Callie eased herself back, leaning her head against the wall. He would have to wait if he'd wanted to talk to her. She was busy being a…mother. The word moved through her like an angel's song, lifting the hairs on her arms.

Later that evening, Callie found a gift-wrapped package next to her dinner plate. She flushed, wondering if John had sent something over in the hopes she would accept his dinner invitation. As she turned the small box over in her hand, David entered the dining room and eased into his chair.

"I wonder where this came from?" Then she saw the look on his face, and knew.

"Just a small token."

A tenderness that filled his eyes caught on her heart strings and, like a kite, tugged and pulled until she let the string go, her love lifting to the sky. "For what?"

"Do you have to ask? I picked it up the other day, and was waiting for the right moment. I saw the perfect moment today. You, with Nattie sleeping on your lap."

"Sorry to ruin the lovely picture, but I don't think Nattie feels well. When I tried to get her ready for dinner, she said she didn't want anything to eat. Her cheeks are a little flushed, too. I'll take her some soup later."

"You can't wiggle out of it, Callie. I saw you holding her in your arms. Please accept my little gift."

She studied the box again, turning it over in her hand. "Thank you. May I open it?"

"Sure, what do you think I'm waiting for?"

She grinned and pulled the tissue from the box. When she lifted the lid, a delicate rosebud lapel pin lay on a cushion of blue velvet. A rosy shade of gold shaped the bud, and the leaves and stem contrasted in the traditional golden hue. "It's beautiful. I've never seen anything like it."

"The clerk told me the pin was designed in one of the

Dakotas. Apparently, they're known for three shades of gold. Sorry, this only has two."

She raised her eyes from the lovely brooch, heat flushing her cheeks. "I do feel deprived. Only two shades of gold, huh?"

"I promise. Your next gift will be three." He locked her in his gaze.

Your next gift. She raised her trembling hand to her heated flesh. "I believe I have two-toned cheeks at the moment."

"I seem to embarrass you, don't I?"

Embarrass? He thrilled her. Her voice bunched in her throat. If she spoke, only a sob would escape. Regaining control of herself, she murmured a simple "thank you."

David rose, and in one stride, stood at her side. He lifted the brooch from the box, unlatched it and pinned it to the wide lapel of Callie's simple summer blouse. "There, now we can eat."

When he sat again, he reached toward her. She glanced at his hand in confusion. But when she saw his bowed head, she lay her icy hand in his, and he asked the blessing. The warmth of his fingers and of his prayer radiated a comforting quiet through her. She whispered her "Amen" with his, then concentrated on dinner, afraid if she thought about anything else, the sentiments of the day might overwhelm her.

As she sat on the wide porch, Callie raised her head from her book at the sound of a car motor. Her stomach tumbled, as Mary Beth stepped from her automobile and crossed to the walk.

"Good morning," she called. "I was passing by and noticed you on the porch. I hope you don't mind that I stopped by."

Callie rose. "No, not at all." If God had wanted to punish her, he could have zapped her with a bolt of lightning for her lie. Of all the people in the world Callie *didn't* want to see, Mary Beth topped the list.

"Beautiful summer day, isn't it?" Mary Beth commented, flouncing up the porch stairs.

Callie cringed. The woman brought out the worst in her. She summoned her Christian manners. "May I get you some lemonade?"

Mary Beth stood uneasily on the top porch stair. "That would be nice."

"Have a seat," Callie said, pointing to a chair near hers, "and I'll be right back."

She dashed into the house, raced up the stairs, pulled a comb through her hair, smeared lipstick across her lips, then flew down the stairs to the kitchen. Holding her chest, she gasped to Agnes, "A glass of lemonade, please."

Agnes stared at her wide-eyed. "Something wrong?"

"No—yes. Mary Beth Spiers dropped by for a visit."

Agnes didn't seem to understand, but filled a glass with ice cubes and lemonade. "Here you go," she said, handing it to her.

Callie stood a moment to regain her composure, then

turned and did her best to saunter back to the porch. Pushing open the screen door, she glued a smile to her face and handed the drink to Mary Beth. Nattie, playing in the yard, glanced at them, but kept her distance.

"The child seems more adjusted now than when I first came to Bedford," Mary Beth said as she eyed Nattie.

"Yes, she is. We thank God every day."

Mary Beth stared at her lemonade, then turned to Callie. "So then, what will you do with yourself?"

"Pardon me?" Callie got the drift of her remark, but she wasn't going to admit a thing.

"I mean, you're a nurse. If the patient is well, the nurse usually finds a new patient, right?" Her eyes widened, and when Callie didn't respond, she blinked. "Wrong?"

"No, for a physical illness, you're right. Nattie's problem is more psychological. Healing is different."

"So you're planning to stay, then?" Her face puckered.

"For a while." Seeing the woman's face caused her to wonder about her own. She struggled to display what she hoped was a pleasant expression. "I'll leave eventually," she added, not wanting to utter the words. "Why do you ask?" Callie already suspected why, but she wanted to hear the woman's explanation.

"Well, uh, I suppose I should be out-and-out honest with you." Her shoulders raised, and she gave a deep, disgruntled sigh. "David is an attractive man, and available. Nattie needs a mother. Someone to give her love and affection. I realize right now that you're providing for her care, but

David needs...well—I don't know why I'm explaining this to you."

Callie stared at her in amazement. "I'm not sure why you are, either."

Mary Beth rose, fists clenched at her side. "As long as you're here, David isn't going to realize he needs a wife and a mother for Nattie. I would make him a good companion. You're hired help, Callie. He certainly can't marry his child's nanny, now can he?"

Her words smacked Callie across the face. Struggling for composure, Callie concentrated on keeping her voice level. "I don't think you or I have any business deciding who David should marry." Mary Beth's hand clutched her chest, but Callie continued. "Am I to understand you want me to leave so David will come to his senses and marry you?"

"I didn't say it quite that way. I said, as long as you're here taking care of—"

"Of Nattie. That's what I do here." Callie raised her hand and fondled the two-tone gold rosebud pinned to her summer sweater.

"Well, I wasn't suggesting...I find it very difficult to talk to you."

"If you're waiting for me to leave, I have a piece of advice for you. Don't hold your breath."

Mary Beth's face reddened, and she bolted from her chair. "That's what I get for being honest. If you cared at all for that little girl and her father, you'd feel differently. I'm sorry you don't understand."

She swung on her heel and rushed down the stairs. When she reached the sidewalk, she turned and faced Callie again. "And thank you for the lemonade. It was very good." With that, she spun around and dashed to her car.

Chapter Fourteen

Nattie had made wonderful progress on the piano for a six-year-old. She'd begun her second book in only a few weeks, and Callie listened in awe to her obvious talent. The lessons continued to be their secret, so Nattie practiced during the day when David was at work.

While she practiced, Callie sat nearby, her mind filled with Mary Beth's words. Despite her irritation with the woman, Mary Beth had pinpointed the truth. As long as Callie lived in the house, David wouldn't look for a wife and mother for Nattie.

The image of David falling in love with someone else seeped like poison through Callie's thoughts, making her sick at heart. An inexpressible loneliness surged through her. If she had nothing to offer David, she would be kind to leave. Maybe Mary Beth wasn't the woman for him—but somewhere in the world a lovely young woman waited for a man like David and a beautiful child like Nattie.

Callie pulled herself from her doldrums and eased her way across to the piano, as Nattie finished her piece.

"Was that good?" Her shy eyes sought Callie's.

She rested her hand on Nattie's shoulder. "That was wonderful. Your daddy is going to be so proud of you."

Nattie turned on the bench and faced Callie. "I'm tired of practicing."

"You can stop if you want. You practiced a long time."

She placed her hand in Callie's. "Can we go outside now?"

"Sounds good to me. But first, let's go see what Agnes is doing. I think I smelled cookies earlier."

The child's eyes brightened, and she dragged her tongue across her upper lip. "Yummy. Cookies."

Callie pulled her by the hand. "Let's go see if we can have a sample."

Like two conspirators, they marched toward the kitchen. Agnes, apparently hearing their giggles, waited for them as they came through the door. She placed a plate of cookies on the table, then headed for the cabinet and pulled out two glasses. "Milk goes good with cookies, don't you think?"

"I think you're right, Agnes," Callie said, sliding into a chair next to Nattie.

Before Callie could reach for a cookie, Nattie had one half eaten. Agnes put the glasses of milk on the table, and they munched on cookies and sipped milk until the plate was empty.

"Good thing I only put out a few," Agnes said with a grin, shaking her finger at them. "You wouldn't have left any for the man of the house."

"My daddy's the man of the house," Nattie announced.

"None other," Callie agreed, tousling her hair. "Thanks, Agnes. They were delicious."

"Thanks, Agnes," Nattie echoed. They rose and headed for the side entrance.

Callie halted at the screen door. "We're going for a walk up on the hill, Agnes. Tell David we'll be back in a while, if he gets home before we do."

The housekeeper nodded, and the screen slammed as they made their way down the steps.

Nattie skipped on ahead, and as she watched from behind, Callie marveled at the change in her. Only months ago, Nattie had been silent and withdrawn. Today she behaved like any six-year-old. Only on occasion did she slip into a deep, thoughtful reverie that filled her young face with dark shadows of sadness. Callie thanked God those times grew fewer and farther apart.

But today, the child skipped on ahead, and only when she reached the highway did she stop and look over her shoulder, waiting for Callie to catch up with her.

Hand in hand, they crossed the street, then raced up the hill and through the trees to their favorite spot, the spot where Nattie had spoken her first words to Callie. Now the fields were overgrown with wildflowers, and wild raspberry bushes bunched together along an unshaded path. Nattie plucked a black-eyed Susan as she twirled through the field, holding it out in front of her to show Callie.

They plopped down to rest under the shade of an elm,

where the leaves and sun left speckled patterns on the green grass.

"Can I pick some more flowers? For Daddy."

"You can, but wait until just before we leave, okay? Wildflowers need water. We don't want them to get limp and die before we get them home."

Nattie agreed, then flopped back onto the grass and raised her hand over her head, staring into the cloudy sky. "I can see pictures in the clouds, Callie."

"You can?"

"Uh-huh." She pointed to a large fluffy cumulus.

Callie stretched out on her back next to Nattie, and together they pointed out dragons and elephants and ladies with long hair. The sun spread a warmth over her body, but not as completely as did the glow of her precious moment with Nattie.

As she lay there, Callie's mind filled with old, old songs she remembered her father singing when she was a child. "Buttermilk Sky." "Blue Skies." Then a hymn came to mind, and she sat up cross-legged, humming the tune.

Nattie rolled over on her side and listened for a while in silence, until she touched Callie's leg and said, "Sing."

Callie closed her eyes, and the song filled the air. *"For the beauty of the earth, for the beauty of the skies, for the love which from our birth…"* As Callie sang, Nattie's face glowed. The soft blue of her eyes sparkled with dots of sunshine. If ever in her life Callie had felt fulfilled, today was the day.

Somewhere in the reaches of her mind, the words to the song tumbled out. On the third verse, she rose, lifting her hands to the sky, and Nattie followed her, twirling among the wildflowers.

"For the joy of ear and eye, for the heart and mind's delight."

Then she heard a voice in the distance singing with her, drawing closer. *"For the mystic harmony, linking sense to sound and sight."*

Nattie said the words first. "It's Daddy." She raced from the spot and darted into the grove of trees. Callie stood transfixed for a moment, then thought better and hurried after Nattie. But she had taken only a few steps, when David came through the elms with Nattie in his arms.

A smile filled his face, and as he neared Callie, his rich, resonant baritone voice finished the verse. *"Christ, our Lord to You we raise this our sacrifice of praise."*

When he finished, Nattie giggled in his arms, hugging his neck. "I knew that was you, Daddy."

Callie stood in a daze. "But I didn't."

He unwound Nattie from his arms and slid her to the ground. Then he sank onto a grassy patch, stretching his legs out in front of him. "This is the life."

Callie, still astounded, sank next to him. "You should sing more, David. You talk about me? You have a tremendous voice."

"Not great. Adequate. I can carry a tune."

Callie looked at him and rolled her eyes. "And I gave Sara all the credit for Nattie's talent."

David checked her statement. "We should give God the credit."

Callie stopped in mid-thought. She turned slowly toward him. "You're right." Since the day David had told her about his anger with God, Callie had worried. But his words today eased her mind. And she leaned back on her elbows and breathed in the fresh, sun-warmed air.

David had surprised himself with his comment. But what he said was true. Neither he nor Sara could take credit for Nattie's talent. He'd given the glory to God. He eyed the child, her face glowing and her golden hair curling around her head like a bright halo.

He had an idea, and with a chuckle, he clapped his hands together. "Nattie, pick some daisies for me. With long stems. I'll make something for you."

She dashed off, bringing back a flower on a long spindly stem. "Is this a daisy?"

"That'll do. It's a black-eyed Susan." He pointed to the patch of white flowers nearby. "Those are daisies over there."

She darted away, then hurried back with a couple of the milky-colored blossoms with yellow centers. He sat and wound the stems together, fashioning a daisy chain. Sara had often created flower garlands, but today, as if God had given him another gift, the thought of her didn't press on his heart. Instead, he longed to make a wreath of flowers for Nattie's hair.

As his fingers worked the stems binding the flowers together, he eyed Callie and saw a look of wonderment on her face.

Amazement trickled through him, too, as he pictured

himself immersed in blossoms. "I suppose you never thought you'd see the day that I'd sit and make flower garlands, huh?"

She laughed. "No, you're right. Maybe in a hospital for mental therapy—but not sitting here on the

grass. Couldn't have imagined it in a million years."

"See, you just never know."

Nattie darted back and dropped a few more flowers in his lap, and then headed off again.

"Look at that child, Callie. Can you believe it? I hoped for so long, but I had dark moments when I thought she'd never come out of it. Now here she is—like new."

"I know. Watching her lifts my spirits higher than anything."

He raised his eyes to hers. "I'll tell you what lifts my spirits."

She sensed what he would say, and her chest tightened in anticipation.

"You. I believe Nattie came around because you've given her the tender love she needs. Not her mother, maybe. But you're soft and gentle like Sara. You're fair, blond hair, blue eyes."

"Spitting image?"

David shook his head. "Not spitting," he said, giving her an amused grin. "Only a faint resemblance. And you're a whole different person. Sara was quiet, sometimes too thoughtful. Even before her illness, she concentrated too much on things. She had fun, but…you're full of life and laughter."

Her face filled with surprise, and for the first time, he realized Callie had no idea how lovely she was.

"When I first met you, the word *spunky* came to mind."

"Spunky? I always thought I was a bit drab and boring."

"You?" David stared at her, amazed. Never in his life would he think of her as drab and boring. Lively, unpredictable, perhaps a little irritating at times—but never dull and lifeless.

"So what's the grand pause for? You're thinking bad things about me, aren't you?"

Pleasure tumbled through him. "I plead the fifth."

"Swell." She gazed down at the grass and plucked at a blade with her fingers.

"You'll only blush if I tell you what I was thinking. Except for the part about 'irritating.'"

Her head shot upward. "Irritating?" Her brows squeezed together, and she peered at him. "What do you mean 'irritating'?"

"Occasionally."

She arched an eyebrow.

"Once in a while."

She leaned closer, squinting into his teasing eyes.

His heart thundered at their play. "Rarely. Hardly ever. Once in a blue moon." He shrugged. "Okay, never."

She flashed him a bright smile. "See, I knew it."

He felt as if he were sailing into the clouds. He watched Nattie picking daisies, and Callie smiling at him with her glinting, delphinium-blue eyes. He wondered if he'd ever been so content.

When Nattie returned, he rested the daisy chain on her hair and kissed her.

"Am I pretty, Daddy?" She twirled around the way she and Callie had done earlier.

"You're absolutely beautiful."

Her eyes widened. "Like Callie?"

His heart lurched with awareness. "Yes," he murmured, glancing over at the woman who brought unimagined joy to his life. "Just like Callie." He allowed his gaze to sweep over her before he turned back to Nattie. "But we aren't finished here, Nattie. We have another lady who needs a crown."

Nattie regarded Callie with excitement and ran off again, as David's fingers manipulated the stems in his lap.

After a few concentrated minutes, he rested a laurel of flowers on Callie's head, too. Then he rose. "And now, my two princesses, I think we'd better get home. Looking at my sundial, I see Agnes is probably wondering how to keep our dinner warm."

He reached down, extending his hands to Callie. She looked up and took his hands. With one slight pull, she rose as easily as if she were a feather pillow. David smiled at the two most important women in his life, each with sun-speckled hair adorned with a flowered garland.

That night when Callie went to her room, her thoughts drifted back to the three of them in the meadow earlier that day. Each memory brought a warmth to her heart, as she witnessed Nattie stretching herself back into a normal life. But most of all, Callie pictured David, sitting on the grass, weaving flowers into crowns for their hair. She chuckled to herself, remembering the day they had met and his stern, pinched face.

Yet her joy changed to apprehension when she thought about the future. For them, she saw no hope of a life together. Mary Beth had planted a seed in her mind that continued to grow. When September came, whether she wanted to or not, she must leave.

Going home would be the best for David and for Callie. Though she'd warned herself many times, she had done the unthinkable. She had fallen in love with him.

At first, she wondered if her love for Nattie had made her think fondly of David. Yet the more time she spent with him, the more she was sure that wasn't true. She loved him as a man, not as Nattie's father. He excited her. His touch thrilled her.

Yet her old fears crept into her mind when she least wanted them to. Like her haunting dreams, they covered her with empty, hopeless thoughts.

She rose and turned on the lamp in her bedroom. A shower would relax her, and maybe she could sleep. She turned the nozzle on full blast and stepped into the steaming water, letting it wash over her and soothe her tightened muscles. Afterwards, when dry, she massaged her skin with the vanilla-and-spice-scented cream that reminded her of Agnes's cookies. Her stomach growled, and she chuckled to herself.

Slipping her feet beneath the blankets, Callie fluffed her pillow and snapped off the light. Behind her eyelids, she saw again the afternoon sky filled with puffy white clouds: animals, people and wonderful imaginary shapes.

Then David appeared, lifting a garland of flowers and resting it on her head. In her imagination, his hands touched her face tenderly and his arms reached out, pulling her to him.

But then as sleep descended, the clouds, too, lowered, turning to a gray, swirling mist, and Callie heard the *click* of a lock. The black dream enveloped her, and David's handsome face changed into the face leering from the shadows.

He winked and placed his hot hand on hers. "You just relax there. I can hear you have a pretty voice. Take a nice deep breath. Throw out your chest and fill those lungs."

She drew a deep breath, her blouse buttons pulling against the cloth as her lungs expanded and her diaphragm stretched.

"That's better." He smiled, gazing at her with admiration.

But when she saw his eyes resting on the gaping buttons, the air shot from her.

His fingers moved across the keys, his body swaying on the bench, as she sang. When he played the final cord, his hands rose immediately into applause. "Why, you're a little meadowlark, aren't you?"

He rose and beckoned her with a finger to a sofa across the room. "Have a seat here so we can talk." She froze in place, his leering eyes riveting her to the floor, and as he reached toward her, a soundless scream rose in her throat.

Callie opened her eyes, her body trembling as she stared

into the darkness. *It's only the dream. I'm dreaming.* She wiped the perspiration from her brow and rolled over on her side. Someday the dream would fade. It had to.

Chapter Fifteen

"Well, what do you think?" Callie asked, as Nattie grinned from the piano bench. "Is tonight our surprise concert?"

Her golden curls bounced in the sunlight streaming through the windows. "Uh-huh," she said, giving a nod, "and we'll really surprise him, too."

"We sure will. You play so well already, Nat. I'm proud of you." She rose from the chair and gave the child a squeeze. "Right after dinner, we'll tell him to come into the parlor. Then, I'll be the announcer, and you stand up and take a bow."

Nattie giggled, as Callie described the scene. Filled with their conspiracy, they tiptoed from the parlor and raced up the stairs to wait for David to come home.

They filled their time with puzzles and a storybook, until a car door slam alerted them.

"Daddy's home," Nattie said, peering out the window

and turning to Callie with her hand over her mouth to suppress her giggle.

"I heard, but don't forget, we can't let on about the secret."

"Okay," she said, a mischievous twinkle in her eye.

Shortly, his footsteps reverberated on the stairs, and Nattie jumped up and raced to the doorway. "Daddy." She lurched into his arms.

As she did daily, Callie watched their reunion. Since Nattie's return from her quiet world, their day had established a few pleasant routines. At the sound of David's arrival, Nattie dropped whatever she was doing to greet him. Best of all, David's love, once shrouded by his own knotted emotions, had opened as widely as his arms now stretching toward his daughter.

With Nattie captured in his embrace, he looked at Callie over her shoulder. "So what have the two of you been up to, today?"

Nattie let out a giggle and glanced at Callie.

Without giving away their secret, Callie shushed her with a look, then said to David, "Just our usual fun-filled day. Nothing special—puzzles, storybooks, the usual." She figured "the usual" covered the piano practice.

David eased Nattie to the floor. "Well, I think I'll change. Agnes said dinner's in a half-hour."

"We'll see you there," Callie said, grasping Nattie's hand and pulling her back into her room before she burst with the news.

Callie tempered Nattie's excitement at dinner. But as the

evening progressed, the child's gaze lingered on her, beseeching her to conclude the meal so the surprise concert could begin.

David, for a change, filled the time with talk about some new business opportunities. Rarely did he bring his work to the table, but tonight Callie listened with appreciation, knowing that the chatter distracted Nattie from blurting their after-dinner plans.

"I have an idea," Callie suggested. "Let's have dessert in the parlor a little later. Agnes made homemade peach pie, and I suspect we all need to rest our stomachs before dessert."

"Sounds good to me," David said, folding his napkin and dropping it alongside his plate. He slid back his chair and rose. "How about you, Nat? Willing to wait for dessert?"

She eyed Callie before she commented. "Yes, because I want to show you something now."

"Show me something? Hmm? What could it be? A picture?"

Nattie jumped from her chair. "Nope. Come on, Daddy, and I'll show you our surprise."

David glanced at Callie. She only shrugged innocently. But when he turned his back, she gave Nattie a wink. The child giggled and skipped off to the parlor.

Callie expected to find Nattie seated at the piano when they caught up with her, but she had remembered their plan and now waited in a chair, her hands folded in her lap. Callie delighted in the heartwarming picture.

"So where's my surprise?" David asked as he entered the room.

"Don't rush us," Callie cautioned. "You sit down right there." She pointed to the chair in good view of the piano. "Are you ready?"

He looked at her, a confused frown knitting his brows. "As ready as I'll ever be."

"Okay, then, let me introduce our entertainment for the evening. Da-da-da-dum!" Callie imitated a drum-roll. "Give a warm welcome to Nattie Hamilton, who will perform for us on the grand piano." She began the applause.

David gaped and looked at Nattie, who rose from her chair, bowed and scurried to the piano.

She grinned at her father, then slid a book from under the seat and propped it on the music stand. Easing onto the bench, she adjusted the music book, arched her fingers over the keys and began the song she had prepared: Bach's e´´tude, "Minuet." Her small fingers struck the keys, sending the spirited melody dancing across the room.

With his mouth hanging open like a Venus flytrap, David's attention was riveted on his daughter. When she struck the final note, his quick look at Callie's amused expression prompted him to snap his mouth closed with embarrassment.

Callie burst into applause, praying that David wasn't angry. But in a heartbeat, his surprised expression turned to joy, and he leaped from the chair in a thundering ovation and a cry of "Bravo!"

Nattie slipped from the piano bench, pulled out her pant legs as if she wore a skirt, and took a deep bow.

He bolted to her side and knelt to embrace her. "Oh, Nat, I'm so proud of you. Just like your mom." Turning, his eyes focused on Callie, who was standing in the distance and observing the scene. "And I know I have you to thank for her lessons."

She lowered her lids to hide the tender tears that rose in her eyes. "You're welcome."

"Nat, this is the best concert I've ever heard. You are my personal star."

Nattie grinned and wrapped her arms around his neck. "I'm your star."

"You sure are. Best gift in the whole world." He rose, taking one of her hands. "So when have you been practicing?"

"Every day," Nattie told him. "After you go to work. But we couldn't practice on Saturdays or Sundays. Otherwise, you'd hear me. I'm on my third book already."

David turned to Callie. "You've been buying her music books?"

She nodded.

"You are a gem, Callie. A real gem."

"She's a diamond, just like me." Nattie's voice burst with excitement. "Callie told me I was her gem. Did you know that means a 'diamond,' Daddy?"

David raised his hand quickly and wiped what Callie guessed was a tear that had escaped his eye. "I do. You're both my diamonds."

Nattie ran to Callie's side, hugging her waist. "We're Daddy's diamonds, Callie."

She looked down at the child's beaming face. "I heard. That makes us both pretty special."

"Yep," she said, her head resting against Callie's hip.

Callie looked at David. "Before our throats are too knotted to enjoy dessert, I should probably ask Agnes to bring in the pie. What do you say?"

He grinned, his eyes glistening with moisture. "I say, you're not only a diamond, but a very wise woman."

When John Spier called, Callie could think of no excuse. She agreed to attend a jazz concert at the historic Opera House in Mitchell. When she accepted the invitation, he suggested dinner, as well.

A whole evening with John didn't excite her. But she'd told him to call, and he'd done what she asked.

Telling David was difficult. She had no idea whether he cared or not, but *she* cared. And she took forever to harness her courage.

"Tonight?" David asked.

"Yes." She wanted to tell him she'd rather stay home and sit in the parlor with him, but her truthfulness would only embarrass her, and lead nowhere. "But if it's a problem, I'll call him and explain. I didn't give you much notice."

"No, that's fine, Callie. I, ah…I have no plans for the evening.

Disappointment filled her. She wished, at least, that he looked upset or inconvenienced.

He peered at his shoes. "You need a private life. You devote a lot of time to us."

"All right, if you don't mind." She had so much more to say—but if he didn't care, why should she? "I'll go, then. Thank you."

"You're welcome," he said, glancing at her. "Have a nice time."

Suddenly her disappointment turned to irritation. "I'm sure I will," she said, her voice picking up a spark. "I'll go."

"Good."

This time his tone sounded edgy. She turned and left the study. Nattie stood in the hallway, peering at her, as Callie came from the room. She had more than two hours to get ready, but she wasn't going to sit there and feel sorry for herself. She had a date, and she'd enjoy herself if it killed her.

With a final look at David through the doorway, she charged up the stairs and into her room. Plopping on the edge of her bed, she stared into her open closet. What should she wear? Hardly anything she owned seemed appropriate for a date. She needed to go on a shopping spree—but where around here? Shopping meant a trip to Indianapolis. More guilt rose as she thought of her mother.

Though they talked on the telephone, Callie hadn't been home to visit Grace in a while. She should arrange a trip. *Trip?* In September, she would be leaving Bedford altogether. Bleak dread raked through her. But it was a cold, hard fact.

She rose and maneuvered her outfits along the wooden rod, glancing at skirts, blouses, dresses. The Opera House. Was it dressy? She was positive she didn't have anything appropriate. Taking care of Nattie didn't require fancy dress, only casual. She searched through the clothing again, but stopped when she heard a noise at the hall door.

She turned and saw Nattie peering in from the sitting room. "Come in, Nat."

Nattie rarely came to Callie's room, and today she edged through the door.

"Did you need something?"

Nattie shook her head, her eyes focused on the closet. "Are you going away?" she asked.

"Uh-huh," Callie said, peering at a summery dress she held in front of her on the hanger.

"Please, don't go away." Nattie's voice quivered with emotion.

Callie spun around and faced her. Nattie's lower lip trembled, leaving Callie confused. "What's wrong? Don't you feel well?"

She shook her head. "I don't want you to leave. Who will take care of me?"

Callie crossed to her and knelt to hold her. "No, I'm not leaving for good. Just for tonight, Nat. Your daddy's home, and Agnes. They'll be here. I'll be back later."

Nattie's misty eyes widened. "Oh…I thought you were going away."

"What would make you say that? Heaven forbid. I wouldn't leave you." Nattie lay her head on Callie's shoulder, and the unintended lie she had uttered, like a boomerang, spun back, whacking her conscience. Hadn't she just decided she would leave Bedford in September?

She gazed into the child's sad face and couldn't bring herself to say any more. Instead, she held Nattie tightly to her chest until she felt her relax, then tickled her under the chin. "So, you thought I was leaving you. You silly. Wouldn't I tell you if I were going away for good?"

"But you and Daddy hollered. I thought—"

"No, we were just talking loudly. There's a difference. And don't you worry about that, anyway. I'm not going anywhere, except out to dinner and to a concert with Pastor John."

Nattie tilted her head, staring directly into her eyes. "Why don't you go with Daddy?"

The child's look of sincerity tugged at Callie's heartstrings. Yet, the words made her smile. Sometimes she wondered the same thing. What might it be like to spend an evening with David—on a real date? She took a minute to find her voice. "I suppose because your daddy didn't ask me—"

"Didn't ask you what?"

Her head shot upward, and she felt a flush spill over her face like a can of rose-colored paint. "I didn't hear you."

David stepped into the room. "Yes, I know. So what didn't I ask you?"

"You didn't ask Callie to go to dinner," Nattie offered, still hugging Callie's neck.

"And why would I do that?" He glowered at Callie.

She unleashed Nattie's arms, then rose. "You shouldn't. She's upset because she thought I was leaving—for good. I explained I was going out with John."

"Ah," David said. "She thought that because you were yelling at me."

Callie lifted her chin. "*I* yelled at *you?*"

"Yes. And now she wants to know why I don't take you to dinner and the concert?"

Nattie shook her head, her eyes wide, certainly not understanding all the innuendos.

Callie glared at him. "Yes, that's what she asked." She waited for his arrogant, stinging response.

"I guess," he said, kneeling down to Nattie, "that I didn't think of it first."

Callie's mouth dropped open wider than David's had days earlier at Nattie's concert. Her pulsed raced like an *arpeggio.*

He raised his soft, apologizing eyes to hers, and she faltered backward, grasping the dresser to steady her trembling legs. "You've caught me off guard."

His full, parted lips flickered to a smile. "Yes, I see that. You can close your mouth now." He scooped Nattie into his arms, as she let out a squeal. "We'd better let Miss Randolph get herself decked out for her *date,* Nattie."

"Who's Miss Randolph?" Nattie asked, as he carried her, giggling, toward the door.

He glanced at Callie over his shoulder. "I'm not sure myself, Nattie. I have to figure that one out."

Chapter Sixteen

When Callie arrived home from her evening with John, David's study light glowed through the tower room window. She said goodnight to John and hurried inside. Stopping outside the study door, she paused. She longed to talk to him, but couldn't bolster her courage, so instead she headed upstairs to her room.

The evening had been a strange one. She wondered if, instead of being interested in her, after all, he hoped she could be a liaison between David and the church. Though John said how much he enjoyed her company, the conversation continued to backtrack to the church, the broken organ, and a variety of other congregational concerns.

Callie had decided a pastor's life must be a difficult one, and her heart softened a little as she'd listened to him. She knew the pianist was leaving, and he needed a replacement or, at least, a substitute until a new pianist could be found. Callie sat beside him feeling guilty. He knew she played the piano, and by the end of the evening, she suggested that she might consider helping out "in a pinch."

As well as addressing John's concerns, Callie had her own. She couldn't get Nattie's question out of her mind: *"Are you going away?"* Thinking of the situation, she ached. It was no-win. If she stayed with Nattie, David would eventually fall in love and find a wife. She didn't know if she could bear it.

Still, she knew David's feelings for her had grown. At the thought, her heart soared—until reality smacked her in the face and her feelings nosedived to the ground. How many times did she have to tell herself she had nothing to offer him? She could never allow him to fall in love with her—nor she with him.

With her mind in a turmoil, she climbed into bed. She lay for a long time, her thoughts pacing back and forth like someone waiting for a last meal. She knew she was a loser no matter how she looked at it—and was suffering because her actions would also hurt Nattie.

Finally her eyes grew heavy, and she drifted to a near sleep, awakened again, then succumbed. And as her mind glided into sleep, so the shadows rose from her subconscious.

With his hot hand on hers, she heard him. "You just relax there, little lady. I can hear you have a pretty voice. Take a nice deep breath. Throw out your chest and fill those lungs."

She drew a deep breath, her blouse buttons pulling against the cloth, and she saw his eyes resting on the gaping buttons.

"That's better." He smiled. "Let's try a song.

We'll do one you know." He handed her some sheet music. "Pick something you know well."

She made her selection and handed him the music. She heard the introduction clearly and filled her diaphragm with air. She opened her mouth, and her pure, natural voice, filled with strength and joy, soared from her.

He gazed at her with admiration, swaying on the bench, as she sang. When he played the final cord, his hands rose immediately into applause. "Why you're a little meadowlark, aren't you."

He rose, beckoning her to follow him across the room to the sofa. "Have a seat, my little Meadowlark, so we can talk business. Her heart raced at first, then the hammering began. He settled next to her, placing his hand on hers. "Are you more comfortable now?"

"Yes," she said, trying to extract her hand. "A little nervous, I guess."

"How old are you?"

"Just turned nineteen. I'm a sophomore at the University of Indiana."

"You'd really like to sing with our group, wouldn't you? Travel with us in the summer? I'm sure you'd be grateful for a place in our choir."

"Oh, I would. Yes, my father thinks you're wonderful."

"And you? Am I wonderful, Meadowlark?"

His hand slid across her knee, and she grabbed it, holding him back. But his strength overpowered her.

"You want to make your daddy proud, don't you? If you want your daddy to be proud, you have to please me a little. How about a kiss?"

*His face loomed above her. Her chest hammered, thundered inside her, and she opened her mouth to scream, but she had no voice. Instead, she couldn't breathe, she was sinking into some deep swirling ocean of icy black water. She heard her blouse tear*ing and felt her skirt rising on her thighs, and she died beneath the blackness.

When Callie woke, her hands clasped the blankets and her arms ached from fighting off the monster in her dream. She had kept her secret from everyone. No one knew why she had stopped singing. No one knew what had happened—only she and Jim McKee.

She rolled on her side and snapped on the light, squinting at the brightness. Why had she not pulled herself from the dream sooner? Lately, she'd been able to stop the dream before the end, but tonight the horrible memory wrenched through her. All the filth and pain she had felt these past years lay on her shoulders.

Callie rose from her bed and went into the bathroom, ran cool tap water over her face and arms. She returned to the bedroom and eased herself to the edge of the bed, noticing the clock. Only twenty-five minutes had passed since she'd crawled under the sheets. She needed to talk to David, to do something to make the terrible thoughts go away. But if she talked tonight, she might regret it. The burden she had carried so many years struggled for release.

She leaned back again on the pillow and dimmed the bulb to a soft glow. As she folded her hands behind her head, her mind wandered, and while it strayed, she heard faintly, a soft, lilting melody drift through the room. Her radio? Had she accidentally set the clock-radio alarm?

She rose and strode to the sitting room. The sound was stronger there, louder than in her bedroom. Television? A recording? She listened more closely. A piano coming from below. Was David playing the piano? She had never heard him play. The music rose through the walls, poignant and beautiful.

She slipped into sweatpants and shirt, and opened her sitting room door. The hallway was empty. No light glowed beneath the second-floor doorways. She followed the stairs down to the dimly lit foyer. A light still shone beneath David's study door, and from outside, she heard the lovely, haunting melody.

Whether wise or not, she turned the knob and eased the door open. Barefoot, she tiptoed into the room, following the music coming from the piano. As she reached the archway, she stood back and watched David's shadow dip and bend as his body moved with the rapture of the music. Her heart soared, yet wept at the haunting sound.

When the last strain died away, he sat with his head bowed, then, as if he sensed her presence, he turned. She stepped through the opening, and his gaze lifted to her face, caressing her, his eyes glistening with emotion.

"Callie, I thought you were sleeping." He rose and moved toward her. "Is something wrong? Did I wake you?"

"No. A dream woke me." She closed the distance between them. "David, the song was beautiful. What is it?" She glanced toward the piano and saw his manuscript spread out on the music stand. "You wrote that, David?" Callie dashed to the paper and lifted the music. "You wrote this." She swung to face him.

He rested his hands on her shoulders. "Yes, I wrote it. It's been playing in my mind for months, but I hadn't written in so long, not since…since Sara died. I didn't think I'd write again. But I couldn't make the music stop roaring in my head until I put it on paper."

Swirling emotion drew her eyes to his, and in them, she searched for an answer. His words promised a release for her. He couldn't make the music stop until he put it on paper. Would her dreams stop if she said them aloud?

She struggled with her thoughts. The truth lay in his heart and in hers. If he knew, could he love her? If she told him, would she be released from her self-made prison? Could she take the chance? She slid the music back on the stand.

"Callie, I could no more fight the music in my head than I can fight the feelings inside me. You should know that I love you. I've been falling in love with you ever since the day we met."

"Oh, please, David, don't say anything that will hurt us."

"Hurt you? Never. My feelings are far too powerful to hide any longer. I've tried to sense how you feel about me. I'd hoped you were learning to love me, too."

"There are too many things you don't know about me, David. Awful things. If you knew them, you wouldn't say you loved me. I've struggled with them in my dreams, but not aloud. They hurt too bad. Please, don't say you love me."

David looked into her eyes, trying to fathom what terrible things she could mean. Her eyes glowed, but with fear. He felt her trepidation in the tension of her shoulders. He drew her to him and wrapped his arms around her.

"Please, Callie, tell me. Do you love me? If you love me, I can handle anything. Whatever you need to tell me. I promise."

She clung rigidly to his arms, and he sensed her panic.

"Don't promise anything until you know the truth," she pleaded. "I couldn't bear to have you reject me."

"Then you do love me? Say it, please."

"I've tried not to love you. For a long time, I told myself I only loved Nattie, but I can't lie. Yes, I do love you, but I can never marry you…or anyone. Never."

He caught her face in his hands and lowered his lips to hers. Her mouth yielded to his, but just as quickly, she pulled away. Instead, he kissed her cheeks and her eyes, tasting the saltiness of the tears that clung to her lashes.

"Callie, if you love me, you'll tell me what's wrong. Let me know what's hurt you so badly. Maybe I can help you."

"Please, let me think about it, David. Play your music for me again. I'd love to hear your song once more. I'll sit right here." She backed up and lowered herself into a chair.

"Promise you'll tell me?"

"I promise I'll think about it."

"Promise you'll tell me, Callie."

"Play for me, David, and I'll try."

David looked with longing into her eyes, and didn't argue, but wandered to the piano and slid onto the bench, shifting the music on the stand. He glanced at her, then lifted his eyes to the music. He played, and the love he'd felt for these past months rose from the keys and drifted through the room.

He sensed her watching him, and he trembled at the thought. As his attention drifted to the last phrase of music, she rose and moved across the floor to stand behind him, her hands resting on his shoulders. He felt the warmth of her hands on his arms, and his fingers tingled with the fire burning in his heart.

On the last chord, he turned to her, and tears ran down her cheeks. Her eyes were focused on the sheet of music resting on the stand. Almost imperceptibly, he heard her whisper, "'Callie's Song.' You named it for me."

He swiveled on the bench. "The music is you, Callie. All the longing and joy, fear, confusion, wonder you brought into our lives here. Nattie, you, me, everything."

She stared at him in disbelief. "Thank you," she whispered.

He stood and placed his hands on her arms. "Thanks to you, Callie." He took her hand and led her toward the door. "Let's sit in the parlor. It's more comfortable there. We need to talk. I'll make us a cup of tea. How does that sound?"

She nodded and followed him, his arm guiding her. When they reached the foyer, he kissed her cheek, aiming her into the parlor as he turned toward the kitchen.

Callie wandered through the doorway, wondering what she would do now. Where could she begin? She had so much she should tell him, yet so little she wanted to admit. He loved her. And she had finally told him the truth: she loved him with all her heart. And Nattie, too. But…

She eased herself onto the sofa, her gaze sweeping the room. The grand piano stood in silence in the bay window, and she thought about the wonderful day, not long ago, when Nattie had played her concert. What happiness she had felt that day. But tonight, though David's song touched her with tenderness, her pulse tripped in fear at the story David wanted her to tell.

Hearing his steps in the foyer, she looked toward the doorway. He came into the room carrying two mugs, and sending a steamy, fragrant mist into the air. Handing one mug to her, he sat by her side, stretching his legs in front of him. "Be careful. This stuff's really hot."

She blew on the beverage before taking a cautious sip, and curled her legs underneath her.

David studied her. "So. Where do we begin?"

She stared at her hands folded in her lap. "I was trying to decide while you were getting the tea. This is very difficult for me. Harder than you can ever imagine. If I get through this, David, you should know you're the only person in the whole world I've told this to."

"I know. You've suffered far too long for whatever this is about. I'm honored to be the one you trust enough to tell."

A sigh tore through her, and an unbelievable desperation raged inside. A sob escaped from her throat. She swallowed it back, choking on the emotion.

He took her hand in his and brushed her skin with his fingertips without speaking.

Another sigh rattled from her. With a gentle touch, David caressed her hand. Then she began, slowly at first.

"Seven years ago I sang in church, in college—anywhere an audience would listen. I studied music in college. Even thought I might like a career as a musician or singer. But my father longed for me to audition for the Jim McKee Singers. It was made up of college-age students who traveled in the summer. My father was a powerful Christian, and his greatest joy was for me to sing with them during one of their summer tours."

Callie closed her eyes, wondering how far she could get before she lost control. David shifted his fingers to her arm, caressing her the way a father calms his child.

"I arranged for a tryout and waited in an office set up near the college for the local auditions. I felt more and more nervous as each person went in and left. Soon, I was alone. He came to the door and called me in."

"Who, Callie? Who was he?"

She swallowed, struggling to speak his name. "The director...J-Jim McKee." Her lips stammered the name.

"So what happened?"

She felt David tense, almost as if he could guess what she was going to say, but his eyes only emanated tenderness.

She returned to the story beginning with the *click* of the lock. "'You're nervous enough, I'm sure,' he said to me as he bolted the door. 'We don't want anyone popping in and making things worse, do we?'"

As if marching through her dream, she led David through the audition. "Then Jim McKee led me to the couch, and kept calling me his 'little meadowlark.' My poor mother called me that a few months ago, and I panicked. I can't hear that word without remembering."

David leaned over to kiss her cheek. "It's okay, Callie. I love you."

"How can you love me, David? You already know what happened." The sobs broke from her throat, and she buried her face in her hands. "I was a virgin. And he took the most precious gift I longed to share with a husband someday. He raped me, David."

Chapter Seventeen

David drew her into his arms, holding her as she wept and rocked her as he would a child. "It wasn't your fault, Callie. You didn't make it happen. It wasn't your fault."

Seven years of pain and sorrow flooded from her in a torrent of hot tears. His murmured words lulled her. When she gathered her strength, she lifted her head, fearing to look in his eyes, but there, she saw only his gentle understanding.

"I've kept that a secret so long, David."

"Why? That's what I don't understand. Why? How many other young women's lives did that demon destroy?"

"I didn't have the courage to tell my parents. My father idolized the man. He wouldn't have accepted that Jim McKee would do something like that." She searched his face for his understanding. "I thought my dad would blame me, think I had been so awed that I was a willing partner. I don't know.

I thought I could wash it away with soap and water and prayers."

"Callie, my love, you suffered too long."

"I read in the paper a few years ago that he died suddenly from a heart attack. *David, I was happy.* I'm ashamed of myself, but I was happy he died."

David buried his face in her hair. She didn't know what he felt. But his eyes had said he understood, and that's what mattered.

She filled her lungs with healing air and released a ragged sigh. "You know, deep inside I've felt so much guilt. I've wondered if I *did* do something to make him think I wanted him." She sighed. "Do you know what sticks in my mind?"

He shook his head.

"I remember my deep breath and the buttons gaping on my blouse. I kept asking myself, did I tempt him? Did he think I did it on purpose, that it was a come-on?"

David closed his eyes and shuddered. "Callie, how many women in the world take deep breaths and their buttons pull on their blouses? Do you think it's their announcement to the world that they want to be raped? I can't believe you've worried all these years about that."

"I was barely a woman then, naive and so innocent... until that terrible day."

Helplessness washed over her again as she recalled the day she realized she was pregnant. How could she tell her parents then about the horrible event she'd kept from them? That was the moment she decided to let them think the baby growing inside her was fathered by a college student. Why destroy everything they believed? She let them accept her lie.

And now, how could she tell David? He and Sara had chanced everything, even Sara's life, to have a child, and Callie walked away from hers. Maybe the rape wasn't her fault. But losing her child was.

An abortion had been out of the question. God would never forgive her for taking the life of an innocent child. Despite her supposed wisdom, she'd never forgive herself for agreeing to the adoption. How could she tell David?

The silence lingered, and David held her close in his arms.

"David?" she murmured.

"Yes." He pulled his face from her hair and looked into her eyes, questioning.

"Do you understand why I'm afraid? I don't know if I can ever love a man fully without those memories filling my mind. Even your innocent touch scares me sometimes."

"I sensed your fear, Callie, and I didn't understand. I thought it was *me*."

"Oh, no, it isn't you."

"I know that now. And now that I understand, we can work on it, Callie. We'll take it slow. One step at a time. You can learn that being loved is a gentle, powerful experience. *Love,* Callie—love is a gift from God. A wonderful, pure gift."

Tears rose in David's eyes, and for the first time, Callie saw them spill down his cheeks. Her stomach knotted when she saw his sorrow—sorrow he had hidden for so long.

"You're crying." Callie reached up to wipe away the tears from his cheeks. She kissed his moist eyes and buried her face in his neck.

David's heart reeled at her tenderness. She was not alone in bearing shame for so many years. "I'm crying for both of us. We've both carried secrets longer than we should."

"Secrets? You mean Sara's pregnancy and—"

"Yes, I went against God's wishes and demanded an abortion. I didn't want her to die, and I knew if she carried the baby, she couldn't have the treatment she needed. But Sara refused, and we waited too long. God punished me for my selfishness."

Callie looked at him, her face filled with confusion. "She was too far in her pregnancy for an abortion?"

He didn't comment, leaving her to accept his silence as his answer. Sara had wanted a baby so badly. He remembered the anger he had felt shortly before she died, how he blamed her pregnancy for her short life. Shaking his fist at God for their losses.

David pulled himself from his sad musings. "Callie, we both have some issues to deal with, but doing it together will give us strength. Love is a mighty healer."

He saw in her face understanding and acceptance. He lowered his lips to hers, and this time, she didn't recoil, but raised her mouth to meet his. Gently their lips joined, and she offered him the love that had lain buried inside her.

When they parted, he held her close, praying that the healing for both of them had already begun.

* * *

Callie leaped from bed the next morning. The clock read ten. She'd not slept that late in years. What about Nattie? She threw on her robe and darted across the hall. Nattie was not there. Her bed was unmade, her pajamas in a pile on the floor.

Callie hurried back to her room, completed the most rudimentary cleansing ritual and threw on a pair of slacks and a top. As she dashed down the staircase, she saw David and Nattie at breakfast. Embarrassed at her lateness, she slowed her pace and worked at regaining her composure.

At the bottom of the stairs, a bouquet of fresh flowers sat on the foyer table. At its base lay a card with her name scrawled on the envelope. David caught her eye as she stood in the foyer, and she nodded, touched that he had sent her flowers already, so early in the morning.

But the biggest surprise occurred when she opened the card. The flowers were from John. She flushed, knowing she had to call him immediately after breakfast, to thank him and give him some kind of explanation as to why she couldn't go out with him again.

She hurried into the dining room.

"Callie." Nattie giggled. "You didn't wake me up. Daddy said you overslept."

"Good morning." David eyed her with a searching look. "I believe you overslept."

"I did, didn't I. And why aren't you at work?"

He grinned. "Guilty as charged. And the flowers?"

"You got flowers," Nattie chimed.

Callie nodded. "From John." She wrinkled her nose. "I guess I owe him a telephone call."

"I guess," David said with a hint of jealousy. "What would make him send you a bouquet, I wonder?"

"Guilt? Payola?"

"Blackmail?" His grin grew. "Whatever. Call him, please."

"I will. I promise. By the way, I agreed to fill in as the pianist. Pam Ingram is leaving. She's expecting a baby and doesn't have time to handle the piano and choir right now."

"Pianist and choir director?"

"No. You heard me. *Pianist.* You're the choir director."

"Was."

"We'll see."

"I repeat, *was.*"

She gave him a grin, not saying another word. They enjoyed breakfast together, then David hurried off to work. Later in the afternoon, Agnes called Callie to the front door. She descended the stairs with Nattie on her heels and halted in surprise halfway down.

"More flowers?" she asked, gaping at a delivery man holding a huge package wrapped in floral paper.

"Must be a special occasion," he said. "This is the second bouquet I've delivered here."

She swallowed. "Not really. Just a coincidence." She took the bouquet from him and closed the screen door.

Nattie skipped around her in excitement. "More flowers?"

"Looks like it, doesn't it?"

Callie pulled the protective paper from the magnificent arrangement of mixed flowers: lilies, orchids, roses. John's simple vase looked sad by comparison. She didn't need to open the card to know the source. A grin crept to her lips.

"Who are they from, Callie?"

"Your daddy, I think." Callie pulled the card from the envelope. *I love you. Never forget. David.* She laughed, seeing the sense of competition John's bouquet had aroused. Then her stomach churned as she recalled her promise: she needed to march to the telephone without delay and talk to John.

Callie thanked John by telephone for the flowers and made arrangements to practice on the church piano. Though two pianos were available at the house, her "practice" was an excuse to see him. She reviewed a variety of ways she might tell him about David and her, but nothing felt comfortable.

A cooling air washed over her as she entered the church. The stained-glass windows held the sun's scorching rays at bay. She headed down the aisle, and by the time she reached the piano, John was coming through a side door. But to her dismay, Mary Beth followed behind him.

His sister wore a bright smile painted on her lips, and the look gave Callie an eerie feeling. In a flash, she knew what Mary Beth was thinking. If Callie was dating John, David was "available." She had bad news for both of them.

John stepped to her side. "I appreciate your willingness to fill in here. I'm looking for a regular pianist, I promise, but it may take some time. We don't have too many accomplished musicians hanging around Bedford."

"As long as you know this is temporary," she reminded him.

Mary Beth fanned her face with her hand. "Whew, you saved me, Callie. I play a little, and John was trying to coerce me."

Callie bit her tongue. If she had had any idea Mary Beth played, she wouldn't have volunteered—but it was too late now. "Well, I'm glad to hear you can play, Mary Beth. I do plan to visit my mom in Indianapolis. I haven't seen her in a while, and I'm feeling guilty."

Mary Beth raised her hand to her throat with a titter. "Oh, my, I guess I shouldn't have spoken."

She leaned intimately toward Callie. "And how are things with you? I understand you had a nice evening. And flowers. He sent you flowers." Her voice lilted with feigned enthusiasm.

"Yes, we had a nice time, but I didn't expect flowers."

Mary Beth took a step backward. "I suppose I should leave and let the two of you talk privately."

She needed to act now or never. "No, Mary Beth, don't go. I have something to tell both of you."

John's face brightened, then faded when he looked at her expression. Mary Beth had a similar reaction.

Callie cleared her throat. "I don't want to mislead you.

I had a lovely time. The food was excellent, and I enjoyed the concert. But I'm afraid I can't accept any more invitations."

"You can't?" John asked.

Mary Beth's head pivoted from one to the other.

"That evening, David and I came to…an understanding."

Mary Beth gasped. "An understanding?"

"Yes, we realize that we've grown to…care very deeply for each other, and we—we've fallen in love."

"Fallen in love." The words escaped them in unison like the chorus of a Greek tragedy.

Callie looked at them. "I hope you can be happy for us."

"Happy?" John looked bemused, then his brows unfurrowed. "Happy, yes. I'm happy for you."

She watched him struggle to maintain a neutral expression. Mary Beth's face registered pure frustration.

"Well, I hope under the circumstances," Mary Beth said, her face pinched, "that you don't plan to continue living together in the same house."

Callie's heart dropped. The thought hadn't occurred to her. But she had to live here. How would she and David know if they could work through their problems? Yet how could she explain the situation to others—once Mary Beth spread the news?

Callie leveled her stare at Mary Beth. "We don't live in the house alone, as you know. Agnes and Nattie are both there. I don't believe in premarital relationships, Mary Beth, if that's what you're insinuating." She almost became catty, wanting to add the words, *"Perhaps you do."* But God intervened and removed the words from her lips.

"I'm not insinuating anything. I just wouldn't want others to think differently."

John pressed his sister's arm. "I don't see how others will think anything, Mary Beth. No one knows this, except you and me. And we won't spread idle gossip, will we?"

Mary Beth grasped the neck of her blouse for a second time. "Why…no. I certainly wouldn't spread gossip."

"Then I don't believe we have a problem at all."

Callie wanted to hug him, but instead, she extended her hand. "Thank you, John, for understanding." Mary Beth hovered as if waiting to receive her thank you, but Callie sat at the piano to practice.

Chapter Eighteen

No matter what John had said to make things better, Callie couldn't forget his sister's words. Was it wrong for her to stay at the house now that she and David had admitted their love for each other? Wonderful, fulfilled days passed by, and though they said nothing to Nattie, the child seemed to understand changes had occurred. And her joy had grown as much as theirs.

September was nearly on their doorstep, and Nattie would soon begin school. With her debut into the world of education, Callie faced a decision. What reason did she have to stay in Bedford? The time had come to talk honestly with David.

But Callie's procrastination had blossomed into avoidance. Today she set a deadline. One week. Within the week, she had to broach the subject of leaving. She couldn't stay in the house under the circumstances, no matter what her heart said.

Callie descended the staircase to a flutter of activity. Yesterday David had announced he'd invited their old housekeeper, Miriam, to dinner. With improved health, she had come to Bedford to visit her sister.

At the bottom of the stairs, Nattie clung to the banister, staring at the door and awaiting Miriam's arrival. At the sound of an automobile, Nattie raced to the door and tugged it open.

As soon as Callie saw her, she understood why Miriam held a special place in their hearts. Stepping from the car was a woman who fulfilled everyone's dream of a roundish, warm, lovable fairy godmother. Her face glimmered with animation and love as she threw her ample arms around Nattie and David.

Callie waited inside, allowing their welcome to be unburdened by introductions. David helped Miriam through the door, and Callie met her in the foyer.

The elderly woman moved cautiously forward, a cane in her left hand, and Callie joined her in welcome. "I'm so happy to meet you. I've heard nothing but wonderful things about you."

Miriam's eyes twinkled. "And I've heard nothing but wonderful things about you." She wrapped one arm around Callie's shoulders, giving her a warm hug.

"Come into the parlor, Miriam. We'll sit until dinner's ready." There, David guided her to a comfortable chair. Nattie clung to her side and leaned against the chair arm, as Miriam settled herself.

"I'd hold you on my lap, precious, but I'm not sure my old legs will bear the weight. You've grown so big since I last saw you. It seems years, rather than months."

Nattie stood straight as if pulled by a string. "I forgot. Agnes said I could help set the table." She skipped from the room, as the others chuckled at her enthusiasm.

"David, what a joy to see her so well." Miriam turned toward Callie. "I know we have this young lady to thank."

Callie murmured a thank you, as Miriam continued.

"When I left, my heart was nearly broken, seeing Nattie so distraught. David had already gone through enough without that burden."

"I've enjoyed every moment I've spent with Nattie," Callie said. "I've had the rare pleasure of watching her blossom. It's like a special gift from God."

"I'm sure it is," she said. "And now, David, what's happening with you?"

"Seeing Nattie get better has been amazing. And I might add, meeting Callie has been a blessing for me, too."

A healthy grin curved Miriam's mouth, and her eyes twinkled. "Am I to understand you two have— how should I put it—an understanding?"

Callie glanced at David with a shy grin.

He nodded. "Yes, you could call it that. Callie has brought me back to life as much as she has Nat."

Miriam turned to Callie. "Then, I thank you. You've made an old woman feel very happy."

Callie laughed. "Thanks. We're a pretty happy bunch."

"And we'll be even happier when we eat. Let me check on dinner." David jumped up and left the room.

Miriam checked the doorway, then faced Callie. "While he's gone, I want to thank you privately. I love this family like my own, and my heart was heavy with all the sadness in this house. But today, I feel love—and best of all, promise."

"Thank you. When I first came, I thought David was a grouchy, unloving, hard-nosed man. At times he was, but I soon found the real David underneath all that cover-up."

"David hardened himself. He blamed himself for Sara's death, I know. Letting her get pregnant, and then losing the baby. But when they got Nattie, what joy! She was the answer to their prayers."

"Losing the baby? You mean Sara had a miscarriage. I didn't know that." Callie's stomach knotted. David's words echoed in her mind, *"God punished me for my selfishness."* Is that what he'd meant?

"Oh, yes, such sadness that day."

"I can imagine their joy when Nattie arrived."

"Yes, but short-lived." Miriam's old grief resurfaced in her voice.

"Only four years, I understand."

Miriam lowered her eyes and a look of disapproval swept over her. "Yes, Sara was a lovely woman… David knew she had cancer when they married."

Callie nodded. "Yes, he told me." Obviously, Miriam had stronger feelings than she allowed herself to say.

The older woman regrouped. "But the four years with Nattie were wonderful years for them both. Right up to the end."

David's footsteps signaled his return. He came through the doorway with his hands outstretched. "Dinnertime. Have you ever heard sweeter words?"

Callie helped Miriam from the chair and whispered in her ear, "I always thought the sweetest words were 'I love you'—but you know men."

The two women chuckled, and David raised an eyebrow at them.

They lingered over a dinner of good food, reminiscences and laughter—until the telephone rang.

Agnes summoned Callie.

It was Ken. "It's Mom," he said. "She had another stroke. More serious this time."

"Oh, no, Ken. I've been meaning to visit, but I haven't. I feel so terrible. I'll leave right away."

"You can wait if you'd rather. I'll keep you posted. No sense in rushing here tonight."

Callie clenched the receiver. "No, I want to come now. I'll feel better. I won't sleep a wink if I stay here."

"Okay. Give me a call when you arrive. If I'm not home, I'll be here at the hospital."

"It'll take me three hours or so, Ken. It'll be late. Nine-thirty or ten, maybe. So don't worry."

"Callie, drive carefully."

She placed the receiver in the cradle and turned toward the dining room. She hated to put a damper on the visit.

As she entered the room, David rose. "Is something wrong?"

When the words stumbled from her tongue, she fought back her tears. "My mom's had a bad stroke. I have to go home tonight."

"Get ready, Callie, and I'll drive you," David said. "I don't want you to go alone."

"No, I need my car while I'm there. I'm fine, please. You go ahead and enjoy your visit. I'll run up and pack. As soon as I know something, I'll call."

When Callie arrived, she went directly to the hospital. Grace lay sleeping, connected to a machine that hummed and flashed numbers measuring her vital signs. Ken stepped from the bedside and wrapped his arm around Callie.

"She's about the same. She seems to be out of danger, but you can see the stroke has affected her this time."

Callie leaned over the bed and saw her mother's mouth twisted to one side. "So how much damage? Can they tell yet?"

"No. They'll run some tests in the morning. The doctor said her speech will be affected, at least for a while." He motioned to the chair. "Sit here for a few minutes. I'll take a walk and stretch my legs."

Callie nodded and eased herself into the chair. Pushing her arm through the bed's protective bars, she patted her mother's hand. Tears rose in her eyes, and she felt angry at herself for not having taken the time to come up for a visit.

She rested her head against the high chair back, and her

mind filled with prayers. As her thoughts turned to God, she remembered her quandary— whether to stay in Bedford or come home. Maybe this was God's way of intervening. Perhaps her decision would be made for her.

Ken returned, bringing her a cup of coffee. They stayed by their mother's side until their eyelids drooped, then agreed that sitting there all night was foolish. Grace was out of danger, and they needed their rest.

Walking into the night air, Callie looked up into the sky, wondering if indeed God was directing her. If her mother needed her here, she would move back to Indianapolis. She had little choice.

In the morning, Callie called the nurse's station. Grace had rested during the night, and remained the same. Before leaving for the hospital, Callie called David and promised to phone later when she knew more.

By the time she reached the hospital, Ken had not arrived, and Callie stood alone in the doorway of Grace's room. Her mother's eyes were closed, but as Callie neared the bed, Grace opened them with a look of confusion.

"Everything's fine, Mom. You're in the hospital."

Grace opened her mouth, but the muddled words filled her eyes with fear.

"Don't try to talk, Mom. Just rest. The doctor will be in soon, and we'll know more then." Callie adjusted the chair and sat beside her. "If you need me, I'm right here."

She took her mother's hand and gave it a squeeze. And

to her relief, Grace exerted a faint answering pressure. Callie clasped her mother's hand, thanking God.

Grace drifted into a fitful sleep, and Callie waited, speaking with nurses as they came in and out to check machines and the IVs, but they said little about her mother's condition.

Ken arrived, and two doctors followed on his heels, then conferred outside the room. Callie rose and met them in the hallway, while Ken stood beside Grace. When they entered, Ken kissed his mother's cheek and joined Callie.

"They suggested we go down for coffee while they examine her. He'll catch us later. Okay?" Callie asked.

Ken agreed, and they hurried to the cafeteria and moved quickly along the food line. Balancing her tray, Callie found a table near an outside window. They ate in silence, until Callie could gather her thoughts.

"I'm trying to decide what to do, Ken. Nattie has improved so much. She'll be starting school in a couple more weeks, and I suppose I should come back home and stay with Mom."

"I thought the last time I talked to you things were going well with you and David. Didn't you say a little romance was cooking?" Ken lifted his coffee cup and drank.

"That's another issue. I'm not sure if I should stay at the house under the circumstances. What will people say?" She leaned back against her chair, her fork poised in her hand. "But if I'm not there, we have little hope for a relationship, either. A two-hour drive each way doesn't encourage a budding romance."

"It's your call, sis."

"I know. But I'm so confused." She placed the fork on her plate and rubbed her temples.

"Well, don't try to make decisions now. Let's see what the doctors say. Mom may be in better shape than we think."

"I don't know if that really solves my dilemma. I still think I should come home." Her hands knotted on the table.

He placed his hand on hers. "Don't ruin your life, Callie. You overthink things sometimes. Try to be patient. Let's take one problem at a time. We're worried about Mom right now."

When they finished eating, they returned to Grace's room and met the doctor outside her door.

"So what do you think, Dr. Sanders?" Callie asked. "Any idea yet what happened?"

"Let me use layman's terms."

"Thanks. But I might mention I'm a nurse."

"Good. That could be helpful. Your mother apparently had an embolism. A blood clot broke loose from somewhere in her body, perhaps the heart. It often travels through the arterial stream into the cerebral cortex. When the clot lodges somewhere along its path, it can stop the flow of blood to the brain. In your mother's case, it did, and the stroke resulted."

Ken's face tensed. "So what happens now? Do you know how bad it is?"

"We'll run more tests, but we know she has some paralysis. She'll need physical therapy, and we'll begin that as soon as she's strong enough. Speech therapy will begin as soon as she's alert. Sometimes we have to wait two or three months before we see if she'll have permanent damage."

Ken's eyes widened. "Two or three months? You mean, we just have to sit and wait?"

"We'll do what we can." He looked at Callie. "And you might be able to speed up the process if you're willing to handle additional physical therapy at home."

Helping with Mom's treatment meant staying in Indianapolis. Nattie's face rose in Callie's mind, and a lonely feeling engulfed her.

"Good. Right now, your mother has IVs, but later she'll be on a variety of medications. An anticoagulant to keep her blood from clotting, and a vasodilator to keep the arteries open. If she has a narrowing or blockage in the carotid artery, she'll need surgery. Right now, your guess is as good as mine. The test will answer a lot of questions."

Ken glanced at Callie.

She shrugged. "We'll wait, then, until you have more information."

The doctor nodded. "You're welcome to visit for a while, but I suggest you let your mother rest as much as possible. Later today, we'll run the tests. Why not stay for a few more minutes, and then go on home? Come back this evening, if you like, and by tomorrow we should have some answers."

Ken nodded. "How about it, Callie?"

She heaved a sigh. "Not much we can do now, I

suppose." She looked at the physician. "And we should follow doctor's orders."

With a gentle grin, the doctor rested his hand on her arm. "I only hope your mother's as good at following orders as you are."

According to the test reports, Grace's prognosis gave Callie hope. The week passed during which she was scheduled for daily therapy. Another week or so in the hospital, Dr. Sanders said, and her mother could go home.

The news still lay unsettled in Callie's mind. She sat in her mother's house, staring at the telephone. She had promised to call David, but she had delayed for a full week, wanting to clarify her decision.

David had sent flowers to Grace at the hospital, and another lovely bouquet sat on a nearby table. The brilliant colors should have brightened Callie's evening, but they didn't. Her thoughts were too muddled. She missed David and Nattie. But when Grace was released, she'd need help. Callie knew she had to provide it.

She raised the receiver and punched in the numbers. David's voice echoed across the line.

"How are you two?" she asked.

"We miss you. How are things there?"

"Better. Mom started therapy, and I'm happy to say, she's doing pretty well. Her speech is slurred, but I can understand her. And she forgets words once in a while."

David chuckled. "I do that without a stroke. How about movement?"

"She can't walk by herself yet. But things are promising. It'll take time. She'll have to continue therapy when she gets home."

He sighed. "So that means…?"

"So that means, I'll be coming to Bedford for my things."

Silence.

David finally spoke. "Then you'll go back for a while. I understand. Your mother needs you."

Callie closed her eyes to catch the tears that formed. "Not for a while, David. I'm coming back for good."

Chapter Nineteen

David hovered in her doorway, the blood in his veins as frozen as if he were an ice sculpture. Callie stood at the closet, packing. His wonderful new life was melting away; where his hopes and dreams had been, he saw only empty space.

"Callie, can't you listen to reason?"

"You mean *your reason,* David, not mine."

He strode across the room to her side. "I know your mother needs you now, but not forever. Please, we can't manage here without you, and I don't mean taking care of Nattie. We both love you. You're part of our lives."

She swung to face him. "Please, don't make this harder than it is. I love you, too, David, but we're both dealing with issues from the past. I'm not sure this relationship can go anywhere. Especially now, since someone made me think." Her eyes closed for a heartbeat. "I can't ruin your reputation or mine."

"What are you talking about? 'Ruin your reputation or mine'? That doesn't make sense."

"Yes, it does. Nat's fine now. She doesn't need me. So what purpose do I have living here? I'm a paid…what? You tell me." She grasped his arms. "I'm a pretty expensive baby-sitter, wouldn't you say?"

Tears spilled from her eyes and ran down her cheeks.

"Oh, Callie, what do you think you are—a kept woman?" David slid his arms around her back. "God knows that we need you here. I don't care what others might say. And why would they? Who would say anything?"

Callie shook her head without answering.

"Everyone knows about Nattie's problems. For you to walk in and out of our lives when you mean so much to her is unthinkable. She lost her mother, and now you—someone she's grown to love. Who would put such crazy thoughts in your head?"

David's mind swam. *Pastor John? Agnes?* None of it made sense. "You're a Christian. You serve the church. No one would think wrong of you for being here. And what about Nattie?"

"But she's well, David. She doesn't *need* me anymore."

He dropped his arms to his sides and spun away. "No? You think she doesn't need you. Do you know where she is right now?" He whirled around to face her. "She's crying in her room. Nattie loves you. When you came, I didn't think about her loving you. All I thought was that I needed someone to make her better. I never thought I would hurt her."

Callie covered her face with her hands, and remorse spilled over him for the sorrow he had created by his words. "I'm not trying to make you feel guilty. I'm only trying to help you understand how much we love you."

"I'm sorry, David. I've given this a lot of thought. I pray I'm doing the right thing. If I'm wrong, I hope God will help me make it right. That's all I can say. I spent my life bearing a secret anger toward my parents. My mom is the only parent I have left to whom I can make retribution for my feelings. I have to do this."

David closed his eyes and filled his lungs with air. Why did she feel anger toward her parents? He didn't understand her cryptic comment. "I know you want to be with your mother, Callie. And Indianapolis is only two hours away. We'll work things out. Remember our 'deal' a while ago? We agreed to pray for each other. Like Jesus said, 'Where two or three are gathered in my name, I am with them.' We'll leave it in God's hands."

He moved to her side again and held her close. Her heart pounded against his chest, answering his own thudding rhythm. "I love you, Callie." He tilted her face to his. "I have faith in us." His lips touched hers lightly, then he backed away and left, knowing his life would soon be as lonely as the room she was vacating.

Callie struggled to see the road through her tears on her return to Indianapolis. Signing adoption papers had been the hardest thing she'd ever done. Saying goodbye to Nattie was the second. And saying goodbye to David… Callie had no words for the way she felt. She loved them both, but too many things stood in their way. Mary Beth's words hammered in her mind. David still struggled with Sara's death, and Callie had yet to heal from the rape and the adoption. Like someone who carries baskets of bricks up a hill, she carried the weight of Jim McKee's sin on her shoulders.

So often when she looked at Nattie, she imagined her own child. Did her daughter have a halo of blond curls? Was she loved? Was she learning about Jesus? Callie couldn't bear to think the worst. She longed to know—her heart ached. And all the love she had denied herself for years had risen like a wonderful gift and showered down on Nattie. And again Callie was letting a child go. Callie longed for a release. Would telling David about her own child help to heal the wounds? Now she would never know.

Since the telephone call, her thoughts had been filled with worry about her mother. But as she left Bedford, her talk with Miriam drifted into her mind. David hadn't told her Sara had miscarried. Yet he'd told her about wanting the abortion. Callie's head spun with disjointed bits of information, spilled out like pieces of one of Nattie's puzzles. Why didn't David feel God's forgiveness when Nattie was born? Why did he cling to his anger? God had given him a second chance—Nattie.

Finally, she turned her concerns to her present problem—Grace. Would Mom listen to her—as her nurse, and not as her daughter? What might that do to their relationship, which she had hoped to heal? Her head ached with wondering.

* * *

The next days flew past with preparations for Grace's return: a hospital bed, therapy training, treatment scheduling, grocery shopping. Yet keeping busy didn't help Callie feel less sad or lonely.

David persisted. He phoned, sent flowers and wrote notes on Missing You cards, but Callie clung to her decision. She believed God's hand had guided her.

Grace's day of homecoming arrived, and Callie stood beside her hospital bed packing her belongings. "Anxious to get home, Mom?"

Grace nodded as she had begun to do, avoiding her distorted voice.

"Talk, Mom. No head-nods. The more you talk, the quicker you'll have your old voice back."

Grace clamped her lips together like a disobedient child.

"Very adult of you, Mom." Callie shook her head in frustration. She had watched hospital films and talked to the psychologist for tips on helping Grace and being supportive. She already felt like a failure.

As she finished packing, Dr. Sanders appeared at the doorway. "So today's the big day? How are you feeling?"

Grace shrugged, then struggled to get out a thick-sounding "Fine."

"Good. I have your prescriptions written out for you. And you're a lucky woman to have a daughter who's a nurse."

"I'm not sure that will go over too well," Callie said. "She's going to resent me."

Dr. Sanders patted Callie's hand. "She'll be fine." He turned to Grace. "Now, you'll listen to your daughter, right? She's trained to help you, and you'll have to mind her. If not, you'll end up back here. I know you don't want that."

Grace's eyes widened, but she kept her lips pressed together.

Dr. Sanders pointed to her mouth. "And you have to speak, Grace. You'll never talk if you don't practice."

He turned to Callie. "We'll send the speech therapist out three times a week, and then count on you to do the rest."

"That's fine. I've had instructions, and I can handle the therapy—if she'll listen." She directed her last words to Grace.

He spoke for a moment with Grace, and when he left, Callie gathered up the overnight bag and parcels and headed to her car.

Grace was wheeled outside and eased into the car. The trip home was silent, except for Callie's own running monologue. And she breathed a relieved sigh when Ken's car pulled into the driveway behind them.

"Glad you're here," she said, sliding from the car. She closed her door. "I didn't know if I could get Mom in alone. Besides, I need a little moral support."

"You look beat already," Ken said, standing at the trunk, as they unloaded the wheelchair.

She looked at him, shaking her head. "I'm afraid this'll be the undoing of Mother and me. I hoped, coming home, we could smooth out our differences, but she's being terribly belligerent. Like a child."

Ken rolled his eyes. "We'll just have to be patient. She'll come around."

She rested her hand on his shoulder. "And don't forget, I'll need a break once in a while. I can't do this alone or I'll end up in a hospital...and it won't be *medical* hospital."

Ken slammed the trunk. "No one would ever notice."

"Thanks." She poked his arm.

He rolled the wheelchair to the car door, and with his strong arms settled Grace into the seat. Together, they hoisted Grace up the porch stairs into the house and into the hospital bed, as the patient grunted and pointed.

Hands on her hips, Callie stood beside them. "Make her talk, Ken." She scowled at her mother. "We'll have no grunting or pointing in this house."

Grace glowered back as much as her face would allow, and Callie covered a snicker. Her heart broke for her mother, but she knew she'd better learn to laugh if they were to survive.

When Grace was settled, Callie invited Ken into the kitchen for a sandwich. He stretched his legs in front of him, twiddling his thumbs, as Callie buttered the bread. "Do you think you can do this?" he asked.

"Oh, they say God never gives us more than we can handle." She turned to face him. "But I think He's pushing it this time."

Ken threw his head back and laughed. "I was thinking

the same thing. Hang in there, and I'll do what I can to help."

"Great, but I won't hold my breath."

David sent two more bouquets the following week—one for her, and the other for Grace. Callie missed him more than she could say. The situation hadn't eased. Grace fought her at every turn, and her nerves pulsed like wired dynamite.

One day, Callie was sitting in the kitchen, nibbling a sandwich that she could barely swallow, when the telephone rang. When she heard David's voice, her hand shook. She longed to tell him how awful things were, but instead she inquired about him, avoiding what was in her heart.

Finally she asked, "How's Nat?"

"Lonesome." A heavy silence hung on the line. "So am I, Callie. Nothing seems worth much anymore."

She refused to respond. She'd say far more than was safe to admit. "How's Nat's school? Is she doing okay?"

She waited. A chill ruffled through her. "Is something wrong, David?"

"I don't want to burden you. You have enough problems."

She stiffened. "Don't leave me hanging, David. What's wrong." Her voice sounded strained to her ears. "I'm sorry, David, but you've upset me. Is something wrong with Nattie?"

"She's…beginning to withdraw again. Not like before, but she's not herself. I know she misses you. It'll pass with time. Her teacher was concerned, but I explained that...well, I didn't want to get into a lengthy discussion. I said her mother had died recently. I figured that would explain it."

If she'd felt stress before, she felt a thousand times worse hearing his words. "I don't know what to say. Even if I wanted to come back, I can't. Mom needs too much right now, and Ken works full time. He gives me a break once in a while, but I'm it, David. I'm the caregiver here."

He sighed. "I know. I know. I'm trying to think of something."

When she hung up, she covered her face and wept. She felt pity for everyone: Grace, David, Nattie and herself. When her tears ended, she splashed water on her eyes and planted a smile on her lips. Her wristwatch signaled Grace's therapy—and if Callie didn't smile, she'd scream.

"Look at you, Mom," Ken said, as Grace shuffled her feet across the floor while leaning heavily on her walker.

A twisted grin covered Grace's face; she looked as pleased as a toddler learning to take her first steps.

Callie stood nearby, watchful for any problems, but Grace moved steadily along. "Mom's worked hard," she said to Ken. "It makes it worthwhile, doesn't it, Mom? At least, you can get up and move around a little."

Grace grunted a "yes." Her speech had improved, too, turning their hope to reality.

Callie kept her eyes focused on Grace. "See if you can make it to the living room, Mom. You can sit in there for a change."

Grace heaved her shoulders upward as she moved the walker. When she was seated, Callie made a pot of tea and brought out some freshly baked cookies for a celebration. As difficult as it had been, she could see that Grace was mending.

As they talked, the telephone rang, and Callie left the living room to answer it in the kitchen. Something inside her told her the caller was David.

"Don't say a word, Callie, but Nattie and I are coming to Indianapolis to see you."

"Please, David, no. I'm still miserable. I don't think I could bear to see you…and not Nattie. I'll cry for sure."

"Good. Tears soften the heart, Callie, my love. You might as well give up. I'm coming. Nattie will be terribly disappointed if I tell her you don't want us to come."

"Oh, David. Don't say that. Come, then. I'll be here… forever."

"Maybe not. I think I have a solution."

Chapter Twenty

Callie's heart did cartwheels when she saw Nattie through the window. The child darted up the porch before David could catch her. Callie flung open the door and knelt to embrace her; Nattie flew into her arms and buried her face in Callie's neck.

Her small, muffled voice sounded on Callie's cheek. "I miss you."

"I miss you, too, Nat. Terribly." Callie raised her eyes toward David. "I miss all of you."

"Aren't you coming home?" Nattie asked.

The word *home* tore through her. Bedford was more home to her than her mother's house. The answer caught in her throat. She swallowed, and avoided a direct answer. "My mom is sick right now, Nat, and I have to take care of her."

Nattie tilted her head back and searched Callie's face. "Is she going to die?"

"No, she's getting better. But you know what? She won't

talk much at all. Do you remember someone who didn't want to talk much a while ago?"

Nattie hung her head shyly and nodded. But her head popped up with her next words. "Is your mommy sad?"

Callie grinned. "No, not sad." She glanced up at David. "More like 'mad.' As mad as a wet hen, in fact."

Nattie giggled at the old saying.

"Well, let's not stand in the doorway. Come in." Callie rose, took Nattie by the hand, and moved so David could enter.

He stepped inside and slipped his arm cautiously around her waist, as Nattie eyed them. "How are you?"

Callie lowered her eyes. "Miserable. And you?"

"Terribly miserable."

Nattie pushed her shoulders forward, squeezing her hands between her knees, and chuckled. "I'm miserable, too."

Her words made them smile. Callie gave her another hug. "Well, that's good, then. We're all miserable together." She gestured them into the living room. "Have you eaten? Anyone starving?"

"No, we had some breakfast on the way."

"We stopped at Burger Boy," Nattie added.

"Burger Boy, huh?" Callie gave David a disapproving look.

He wiggled his eyebrows. "They have biscuit breakfasts."

"Ah. Well, then, how about something to drink and maybe a cookie or two?"

They agreed, and while they waited in the living room,

Callie gathered the drinks and cookies, taking deep breaths to control her wavering emotions. She loved them both, and seeing them today, though wonderful, felt painful, as well.

"Here we go," she said, carrying a tray into the living room and putting the cookies closest to Nattie.

Sinking into a chair, Callie studied David's face. His usual bright, teasing eyes looked shadowed. She gazed at Nattie, longing to speak privately to David. Then an idea struck.

"David, would you and Nat like to say hello to Mom?"

"Sure, if she's up to it."

"Nat, you've never met my mother. I might have a book around here somewhere, and you could show her the pictures and tell her a story. Would you like that? She gets pretty lonely in her room."

Nattie nodded, and Callie hurried to her room. On her bookshelf, she'd kept some favorite children's books. She shuffled through them and located a book of well-known tales and stories illustrated with colorful pictures. Before she returned to the living room, she popped into Grace's room to announce visitors, then left without giving Grace a chance to say no.

In the living room, she handed Nattie the book. "When I was young, this book was one of my favorites."

As soon as Nattie held the book, she flipped through the pages. "I know this story, and this one," she said.

"Good, then let's go in to see my mom."

She took Nattie by the hand, with David following, and

headed down the hallway. Grace was staring at the doorway as they entered, looking stressed, probably over Callie's announcement. But when her gaze lit upon Nattie, her face softened. Only the slight tug of paralysis distorted her usual expression.

"Mom, here's David. And Nattie. You've never met her."

David stepped forward, extending his hand. "It's good to see you, Grace. Callie says you're doing great. A little more time, and you'll be back to normal, huh?"

"Oh, I don't know," Grace said, her speech thick and halting.

Nattie stared at Grace and then glanced at Callie. "I thought your mommy didn't talk."

Callie snickered. "Maybe she just doesn't talk to *me*, Nattie." She peered at Grace. Her mother averted her eyes. Instead, she watched Nattie.

"When I was younger, I didn't want to talk," Nattie said, leaning her folded arms on Grace's bed.

"No?" Grace said, not taking her eyes from the child.

"I was too sad."

"Happy now?" Grace laid her hand on Nattie's arms.

"Uh-huh, except Callie went away to take care of you." Nattie glanced at Callie over her shoulder. "I miss her."

Grace's skewed face formed an angled smile. "You do, huh?"

"Yep." Nattie leaned forward and whispered at Grace. "But we came for a visit to tell her to come home."

Grace raised her eyes toward Callie. "Home?" She

reached out and drew her hand over Nattie's blond hair, then nodded. "Yes, I suppose that is her home."

Tears burned behind Callie's eyes, and she quickly changed the topic. "Mom, Nattie wants to show you a picture book. You want to get up in a chair, or would you rather have her up there on the bed with you?"

Grace patted the coverlet beside her, and David boosted the child to the edge of the bed.

"You can get up for lunch, okay? We'll be in the other room for a few minutes. Can you get down by yourself, Nat?"

"I think so." She stared down at the floor.

"If not, give a call, and I'll come running," David said, patting her cheek with his fingers.

Callie and David walked out of the room, leaving Nattie to entertain Grace.

"I think Nat could work wonders with Mother. I haven't seen her so talkative since the stroke. She buttons up when I'm the one she has to talk to."

"But you're the nurse. No one likes nurses. They're too mean, and they make you take medicine and do things you don't want to do."

She returned his tease, rolling her eyes. "Thanks."

"And they always say, 'It's time to take *our* bath.' Have you ever seen a nurse—other than yourself, that is—take a bath?"

She listened to David's chatter, but inside, her stomach dipped on a roller-coaster ride. What would happen now that they were alone? David answered her question. He slid his arm around her waist, drawing her against him. His hand ran up her arm to her face, and he touched her cheek, drawing his fingers along her heating skin to trace her lips.

Her knees wanted to buckle beneath her, and a sensation, beginning as a tingle, grew to an uncontrollable tremor, as his face neared hers. She thought of pulling away, but her desire overpowered her intentions. She met his lips with hers, eagerly savoring the sweetness, and a moan escaped his throat, sending a deepening shudder through her body as her own sigh joined his.

Out of breath, she eased away and gazed into his heavy-lidded eyes. "David, you can't kiss me like this. I can't handle it."

"Good. Let *me* handle things. I refuse to leave this house without knowing you'll come back to us."

"How can I do that? Tell me." She raised her voice overwhelmed by a sense of futility. She longed to be with them in Bedford. No matter what others thought, she loved them and belonged with them.

"Let's sit, and I'll tell you how. I've figured it out. Come." He took her hand and guided her into the living room, and together they sank onto the sofa in each other's arms.

Her first thought was Nattie. What if she saw David's arms around her? "What if Nattie see us?"

"I told her I love you, Callie. And guess what she said."

She could only shake her head.

"She loves you, too. That was her response. And she

needs you. She's been so quiet. But as soon as she saw you today, she opened again. Look at her with Grace. She's good for Grace, too."

Callie couldn't deny that. Grace hadn't been so receptive to anyone. Maybe a child's exuberance would bring her out of her self-pitying mode. She thought of her own situation. Nattie had worked a miracle, making her a whole person again.

"So," Callie asked. "What's your plan?"

"Bring your mother to Bedford."

"What?" She scanned his eager face. "I can't do that."

"Why not? Bring her to the house. We have tons of room."

"But it doesn't make sense...does it?"

"It makes all the sense in the world. I've already made arrangements. We'll set the library up as her room. She'll have an easy chair, television, books if she likes to read. There's a telephone there. A bathroom nearby."

"You're overwhelming me." She shook her head in confusion.

"I realized there's no shower on the first floor, except in Agnes's quarters. She said, 'Great, no problem.' So that's solved."

"What about her doctors and medication?"

"Once she's able to get around more, you can bring Grace here for her appointments. And her prescriptions can be filled in Bedford or here. That's not a problem."

Callie stared at him, dazed. "You've thought of everything, I take it."

"Please, don't get upset with me."

"I'm not upset, really. I'm stunned, David. I made a decision that staying in Bedford was the wrong thing to do, and now you're organizing and arranging my life."

"I'm sorry. That was selfish of me to assume that—"

"No, no, I'm not angry. I love you for it, because it means you love me. But I need to think things through."

"I understand, and you'll want to wait until the doctor says it's okay for Grace to travel. But, Callie, we can handle things if we know you're coming home."

"Home?" she said.

"Yes, home." He turned her face to his, and their lips met.

Past fears of intimacy rose inside her, and she tensed for a flickering moment. Then, as quickly, she relaxed her shoulders. With David, she experienced what God meant by loving…giving herself to a special someone and feeling complete.

With his kiss still warm on her lips, Callie rested her head against his shoulder. "David, I can't do anything without Mom's approval. I don't know if she'll be willing to come to Bedford."

"I've prayed." He ran his hand across the back of his neck. "I've prayed, and I believe God heard my prayers. I think Grace will come, Callie. Give her time, but I think she'll come."

She closed her eyes, adding her prayer to David's. Life was nothing without him and Nattie. That's where she belonged. But in all the confusion, she had yet to accomplish what she had set out to do: resolve the hurt that affected her relationship with Grace. She had to forgive and be forgiven.

Forgiving and being forgiven. Such complicated concepts.

She hadn't been totally honest with David, either. Would he forgive her when he learned about her child and the adoption? If only she knew her daughter was happy, maybe she could forgive herself.

But God had given her another child: Nattie. Was this her second chance to make things right?

Chapter Twenty-One

David checked the library for the fifth time. The room looked comfortable. Bed, bedside table, small dresser, all hauled down from an upstairs bedroom. He'd added a television set, and today, a bouquet of fresh flowers had been delivered. He wanted Grace to feel welcome.

The move had been difficult. Callie had been met with resistance from her mother, but finally, Grace had a change of heart. He didn't question the cause, but Callie said it followed on the footsteps of Nattie's second visit to Indianapolis. Nattie had latched onto Grace as she had the first time and had remained at her side. One evening, they sat together in the living room. As David and Callie talked, they grinned, overhearing Grace's and Nattie's conversation from the sofa.

"Tell me about school," Grace said, her speech clearer than it had been on their first visit.

Nattie tilted her head and thought. "Well, the teacher said I'm a good reader for first grade. And I can print my name and some other words…" She paused and raced across the room to Callie. "Do you have paper and a pencil? I want to show your mommy how I can print."

"Sure, I do," Callie said, and pulled a pad of paper and pencil from a lamp table drawer. "Here, you go."

Nattie returned to Grace, nestled at her side and proceeded to demonstrate her printing talents. David listened to Grace's encouraging comments and then returned to his own conversation.

"Any progress with Grace?" David asked in a near whisper, knowing his plans for them to move to Bedford had not set well.

"She's stubborn, David. I suppose I understand. But I haven't given up."

"She seems to be doing well."

"She is. She's using her own bed now, and she walks with the cane, though one leg still isn't cooperating totally."

"I'd hoped once she got around a little on her own, she might think of Bedford as a vacation," he said.

Callie rolled her eyes. "There's where you made your second mistake. Mom isn't crazy about vacations. She's a homebody."

He glanced at Grace and Nattie, the weight of hopelessness on his chest. His life had been empty and futureless without Callie. Though Nattie had withdrawn after she left, their visit two weeks earlier had seemed to work a miracle. All he could think about was his prayer that Callie would come back to Bedford.

Muddled in his thoughts, Nattie's words pulled him back to the present.

"Could you be my grandma?" she asked, looking into Grace's attentive eyes.

David's heart kicked into second gear. He glanced at Callie and saw that she had heard. He waited for Grace's response, his heartbeat suspended.

She lifted her gnarled hand and patted Nattie's leg, which was snuggled close to her own. "I'd like that, Nattie. You can call me Grandma Grace." Her eyes hadn't shifted from the child's face.

"Could I just call you Grandma?"

Grace's face twisted to a gentle smile. "Whatever makes you happy, child."

"Good," Nattie said, and lifted herself to kiss Grace's cheek.

David's heart melted at the sight, and when he turned to Callie, she was wiping tears from her eyes.

"Sentimental, huh?" she asked.

"Just plain beautiful," David responded.

That day had replayed itself over in his mind for the past two weeks. A week after their last visit, Callie had called to say Grace was becoming more receptive to a trip to Bedford. Today, his dream would become a reality.

Now, glancing out the window once again, David grinned, as he saw Nattie gallop through the autumn leaves gathered in mounds under the elms. She was as anxious as he.

Tired of waiting inside, David tossed on his windbreaker

and joined Nattie in the yard. Seeing him, she giggled and filled her arms with leaves, tossing them into the air. As the burnished leaves settled to earth, Callie's car came up the winding driveway. Nattie let out a squeal and ran toward him. Together, they followed the car until it stopped in front of the wide porch.

"Grandma. Callie," Nattie called, racing to the car door.

Callie climbed out and gave Nattie a hug. David opened the passenger door and helped Grace from the car.

He longed to take Callie in his arms, but Grace leaned heavily on him, so he controlled himself. Later, when they were alone, he could welcome her as he longed to do. He eased Grace up the wide steps and across the porch. Agnes greeted them at the door and held it open so Grace had easy access.

"My, now this is what I call a foyer," Grace said, looking wide-eyed around the vast entrance. "Callie didn't quite prepare me for something this elegant."

Nattie jigged around her, encouraging her to follow. "Look, Grandma, here's your bedroom. It's the lib'ary, but now it's your room."

"David didn't want you to climb the stairs," Callie explained. "He has extra bedrooms upstairs. When you're up to it, we can move your things up there, if you'd like."

Grace concentrated on her steps, but shifted her focus for a moment from the floor to Callie's face. "When I can climb those steps, I'll be ready to go back home." She grinned at David. "And you'll probably be ready to kick me out."

Nattie spun around, hearing her words. "We won't kick you out, Grandma. You can stay with me forever."

With a knowing eye, she glanced at Nattie. "Thank you, child. That's the sweetest thing I've ever heard."

Callie leaned close to David's ear. "That's because she doesn't listen to me. Believe it or not, I have said some pretty sweet things."

David winked at her. "I'm sure you have."

Grace raised her head and looked at the two of them. "I may have had a stroke, but I'm not deaf. So quit talking about me."

Nattie grasped her hand. "We have to be nice to Grandma. She's sick."

David and Callie burst into laughter, with Grace's snicker not far behind. Nattie looked at the three of them, then tucked her hands between her knees and joined them with her own giggle.

Callie hung up the telephone and turned to David. "I gather you told Pastor John I was coming back."

He nodded. "Why? Was it supposed to be a secret?"

"No, but he just called to ask me to sing on Sunday. And he told me about the organ, David. I'm really pleased."

"Give thanks to God, not me. He brought me to my senses."

"What do you mean?"

David took her hands in his and kissed them. "My anger was focused in the wrong direction. I've been angry at God for taking Sara and for Nat's problems, instead of being angry at myself. We knew Sara had cancer, but I expected God to work a miracle."

She nodded. "We can't expect miracles."

"No, we can't expect anything, but we need to have faith. It's the faith that works the miracles. And God hasn't let me down, even when I was being bullheaded. I wanted instant gratification. But sometimes, we have to do a bit of soul-searching before we can appreciate God's will."

"So after some soul-searching, you decided to donate to the organ-repair fund."

"Paid for the repair. I can afford it, and the congregation enjoys the organ music as much as I do."

"It's nice for everyone. I'm glad, David. Oh, and Pastor John mentioned the new organist…with much enthusiasm, I might add." She suspected John valued the organist for more than her musical contributions on Sunday mornings.

"Wait until you see her. She's cute and single. And the right age."

Teasing, Callie arched an eyebrow. "The right age for whom?"

"For Pastor John." He caressed her cheek with the back of his fingers. "*Whom* else?" He gave her a wink.

"Well, I'm glad." She sat next to him on the sofa. "She doesn't happen to have a brother Mary Beth's age, does she?"

"Jealous, are you?" He clasped her hand.

"Should I be?"

"No, but I forgot to tell you what happened while you were gone."

Callie raised both eyebrows this time. "Ah, true confessions?" She curled her legs beneath her and faced him.

"Not quite." His words were accompanied by a chuckle. "But this is about Mary Beth."

Callie's eyes glinted in jest.

"And?"

"A day or two after you left, she called, inviting me to dinner." "And you accepted, I'm sure." "Anticipating her motive, yes. I wanted to clear up the issue once and for all…and for no other reason." "I'm certain." Callie batted her eyelashes at him. David grinned. "Anyway, to get back to the subject—as I intended—" "Ah, as you intended." "Yes, as I intended, she let me know she was in terested in making my lonely life less lonely." "Beautifully said." "Thank you." Callie draped an arm around his neck. "And what did you say to that?"

"I thanked her graciously, but declined her offer." He filled his lungs. "Actually, I felt terrible for her. She was embarrassed and flustered. She wasn't quite as blunt as I made her out to be, but she did let me know how she felt."

"I hope you were nice when you rejected her."

"As nice as a rejection can be. I said I was in love with you—but that if I weren't, she'd be a likely second." He tilted his head, giving her a coy look.

"Now that's a rejection."

"I didn't really add the last part." He chucked her beneath the chin. "And I told her I planned to do all I could to bring you back to Bedford."

"You did? Really?"

"I did. She handled it quite well, I'd say."

"No weeping or gnashing of teeth?"

"Only a little."

"Good. She can probably handle it better than I can. With weeping, I'm skilled, but gnashing…?" She gave him a silly grin.

After church on Sunday morning, Callie slipped into her casual clothes and went outside. More leaves had fallen overnight, and winter's chill had put a coating of hoarfrost on everything. She drew in a deep breath of frigid air.

In less than a month Thanksgiving would arrive, then Christmas. On Christmas Day her child would be seven, and little more than a month later, Nat would celebrate her seventh birthday. All the love Callie had kept bundled inside for her own child, she lavished on Nattie. Still, she clung to her secret. And until she had the courage to tell David and Grace, the secret was a barrier between them.

Without question, Nattie had wrought a change in her mother. Grace's critical martyrdom had faded, and in its place, she seemed to have found a joy in living. She would have made Callie's child a wonderful grandmother, after all.

No wedding had been mentioned, but Callie was sure marriage was David's intention. They had settled, without words, into a warm, committed relationship.

But marriage was built on honesty. She wanted to start the new year with the truth. And the longer she waited, the more difficult it would become. The last time she'd set a deadline for herself, she had sensed that God worked to bring it about sooner. Now, she set a second deadline. She would summon her courage, and by the first of January she would tell David about her baby.

Chapter Twenty-Two

Callie and Grace sat in the parlor, a fire glowing in the fireplace. Thanksgiving was still a week away, but the first snow had fallen early and muted the world outside. With David at work and Nattie in school, the house was also quiet.

Callie studied her mother, seated cozily in front of the fire reading a magazine. A year earlier, she would never have believed that her feelings for Grace would change so radically, but they had. And with a renewed fondness welling inside her, she knew the right moment had arrived.

"Mom, could we talk?"

Grace glanced up from the magazine, a look of tenderness etching her face. "I've been wanting to talk to you, too."

"You have?" For the first time in years, she saw her mother with clearer eyes. Grace had always loved her, but her love had seemed doled out in controlled portions, as if she were afraid she might give it all away at one time and have nothing left. Today she seemed different.

Grace tossed the magazine to the floor and leaned back in the chair. "I didn't want to come here at first. You knew that, of course. And I suppose you saw what changed my mind. That wonderful child. I can understand why you wanted to come back here, Callie, not only because of David, but for Nattie."

"I know. She stole my heart."

"And I think David has, as well. He's a loving man. Kind and generous. You couldn't find a better husband." She peered into Callie's eyes. "I pray that's what the two of you have in mind."

"I pray so, too, Mom. And I'm glad you like him."

"I do. But God gave both of us a gift in Nattie. I look at her, Callie, and all I can think is somewhere in this world there's another little girl just like her. Nattie's so much like you, Callie." Her lips trembled, and she paused, her voice hindered by emotion. "I can imagine what your own little girl is like right now."

Tears stung Callie's eyes. "That's what I want to talk about, Mom. Part is a confession—a terrible secret I kept from you for so many years. Part is to help you understand my hurt and anger toward you and Dad."

"What are you talking about?" Grace's face paled, her eyes narrowed.

"I kept things hidden from you, and I've done the same with David. He doesn't know that I had a child. But I'm going to tell him. He and Sara wanted a child so badly that they took life-threatening chances to have a baby. Sara couldn't continue her radiation or chemotherapy without harming the baby, and without it, she endangered her own life. How could I tell him I had one that I gave away?"

"Oh Callie, that was a whole different matter. You can't compare the two situations."

"But I can. What would he think of me? I've worried that I'll disillusion him. He expects more of me. I always thought that you and Daddy felt that way, and I couldn't endure that rejection again from someone else I love so much."

Grace threw her hand to her mouth, and her eyes brimmed with tears. "Not rejection, Callie. Your dad and I were so hurt for you. We were irritated that you protected the young man. That's the part that upset us. And naturally, we were disappointed."

"And that's the part that hurt me so much, Mom."

"We had such dreams for you—with all your talents and gifts from God. And your refusal to sing. We felt you were punishing us because we forced the adoption. But we always loved you and thought we were doing the right thing about the baby."

"I know. And my anger at you wasn't fair. Because I never told you the whole story."

Grace's body stiffened. "The whole story?"

"I couldn't tell you the truth, because I knew both of you would be crushed. And to be honest, I wondered if you'd believe me, because I felt guilty thinking I might be partly to blame for what happened." Pressure pushed against her chest and constricted her throat.

"Callie, you're talking in circles. Please, tell me what you mean. You're scaring me."

Strangling on the words, Callie whispered, "The baby's father wasn't a college boy, Mother."

"Not a—" She faltered and clung to the chair. "Then, who?"

"I was raped." The word spilled out of her along with a torrent of blinding tears. Her body shook with the knotted, bitter hurt that had bound her for so many years. Telling David had been difficult, but telling her mother was devastating.

Grace rose with more speed than Callie could have imagined possible, and made her way to the sofa. She wrapped her arms around Callie and held her with every bit of strength she had. She asked no questions, but she held her daughter with the love only a mother could have for her child.

When Callie had regained control, she told Grace the story, in all its horror. Her mother listened, stroking and calming her until the awful truth was out. A ragged sigh raked through her shaking body.

Tears rolled down Grace's cheeks. No words were needed—Callie understood her mother's grief as well as she knew her own. They talked through the afternoon in a way they had never talked before. Their tears, like a cleansing flood, purified them, purged their past hurt and anger, and united them in love.

Ken joined them for Thanksgiving, and Grace had been content until then. But as Christmas approached, she urged Callie to take her home.

"Look how well I'm doing. My bedroom's upstairs now. I'm getting around. The cane is only a prop—see?" She lifted the cane and took a few steps. "I miss my house. And my things."

"That's why I don't have things, Mom. I've learned to live everywhere without a bunch of trappings."

"That's because all your trappings are with my things—at the house."

She chuckled at the truth. "I'll tell you what, Mom. Christmas is less than three weeks away. Why not stay here through the holidays, and then we'll take you home. You'll have nearly three weeks to get stronger."

"No sense in spending Christmas alone, is there?" David asked.

Grace eyed them both. "You promise? If I shut my mouth, you'll take me home after the holidays?"

"Promise," Callie said. "And think of what a nice Christmas you'll have this year with Nattie around. Christmas is always special with children."

Grace's face softened. "It has been a long time, hasn't it. You were my last baby."

David folded the paper and dropped it beside the chair. "And she's sure not a baby anymore." He winked at Grace.

"Me?" Nattie asked from the doorway, her brow puckered. "I'm not a baby anymore."

David opened his arms to her. "You sure aren't, Nat. But no, we were talking about Callie. She's no baby, either."

Nattie laughed. "I wish we had a baby."

Callie looked from Nattie to David, wondering what his response would be.

"First, we need a husband and wife. Then babies can come."

Nattie glanced at Callie. "You can marry Callie, Daddy. Then you'll be a husband and wife."

David gave her a giant hug. "My girl. She's making all the arrangements." His amused eyes sought Callie's. "We'll have to see about that, won't we?"

"Okay," Nattie said, and dropped the matter without another comment.

But Callie's heart pounded. Marriage seemed the next step for them, but the words were yet to be spoken. And Callie couldn't answer yes—not yet.

"I have an idea," Callie said.

Three pairs of eyes turned toward her. Surprise lit Grace's face. Callie grinned to herself—did Grace think Callie was about to propose? "Let's go out and buy a Christmas tree."

"Goody," Nattie said, jumping in place at David's side. Her enthusiasm was contagious.

"Before this child knocks me out with her exuberance, I suppose we ought to do just that. A Christmas tree, it is," David said.

For Callie, many years had passed since she'd decorated a house. But this year, she joined in the excitement. The tree stood in the family parlor, covered in lights and bulbs. The house smelled of ginger and vanilla, and every day Callie and Nattie tiptoed into the kitchen to snatch a cookie or two from Agnes's baking.

Four days before Christmas, to Callie's dismay, David had to squeeze in a two-day business trip, returning Christmas Eve.

With David's absence, Callie felt lonely. The house was silent, and she opened her door and glanced across the hallway. Nattie seemed too quiet, and she wondered if the child missed David, too, or if something else bothered her.

She tiptoed across the hall and peeked through the doorway. Nattie was curled on bed with a book on her lap. She looked up when Callie came into the room.

"So, how are you doing?" Callie asked, sitting on the edge of her bed.

"Okay."

"Just okay? And with Christmas coming so soon? I thought you'd be all excited."

She looked at Nattie's face and saw a question in her eyes. "Is something wrong, Nat?"

Nattie snuggled down into her bed, turning her head on the pillow. "If you marry my daddy, would you have a baby?"

Callie's pulse skipped a beat. "Only God can answer that, Nattie. Would you like a new baby?"

She nodded yet her eyes blinked as if a fearful thought hung in her mind.

"What are you worried about, sweetie?" Did she wonder if Callie and David had enough love to share?

Nattie lowered her eyelids. "Would you die if you had a baby?"

A ragged sigh shivered through Callie, and she slid her legs onto the bed and curled up next to Nattie. "No, Nattie, I wouldn't die. Are you thinking of your mom?"

Her head moved against the pillow, nodding. "When my mommy was sick, Daddy said he was sorry that I was born, because it made Mommy die."

Callie struggled to contain her gasp. "Oh, Nattie, your daddy wouldn't say that. He loves you so much. Your parents wanted you so badly, and Miriam said that you gave your mom and dad so much happiness. No, no, you couldn't have heard your daddy say that. Maybe you misunderstood."

"Because my mommy was having a baby, she couldn't get her medicine, and she died. So I made her die, didn't I?"

"Is that what's made you sad all this time, Nattie?"

Nattie didn't have to speak. Her face reflected the answer. Callie understood now—Nattie's silence for so long, her burden of guilt that she had caused her mother's death.

She wrapped Nattie in her arms and held her tightly against her chest. Looking at the little girl's blue eyes, nearly the color of her own, she knew this would be what she'd feel for her own child. She couldn't love her own flesh any more than she had grown to love Nattie. And Nattie's hurt was her own.

"Whatever you heard, Nattie, I think, you didn't understand. Your mom had a bad disease for a long time. God was so good to her and gave her four years to spend with you before she went to heaven. Do you remember how much she loved you?"

"Uh-huh," Nattie whispered. "She hugged me like you do." Her small arms wound more tightly around Callie's neck. "Callie?" Her voice was a whisper.

"What, sweetheart?"

"Could you be my mommy?"

"I think I am already, Nattie. I love you as if you were my own daughter. I couldn't love you more." The words caught in her throat. "And your daddy thinks you're the greatest in the whole wide world.

So does Grandma Grace."

Nattie nodded. "Grandma loves me. She told me."

"She did, huh? You go to sleep. Your daddy'll be home tomorrow." She nestled Nattie in her arms, singing softly in her ear.

What could Nattie have heard? When David returned, Callie would know.

Chapter Twenty-Three

David stepped into the foyer loaded with packages, and Callie rushed into his arms, suppressing her questions. He lowered the bags, and, despite the snow that clung to his coat, he pulled her to him and pressed his icy lips against her warm, eager mouth. "What a greeting. I should go away more often."

"Don't you dare." She dodged from his damp, chilled arms.

"So where's my favorite daughter?"

He heard a giggle, and Nattie leaped through the parlor doorway into his arms and planted a loud kiss on his cheek.

"You're freezing, Daddy."

"And your snuggly warm, Nattie."

She wiggled until he released her.

David slid off his coat, and Callie took it from him as he retrieved his packages.

"What have you got there?" she asked, eyeing the parcels.

"Wouldn't *you* like to know?"

"Yes, I would."

"Me, too," Nattie added. "Did you buy me a present?"

"Both of you are nosy. Yes, they're all Christmas surprises, so you'll have to wait. And before I let you two bury your noses in the bags, I'm taking them upstairs right now."

Callie and Nattie pretended to pout, but David ignored them and scooted up the stairs, carrying the bulging shopping bags.

He tossed them into his closet, then changed into his khaki slacks and a rust-and-green pullover. Before closing the door, he glanced with an anxious grin at the packages.

While in Bloomington, he had wandered through a jewelry store, finally selecting a gold locket for Nattie as delicate and lovely as she was.

His heart tripped when he thought of Callie's gift. As well as a gold chain with pearl and garnet beads, David had selected an engagement ring. Christmas Day, he would propose.

After he dressed, David returned to the first floor, admiring the holiday decor. For two years his Christmas spirit had lain dormant. Today, with Callie at his side, he felt complete.

As he neared the bottom of the stairs, Callie beckoned him through the library door, a strange look on her face.

"Something wrong?"

"Push the door closed, would you?" she asked. "I want to make sure we're alone before we talk."

Feeling his pulse quicken, he gave the door a push.

Her face told him she was terribly concerned. "What is it?"

"Something happened while you were gone, and I've been anxious to talk to you." She glanced over her shoulder at a chair. "Let's sit, okay?"

"Sure," he said, folding his tense body into a nearby recliner. "I see you're upset."

"It's something Nattie said. I think I know what's been bothering her all this time."

His pulse throbbed in his temples. "What is it?"

Callie blurted her story. Confusion and worry tangled in her words, and as he listened, he forced his mind back nearly three years, trying to decipher what Nattie might have heard.

"Callie, I don't know. I can't imagine what she heard. We never talked in front of her. Sara and I were very open about her illness and about her ill-fated pregnancy, but not with Nattie around. I was so angry and guilty when Sara had the miscarriage. But that was a year before Natalie—"

"Could she have overheard you talking when Sara was...really bad. Near the end?"

"If Nattie was listening, I didn't know. Yes, I was terribly upset. I knew Sara's pregnancy was a mistake. Stopping her treatment risked her life, and then we lost the baby, anyway. Oh, Callie, I probably yelled at her, telling her how foolish we were to try and have a child. I was a maniac right before she died."

"If Nattie heard it, she blamed herself."

"But she wasn't to blame. And Nattie should know that. She couldn't have been to blame."

Callie's eyes questioned him, her forehead furrowing in confusion. "Why, David? Sara couldn't have treatment during either pregnancy. Why *wouldn't* Nattie feel to blame?"

David's world crumbled around him. Words he hadn't said since Sara died rose to his lips. Nattie had been told, but she had been young. Maybe she'd forgotten. They had to raise her to know the truth.

"Answer me, David. Why?"

He struggled to say the words. "When Sara lost the baby, we knew that was our last chance. Nattie isn't my biological child, Callie. She was adopted."

Callie stopped as if struck by a sniper's bullet. Blood drained from her face. Trembling uncontrollably, she raised her hand to her chest. "Adopted?" She rose, her legs quaking. "Adopted?" she whispered. "And you never told me."

"Oh Callie, to me, Nattie was our own. I rarely think about—" He stopped speaking. Callie had dashed from the room and up the stairs.

Weakness overcame her. Callie stood in her room, holding her face in her hands, disbelieving. Why had David lied to her? But...he hadn't lied. He hadn't told her, that was all. A wave of sorrow washed over her. Neither had she told *him* the whole truth.

Adoption. Had David not spoken of it for a reason? Was he ashamed? Her chest tightened, restricting her breathing. She closed her bedroom door and locked it, then threw herself across the bed. Callie's own sorrow tore through her. *Nattie.* This beautiful child, like her own daughter, had been signed away—placed in someone else's home. And somewhere, another mother wondered about *her* lost child. The paradox knifed her. *Why Lord? Why should mothers feel such pain?*

She needed to calm down and reason. Callie closed her eyes, whispering a long-needed prayer to God. Compassion, wisdom, understanding. She needed so much. Yet, so often she wore herself out trying to solve every problem on her own. God had guided her to this house. Was this His purpose?

She loved Nattie as her own, and the child almost could be hers: they had the same coloring and talents. But she knew in her heart, Nattie wasn't. She belonged to someone else.

She curled on her side and prayed aloud. *"Lord, please help me to understand. You tell us to seek You and You'll hear us. With all my heart Lord, I need to find peace and comfort. I want to understand."*

A light rap sounded on the door. *David.* She ignored his knock and his hushed voice, calling her name. For now, she had to think on her own. She could apologize for her behavior and explain her strange reaction later.

Finally, she rose and washed her face, staring at the pale image in the mirror that gaped back at her. Tonight was Christmas Eve, and Ken would arrive soon. This was not the moment for confessions and confusion. Now she needed to look presentable.

She retouched her makeup and tossed a teal-blue dress over her head, cinching the belt around her waist. The rosebud brooch from David lay on her dresser, and she pinned it to her shoulder. *Better? Yes, I look better.* She unlocked the door and descended the stairs.

Ken had already arrived, and called to her from the bottom landing. "Merry Christmas, Callie."

"Merry Christmas, Ken," she echoed.

David watched from behind her brother. Though handsome in his navy suit, tension ridged David's face, and he looked less than merry. She gave her brother a kiss on the cheek, then spoke to David. "I see you're ready for church."

"Yes. You look lovely, Callie." He gave her brother a friendly pat on the shoulder. "Go ahead, Ken. Let's sit in the parlor with the Christmas tree."

Ken went ahead, joining Nattie and Grace, and David leaned close to her ear as they followed him. "We need to talk."

"Later, David, please. I owe you an explanation."

He nodded, but she felt his arm tense. Tenderly, she pressed his forearm, hoping he understood and forgave her. A faint movement flickered at the corner of his mouth, and she relaxed, believing that he did understand.

With conversations flowing in many directions, the time passed, and Agnes soon announced their early dinner. The children's Christmas program began at seven-thirty, and Nattie had to arrive by seven.

At the church, they sat near the front. Beginning with "Oh, Come Little Children," the youngsters proceeded down the aisle, dressed as shepherds, wise men, Mary, Joseph and the angels.

Nattie's halo bounced as she marched past the rows in her white flowing robe and sparkling angel wings. When she saw the family, she raised her hand in a tiny wave.

The children took their places, and families beamed as the little actors spoke with practiced precision. When the angels chorused, "Peace on earth; goodwill to men," Nattie's voice rose above the rest, every word clear and distinct.

At the end of the program, they descended the stairs to the Sunday School rooms, while the children stripped off their costumes.

Nattie dashed to them when they hit the landing. "Was I good? I knew all my lines."

David crouched down and gave her a hug. "We were all very proud of you."

Callie's heart twisted, watching him with Nattie. So much love and devotion for his daughter. Natural or adopted, she was his child.

When David retreated to locate Nattie's coat, a familiar voice sailed toward Callie.

"Well, Merry Christmas."

Turning, Callie cranked her facial muscles into a smile. "Hello, Mary Beth. Merry Christmas."

A man was attached to her arm, and she batted her eyes toward her escort. "Callie, do you know Charles Robinson?"

"Not formally, but I know you from church. It's nice to meet you. And this is my brother, Ken." They shook hands. Saving further conversation, David returned just then with Nattie, now buttoned into her coat. After final amenities, they headed toward the door.

Once home, as they entered the foyer, the parlor clock chimed ten, and eager for Christmas Day, Nattie headed for bed with David's promise to tuck her in. Callie longed to talk with David but she had to join the others for Agnes's homemade cookies and coffee.

The conversation flowed until Callie yawned, followed by David. Finally, they agreed it was time to turn in.

David rose first. "I'd better call it a night. I still have a few 'Santa' things to do for tomorrow morning."

Ken followed and helped Grace up the stairs. As they made their way, Callie turned to David. "Can we talk now?"

He hesitated. "Let me get this stuff set up, so I won't feel hurried. I'll knock on your door when I'm finished."

Disappointment needled her, but he was right. They didn't need to be rushed. Their talk would be important, and she wanted to be emotionally ready. "Okay. I'll be waiting."

Upstairs, Callie paused outside Nattie's room. In the glow of the pink night-light, the child lay in a soft flush of color. Callie stood over her, her hand stroking the golden curls fanned out on the pillow. Nattie slept soundly.

Callie leaned over, brushing Nattie's cheek with her lips, then whispered, "I love you, Nattie." Her heart stirred with loving awareness. It didn't matter whose child she was—Nattie was loved and cherished. God had guided the baby to this house and to a Christian family who loved her.

Brushing the tears from her cheeks, Callie crossed the hall and slipped into a caftan, then waited. Her nerves pitched at each creak of the house, wondering if it was David. Tonight she would tell him about her daughter. How would he feel? And how did she feel? *Peace and understanding, Lord.* Her prayer lifted again. She pushed her door ajar and moved her chair so she could see David approach.

When he appeared, he passed her room and crossed to Nattie's. Surprised, Callie rose, padding softly to the doorway, but he only peeked in and then turned.

"You're waiting. I'm sorry it took so long. You know how it is assembling toys."

A knot tightened in her stomach. No, she didn't know.

"Let's sit," David said, drawing the desk chair beside her recliner. "We have lots to talk about."

Callie sank into the cushion. "I'm sorry, David. I was shocked. I—"

"First, let me explain, please. I wasn't hiding Nattie's adoption. When you first came, the thought entered my mind. But I didn't know you and wanted you to treat her as my own. Then, you grew to love her as I do, and the thought faded. She is my daughter. I love her no differently than I would a natural child."

"Please, David. My shock is more complex than you can imagine. Yes, I was startled when you told me. And then I wondered if you were ashamed of her adoption, and—"

"Ashamed? How could I be? Sara and I chose her. She was ours from her first days on earth. We nurtured her, loved her, cared for her. How could I be ashamed? I thank God for my beautiful daughter, Callie."

Her tears flowed, dripping to her hands knotted in her lap. She raised them to cover her face.

David rose and knelt at her feet. "Don't cry. Please. I don't understand what's happened."

"David, I didn't know how I was going to tell you this. I was so worried you'd hate me or wonder what kind of person I am."

David pulled her hands from her face. "Whatever it is, just tell me." He held her hands captive in his.

She closed her eyes, tears dripping from her chin. "After I was raped, I found out I was pregnant."

"Pregnant—oh, Callie, my love." Tears rimmed his eyes.

"My parents thought the father was a college boy, and I let them believe it. I had a baby girl, David, born on Christmas Day. I placed her up for adoption."

"My love, how could I hate you? You were blameless. And hurt far more than I ever knew."

"But you did so much to have a baby—taking horrible chances. And I didn't fight to keep my child. I haven't forgiven myself. Every day I ask God why it happened—and if she's okay. Is she happy? Do her parents love her?"

David rose, lifted her from the chair, and cradled her in his arms. "Oh, my dear, look around you. Look at the beautiful child that gave Sara and me such joy. Wouldn't God do the same for your child? Trust in the Lord, Callie. You have strong faith in so many things. Believe that God placed your daughter in a home as filled with love as this one."

"I want to believe that." Music stirred in Callie's mind.

She paused. The sad song that played within her heart faded, and a new melody filled her—a sense of peace and understanding. And love. "I went to Nattie's room when I came up and looked at her sweet face." The music lifted at the memory. "I couldn't love my own child more, David. I almost feel as if God has given me another chance."

"He has, my love, He has. And He's given us another chance. You've brought such joy to our lives. Nattie and I were shadows when you came, but you breathed new life into us—just as you gave life to your little daughter years ago."

The grandfather clock in the parlor began to chime. *One. Two. Three*… They paused, listening for the last. "It's midnight. Christmas Day." She didn't say what else lay in her heart. His eyes told her he knew.

"Doubt is part of life, Callie. When we first brought Nattie home, I wondered if I could love her. *Really* love her—like a true father. And—"

"You don't have to say it. If anyone was ever a true and loving father, it's you."

"And if anyone was ever a true and loving mother, it's you."

Callie looked into his face, and saw love glowing in his eyes. Her heart felt as if it would burst, and joy danced through her body. "A mother. It's a beautiful thought."

"A mother." Trance-like, David repeated her words and kissed her hair. He tilted her chin upward until their eyes met. "Callie, this is perfect. I planned this for tomorrow, but wait. Wait. Don't move."

He darted from the room, and in a moment returned to

drop to his knees in front of her for the second time that night. "I've loved you for so long. You've brought happiness and completeness into our empty world, and, praise God, you've given me a healthy daughter. Nattie loves you so much and so do I. We would like to marry you, Callie. Will you be my wife? And Nattie's mother?"

Tears rolled down his cheeks as he handed her the blue velvet box. Callie knew what was inside, and without hesitating, she whispered her answer. "You know, I love you both with all my heart. Please forgive me for my foolish doubts and fears. I'm so filled with happiness—"

"And?"

She looked into his loving eyes. "And yes, I'll marry you."

His face brightened; the tension melted away. "Open the box, Callie." He turned it in her hand to face her.

She lifted the lid. Inside, a roping of three shades of gold entwined three sparkling diamonds. She raised her eyes. "Three shades of gold. And three diamonds. One for each of us."

"One for each of us. And we can always add a fourth."

His eyes glowed, and with quivering fingers, he took the ring from her and slipped it on her finger. "Perfect." His gaze caressed her face. "Yes, perfect."

She opened her mouth to speak, but he quieted her with his warm, tender lips. Captured in his arms, Callie's fears and shame were gone. Her black dreams could hurt no more. She nestled securely against David's chest, finally whole and at peace.

When their lips parted, they tiptoed, hand in hand, across the hall to gaze at their beautiful child, sleeping peacefully in a rosy glow of light.

Epilogue

On Christmas Day, a month before Nattie's ninth birthday, the family gathered in church. Even Callie's sister, Patricia, and her husband had come from California for the holiday. They arrived, eager to see Randolph David Hamilton, who'd been born in early November.

Grace held the baby in her arms, with Nattie nestled as close as she could without sitting on Grace's lap.

David and Callie stood at the front, their faces glowing with wide, proud grins. David's gaze drifted with admiration to his wife, almost as trim again as she had been before her nine months of "ballooning," as they'd called it. He couldn't take his eyes from her.

"What?" Callie whispered. "Why are you staring at me?"

"Because you're beautiful, and I'm the happiest man alive." He squeezed her arm and tilted his head toward the children, sitting in the third pew.

She teased him with the nudge of her hip. "Well, you'd better focus on the music. We have to sing in a minute."

The organ music voluntary ended, and the ushers brought the offering plates to the front. As they retreated down the aisle, the organist played the introductory notes to the duet.

The opening strains began, and Callie's mind soared back to a Christmas midnight two years earlier—to the moment her past vanished and God's purpose became clear. On that day, a new life began.

Her gaze drifted to Nattie, growing lovelier each day, now looking at her with pure, joyous love. Somewhere on this Christmas night, another young girl celebrated Jesus's birth and her own birthday. Assurance filled Callie, as she trusted that God had guided her own baby daughter to a loving, Christian family.

Callie wiped away an invading tear. Today, with happiness, she looked at her son, the image of his handsome father. Raising her eyes to David's, she felt complete and wonderful. His smile captivated her, and she sighed.

As the last note of the introduction sounded, they each drew in a deep breath, then lifted their voices in the familiar words of an old carol that now rang with new meaning. *"It came upon a midnight clear, that glorious song of old…."*

* * * * *

Dear Reader,

Sometimes a story weaves through a writer's mind, and when hands touch the keyboard, the story writes itself. This was my experience with *Upon a Midnight Clear*. Though I have never lost a child through death or adoption, I have experienced both of those deep hurts through family and friends. At times like this, sorrow can take over a happy heart and create secrets that wound the spirit.

Many of us cling to our deepest fears, sorrows and sins because we do not trust. Yet love can heal the worst transgression, making us whole again, just as our Savior has washed us clean and made us snow-white with His forgiveness.

I hope you've enjoyed Callie, David and Nattie's story. Their experience offers comfort and hope to us all. Don't suffer alone. Sharing pain and hurt with others draws us closer together and heals our secret wounds. And talk to the Lord. We can experience God's undying love by asking forgiveness and accepting His grace.

Gail Gaffner Martin

SECRETS OF THE HEART

And the secrets of his heart will be laid bare.
—*Corinthians* 14:25

To Jill and Debbie,
who so willingly shared their stories
Thanks to Shelly Thomas at
Lutheran Social Services for her help

Chapter One

Kate Davis jerked her head, pulling her gaze from the delicate anthill growing at the base of the glider swing. With a wry chuckle, she rolled her eyes. "I can't believe I'm sitting here watching ants have more fun than I am."

Though the old oak offered her shade, the May sun sneaked beneath the tree branches and warmed her arms. She stretched her legs in front of her and scanned the backyard, admiring the veil of purple blossoms weighting the lilac trees and filling the air with a rich, sweet scent. This year spring came late to Michigan, and a small bed of mixed tulips added a splash of color in the morning sunlight.

Everything was bright and cheery, except Kate. Spring meant new birth, a new surprise every day, but her life seemed to drag on with endless mediocrity. She'd spent the past hour comparing her rather boring personal life with her overly impassioned career and wished her days lay somewhere in the middle of those two emotions.

A lazy Saturday afternoon wasn't too bad, but those long, empty evenings were another story. She sat too many nights in front of the television or played board games with her housemate, Phyllis Ryan.

Wondering about this particular Saturday, Kate noticed again the column of industrious ants. As a row paraded over the sand and into the hole, another army marched back out. At least the ants were doing something. Kate pushed herself up from the swing. Enough of this, she thought as she strode across the grass and headed for the back door. I refuse to spend another minute mesmerized by insects. Something had to change. She needed a plan.

"Phyllis," she called, stepping into the back hall. "Let's do some—"

A piercing shriek shot from the front of the house. With her heart hammering, Kate dashed to the kitchen doorway and barreled toward her friend's heartrending screech.

Stumbling into the living room, Kate froze, witnessing her housemate clutched in a powerful set of arms with her feet flailing above the carpet at the open front door.

Kate grabbed the first thing she laid her hands on and Kate darted toward them, raising the weapon over her head. "Take your hands off her," she shouted.

Kate's last word was jumbled in Phyllis's hysterical cries of "No."

Phyllis bolted from the man's arms, panic covering her face, and raised her hand in protection. "Kate, no, this is my brother, Scott."

Her cheeks on fire, Kate gaped at the two startled faces and lowered the flowered umbrella. "I'm sorry, Phyllis." Kate's look darted from her friend to the widened nutmeg-brown eyes of her dazed brother, then to her pitiful weapon and back to Phyllis. "I had no idea you were expecting anyone. I heard the scream and—"

"It's okay, Kate. I wasn't expecting him, either." Phyllis turned her head to peer good-naturedly at the square, solid male at her side. "Was I?"

"No," he said with a chuckle, "I wanted to surprise you. But I was the one surprised." He eyed Kate. "You could have fractured my skull with that pretty umbrella."

Kate scrutinized the pathetic weapon and offered a half-hearted grin, adding, "I'm sorry." But, inwardly, she cringed with embarrassment, thinking that at thirty-four she should have better sense than to attack without knowing the situation.

With the two still gawking, Kate edged backward and slid the umbrella into the stand. When she looked up and caught his gaze, an unwelcome, unpleasant memory of her adolescence inched into her thoughts. "Please," she said, "come in...while I silently vanish into the sunset."

"Don't you dare," Phyllis said. "I want you and Scott to get to know each other."

Phyllis wrapped her arm around her brother's waist. "It's been too long, hasn't it?"

"More than a year, I think" he said.

"How about something to drink? And maybe a sandwich?" Phyllis beckoned him toward the kitchen.

Scott gave Kate a fleeting grin as he passed and followed his sister.

Addled, Kate held back, struggling with her reaction to the strapping man. With one lengthy look, she had flown back in time. Back to high school. Back to her nonexistent confidence and her naive desires.

What had caused her to sink into an abyss of miserable memories? The answer hit her before the question left her mind. Scott's build. Not his near six-foot stature, but his broad, square frame like a football player. Thick neck, powerful chest, strong muscular legs, and the bulging arms she saw wrapped around Phyllis. She cringed with a painful recollection.

"Kate?" Phyllis's voice sailed through the archway, and Kate pushed away the nagging, guilt-ridden memories and planted a pleasant expression on her face. Straightening her shoulders, she strolled into the kitchen.

"You're not embarrassed, are you?" Scott asked, his voice brimming with amusement.

"Nothing I can't handle," Kate said, sinking into an adjacent chair at the table.

"I commend you for protecting my baby sister."

She gave him a feeble grin. "I doubt if an umbrella could've done much damage."

Without comment, he leaned against the chair back and chuckled.

Putting an end to their silly conversation, Kate eyed Phyllis at the counter. "Can I help?"

"No, you two talk while I make up some tuna salad." She turned toward them. "Does that sound good?"

With their agreeable nods, Phyllis returned to her task.

Avoiding Scott's scrutiny, Kate lifted the pitcher and poured a tumbler of lemonade. "So, what brings you to town?" she asked, focusing on the condensation forming on her glass. With the first sip, her cheeks puckered at the zesty, tart tang that rolled on her tongue.

"I'm doing my residency at County General."

"Residency?" She hesitated, then remembered. "Ah, Phyl mentioned you're a doctor." Her finger traced the rim of the glass. "What's your speciality?"

He shook his head. "General practice."

Surprised by his response, she straightened in the chair. "No specialty, that's rare."

"Threw you a curve?" he said. "Financially, I could earn more as a specialist, but I like the idea of family practice."

She liked what he said, and a warm feeling settled over her. Kate leaned back, studying his animated, handsome face. "That's nice. Family practice seems to be vanishing, but specialists are too costly for young families. Especially single parents."

Seeing a scowl dart across his face, curiosity needled Kate. "Did I say something wrong?" she asked.

"No, I, ah, well, you're not a single parent, are you?"

His question left Kate with an uneasy feeling. "What would make you ask that?"

He shrugged. "I don't know. You sounded serious."

"It's a serious problem."

He nodded, and they sat in silence. Kate wished she'd not interjected her ever serious concerns. He was fun and light-hearted, and she'd put a weight on the conversation.

Phyllis slid them each a tuna sandwich, garnished with lettuce and a dill pickle spear. "Pretty fancy," she said cutting the heavy silence that had risen between them. She settled into a chair. "Don't let Kate fool you. She's not always this serious."

Scott hesitated, as if waiting for her to respond.

Kate's mind went blank, unable to think of anything to say. For a moment, her thoughts were tangled in the past and the present, unsorted and unwelcome.

"Kate works with me," Phyllis said, "at Children's Haven."

Kate could have hugged her for covering her growing discomfort.

"Ahh, that explains your comment, then," Scott said, relaxing against the chair. "So, what do you do there?"

Hating to be the center of attention, Kate felt pinned by his gaze. "I'm a social worker."

"Then I can see what you mean. Lots of tension, I imagine. Innocent children hurt by troubled parents."

Kate nodded. "Some, but often it's just a sad situation that time can heal. The problems vary."

"Last year when I was an intern, I ran into all kinds of problems. My skin crawls when I remember some of the abused kids we treated." He blew a stream of air from his lungs.

"Let's talk about something more pleasant," Kate suggested, hoping to turn the attention to someone else.

His scowl faded, replaced by a smile. "Okay, let's talk about you...away from Children's Haven."

Noting her failed attempt, Kate's stomach sank. She shook her head. "I said pleasant, not pitiful." She sent him another halfhearted grin.

"Oh, don't be modest," Phyllis inserted. "Kate does all kinds of wonderful things. When I lost my roommate, she offered to share this house with me. She didn't even know me that well."

"I did, too. Anyway, it helps with expenses. It's worked out great." Determined to change the subject, she picked up her untouched sandwich. "Isn't anyone going to cat?"

They complied, and for a few minutes, they concentrated on lunch. When the conversation returned, Scott and Phyllis chatted about his internship experiences and their family.

Kate contemplated their easy rapport. She envied what seemed to be a real friendship. Her only sibling, Kristin, and she were as different as country music and opera...and about as conflicting. Kate had never known that kind of relationship with her sister.

Feeling a little like an eavesdropper, Kate listened to their reunion for a while. But after finishing her sandwich, she drained her glass and carried the dishes to the sink.

When the conversation lulled, Kate prepared her escape. "I have some things to do so I'll let you two reminisce." She jutted her hand toward Scott's. "Nice to meet you."

He captured her fingers with his massive hand.

Fighting not to recoil, Kate felt swallowed in his grasp.

"Don't hide because of me," he said. "When you finish, come back."

She nodded, knowing she wouldn't, and fled for the safety of her room.

Closing the door, a sigh rattled from her chest. She hated envy. And watching Phyllis and her brother filled her with it.

One thing she learned in Sunday school was coveting is a sin. Still, she'd spent her youth yearning to be her older sister. Kristin seemed perfect, while much of Kate's life centered around her transgressions, especially in her parents' eyes.

She sat on her bed and folded her hands in her lap. Why did she allow herself to sink into a state of self-pity when she talked with Scott? Instead of enjoying the conversation, she spent the time trying to block the memories he aroused.

He'd been amiable and warm. She recalled his teasing eyes and generous smile—and his huge dimples. She pictured the deep indentations in his cheeks when he gave her an amused look.

Imagining Scott as a physician settled in her mind. His sincere face would soothe a mother's concern, and his boyish charm would appeal to children. He'd make a good family doctor.

Falling back against the mattress, Kate closed her eyes. What kind of face did she have? Worried? Serious? No, she laughed when situations were comical. But...sometimes, things didn't seem funny to her. Maybe, the problem was her occupation, as Phyllis had suggested. Sad, depressing situations and frightened, rejected children.

No matter, she tried to act positive. That was one thing for which she prided herself. Thinking back to her youthful mistakes—she added a capital *M* to the word—she'd made the best of her senseless, shameful offense. She thanked God for lifting her from depression and guiding her to a purposeful career. Social work was the best part of her life.

Interrupting her musing, a tap sounded against her bedroom door. She noted the comfortable, safe barricade and, against her will, slid from the bed. When she turned the knob, Phyllis pushed open the door without waiting.

"Not feeling well?" Phyllis asked, her brows knit with concern.

"Resting. I'm lazy today." Kate distorted the truth to cover her wavering emotions.

"Then you'll like our plan. Scott wants to take us to dinner. What do you say? And he said no's not a choice."

The invitation made her grin, but apprehension nipped at her. "Okay," Kate said, praying she could view Scott with clearer eyes.

"Great," Phyllis said, then added in a whisper, "and I hope you don't mind I invited him to spend the night in the guest room. That way I can get him to go to church with us tomorrow. He's a natural sloth on Sunday mornings."

Her eager eyes searched Kate's, and she couldn't disappoint her friend. Anyway, the house seemed as much Phyllis's as hers.

"Sure," Kate said, hoping she sounded sincere.

* * *

Sitting together in a restaurant booth, Scott observed Kate throughout dinner. Though she seemed amiable, he sensed she was uncomfortable, and he wished he could help her relax.

Kate stared at her half-full plate. Direct eye contact seemed to fluster her. Scott had tried to keep from making direct contact, but he couldn't stop himself. Her eyes were captivating—a soft, misty brown with flecks of green and yellow. Hazel, he guessed.

Shifting his focus, he admired her sun-streaked hair hanging straight and shoulder length with a part to one side. Occasionally, she lifted her fingers and pushed the loose strands from her forehead. She was a beautiful woman. Admiring her aroused many questions. For one, why wasn't she married or, at least, going with someone?

"So what are you planning to do with yourself, Scott?" Phyllis asked. "I mean other than your residency."

"First thing, I need an apartment. Mom offered my old room, but that seemed too...adolescent." He grinned. "I'll find someone to share expenses. Like the two of you are doing. Once I have my own practice, I'll buy a house."

"I feel smothered in an apartment," Kate said. "No fresh air, except a window or one of those tiny balconies. A house gives you lots of room for privacy...or companionship, if you want it."

"A house would be nice," Scott agreed.

Silence fell over them, and he peered at his sister, then at Kate who again averted her eyes. Knowing Phyllis, he could almost hear the wheels turning. In a moment, she'd have some kind of plan. If he were a betting man, he'd make a secure wager.

His sister's pensive face edged upward, then a smile crept to her lips. "I've got it."

Hearing Phyllis's excited voice, Kate's attention left her plate.

"Why not stay with us?" Phyllis said. "Pay rent until you find a place?" She pivoted from him to Kate's astonished expression. "What do you say?" she asked.

Kate seemed to shrink into her seat. Obviously, she hated the idea.

"No, I can't do that," he said, hoping to smooth the tension. "Too much like living with Mom and Dad."

"It is not," Phyllis said. "We're nearly the same age. Thirty-two and twenty-nine. We're contemporaries." She flashed them a bright grin. "So what do you say?"

"I might be your brother, Phyllis, but the house belongs to Kate, too." He hoped his sister would catch on and back off.

"She won't mind, will you?" She turned to Kate whose expression flickered from startled to defeated.

Kate faltered. "If, ah, that works for you, Scott, we can manage...I mean, we can work things out. It's only temporary."

He studied her, wondering why she was agreeing to a plan she obviously despised. He knew the answer without asking. She was plain old nice. Truly compassionate. It went with her job.

"Okay, then," Phyllis said, grasping his arm. "You're our

new roomie. I think the guest room will work fine. You and I will share the bathroom upstairs. Kate's bedroom and bath are on the first floor."

Kate had agreed, but the plan was obviously putting her out. From her expression, Scott figured he'd be smart to start apartment hunting tomorrow morning...right after church. *Church.* Somehow, he'd conceded to go there, too.

The next day, Kate ignored the anthill and leaned back in the glider. She felt more optimistic. Maybe things would work out after all. The worship service that morning had lifted her spirits, and though Scott taunted Phyllis about making him go to church, he'd been a good sport. At first, he stumbled through a couple of melodies, but many of the hymns he sang out in a confident baritone voice that she had to admit was pretty good.

On the way home, they sang one of the morning's hymns at the top of their lungs. The words lingered in her head. Yes, they'll know we are Christians by our love. The experience felt nice. Like family.

A scowl edged across her face and she pushed it aside. No room for self-pity. She wanted to enjoy the rest of the day before she returned to work tomorrow.

A shadow feel across her legs, and Kate snapped her head upward. She found herself gazing into a pair of mischievous eyes that sent her heart pitching like a rowboat in a storm.

"You look too relaxed," Scott said, dropping down beside her on the glider. "Thought I'd bug you a little. Plus I can use some rays."

He shifted on the seat, stretched out his legs, and lifted his nose in the air. "What's that wonderful smell? You?"

His bluntness made her laugh. "I should say yes, but it's probably the lilacs."

He scanned one side of the yard, then the other. "I suppose you're right. There's sure a lot of them." He leaned toward her and sniffed. "But you smell pretty sweet yourself."

"Thanks." His innocent frankness amazed her.

"Silliness aside, Kate, I really want to thank you for letting me stay here. I promise I'll find an apartment soon. I know that you weren't thrilled—"

She squirmed against the seat, mortified that her feelings had been so open. "I didn't mean to be unkind. To be honest, all I could think of was confusion with the three of us trying to share the house, but I've had time to let the idea settle in." She noted his serious eyes. "It's fine. Really."

"Well, I appreciate your generosity. My folks are great, but living at home when I've been away so long—"

Kate touched his arm. "You don't have to explain that to me. I'd feel exactly like you do. Maybe more so." The tense teen years filled her mind. "You're welcome to stay until you find someplace you really like."

"That's a deal," he said, reaching toward her for a handshake.

She grinned at his amiable gesture and tucked her smaller palm against his. His smile and the feel of his large, warm hand pressing against her skin radiated up her arm. Heat rose to her cheeks. She felt foolish. Why did she flush at his touch?

Scott released her hand and relaxed against the glider. “I’m not looking forward to the next few days.”

“No?” His comment aroused her curiosity. “Why?”

“Nothing, really. Tomorrow I start work. Every hospital has its own idiosyncrasies. Its own hierarchy. You know how it is.”

Thinking of her own situation, she nodded. Now, she felt at home at the Haven, but her first months there were filled with uncertainty while she learned the rules and protocol. Only the laws remained the same.

“I don’t know what I’ll be doing yet. Except rotating floors,” he added.

“Dr. Barlow’s a resident at County General, and he has hours at Children’s Haven. He does physicals on the intakes and handles the usual cases of measles, colds and head lice.”

“Head lice. Thanks.” He raised his arms and stretched them across the back of the glider. “For a while, I’ll be doing all the dirty work that the practicing physicians don’t want to do.” He shot her an apologetic grin. “Sorry, I sound like a prima donna.”

“No, you don’t,” she said.

Amazed, Kate stretched her legs into the sun and leaned back. She felt relaxed sitting beside a man with no expectations, no come-ons, no false flattery. Despite her qualms, Scott gave her interesting conversation and good honest fun. She might enjoy having a real male friend.

Chapter Two

A wooden chair scraped against the bare floor, and Kate leaned back, studying the angry ten-year-old who was scowling in front of her desk.

"Then if you don't want to talk, Eddie, I'll have to see you again on Thursday."

"An' I won't talk then, either," he declared.

With his fists knotted, the boy spun around and charged toward the exit like a freight train. But as he approached the doorway, Phyllis stepped into Kate's office and did a quick two-step to avoid being run over.

Eddie shot through the doorway without looking back.

"What was that all about?" Phyllis asked.

"Eddie's in a bad mood today. Glad he didn't run you over."

Phyllis's halfhearted smile echoed Kate's feelings. She dealt with too many angry children wanting to punch their way out of every situation.

"So what's up?" Kate noticed the manila file folder and assumed Phyllis hadn't dropped by to visit.

"A new six-year-old girl arrived today. You may want to work her into your schedule tomorrow." She dropped the file on Kate's desk. "Amber's really timid and having a hard time."

"Why is she here?"

"She lives with her grandma, but her grandma's in the hospital. There's no one else. That's all I know."

"Sad." Kate shook her head. "When you get back tell the housemother to bring her down. I'll see her now."

Phyllis squeezed Kate's forearm. "Great. I figured you would."

Kate shook her head. "You're getting to know me too well."

An uneasy expression rose on Phyllis's face, and she paused. "Ah, speaking of that, I've been wanting to ask you. Are you okay with Scott at the house? After I invited him, I realized I should have asked you first. In private."

"It's fine, Phyl. It's temporary, and he's been very considerate." Discomfort threaded through her, remembering her first unhappy reaction.

"Whew! I'm relieved." Phyllis blew a stream of air from between her pursed lips. "Scott nailed me to the wall the other day, saying I had overstepped our friendship."

"It's temporary. And it's been fun." She tried to picture Scott angry at Phyllis, but couldn't. Jolts of envy pricked her conscience. "You two have such a great relationship. Honest and...sort of, looking out for each other."

"We do," Phyllis said, her voice growing tender.

"I never had that kind of relationship with my sister," Kate admitted, then wished she hadn't. Talking about her association with Kristin was too difficult.

"No? That's too bad. Scott's been a really great big brother."

"I can see that," Kate said, fingering the file on her desk.

Phyllis backed toward the doorway. "See you at lunch."

"Don't forget to send Amber down," Kate reminded her.

"I'll have Denise bring her here right away."

Kate nodded, pushing their conversation out of her mind. She opened the child's folder, then thumbed through the pages, searching for a relative, but found none. Only the ailing grandmother.

Closing the folder, Kate rose and wandered to the window, longing to be outside under the powder-blue sky. Unbidden, her thoughts turned to Scott. Living with them for the past five days, he'd been considerate and kindhearted. Since he began work, Scott spent his days at the hospital. When he arrived home, they had dinner together, then he vanished. He seemed to respect her privacy.

At times, Kate wished he didn't. When he exited the room, loneliness filled the space he'd left empty. Until last Saturday, the house had never rung with so much good cheer and laughter.

Yet, once in a while when she looked at Scott a certain way, the old sorrow rose in her—sorrow she presumed she had overcome long ago. His sturdy body was so much like her memory of Ron from her teens. Kate bit her bottom lip, wishing she would stop comparing. Forget Ron. She'd learned from her terrible experience and directed her energy toward doing good for others...even though she'd not done right by herself.

A firm rap on the doorjamb snapped Kate to attention. The housemother leaned into the room, prodding a tiny blond child through the doorway.

"Here's Amber," the woman said.

"Thanks, Denise." Kate stepped toward the child.

Denise nodded and vanished around the corner.

Confusion and fright etched the girl's pale face, and she stared at Kate with wide eyes.

"Amber, I'm Kate. Would you sit with me, please?" She beckoned the child toward the chair.

The girl froze just inside the doorway, glancing behind her for the housemother, then looking back at Kate with helplessness.

Kate ambled toward the door, praying the girl wouldn't bolt in fear like a startled fawn. She rested her hand on the child's back and guided her to a seat.

Instead of sitting behind her desk, Kate grasped a stuffed toy lamb from a nearby shelf and joined the child in a second chair.

Amber focused on the stuffed, curly-haired animal.

As a diversion, Kate petted the toy while she distracted the child with quiet conversation. When she sensed Amber had relaxed, she placed the stuffed animal in the girl's lap and began in earnest.

"Tell me about your grandmother."

Amber's gaze clung to the lamb. "She's sick."

"I know. I'm sorry." She studied the sorrowful child. "What happened?"

"She wouldn't wake up," Amber murmured.

Kate leaned forward and spoke tenderly. "I bet you were frightened."

Amber nodded.

"What did you do?" Kate asked.

"I called 911 like Grandma taught me."

From the report, Kate recalled the woman had a stroke. "You were very brave."

Her eyes widened. "I was?"

"Yes, you were very smart to call for help." Kate hesitated with her next question, then plowed ahead. "Where are your mother and father, Amber?"

The child's upturned gaze swept the room, then she shrugged.

"You don't know?" Kate asked.

Lowering her eyes, Amber shook her head.

"Has it been a long time since you've seen them?"

A deep scowl worked across the child's face.

Kate waited. Then, she tried a different tack. "Did you see your parents at Christmas?"

"No." She responded without delay.

Kate searched for a new approach. "When's your birthday, Amber?"

"March 19."

"Did you see your mother or father then?" Kate asked.

"I don't have a mother or father."

Caught off guard, Kate swallowed her startled gasp. "Did they die?"

Amber shrugged again. "I don't know."

Kate slumped against the chair. Amber's resemblance to Kate as a child was uncanny. Kate searched the girl's face. Though she knew better, Amber, with her fair skin and blond curls—especially her hazel eyes—could have been Kate's own child. She pushed away the longing.

What a heavy burden, Lord, to place on such tiny shoulders. Kate's sorrowful past rose again in her appreciation...contemplating where her daughter was now.

"Okay, here's my deal."

Hearing, Scott's voice, Kate spun away from the television. An unexpected sensation rippled up her arms, and she ran her hand down its length to erase the feeling.

He dropped beside her on the sofa. "I need a woman's opinion on this apartment thing. I've found a couple in the paper that sound interesting."

She looked toward him for the want ads, but he was empty-handed. "Well, let me see the paper," she said.

Dimples appeared with his amused grin. "No, I mean *look* at the apartments. I can read the ads by myself."

Taming her confusion, Kate sorted her thoughts. "Did you ask Phyllis?"

His smile faded. "She's busy Saturday. So how about you—"

"I'm busy, too. Sorry."

"Oh." His voice sagged as quickly as his face.

She'd never seen him so disappointed, like a kid who's been told he can't have a puppy. Feeling the need to explain, she added, "Phyllis and I are both involved with HELP this weekend."

A quizzical expression replaced the frown. "What's help?"

"It's an acronym for Helping the Elderly Live Proudly. A group of us from the church do whatever needs to be done for the senior citizens in the community. Yard work or painting walls. Grocery shopping."

"You're kidding?"

"No." She weighed what he meant. "Sometimes we just visit and listen to their stories. A lot of them live alone and love for someone to stop by just to say hi."

"Now there's something I can do."

"You think we're silly?" Kate asked.

Scott studied her concerned face and wanted to laugh, but he'd already hurt her feelings. "I'm only teasing you."

Her shoulders relaxed, then shifted toward him on the sofa. "You think it's a good idea?"

"Sure." He really couldn't understand how one person wanted to give so much to others. "You're just full of surprises, aren't you? I'd think you'd be tired of worrying about people after you work all day. Isn't that enough?"

"No, I enjoy it. It's what Christians are supposed to do." She pushed a few strands of hair behind her ear.

"You make me feel guilty. I'm not that compassionate."

Her face softened, and she touched his arm. "I saw you

at church when that little toddler used your leg for a prop. Your whole face lit up when you knelt down and talked to him. You'll make a great family doctor."

Her candid comment was refreshing. He slipped his arm around her shoulders and gave her a playful hug. "Thanks, you're too generous."

To his surprise, a soft pink flush rose to her cheeks. Watching her smile fade, he discretely slid his arm to the back of the sofa. "So, getting back to my dilemma, I honestly don't want to apartment hunt alone. I'll rent something, and when it's too late, I'll realize it doesn't have closets. Or a shower."

Her face brightened at his silly chatter and he wanted to hug her again. Yet, he faltered, perplexed as to where his mind was headed. He reined his errant thoughts and focused on Kate's pensive face.

"We could go later in the afternoon," she said. "We usually finish early. By one or so. Is that too late?"

"Not at all." A sense of excitement shivered up his back, and he wondered if it were the thought of getting a place of his own...or just being with Kate. "What if I go with you Saturday? Maybe you'll get done faster."

He expected to see her smile again, but she didn't.

Saturday morning Scott slipped into old jeans and a T-shirt. At the bottom of the stairs, noise drifted from the kitchen along with the smell of coffee. When he entered, the two women were peering into cardboard boxes.

"What's up?" he asked.

Like marionette's on strings, they jumped and swung around, clutching their chests.

"Could you make a little more noise when you sneak up on us?" Phyllis asked.

"Next time, I'll whistle," he said, ambling toward them. "What's in the boxes?"

"Stuff," Kate said. "Have some coffee and toast if you want, because we need to get going."

He stepped to their sides, resting a hand on each one's shoulder and peered between them into the boxes. "Let's see what you've got in there."

Kate moved from under his grasp, grabbed a mug from the hook, and set it in his unoccupied hand. "There. Now, drink first, then you can tote."

He arched a brow and marched to the toaster. After he dropped in the bread, Scott leaned against the counter and waited. He enjoyed watching the women bustle around the kitchen, packing what he guessed was a lunch basket. Being honest with himself, Scott knew it was Kate he watched.

Periodically, she paused and pushed stray hair from her cheek, tucking it behind her ear. Her face looked rested and glowed with sleep—or maybe the excitement of taking care of people. She amazed him.

"Why are you staring at me?" Kate asked, her face shifting from quizzical to suspicious.

As he raised his hands in the air like a captured criminal, the toaster popped, and the sound triggered his imagination. He clutched his chest, spiraled as if shot, and grabbed the counter as he sank to the floor. "Tell my wife I loved her," he said in halting words. He jerked two fabricated spasms before his final dramatic death.

When he peeked with one eye, Phyllis and Kate stood over him, shaking their heads like he was an idiot.

"Looks like you're ready to carry out the cartons," Phyllis said.

Embarrassed at his ridiculous, unappreciated drama, he gave them a haughty look, then rose, wiped off his hands on his denim-clad legs and eyed them.

"I haven't had my toast yet," he said.

"Less drama, more food," Phyllis said shooting him a grin.

Feeling foolish, he buttered his toast in silence and wolfed it down with a few swigs of coffee before the two women's toes tapping, let him know it was time to leave.

"So, what can I do for you?" he asked, knowing before he spoke.

"Help us with those boxes. Or are you too weak from loss of blood?" Kate asked, flashing him a smirky smile.

He ignored her, walked to the counter and peeked into two hefty, cardboard boxes, containing spray bottles, buckets, newspaper, sponges and squeegees. He peered at Kate over his shoulder. "I hope this isn't lunch."

She shook her head. "Lunch is in the wicker basket. Pastor Ray called last night. We're washing windows."

He hoisted a box to his chest and headed for the car. When he returned, Scott grabbed the last box, and on his final trip to his car, Kate held the door for him.

As he passed, a whiff of her sweet fruity fragrance filled his senses. Outdoors, he drew in a deep breath to rid his heady thoughts. Phyllis followed on his heels with the food basket, and finally, Kate, lugging a gallon container and locking the door.

Scott stood by the trunk, his mind whirring again at what he'd gotten himself into. Spending the afternoon with a group of church people and lonely senior citizens wasn't quite what he had in mind as a relaxing day off with Kate. But if the afternoon didn't thrill him, Kate did. He found her intriguing. A real paradox of a woman.

In the church parking lot, Kate stood beside Scott's broad frame, caught again in the memories that hauled her back to high school. Shamefully, she recalled her pride when she stood at Ron's side, praying her sister would pass by and see her with one of the popular football players.

When she introduced Scott to her friends, she sensed he was distracted despite his handshake and pleasant expression. Once in a while, she detected him staring at her, and a wave of self-consciousness washed over her.

While she talked with one of the workers, Scott meandered toward the car. After the woman left, Kate watched him, her curiosity growing. Finally, she headed his way. He had his head tucked beneath the trunk lid, puttering with the cartons.

"What are you doing?"

He lifted his head with a guilty grin. "Nothing."

Kate gave him a poke. "You're into the food basket." The words burst from her when she saw cookie crumbs clinging to his bottom lip. "That's lunch."

"Don't I get some pay for following you around like you're the, uh, Prodigal Son?"

Laughter bubbled up from Kate's chest. "Prodigal Son? I think you mean the Good Samaritan." Kate said, playfully arching an eyebrow.

Scott shrugged. "I knew it was one of those stories."

"Did I hear you say you're a Good Samaritan?" Pastor Ray asked, as he joined them. "That's what HELP needs. More Good Samaritans." He extended his arm toward Scott.

"Scott Ryan," he said, grasping his hand. "Kate's friend."

Kate peered at Scott. "And Phyllis's brother and he's *Dr.* Scott Ryan."

"Doctor? Nice of you to join us," the clergy said as they shook hands. "Everyone's appreciated."

He handed Kate a slip of paper. "Your group is washing windows at the three homes on the list. Oh, and you'll put up their screens if they're not hung already." He pivoted, surveying the crowd in the parking lot. "Who are we missing?" he asked as he ambled toward the next group.

"Ready?" Phyllis asked.

Scott shrugged, "I guess."

"I'll get Darren." Phyllis pointed behind her and darted away.

"She has her eye on him," Kate said, watching her flit across the asphalt. "The poor man doesn't have a chance."

Scott turned to watch them. "Doesn't look like he wants one."

Kate studied Phyllis walking arm in arm with Darren, and a sense of envy rifled through her. She cringed inwardly at the familiar feeling. One of these days Phyllis and Darren would be a happy twosome. And Kate would...live alone.

She rode with Scott while Darren's truck followed with two ladders and Phyllis. A few streets from the church, Kate motioned Scott to slow down. "Here," she said, pointing to a small bungalow in desperate need of paint.

Within minutes, the equipment was assembled on the grass, and Kate knocked on the door.

Scott stayed by the car, watching Kate and questioning his growing fondness. As time passed, a pleasant feeling wove through him, a warm, cozy glow. He'd spent too long with his nose to the proverbial grindstone, buried in textbooks while he learned to diagnose diseases and procedures to treat them.

Moving in with his sister and Kate, even temporarily, helped him return to the real world of fun, family...and friendships. That's what he'd really missed for so long. An old ache cut at his heart when he thought back. He'd pushed all the nagging desires into the "contamination bin" where they belonged. Why did the old wound open again?

Scott reined his negative thoughts and pushed the pleasant moment back into focus. Watching Kate waiting at the door, he admired her figure. In pale-rose slacks and a pink-and-white T-shirt, she looked as delicate and wispy as spun sugar. Probably as sweet, he calculated, seeing her cheerful greeting when a gaunt gray-haired lady answered the door.

The elderly woman clung to the doorjamb with one hand while the other gripped the screen like a crutch. His medical knowledge needled his curiosity, and he edged forward for clearer observation. The woman squinted into the sunlight, her eyes pale and glazed. To diagnose the situation, he needed to talk with her.

With a final pat of the senior's arm, Kate bounced from the porch ready to work and beckoned them toward her.

Scott tucked away his worries for a more appropriate time. He filled the buckets from the outdoor hose, and they attacked the windows—and at times themselves—as they sloshed and dripped their way around the house.

The sun rose in the sky, and heat shimmered off the cement driveway. Scott studied Kate as she descended the ladder, watching a tiny rivulet of perspiration roll down her cheek. He grasped a clean rag and wet it at the tap.

When she stepped to the ground, Scott met her with a moist cloth, pressing it against her cheek.

She jumped at first, then smiled and mopped her face. "Feels good," she said. "See." She drew the damp rag along his neckline.

"You can nurse me to health, anytime," he said, pivoting around to face her. When he looked into her gentle eyes, his breath caught in his throat. Colors like burnished leaves watched him from beneath a shapely brow. Her high, full cheekbones were tinted by the sun, and a few delicate freckles dappled her cute turned-up nose.

Unmoving, Kate searched his face, a puzzled look growing in her eyes.

Lifting his thumb and finger, he tilted her chin, longing to kiss her perfect full lips. She looked real and honest. "You okay?" he asked, grasping for something sensible to say.

"Fine. And you?" Her words were as inane and senseless as his.

Kate's smile sent a warm charge down his spine. He chuckled and dropped his hand, wishing he could feel like this all the time instead of being buried under a pile of medical journals. Kate brought out the best in him—silliness, yes, but also a delight for living instead of only doctoring. He liked that, and he had to remember the difference.

With thoughtful silence, they shifted back to the wet cloths, spray bottles and the fleeting time.

"We'd better finish," Scott said. "We have two more to go, and I'm already hungry."

She chuckled and bent down to gather the equipment.

Hungry? Scott closed his eyes. Yes, he was starving, but for more than food. He'd allow a college relationship to kill his taste for courtship. But the right woman could make him feel complete and whole and loved. When he lifted his lids, Kate's delicate frame filled his eyes.

Chapter Three

Kate leaned against the chair and relaxed the tension that knotted between her shoulder blades. She ached from the stretching and climbing during their window-washing marathon. Otherwise, the morning had been enjoyable. Scott's presence made the job easy, and the time flew by. As always, he added a little humor and a few shining moments to her usually mundane life.

But the afternoon was different. The apartment search had been useless to the point of ridiculous. Scott clowned through the buildings, evading his rising disappointment. Now, allowing his emotions to surface, he sat at the kitchen table, a disheartened expression on his face.

Kate rose and gathered plates from the kitchen table, sensing she needed to say something. "I know you're disappointed. The apartments sure sounded better in the paper than in person."

"I should've been prepared. Things don't always work the way we like."

“Think positive,” Kate said.

Scott shot her a glance. “Okay, Miss Optimistic, make me smile.”

When she thought of the cramped, unkempt places they’d visited, discouragement was logical, but for Kate, hope sprung eternal. “Don’t forget. There’s always next week. And we’re not kicking you out of here, yet.”

“I’m grateful.” Though she’d made him grin, his expression slid immediately to discouragement.

Kate turned back to the sink. “Maybe Phyllis will go with you next week. She might have a more discerning eye.”

Kate said the words, though the idea didn’t set well. She had enjoyed their time together. Even though teasing and laughing at the ugly apartments were a cover-up, the camaraderie felt fresh and exciting.

“You mean you’re willing to miss another adventurous apartment-hunting experience?” He flashed her a facetious grin, but his face grew tender. “You look tired.”

“Just a little. But I enjoyed the day. And the company was nice,” she added after a moment struggling with whether she should say what she felt.

“Thanks,” he said, rising. “The feeling is mutual.”

He rested his hand on her shoulder, sending a charge down her arm.

“Mind if I rummage through the CDs?” he asked.

“Rummage away,” she said, trying to rein in the sweep of emotion that mystified her. Was her mind playing games with Scott? Or was their friendship taking on a new edge?

For so many years, she'd pushed amorous thoughts from her mind. She had built a wall whenever she sensed a man was interested in her. Relationships were too complicated. They required honesty, and she wasn't ready to spill out her past.

Besides, her life wasn't useless or unbearable. She was a good social worker. Her work gave her purpose. She'd decided long ago to let her career be her focus, even though sometimes her personal life seemed too lonely. And too empty.

But she's made her bed, and now—as her mother had so aptly put it—she would lie in it...alone.

As a young teen, she'd longed to be an adult, assuming things would be better, believing that wisdom and charm would suddenly wash over her and all her feelings of worthlessness would go away.

But it didn't happen that way. Instead, she realized that the sins of the past press on a person's soul. She'd lost all thoughts of a husband or family.

"Nice jazz discs."

Kate turned her head toward the doorway. "Thanks, it's good thinking music."

He nodded, leaning against the doorjamb. "Can I help?"

"No, this is it." She slid the last glass into the washer. "How about some coffee? Or tea?"

"Either's fine."

Within minutes, they entered the living room with soft, melodic jazz filling the air and their mugs emitting the rich fragrance of Darjeeling tea.

"Nothing could be nicer," Scott said, easing into a chair cushion.

But, sinking into the sofa, Kate thought differently. The mood would be more pleasant if she could tell him all the things that bothered her. She couldn't. She pressed her shoulders against the cushion to relax.

The music wove through their genial conversation until Scott's concerned expression met hers.

"Did I say something wrong?" Kate asked.

"No, why?"

"You look worried."

He gave her a halfhearted grin. "My face doesn't hide much, does it?"

"What's wrong?" she asked, her curiosity more than aroused.

"I've been thinking all day about the lady whose windows we washed," he said.

"Which lady?"

"The first house. I don't know her name."

"Mrs. Finkell. Why?"

"She's not well. Did you notice how she clung to the door to steady herself? She's really weak."

"Scott, she's old. She's pushing ninety, I think."

"It's more than age, Kate. I need to talk with her."

"We can't interfere with the seniors' lives. We wash windows and rake leaves," Kate said.

"And talk, you told me." Scott leaned forward with his elbows propped on his knees and folded his hands. "I'm a doctor, Kate. I can't help but notice symptoms. We could drop by for a visit sometime, couldn't we?"

"Sure, on the Saturdays when HELP arranges visits. We never just pop in unexpected. And Mrs. Finkell's not talkative anyway."

"Could you mention my concern to your pastor?" He fell back against the cushion, sipped the tea, and waited.

"Sure," she said, studying his worried face. "You must think it's serious."

"I don't know." A thoughtful frown appeared. "Something didn't look right to me."

"You're as bad as I am. You can't leave your work at the office."

"I think you're worse," Scott said. "I've never known anyone like you to want to do things for others. Constantly. You spend all day with those poor kids and then volunteer—"

"They're not poor kids, Scott. They're fighters. They're victims of circumstances. Most of the kids are bright and loveable—"

"I'm sorry, Kate. I chose the wrong word. I'm sure they're great kids...but you're so devoted, you don't have a life for yourself."

Scott's voice faded as a startling insight struck him. Was this the reason she'd never married? She was so busy with other people's children that she didn't have time for her own.

"The children need someone to give them hope. Someone who soothes their hurts and shows compassion and love. That's why I'm devoted."

Scott sensed he should shut his mouth. In some unknown way, he'd overstepped his boundaries or hit upon something that bothered her. Part of the paradox intrigued him. "Let's talk about something else," he suggested. "Why don't you come over here?" He patted the sofa beside him. "You look tense."

She didn't move. "I feel bad for those kids, Scott."

"I know you do. Neither of us like it. We just react differently. I'm a doctor, but I try not to let those situations get me down. You should, too."

"I need to pray that I learn to do that," she said.

"You can," Scott said. "It takes practice." He gave her a cockeyed smile.

A faint smile rose on her lips, and Scott whispered up a word of thanks. The last thing he wanted to do was upset her—and without knowing why.

He slapped the cushion again. "Get over here."

"Why?" she asked. Her chin jutted forward with a "make me" expression.

Scott drew in a relieved breath, sensing he'd distracted her from whatever bothered her. Teasing, he pushed his hands against the cushion, lifting himself an inch above the sofa. "Do I have to come there and get you?"

A full grin shuffled to her face, and she rose from the chair and inched across the carpet, closing the distance between them. "I'm here. So what do you want? More tea?"

He clasped her arm and pulled her to his side, shifting her sideways so he faced her back, then lifted his hands to the tightened cords in her neck and shoulders. "You need to relax."

As his fingers kneaded her taut muscles, his own body reacted at his action. What was he doing? His pulse skipped, then raced up his arm and his chest fluttered inside like a kite, dipping and soaring, on the wind.

As his fingers worked their miracle, a soft, contented moan escaped Kate's throat. She leaned into him, her head rocking from side to side in rhythm to the music that wrapped around them.

"Feel good?" Scott whispered.

"Mmm-hmm," she murmured, seeming to enjoy the melodic silence that blanketed them.

Kate shifted toward him as if his question had broken the intimate spell that bound them. "Thanks. That was wonderful."

Her gaze caught him unaware, and longing rose to his chest. Her mouth was pink and inviting, and as his yearning grew, he relished the thought of its tender sweetness.

Her lips parted appearing to speak, but she only studied him as if reading his thoughts.

Self-control and good sense rode off on the rhythmic waves of comfortable stillness. Scott lowered his mouth to hers, tenderly, his heart thundering like the ocean tide crashing to shore.

A silent gasp moved against her lips, maddening his senses. When he withdrew, her eyes drifted open, glazed with anxious surprise.

Kate shifted backward, but her gaze remained locked to his. No words, only a soft melody filled the air. Then a delicate pink flush rose to her cheeks, and she evaded him.

When she moved to rise, Scott caught her hand. "I hadn't planned that, Kate. It just happened." He longed to see approval in her eyes.

She bit the corner of her lip, the color now heightened, he hoped, from their kiss, and he yearned to cover her mouth with his, again.

"You've addled me. I hadn't expected...I didn't think that..." She inched away from him, her hands clutched at her waist. "It makes living in the same house difficult."

Was she right? "I'm sorry, Kate. I didn't mean to complicate things."

"You surprised me, that's all."

He wanted to hear her say that his kiss touched her as it had him.

"I don't think it should happen again, Scott. It's...for the best."

His heart sank to his feet. This wasn't what he wanted to hear. Not at all.

"I'm sorry you're still having bad dreams, Amber," Kate said, leaving her desk and crouching beside the tearful child. "Are you sure you can't remember even one?"

She wagged her head from side to side, wiping tears from her eyes with the back of her hand.

Kate moved her fingers in gentle, soothing circles across the child's back. For the past month, Amber's nightmares had darkened the child's world. If Kate had any clue as to the content of Amber's dreams, she might be able to explain them away. But all Kate had learned in their time together was that Amber found comfort in the stuffed lamb that she'd handed her the first day they'd met.

"Are you okay now?" Kate asked.

Amber tilted her head upward. "Yes."

"I have a present for you."

"For me?" The child's eyes widened.

Kate rose from her stooped position, swallowing her emotion, and grasped the package from the top of the filing cabinet. "Here you go." She placed the box in the child's lap and propped herself against the desk.

Amber peered at the gift, then raised her questioning face to Kate's.

"You can open it," Kate said, love and concern dominating her senses.

A faint grin etched Amber's disbelieving countenance. With timidity, she tugged at the corner of the wrapping and freed the box. Lifting the lid, her face brightened. "Sparky!" She lifted out the floppy-eared stuffed animal. "My own puppy."

"*Sparky?* You thought of a name already?"

Amber cradled the toy against her chest. "Uh-huh."

"I had a dog when I was your age. A real one," Kate said.

"You did?"

"Sure did. A spaniel with droopy ears like this one."

Amber cradled the stuffed toy against her chest. "I love him." In the sunlight glinting through the window, Amber's hazel eyes sparkled with flecks of gold. "Thank you."

Kate walked around the desk and sat. She rested her back

against the chair, her emotions too tangled with the child's. "Time's about up, Amber. But remember if you have any more bad dreams, they're not real. They go away when you wake up." She glanced toward the doorway and softened her voice. "And don't forget to ask Jesus to watch over you and chase away your scary dreams, okay?"

Amber nodded. "Okay," she echoed.

Kate rose from her chair and rested her hand on the child's shoulder. "You can take the puppy to your room if you'd like."

"Can I leave him here? Cuz he's safe with you."

Tears pushed at the back of Kate's eyes. "I'll take good care of him. Whenever you're ready, he'll be waiting for you."

"Okay," Amber said as she slid off the chair.

Angry at herself for letting her feelings surface, Kate walked the child to the doorway. "See you next week, and don't forget, if you need me, I'm here."

Amber nodded, then turned and marched down the hallway toward her classroom.

Watching her bouncing blond curls, Kate wiped the stray tears from her eyes. Her feelings were not good. Getting herself in an emotional tizzy over Amber was in no one's best interest.

But her aching heart didn't have a choice. As soon as the child had stepped into her office, a medley of sensations churned in her chest. Concern, curiosity, tenderness and love. Kate's empty arms, longing for her own child, yearned to mother the girl and protect her from hurt. And those dreams? What caused Amber's fearful nightmares? Kate longed to talk to the grandmother. She'd be the one to fill in the gaps of Amber's memory.

Kate's mind churned with speculation throughout the day, and when she arrived home filled with questions, she waited for Scott.

After dinner, Kate cornered him alone in the living room. "Can I get your opinion about something?"

"Sure."

"I've told you about Amber," she said, sinking into the chair.

"Right, and if you want my opinion, you're getting too close, Kate. You'll get hurt."

Kate's heart rose to her throat, and she swallowed. "That's not the opinion I needed." Again, his words closed the gate between them. If she didn't need his help, she wouldn't have asked.

His focus dropped to the carpet. "Sorry."

"She has dreams. Nightmares, really. Denise, that's her housemother, says she often wakes at night in tears, but Amber has no recollection of her nightmares."

Scott lifted his gaze and a scowl creased his forehead. "You've asked her?"

"Yes, she tells me she can't remember. I'm not sure if that's true or if she doesn't want to remember."

"How about trying association? Words that might trigger a repressed event."

Kate considered what he'd said. "I don't know. Maybe,

but I'm sure the grandmother could tell me." She bit her lower lip in thought. "I don't suppose the Haven director would let me take Amber to the hospital for a visit."

"And I think he'd be right. She hasn't adjusted to the Haven, yet." He rubbed the back of his neck. "Better hang on for a while. Maybe the grandmother will rally, or once Amber's more adjusted, she might be allowed a visit."

The real question she wanted to ask niggled at her. She already sensed what his reaction would be, but she had to ask. Scott was her only hope. "Until I can visit the grandmother, maybe you could do me a favor."

His suspicious eyes captured hers.

She hesitated. "Well...you work at County General, and, uh, could you, maybe, read her file? Something in it might—"

"I can't do that, Kate." He nailed her with his gaze. "I have access to my patient charts, but I can't scout around the hospital reading files."

"But if you heard something...or maybe asked around."

He shook his head, his lips compressed and drawn. "I'm too new there, Kate. Maybe after I've been there awhile, but for now, sorry, I just can't."

"Sorry about what?" Phyllis asked from the doorway. She faltered, then inched into the room. "Looks like I arrived in time for an argument."

"Not an argument," Scott said.

"No? I never have any fun." Phyllis sank into the cushion beside him.

Scott reached over and rumpled her hair, then told her

Kate's request. Though she sided with Kate, it was obvious Phyllis could see her brother's side, also.

Kate leaned against the chair, studying the honest exchange between brother and sister, so alike, yet so different. She'd never noticed before how unalike they were in appearance. Though Phyllis was tall, she was trim and small boned. Scott, on the other hand, was muscular and solid. And their coloring and features...

"What's so interesting? You're staring."

Discomfort skittered up Kate's back. She disliked people who gawked, and now she was doing the same. "I was noticing how different you are. Not opinions..." She gave them an arched brow. "But looks. No one would know you're related."

"We're not," Scott said.

His abrupt comment startled Kate. She eyed him, expecting to see a smile, but he wasn't smiling. "You're disowning her because she took my side?"

"No," he said, matter-of-factly. He glanced at Phyllis, a quizzical expression on her face. "Apparently, she doesn't know."

Phyllis shrugged. "Never came up in conversation."

Kate's heart thudded against her breastbone, wondering where the conversation was leading. She looked for a joke in their cryptic comments. But they weren't smiling. "You're not making sense."

"I'm adopted, Kate," Scott said.

Chapter Four

An unsettled feeling slid through Scott as he assayed Kate's surprised face. Her look seemed more than surprised. Maybe startled, apprehensive, frightened. But why? He watched her struggle to regain composure, and his mind whirled in its own confusion, wondering what to say.

"We shocked you, I guess," he said finally.

Her paled complexion revitalized, and her wide-eyed stare wilted. "No, I'm, uh, just...really surprised. Certainly not shocked. I don't, well, I'm confused why, uh, this never came up in any conversation."

Phyllis responded, her face as mystified as Scott felt. "It's not something Scott and I think about, Kate. We've been brother and sister since I was born." She turned to Scott as if pleading for support.

"I suppose it's difficult to understand unless you've been there. I wasn't even four when Phyllis was born."

Phyllis chuckled. "You think you're surprised. Imagine

how Mom and Dad felt when they thought they'd never have a birth child...and I came along."

Scott joined her good humor. "She's my sister...only different parents."

As if tempering her comment, Kate lifted her hand to her lips. "I'm sorry to act so stupefied. You really threw me, that's all."

Unsure how to handle the situation, Scott gave her a grin that he hoped was playful and drew a cross with his index finger above his heart. "Promise. We have no more skeletons in our closet."

Beyond the flicker of a grin, Kate didn't respond.

"And speaking of closets," Scott said, grappling to change the subject, "who wants to go over the apartment ads with me? There has to be a place somewhere in this area that can pass our inspection."

"I vote for Kate," Phyllis said, rising. "I have some laundry to do."

Laundry? Knowing it was a feeble excuse, Scott watched his sister leave the room. "You're stuck," he said to Kate whose natural coloring had returned.

"I could do some laundry, too, you know," she said, her tone once again droll.

"Let's put it this way," he countered. "The longer I wait to find an apartment, the longer I'll live here with you."

"Well, if you put it that way," she said, rising and settling beside him on the sofa, "where's that paper?"

She shot him a bright smile, and he sent one back. But

his comment hit him like a wrecker's ball. When he found an apartment, would Kate ease out of his life? Would the distance send her deeper into her secret world—a world that confused him, yet a world he wanted to understand?

Trudging up the final flight of stairs, Kate studied Scott as he reached the landing ahead of her. They had looked at two unacceptable apartments, and she hoped this time her prayers would be answered—a decent rental. She needed to get away from him before her emotions were too tightly wrapped around his.

Besides, she was irritated. She'd asked one favor of him—to help her check the records of Amber's grandmother. He'd refused. Now, here she was like a fool on a sunny Saturday afternoon, dragging her body up another narrow stairway to view an apartment.

"I'm wearing you out," Scott said as she reached the landing. "This is 3A right here. Front of the building for a change."

He took the key he'd picked up from the super and turned it in the lock. When he pushed open the door, Kate scanned the room. For once, bright sunshine poured in from two large windows. But the light emphasized the less than clean walls and carpet. She debated if Scott had noticed. His grimace answered her question.

"You could ask them to paint," she said, before Scott could mutter his contempt for the dirt. "At least the room has nice wide windows." *Dirty* windows, she added in her distressed ruminations.

Kate stepped into the kitchen where the grime seemed more pronounced. Grease glazed the wall behind the range and the stove top was dulled with dirt. "A little elbow grease will help," she said, turning to face an empty room.

Scott had already moved on ahead of her. She followed the sound of his footsteps down the short hall: bath on one side and bedroom on the other.

Defeat. She saw it in his face. "Let's have lunch and regroup," Kate said.

Without question, he headed back toward the living room and into the building hallway. She bounded behind him down the stairway, wishing he'd at least say something. His silence left her feeling disheartened.

After returning the key, they headed outside and sank into the car seats.

"We're going about this wrong," Kate said.

Finally Scott spoke. "Sorry I'm so down. You can tell me what I'm doing wrong while we grab a bite."

She had said what *we're* doing wrong, but she bit back the correction.

Without waiting for her response, he pulled away and drove in silence.

Nearing the downtown Royal Oak eateries, Scott seemed to pull himself from his doldrums. "I need frèsh air. I thought we'd go to one of the cafés in town."

They were nearly there, and Kate felt no need to reply.

He parked the car on Center Street, and they headed for Main Street. The sidewalks bustled with pedestrians ogling the boutique windows and sitting beneath wide, colorful umbrellas.

Scott flagged a hostess, and they were seated at a cozy outdoor table.

The green covering only blocked half the warm July sun, and the rays felt pleasant, warming her arms from the car's air-conditioning. Scott reached into his shirt pocket and pulled out sunglasses, sliding them on his nose while he perused the menu. After a moment, he laid it on the table.

"I hope this place is okay, Kate," he said, looking at her for the first time since they'd left the apartment building. "I didn't ask, did I?"

"No, but this place is okay. Don't worry. We all have bad days," Kate said, not wanting him to feel worse. His bright smile and good nature was Kate's personal dose of medicine. Seeing him depressed stirred her own deeper sadness.

A pleasant breeze ruffled the umbrellas, and the rich aroma of food hung on the summer air. Her stomach stirred and she focused on the menu, instead of Scott's unusually serious face.

When the waiter arrived, Kate ordered a chef salad and Scott, a stacked sandwich. Their sodas were delivered within a minute, and Kate took a sip before she began.

"What are you thinking?" she asked, organizing the musings she had earlier.

Behind his sunglasses, his eyes were hidden, but he lifted his face from the tumbler to hers. "That's the problem. I'm not sure what's bothering me. The sad state of those apartments or...what?"

"What you need first is to find a roommate, I think. Someone to share expenses. Then you can handle a higher rent and find a better place."

"Probably," he mumbled, preoccupied with stirring the drink with a straw. "I like your house. You have room and a yard. I suppose I'm depressed with the idea of being cramped up in a small space again. The rental prices around here are out of sight."

"Then why look for a place now? You've only been here a few weeks. Wait until you meet someone who'd like to share expenses."

To Kate's relief, he pulled off his sunglasses and leaned forward, searching her eyes. "Are you saying I can stay at the house until then?"

His question settled in her empty stomach like a block of ice. The answer *yes* fluttered to her tongue, but wisdom froze the words in her throat.

"I love staying with you and Phyllis, but you'd prefer me gone, I think." He inched even closer. "Be honest, Kate."

The ice melted with his warmth, and unexpected pleasure bubbled in her thoughts, running over into her words. "Sure, you can stay. I can't throw you out on your ear, can I?" Her pulse surged through her like a burst of steam.

Her hand rested on the table, and he slid his palm toward her and covered her fingers. "Are you positive?"

Unbidden happiness eased down her limbs. "Have I ever been anything but positive?"

Her double meaning brought a smile to his drawn lips. A

blast of air shot from his chest and a rich laugh followed. "I feel better already."

At his words, the waiter arrived with their order. While he set their plates on the table, Kate grasped at the seconds to control her wavering emotions. She had just done the opposite of what she had prayed. Why?

Voices of other patrons filled her ears, and she reflected on the nearby window boxes filled with contained flowers reaching toward the light. Was she like those restricted blossoms bound in their small compartments, stretching and yearning for the sun?

She had suppressed her life, focusing on her work and her home. Not much else, except Phyllis who'd been a good friend. But life offered so much more if she weren't so fearful of facing the dark recesses of her past. She sensed God had forgiven her, but she hadn't forgiven herself. How long would she punish herself for her youthful mistake?

"Not hungry?" Scott asked.

She jerked inwardly hearing his voice and realized she'd drifted off in contemplation. "I was admiring the flowers," she said, stretching the truth.

She lifted her fork and dug into the appetizing salad. The large plate brimmed with fresh lettuce and sliced egg with julienne-cut meats and cheeses. The creamy dressing and savory meat dropped to her tongue and reminded her how hungry she really was.

She lifted a crusty roll from the small plate and broke a piece, using it to scoop her salad onto the fork. Her gaze lifted to Scott, opening his mouth to a mile-high sandwich. She laughed at his antics and felt her shoulders ease and soften to relaxed comfort.

When he'd consumed half the deli sandwich, Scott leaned back and plucked a large curly potato chip from his plate. "Did you talk to the pastor yet?" he asked, then bit into the chip.

Kate swallowed and wiped her mouth with the paper napkin. "Pastor Ray, you mean?"

"Right. About visiting the woman I mentioned."

Kate chuckled. "Mrs. Finkell. No, HELP hasn't met again. Next Saturday's our usual weekend. Are you coming along?"

"If I'm not working." His face grew serious. "I'm really concerned about her, Kate. For some reason, I keep thinking about the lady."

"I haven't mentioned anything to Pastor Ray, but I can if you're that worried."

"Would you? I'd be relieved."

Kate watched him tackle the sandwich again and thought about his concern. She had to admire Scott's dedication. The elderly woman had absorbed him since the day he'd met her. Kate reflected on the Haven and her own worries about the children and families with whom she worked. Perhaps she was as devoted as Scott and didn't recognize it.

As Kate forked into her salad, faces of the helpless children whom she'd talked to over the past months marched through her thoughts until Amber rose and settled in her mind. The child's fears and nightmares concerned Kate. She had to do something to find out more about the girl. And if

Scott wouldn't help her, then she'd take it into her own hands. The significant thing was to help Amber.

Feeling resentful, Scott stood in the hospital cafeteria line. He'd gotten stuck working the weekend. And today, Kate was off with the HELP group—to his surprise, where he wanted to be. Worry for Mrs. Finkell rattled through him, but was quickly replaced by Kate's glowing image.

He drifted back to when he'd spent his first full day in her company. A day that changed his life. He'd always concentrated on his career—except for the unpleasant involvement with Lana in college. But since Kate literally charged into his life, he'd found his focus wavering. Wise or not.

Since then, Kate's image pervaded all hours of his day and night. He'd lain in bed knowing she was one floor below him. Some mornings at breakfast, he'd seen her wrapped in a long-sleeved, belted robe with a delicate sheer, pink hem peeking beneath. The picture stirred him as he tried to sleep, thinking she was as soft and fragile as the cloth. And he longed that her inner reflections were as revealing as he imagined her gown.

At the cashier, he eyed his tray, amazed that he'd selected items from the counter while he'd been preoccupied with Kate. He glanced at the filled tables and spotted one unoccupied chair at a table for two.

"Do you mind?" he asked the doctor seated in the other chair.

"Not at all," the man said, jutting his hand forward. "Cass Wentworth."

"Scott Ryan," he said, taking the doctor's hand in a firm shake. He set down his tray and slid into the chair.

"You're new to County General," the young doctor stated.

"Yes, I'm a resident. What service are you in?"

"Internal medicine. I'm up on medical."

"Do you care for stroke patients, by chance?" Scott asked, Kate entering his mind again.

"No, County General has a Stroke Unit. Why? Do you know someone there?"

Scott shook his head. Kate's request weighed on his shoulders. Why hadn't he told her he'd see what he could do? "A friend has interest in a patient there."

"Ah," he said, without further questions.

The young doctor was amiable, and as they chatted, Scott enjoyed his good humor and was grateful to learn a little of the hospital scuttlebutt.

"Where do you live?" Cass asked, tilting his tumbler to drain the last of his juice.

A feeling of discomfort settled over Scott. "Well, I'm, uh, looking. I'm staying with a relative." Annoyed at his own foolish evasiveness, Scott added, "My sister. She and a friend have a house."

"That's worked out for you?"

"I can't stay there. I need to find a place...one of these days."

Cass sat for a moment without comment, then, as if he had settled his thoughts, he focused on Scott. "I'm considering taking in someone to share my condo. I thought I'd enjoy the privacy, but I feel like I'm rattling around in it."

"Where is your place?" Scott asked, wondering if Cass was suggesting the possibility of rooming with him.

"Downtown Royal Oak. Great location. Close to the freeway. You'll have to stop by sometime. See what you think." He rose, lifted his tray with his left hand, and extended his other to Scott. "Nice to meet you."

"Thanks," Scott said, reciprocating. "Maybe, I'll do that."

Cass backed away. "Medical's on the fifth floor. Drop by. I'll show you around." He gave Scott a nod and headed for the tray conveyer and the door.

His proposition settled on Scott like a stamping press. Now that Kate had offered the surprise suggestion that he stay at the house for a while, he'd been in no hurry. Still, Kate's offer had landed in his lap as gently as dandelion parachutes. And possibly as fragile. A wind of misunderstanding could blow the proposal away.

He tucked away Cass's proposition. He didn't know the man well enough to grasp if the offer was serious or just an offhanded comment. He'd think about it later.

"Anyway, we had a great day," Kate said, noticing Scott's silence while she related their HELP chores. She recalled her curiosity that morning. When Kate arrived at Mrs. Finkell's, she'd studied the woman, looking for a clue to Scott's concern. Nothing caught her attention. She didn't understand Scott's insistence to ask the pastor about his disquiet.

"Oh," she added, "and Pastor Ray said he'll find some way to thank us for all our hard work over the summer."

"Did he say anything else?" Scott asked. His pinning gaze confirmed what he meant.

"Well," Kate complied, "if you mean about visiting Mrs. Finkell, he didn't say no, but he did say that you should telephone first. And to make sure you have a legitimate reason to visit other than checking on her health."

Scott's shoulders lifted and his voice sizzled with irritation. "Why else would I go to visit her, Kate? Did you tell him I'm a doctor?"

Phyllis jumped in. "He knows that Scott, but you aren't Mrs. Finkell's doctor."

"You can't just knock on someone's door and do a physical examination," Kate added.

"Thank you, ladies, for your wisdom." He shook his head and sank back against the chair. "I have better sense than that. I'll think of something."

A lengthy silence filled the room, and Kate squirmed against the upholstery, brooding over Scott's aloof manner. A month ago, his distraction would be the answer to her prayer, but now, events had changed that. Instead, longings shifted through her. Hopeless, useless fantasies. And no matter how hard she tried to convince herself, the dream remained. She liked Scott more than she wanted to admit.

"Who's hungry?" Phyllis asked, breaking the silence. She rose and took a step toward the kitchen.

Kate only cleared her throat, longing to stay quiet until she heard what Scott would say. But he remained silent and thoughtful.

Finally Kate gave in. "I suppose we should eat something."

Scott rose and stretched his arms above his head. "I think I'll skip dinner. The hospital staff's softball team plays tonight."

"Okay," Phyllis said, disappearing through the doorway.

"Softball. Sounds like fun," Kate said. Holding her breath, she waited like a child listening to the distant chimes of an ice cream truck.

"I'll pick up a sandwich or something," he said, feeling the back pocket of his jeans as if checking for his wallet. He patted the spot, then stepped to the door.

Filled with disappointment, Kate watched, willing him to turn around and invite her. When he paused and faced her, she froze in place.

"You're welcome to come along...if you'd like." He looked at her with question.

Suspended, she caught her breath, then rose. "A sandwich and softball? What could be better?" She smiled.

"Better? Not much, except add a soda...and your smile." His apprehensive expression changed to a grin.

"And you," he added, sliding his arm around her shoulder.

At that moment, Kate forgot about the sandwich, soda and softball. The only part that hung in her thoughts was, "And you."

Chapter Five

Clutching their fast-food bag in his left hand, Scott steered Kate along the Boulan Park bleachers until they found space on a lower bench. As he opened the sack, he glanced at the scoreboard.

"County General's behind," he told Kate.

"Losing? Who are they playing?"

"Beaumont Hospital. They're our major competitor." Scott handed her a wrapped burger and a soda. He rolled down the top of the bag and slipped it between them. "I left the fries inside." He used his elbow to point.

Kate nodded, her eyes directed toward the team. "Who's up?" she asked.

"Beaumont, but..." He watched the shortstop leap backward and snatch the ball. "Out!" he yelled. "Third out. We're up."

As the teams shifted places on the diamond, Scott spied a familiar face among the team members. He jostled Kate's arm. "See the tall guy warming up over there—with the bats?"

Kate nodded.

"I met him in the cafeteria today. Cass... Wentworth, I think he said. Nice guy. Works on the medical floor." Scott didn't mention Cass's comment about sharing his place. Though he hadn't expected it, the idea left an empty feeling in his chest.

Though Cass's words lingered, the lively game soon captured Scott's attention again. He munched on the fries and swallowed the burger amid his boisterous yells, and soon Kate joined in, getting caught up in the excitement. Her cheeks glowed in the orange rays of the sinking sun. When she cheered as County General moved ahead of Beaumont, she turned to him with sparkling eyes and a brilliant smile.

"We're winning," she yelled, swinging so quickly toward Scott she sloshed some soda on her leg.

Scott snatched a roll of carry-out napkins from his pocket and pressed them against her jeans. She stretched her slender limb forward as he dabbed while they laughed at her exuberance.

"You can dress her up, but you can't take her out," Scott said, dragging the old saying from the recesses of his memory—the way his father always teased his mother.

Kate responded with a grin, but with the rousing yells, she leaped from the bench as a home run added a point to the winning score.

When the cheering died down, Scott rose and gathered the trash while Kate stood and eyed her damp jeans. While they maneuvered through the crowd, Scott tossed the garbage in a basket, then turned and found himself facing his new friend.

"Scott," Cass said.

"Hey, great game." Scott gave Cass's shoulder a friendly shake, then noticed Cass eyeing Kate.

"Cass, this is my friend Kate Davis. She's my, uh, room..." Flustered, he hesitated. "I think I mentioned that I live with my sister and Kate."

"Ahh," he said, flashing Scott a wry smile.

"No," Scott said. "We're just friends."

"No wonder you didn't jump at my offer," Cass continued, as if not listening.

Kate's voice lifted in question. "Offer?"

"I didn't realize it *was* an offer," Scott countered, uncomfortable with the direction of the conversation. Feeling the need to explain, he turned to Kate. "Cass mentioned he's considering sharing his condo."

Her curiosity seemed to shift to rigid politeness. "That's nice."

Seeming unaware of the tension, Cass looked from one to the other. "Are you headed anywhere? My place is only a few miles from here—Crooks Road to Main Street. How about following me home, and you can see the place?"

Scott's stomach tightened. Instead of feeling the pleasure of finding his own place, disappointment reared inside him. He peered at Kate. "What do you say?"

Her expression was unreadable.

"Sure," she said. "That'd be nice." As if miles away, she stared at the ground.

Was she disappointed? The question bounced through

Scott's head. If so, then perhaps she cared more than she let on. Why did he care anyway? He chided himself for his stupid question. He knew why. He liked Kate. More than liked her, Scott was fond of her. He drew in a ragged breath. *Fond?* Why was he playing games with himself?

When he focused, Cass stared at him curiously.

"Well?" Cass asked.

"Sure. Why not?" Scott said. Placing his hand against Kate's back, he guided her to follow Cass toward the parking lot.

The ride from Boulan Park passed quickly, and when they entered the parking lot, Scott scanned the attractive condos that were designed like a neat row of New England two-story bungalows.

"Not bad," Scott said, pulling into a space near Cass.

Kate was quiet.

He opened his door, but Kate exited the passenger side before he could be a gentleman. When Cass joined them, Kate finally spoke.

"I hope I'm not in the way," she said to Cass.

"Heavens, no. I like having pretty ladies around."

The comment may have been innocent, but Scott tensed at Cass's obvious flirtation. Yet, he'd given the man an open invitation by referring to Kate as a friend.

As Kate walked beside Cass to the front door, Scott straggled behind. The two chatted amiably, Scott's presence unnoted. He felt like the outsider and didn't like the feeling. An uneasy sensation prickled his awareness. Cass's comment that he liked pretty women hanging around didn't set well. Did he mean overnight?

And Kate. He studied her, curious if she was returning Cass's interest. Old memories tugged at him. He'd trusted Lana and she'd betrayed that trust.

Cass held the door, waving him in, and Scott followed Kate into a sunny living room. Scott admired the masculine, comfortable area in shades of beige and browns with a bit of rusty red like an old brick. Leather furnishings formed a U-shape and faced a large cabinet where, Scott guessed, he would find a television and CD equipment behind closed doors.

"Nice," Scott said, knowing his co-worker expected him to say something.

"Thanks. I like it," Cass said, turning toward a doorway.

Kate oohed her pleasure over the kitchen with plentiful oak cabinets and almond accessories. A bay window nook held an oak table and chairs.

The second floor housed two large bedrooms with private baths and an open sitting area between. Against one wall, a large oak stand held Cass's computer and printer. A perfect setup, yet Scott found himself searching for problems. He found none.

When they returned to the first floor and accepted Cass's invitation for a soda, they settled in the living room.

"What do you think?" Cass asked. "Roomy enough, I think. Did you see the guest bath off the laundry room?"

Kate chuckled. "This is almost as large as my whole house."

With both pairs of eyes on him and nothing negative to use as an excuse, Scott admitted it was a great place. Still, a nagging feeling caused him to hesitate. What about Cass's overnight guests?

"Would you like to give it a try, Scott?" Cass asked.

"Hmm? It's hard to refuse," he said, still struggling with his thoughts.

"Hard to refuse, but I hear some hesitation," Cass said. "I suppose I don't blame you when you can wake up in the morning to a pretty face like this one." Sitting with Kate on the sofa, Cass nestled his hand against her shoulder. "You're much more attractive than I am."

A pink flush rose up her neck while heat boiled up Scott's spine.

Bristling with indignation, Scott revealed his agitation. "I'm wondering if you have the wrong idea, here."

A puzzled expression covered Cass's face. "What idea?"

"I'm not involved with Kate...if that's what you think." Defending his morals, he'd done it again—let Cass think that Kate meant nothing to him.

Cass fell back against the cushion and lifted his hands in defense. "Whoa, man, I'm sorry if I suggested that. I'm just toying with Kate. I really didn't mean to offend either of you."

Kate's befuddled countenance oscillated like a tennis match spectator's, as she pivoted her head from one to the other.

"You didn't offend me, but..." Scott didn't know what to say. Humiliation slithered up his spine, and he faced a shocking insight. In his heart, Kate was his. No action, words or obvious truth to his feeling, but that's exactly how he felt. "I'm not comfortable with 'toying' around, I guess."

His concerned expression fading, Cass's face filled with good humor. "I get it. Are you worried about me having babes hanging around...night and morning?" He peered at Scott. "I admit I'm a tease, but it stops there. I know that's odd for this day and age, but..."

Cass hesitated, glancing at Kate. "I'm embarrassed to admit this, but I, uh, sort of believe that a real commitment...I suppose I should say marriage, is the time for being intimate."

Scott clamped his mouth from gaping at Cass's words. "You're kidding?"

Discomfort crept to Cass's face. "No, I'm serious."

"Who'd have thought? I agree. That conviction has gotten me into trouble, but to me, chastity's a precious gift between husband and wife."

"My thoughts exactly. So, now that we have that settled, are you interested?" Cass chuckled. "The day we met in the cafeteria, you struck me as an easygoing guy—one I'd enjoy sharing the place with."

"You mean I made an impression on you that fast?"

Cass grinned.

With mixed feelings, Scott struggled to respond. "Well, sure...I'd, uh, like to give it a try. We need to talk rent, but...other than that, why not?"

Scott knew why not, but it wasn't a logical reason. He had no assurance that Kate gave a hoot about him. Why open himself up for hurt again? He didn't need it.

Wondering why she'd been so quiet, Scott looked at Kate. A strange sadness loomed on her face, seeming pale in the lamplight. When he caught her attention, she looked as if she'd been pronounced guilty of some heinous crime.

A weight settled on his shoulders. What had he said or done to cause her to look utterly defeated?

Kate rolled over on her bed and wiped her eyes with the corner of her wilted T-shirt. Friday night and the house was empty, except for her. Earlier, Kate witnessed Phyllis's glowing face as she parading through the doorway on Darren's arm for a long-awaited date.

I'm happy for her, Kate thought, then cringed, hearing her own blatant lie. She knew in her heart she envied Phyllis like she had always envied her sister. Envy. If God wasn't merciful, she'd be in serious trouble.

And Scott. A rustle of tenderness drifted up her arms to her chest. Kate pictured his strong arms, muscles bulging as he toted luggage and boxes from the second floor to his car. Last Sunday, he had emptied the guest room and said goodbye. She hadn't heard a word.

Again, tears bubbled up and spilled down her cheeks. Self-pity. She hated it. Envy. She hated that, too. And that's what filled her—envy and self-pity. And where was her common sense? It had taken a vacation.

Scott's departure should have been a gift. But one that seemed a paradox, like a friend donating a kidney for you—a generous sacrifice, but a tremendous loss at the same time.

In her heart, she knew nothing could come of her relationship with Scott. She'd said it over and over. After their visit to Cass's place, Scott's words settled in her mind like the black plague. "Chastity is a precious gift between husband and wife."

The words struck Kate like an express train, and a deep sob erupted from her throat. She had no precious gift to offer anyone. With youthful ignorance and misplaced passion, she had given it away to a sturdy, good-looking football player. As if her treasure had been a meaningless gag gift, Ron threw it back in her face and walked away, leaving her with the tragic burden and sorrow.

Weighted by her melancholy, she folded her hands behind her head, struggling to control the rush of black memories that rolled through her like smoke from a house fire. The burning image seared her emotions and unable to bear the raging pain, she descended into uneasy sleep.

The telephone's ring pulled Kate from her bed like a police siren. She bolted upward, swung her legs from the mattress to the floor, and rose, grasping the nightstand to steady her reeling body. Her dark mood had settled on her like black fog, and in the unlighted bedroom, she stumbled her way to the door, then to the telephone.

"Hello," she said, her voice unsteady.

"Kate? Is something wrong?"

Her heart skipped as Scott's voice reconciled into reality. "No, I guess I fell asleep."

"See what happens when I move out. Life gets boring."

He chuckled, but his words hit Kate with dire truth.

Without waiting for her to respond, he continued, "Is HELP this weekend?"

"HELP? Ah, yes. Tomorrow." Her pulse raced at his question.

"Great. I have the day off. I'll come by and pick you up, okay?"

"Sure," she said, without thinking—without thinking wisely was more accurate.

"So, do you miss me?"

She faltered, wanting her heart to speak and not her brain. "It's quiet." *Quiet and empty.* The deep cavern of silence surrounded her.

"Sorry, I haven't called. It takes time getting to know a new housemate."

"I imagine." She regretted the bitterness that skipped through her voice.

"Are you okay, Kate?"

"I'm fine, really." Lie. Lie.

"If you're sure." He hesitated, then continued. "Cass is either dragging me out to dinner or filling me in on his life. Time flies. I really meant to telephone."

"I didn't expect you to call." Disgusting self-pity. She loathed it.

"But I meant to," he said, ignoring her response.

Kate grabbed herself mentally by the collar and gave herself a shake. "I'm glad you called, Scott. It does seem lonely here."

"If it weren't so late, I'd come by tonight, but tomorrow's not far away. I'll come by early."

"Okay," she said, longing to keep him on the telephone forever.

When he disconnected, Kate held the receiver, wanting to cling to the moment a little longer. No matter what she said or what her mind told her, she couldn't lose Scott's friendship. If nothing permanent could ever come of their relationship, she didn't care at the moment. He could be her friend. Her very dear friend. That's what she needed.

Chapter Six

Scott finished mowing Mrs. Finkell's lawn while the others completed the edging and trimming. Putting the mower back into Darren's truck bed, Scott wondered how the others would feel if he stayed behind to talk with the elderly woman. Her health concerns nagged at him. Being a doctor, he couldn't walk away without gathering some information.

When Kate came down the walk toward him, Scott's heart skipped a beat. Wondering what had happened, he studied her face. No matter what he said, she seemed tense and distant—nothing like the Kate he met a couple months earlier, flailing her flowered umbrella in his face. That day brightened in his memory, but seeing her now didn't. What could he do to bring back the Kate he once knew?

"Where's your smile, Katie?" he asked, sending her a toying smile.

Her gaze darted upward. "What?" A flickering grin settled on her lips. "How did you come up with that name?"

"I'm gifted, I suppose." He rested his hand on her shoulder. "I've missed you. Do you think it's true that absence makes the heart grow fonder?"

She gave him a swat and tossed her equipment in the truck. "Don't be silly."

But he watched the pleasure rise to her face. She missed seeing him every day, just as he missed her. He was certain.

Recalling his plan, he sidled over to her and lowered his voice. "Do you think Phyllis and Darren will mind if we lag behind so I can talk for a minute with Mrs. Finkell?"

"So that's why you're sweet-talking me," Kate said.

"No. That was the truth. This is a perfect opportunity to see the lady for a minute. You know I've been curious. What do you think?"

She shrugged. "I'm sure they'll understand."

To his relief, when Phyllis and Darren returned with their gear, they were in agreement.

"We won't be long," Scott promised. "Since she knows Kate, I figured she should be there."

Darren nodded as he stowed the gear in the truck bed. "See you in a while," he said, climbing into the cab. With a wave, they pulled away toward the next house.

When they were down the block, Kate headed up the sidewalk to the porch and rang the bell.

Mrs. Finkell answered the door, and when Kate said they had time for a short visit, the woman swung the door wide. "Come in," she said. Her watery eyes narrowed in the late summer sun and she hurried to close the door.

When he stepped inside, Scott scanned the small living room overburdened with lace doilies and dusty knickknacks. A knitted quilt lay over the arm of the sofa, and a bed pillow propped nearby led him to believe the woman napped there.

"Just move that stuff and find a seat," she said, waving her hand as if the magazines and clothing would vanish from the furniture.

Scott shifted a pile of newspapers, leaving a spot large enough for him and Kate to sit.

"Like a lemonade?" Mrs. Finkell asked. "Can't seem to get enough to drink myself."

Studying her with a doctor's eye, Scott tallied up another symptom: hazy eyes, thirsty and open sores that he noticed since they'd entered the house.

"Just half a glass would be nice," Kate answered.

Scott said he'd take the same, and Mrs. Finkell left the room.

Scott waited for the woman to be out of earshot, then leaned toward Kate. "Look at her legs when she comes back. She has open sores above her ankles and they aren't healing. I'd say she has diabetes," he whispered.

"How can you tell from that?" Kate asked with a voice much too loud.

Looking through the doorway, Scott noticed the woman returning, and he signaled Kate. She slammed her mouth closed as Mrs. Finkell stepped into the room.

"Here you are," she said, handing each of them a partially filled tumbler. She stepped back and sank into a rocker that faced away from the window. "That bright sunlight's hard on these old eyes of mine. Can't look at it."

"And you said you're often thirsty," Scott said, initializing his concern.

"Seem to be," she said, then turned her attention to Kate. "Can't thank all you church people enough for all you've done around here. I'll be ninety-two my next birthday. What do you say to that?"

"I'd say you're young at heart, Mrs. Finkell," Kate said.

"Not so young anymore," the woman added. "Figure I don't have too much longer before I meet my Maker, but you know, it's a funny thing." She sent them an eager smile. "As much as I love the Lord, I love this life, too."

"Good for you," Scott said, pleased she'd left him an opening. His concern rose as she mentioned her symptoms. "If you want to be around a few more years, you need to take care of yourself."

"Oh, I know that. Sometimes I'm lonesome, but most times, I'm content, even if it's just enjoying my memories."

Scott wasn't put off by her diversion, not when he'd gotten this close. "When's the last time you saw your doctor, Mrs. Finkell?"

She tilted back in the wooden rocker and focused across the room.

Scott followed her line of direction and spotted a display of framed photographs. One looked like a young girl's senior picture.

The older woman gestured toward the bookcase. "That's my daughter's picture there. High school picture, but I always liked it." She looked down toward her gnarled fingers knotted in her lap. "Since she moved away, it's hard for me to get out. I don't get to the doctor often."

"I imagine you miss your daughter," Kate said, leaning forward from her seat.

"I do, yes. Life gets lonely without family. I have no one around here to run errands or get me where I need to go."

Scott opened his mouth, but Kate jumped in ahead of him.

"But anyone from HELP would be happy to give you a ride to the doctor or anywhere. All you have to do is ask."

A smile spread over her wrinkled face, and she propelled the chair in a gentle rocking motion. "That's mighty nice of you. Guess you've become like family."

Unable to contain himself, Scott announced he was a doctor. Feeling a poke to the ribs, he turned to Kate and winced at her glower. But he couldn't stop. His worry was too great. Touching on symptoms, she'd mentioned—her thirst and her eyesight—Scott pointed out the open sores on her legs.

"I'd recommend you make an appointment, Mrs. Finkell."

A new grin tugged at her creased face. "Then, I can tell that old geezer I have a good-looking young friend who's a doctor."

"You could," Scott said with a chuckle.

Kate was quiet, but Scott explained again his concern for her health while the older woman listened. After obtaining a promise that she'd call her physician, Scott rose and took her hand. "We'll call you Monday evening, okay, Mrs. Finkell?"

She agreed.

Kate jotted down the woman's telephone number, and with a hug, she said goodbye. Scott followed her to the door, washed in relief. His prayers of thanks rose, pleased that the elderly woman had listened.

Outside as they walked to the car, Kate squeezed his arm. "I should be angry at you, but I'm grateful. If you hadn't insisted, she might have ignored you."

Scott paused at the car door and tilted her chin upward. "Thanks. It's hard being a doctor and overlooking the obvious."

His words took a turn, and determination thrust him onward. "And there's another obvious, I can't overlook." His heart compressed. "You're upset with me, I think." He watched her struggle to pull her gaze from his.

"I'm upset with myself...not you," she said. Her face paled and her shoulders appeared tense.

Scott searched her face, longing to know what she meant, but he sensed the distance rising between them. "I wish you could tell me," he said finally.

"It's not important. Really. Just some old trappings hanging on from my youth. Troubles I should have buried long ago. But nothing you can do."

"I don't want to lose your friendship, Kate. I like you too much to have you pull away from me, and I feel a wedge growing between us."

His distress spurred him forward like a foot pressing on an accelerator to race through a yellow light. "I'll be honest.

I hated to move in with Cass, because I was afraid you'd drift away from me. I don't want that to happen."

"I'm not drifting. Look, we're standing here talking."

He felt her lie tangle around his heart. Unless God intervened, she was drifting away beyond his grasp like a helium balloon on the wind. An iron fence had risen between them. He could see her and hear her, but he couldn't draw her into his arms. And no matter how firmly he denied his desire, that's exactly where he wanted her to be.

God intervened. When his director called him into the office, Scott couldn't believe what he heard.

"Since you're going into family practice, I thought Children's Haven might be right up your alley."

Scott closed his gaping mouth. "For how long?"

"Well, Dr. Barlow will need a month or so to recuperate after his surgery. So you'll be there at least five or six weeks, I'd guess."

"Full-time?"

"No, not full-time. Monday, Wednesday and Friday. And then you'll be on call for emergencies. You can handle that I should think."

"Yes, no problem. The change will be interesting." The phrase amused him. Interesting. More like wonderful.

"Fine. You'll begin next Monday, then."

When he left the director's office, Scott smiled widely. If Kate planned to pull away from him, God had another idea. And Scott definitely gave God credit for the amazing event.

After he'd talked to Kate outside Mrs. Finkell's, Scott pulled out of his intellect every reason and incident he could conjure, trying to make some sense out of Kate's behavior. She'd always been a little unsure of herself. He blamed that on her shaky self-esteem. He hoped someday she'd realize what a charming, wonderful person she was.

But since the day Cass had invited them to see the condo, she'd grown more distant. He couldn't put his finger on it. He relived the day. She'd been quiet, he recalled, but once he invited her to the softball game, she seemed to perk up and really come alive at the game.

He chuckled remembering how she'd spilled her drink in her exuberance. His heart tripped again recalling how he'd blotted the soda from her shapely leg hidden beneath her jeans.

Was she upset because they'd gone to Cass's place? When he pictured her animation and smiles, hanging on Cass's every word, rivalry poked at him.

But the problem wasn't then. It happened later—later when she became silent and brooding. What had they talked about? His mind went blank.

At times, he'd thought she was angry because he had been unwilling to help her check Amber's grandmother's records. Then, had second thoughts.

That particular problem he would soon solve. Rumor had been circulating that he'd be going up to the medical floor on his next service. While on medical, dropping into the stroke unit would be easy. Maybe if he told Kate, she'd cheer up.

He grinned, imagining Kate's expression when he appeared unexpectedly at her office door the following Monday. The transfer to Children's Haven would be a secret from her until then.

When Scott peered through her office doorway, Kate's mouth opened like a hungry baby bird's—except no sound came from her lips.

Leaping from her desk, she shot toward him, her hand pressed against her chest, peering at him with disbelief.

"What are you doing here?" she asked.

She stood in front of him, inspecting his doctor's coat, then looked at him with question.

"I'm the Haven's new doctor," he said.

"New doctor? Where's Dr. Barlow?"

"Having surgery." He guided her back to her desk, then dropped into a chair and explained. "I'll only be a here a few weeks, but I knew you'd be thrilled. Right, Katie?" He gave her a million-dollar smile and was relieved when she laughed.

"You're so silly," she said as her shoulders relaxed. "Let me break the news. You've arrived at a good time. This morning, I hear we have two suspected cases of chicken pox. I hope you've had them."

"I have, but thanks for the warning." He rose and rested his palms on her desk, facing her. "I just dropped by to say hi. But I suppose I'd better get back before I find a line of speckled youngsters waiting for the doctor."

At the door, he halted and turned around. "Lunch? Could we eat together...say about one?"

She hesitated before answering. "Sure. In the cafeteria."

When Scott disappeared, Kate fell against the chair and caught her breath. What would she do now? She had tried so hard to get him out of her mind. A useless task, but she'd made a valiant effort.

Now he was here where she'd be with him three days a week. How could she keep her feelings under control? Even today, seeing him in his doctor's coat sent warmth edging through her body.

Scott was always handsome, but in his doctor's coat, he exuded an air of confidence, yet kindness. The white color broadened his already wide shoulders, and his nutmeg hair and deep-brown eyes added the boyish charm she loved—not to overlook his teasing dimples and generous smile. She chided her gushing infatuation.

Still, she really admired him, longing to have Scott's control and poise. In her work, she displayed those attributes, knowing her job backward and forward. Even the unwanted surprises—unexpected problems or serious situations involving the children—those, she could handle.

But beyond her career, Kate lacked self-direction and control in her personal life. Her past rose up like a cobra, ready to strike her, poisoning her thoughts. Kate's memory dragged back to her teen years...and her sister.

Even in junior high, Kristin had been popular. Friends, boys and girls, dropped by or telephoned to make plans or to gossip. In high school, Kristin had a date for every dance or special occasion.

Shrinking with the memory, Kate missed her senior prom. Another horrible occasion arched its ugly head, recalling the time her mother had forced her to go to a junior high dance escorted by her cousin. Kristin made sure everyone knew. Kate had been mortified. Always, Kate longed to be her sister, willing to do anything to be like Kristin. And she did.

The same old shame rifled through Kate again. Why had she sinned? She had disobeyed God's will and her parents' trust. In her heart, Kate believed that Kristin had given herself to boyfriends. Kristin had been streetwise. Kate had been naive. All she had wanted was to be popular.

She closed her eyes and pushed the endless miseries into her Pandora's box. A deep sigh shuddered through her, and she looked at her wristwatch. Almost time for her next appointment. *Amber.* Her heart knotted as the child's image rose in her mind.

Kate stood and pulled Amber's stuffed dog from her bottom desk drawer. Placing it on her desk, she stretched her arms above her head. Sunlight spilled through the French pane window and etched her desktop with dark-edged boxes of sunshine. If she had to be in a box, let it be one filled with light.

As she stared at the pattern, a sound caused her to turn. Amber stood in her doorway, her face pale and drawn, her cheeks blotched with red.

"Don't you feel well?" Kate asked.

The child wandered in, rubbing her glazed eyes. "I'm not sick."

Kate heard her falsehood but didn't press the truth.

The girl headed for the familiar chair and slid to the seat. "I'm tired."

"I see. Why do you think you're tired?"

Amber shrugged, and Kate reached out and pulled the stuffed animal off her desk.

"Do you want to hold Sparky?"

The child nodded and took the stuffed animal in her lap. As she played with the floppy ears, Kate probed her for problems, asked about her dreams and allowed long pauses of silence to suspend on the air.

Realizing she was getting nowhere and worried about Amber's health, Kate rose and rested her hand on the child's shoulder. She inspected the girl's arms for spots, sensing that she might be coming down with chicken pox like the others had done. She saw nothing.

"Can I feel your forehead, Amber? You might have a fever," Kate asked.

She nodded, and Kate lay her palm across the child's brow and felt the heat she suspected.

"I think you have a little fever, sweetie," Kate said, stepping back and crouching in front of the girl.

Amber lifted her thoughtful eyes, her fingers still fiddling with Sparky's ears. "I remember something."

Kate's heart lurched. "About your dreams?"

A distant look washed over Amber's face. "No, not my dreams."

"No?" Kate said, holding her breath. "Then what?"

"I remembered I had a dog like Sparky once when I was a baby. He had long ears like this puppy."

"Are you sure?"

Her head nodded, convincingly. "I remember I cried."

"Did something happen to Sparky?" Kate's heart leaped, thinking if that event came to Amber's mind, maybe she would remember more.

"He ran away...." She paused, her eyes lifting to the ceiling, then back again. "Maybe, he died."

"Either one would make me sad, Amber." Kate recalled how quickly Amber had named the stuffed toy. "Sparky" had flown out of the child's mouth. Could this be the beginning of her recollection?

Kate waited, but Amber didn't continue. "Is that all you remember?"

"I'm too tired." Amber leaned her flushed cheek against her shoulder.

Kate longed to take the child in her arms and hold her until every hurt was gone. But she knew better than to be too affectionate with the child. The Haven had rules. And it was best for Amber.

Kate rose and stepped backward. "Would you like to go to your room, Amber...or—" *Scott.* "Let's take a walk to the clinic. You can meet my friend. He's a doctor who'll be working here a few weeks. And he's very nice. What do you say?"

Amber lifted her glassy eyes and nodded.

Gesturing toward the door, Kate took a step forward, her heart riding on the waves of expectation. Amber could be in no better hands than Scott's. The image sifted through her and rolled into her consciousness. Kate's own problems assailed her like the plague. In whose hands would she be healed?

Chapter Seven

Scott rubbed the nape of his neck, then bent over the desk, filling in the medical chart of his third youngster that day diagnosed with chicken pox. If the housemothers didn't confine those children to an area, the Haven would have an epidemic on their hands.

Putting his clasped fingers behind his head, Scott leaned back in his chair and let his thoughts drift to earlier that morning. Kate's look of surprise amused him. But he wasn't positive that she had been pleased. Kate had a way of covering her true feelings, like a judge attempting to be fair and impartial.

When Scott tilted forward, he caught a glimpse of a small blond child beyond the doorway. When she entered the clinic, Scott was surprised to see Kate follow. Her expression was serious, and his attention returned to the child.

"Dr. Ryan, this is Amber," Kate said, maintaining a professional relationship.

"Hi, Amber," Scott said, observing the telltale flushed cheeks and glazed eyes. He could make this diagnosis in a heartbeat.

Kate continued, "I'm thinking she might—"

"Have chicken pox," Scott said. "If so, she's the fourth this morning."

"That's what I was afraid of," Kate said, biting her lip.

Amber was a pretty child. Her hair, lighter than Kate's, curled in a blond halo around her delicate features. She looked up at him with fearful, glassy eyes—vulnerable and fragile. Now, he understood why Kate seemed so drawn to the girl.

"Should I leave?" Kate asked.

"No, I need someone in the room." He grinned at her over his shoulder. "So you're it."

With Amber's focus riveted to her, Kate moved to a chair and sat.

Scott bent down and touched the child's mottled cheeks. "You're not feeling well, Amber?"

She took a faltering step backward and shook her head.

Scott straightened. "I need you up here," he said, patting the vinyl-covered table. "How about if I give you a boost."

Amber moved backward against Kate's knees, fear hovering in her eyes.

"It's okay, sweetie," Kate said. "Remember. I told you the doctor's a friend of mine. He wants to see if you're getting chicken pox like some of the other kids."

Taking a cautious stride toward her, Scott extended his

hand, and finally, she approached him and allowed Scott to lift her to the table.

He pulled the thermometer from a wall bracket and placed it in her mouth, then examined her neck and face. "Might be an early case? I don't see any polka dots." He winked at the girl.

Amber gave him a shy grin.

The thermometer gave a soft beep, and Scott removed it. "Hmm...102.8 Fahrenheit," he said aloud, for Kate's benefit. He leveled his eyes to Amber's. "No wonder you aren't feeling well, young lady."

"That's bad," Kate said.

He turned toward her. "For adults, but children's temps will often go higher." He pivoted back to Amber.

"Let's pull your T-shirt off, so I can check to see if you're turning into a spotted giraffe."

Giggling at his comment, Amber lifted her arms while Scott tugged off her pink shirt. Though a few faint rashes appeared on her skin, Scott's eyes were drawn to the withered skin below the left shoulder. An old burn scar.

He caught Kate's attention, flagging her to the table. She rose and joined him, staring at the puckered skin marring the soft pink flesh of the child's back.

Though startled at first, Kate's face furrowed with concern, but Scott shook his head, discouraging her from making comment.

The tender look in her eyes tugged at his heart. Kate cared more than she should for the child...as she probably did for every child who came to her office. She was a gentle, warm woman and would make a good mother, he was sure.

Amber held her hands folded tightly in her lap, her slender back rigid.

Scott grasped her shirt from the tabletop. "Well, missy, I'd say you're about ready to turn into a spotted young lady."

"I am," Amber said. "Do I have chicken pox?"

"You sure do. I'm afraid you'll have to take it easy for a few days." He slipped the pink top over her head, and she tugged it down to her waist.

Scott hoisted her off the table and leaned his hip against the edge. "Amber, do you know how you got the scar on your back?"

Her soft brown eyes widened. She shook her head.

"Do you know what kind of scar it is?"

She pressed her lips together and shrugged before murmuring her response. "No."

But Scott wondered if she did. No sense forcing her at this point, but he was anxious to talk it over with Kate.

"You need to get to bed, little lady. I'll talk to..." He peered at Kate for the name of the housemother.

"Denise," Kate said.

Scott nodded. "I'll talk to Denise, Amber, and tell her how to take care of you. Okay?"

Amber remained silence.

With his thoughts whirring, Scott pressed Kate's shoulder. "It's nearly lunch. I'll take Amber back, and I'll meet you in the cafeteria."

With her attention focused on Amber, Kate only nodded.

* * *

"I have to talk to Amber's grandmother," Kate said. "Especially now that we saw the scar." Her chest ached from seeing the wound on Amber's delicate skin.

Scott took a swig of cola to help wash down the sandwich and responded. "Kate, don't be foolish and rush into anything. When I get back to the clinic, I'll review her files."

"I've already looked through her files. I didn't see anything about a scar. It's a burn scar, right?"

He nodded. "First degree."

"What would cause a burn like that?" Kate asked.

"I'm not sure. Children are known for pulling scalding hot pans over on themselves. If it was something thick, like chili maybe, that could cause a serious burn. Or playing with matches. Some of them start their bedclothes on fire."

"Then, the grandmother will know. I'm going to the hospital to see her." She stirred the noodles in her chicken soup, but instead of eating, she dropped the spoon. "Look, the Haven investigates situations all the time when the case calls for it. So I'll cut all the red tape and do it myself."

"What happens if someone finds out?" Scott asked. "Can you get yourself in hot water?"

"No." She spit the word out, then thought better and shrugged. "Well...I shouldn't. Amber's suffered from nightmares since she came here. I'm not going to sit back and let an opportunity go by because I'm afraid of stepping on someone's toes. I'll go to the hospital."

Scott set the tuna salad on the plate and caught her hand in his. "Kate, I know the child means a lot to you. She's a cute little thing, and I can understand how you've gotten caught up in—"

"You'll never understand, Scott. You're not a mother." She bit back the words, but it was too late.

He pinned her with his look. "And neither are you."

She faltered for a response. "But I could be." A long ragged breath heaved from her chest.

"That's true." He squeezed her fingers, then placed his free palm over her hand. "I'm not fighting you, Kate. Don't get on the defensive with me. I'm saying that I can see why this child has captured your heart. She's so like you in many ways. Even your coloring is similar. Your eyes and hair."

Kate shook her head, wanting to halt his line of thinking. Amber might resemble her, but she wasn't Kate's child. Kate's daughter was eighteen now and lived with two loving parents somewhere in the world that Kate didn't know. The ache pressed against her heart.

Scott caught her fingers in his. "Kate, what did I say? I upset you so often without knowing why. Please, tell me. Let me into that mind of yours. You're so important to me, yet you push me away."

"Please don't. It's nothing. I know Amber means too much to me. I suppose I see the same fear in her eyes that I felt as a child. I relate to her. Don't ask why."

He drew his hand away and fell back against the chair. "I'd like to help you. I really would."

Frustration and fear slithered up Kate's back, and she narrowed her eyes. "I asked for your help once, Scott. You said no. I won't ask again."

A look of bewilderment skittered across his face, then vanished. "You mean the grandmother's records?" His voice lifted. "I haven't had a chance to tell you. I've heard rumors that my next service will be in medical. That means I'll be near the stroke unit."

His enthusiasm riled her. Why hadn't he been as eager when she first asked? Why was he so... Kate slammed the lid on her thoughts. She wasn't angry at Scott. She was angry at herself. He didn't realize the memories he dredged up. How could she blame him?

She leaned back, seeking his face, but he looked down, his index finger drawing circles on the tabletop.

"I'm sorry, Scott. You touched a tender spot. I know I've gone overboard with Amber. I'll hurt her with too much affection, and I'll feel lost when she goes back to her grandma."

"That's what I meant, Kate. You have a mother's heart. You're tender, caring and devoted. I don't know how you deal with all that compassion."

Kate drew her hands together on the table and knotted her fingers. "Did you go to Sunday school, Scott?"

"Sure."

"Me, too. And one of the most beautiful pictures that hung in our Sunday school hall was the one of Jesus gathering the little children in his arms. Have you ever seen that one?" The image rose in her thoughts. Jesus' gentle face, his arms outstretched to children of every color, every nation, every child whether good or bad.

"Every kid's seen that one, I suppose," he said. "So why don't I have the same depth of compassion that you do, Kate? I've seen the picture."

She tightened the grip on her fingers like a death knot. "That's because you had parents who doted on you. Phyllis has told me about your folks. I've met them a few times. They're warm, caring people. And whether you were adopted or not, I'm sure they loved you with all their hearts."

"You guessed that right," he said, displaying his wily dimples. "So what about—"

"My parents aren't like yours. I needed Jesus' wide open arms for comfort and security. I knew Jesus loved me no matter what." Kate struggled to rein the emotions that boiled in her throat and behind her eyes.

"Not all parents are like that, Scott." She'd said far more than she wanted to say, and she prayed he wouldn't pry.

He must have read her thoughts, because he drew both of her hands between his and pressed them against his lips without a word.

Kate closed her eyes, afraid that it was only a dream. Afraid to let herself go and relish in his touch. Afraid that if he knew everything he would turn his back and walk away.

Passing through the revolving door, Kate harnessed her courage, lifted her chin, and headed straight for the information desk.

"May I help you?" the volunteer asked.

"Stroke unit. Mrs. Yates."

The woman turned to a computer screen, hit the keys, then nodded. "Annabel Yates?"

"Yes." Kate said, not sure what her first name was.

"Room 614."

Kate thanked her and aimed for the first bank of elevators. When she exited the conveyance, she followed the direction of the sixth floor signs, passed the nursing station, and followed the hallway until she reached the grandmother's doorway.

The room held two beds, and the number indicated that Mrs. Yates was in the one near the window. Passing quietly through so as not to disturb the sleeping patient, Kate rounded the curtain and stood back, seeing an aging face distorted by a stroke.

The older woman's eyes were closed, and Kate peered at the tubing connected to her left arm and the machine monitoring her vital signs. The woman's mouth hung open, and an oxygen tube rested beneath her nose. Her chest rose and fell in ragged breaths.

Kate stepped closer, hoping the woman would sense her presence and open her eyes, but she didn't. A rattled snore rasped from her drooping mouth. Rounding the foot of the bed, Kate slid quietly into a chair and waited.

With her face aged and twisted, the grandmother didn't resemble Amber. Kate guessed her to be sixty—not old, but aged by circumstances. Her wispy salt-and-pepper hair lay matted against the pillow. No cards or flowers sat on the nightstand or windowsill, nothing to give her an identity, nothing to show someone cared.

Restless, the woman moaned and shifted, and the muslin sheet slid from her right arm. Seeing her uncovered, Kate's heart rose to her throat and her breathing shallowed. She gaped at the woman's limb, distorted by a puckered scar, tight shiny red skin amid wrinkled flesh.

Kate rose, moved to the bedside, and scanned the woman's forearm downward to her hand. Kate's stomach knotted with the sight of her gnarled fingers, twisted by some horrible accident—a scorching heat that had scarred her as it had Amber.

What had happened? Kate longed to rouse the woman awake so they could talk. But logic rose and aborted her wild scheme. Kate backed up and lowered herself to the chair. She struggled with her thoughts as time dragged, and when she gave up and rose to leave, a nurse pulled back the curtain.

"Oh, you scared me," the nurse said, staggering backward. "I had no idea Mrs. Yates had company." She moved on quiet shoes to the IV pole and checked the bags. "She's never had company before. Are you a relative?"

"No, I'm, uh, a...I'm caring for her granddaughter," Kate said. "How is she?"

The nurse shook her head. "Not good. She sleeps most of the time. Wakes only for a moment."

"What's her prognosis?" Kate held her breath waiting for the answer.

The nurse shrugged. "You'd need to talk to the doctor."

The disappointment rattled through Kate. Her lone hope drifted out of reach. "And, I won't be able to talk with her?" The answer was obvious.

"She may hear you, but I doubt if she'll be able to answer."

"I see. Then, I suppose..." Kate edged closer to the bed. "I was wondering about this burn. Do you know how it happened?"

The nurse stepped around the bed, lifted Mrs. Yates's arm, and studied the scar. "A burn. I have no idea." She drew the blanket over the woman's arm and shoulder and tucked it beneath her, then looked at Kate. "I'm sorry."

"That's okay, I just wondered," Kate said, backing toward the exit. With longing, she gazed at the elderly woman, wanting so badly to know what happened. Anything to free Amber from her dreams.

Kate lingered in the hallway outside the room, wishing some grand plan would come to her. While standing there, she noticed the placard beside the doorway with Dr. Khodijian written in black marker. Kate tucked the information away for the future. She wished he would have stopped by. At least, he might have some specifics. Finally, she lifted her tense shoulders and stretched them back before heading toward the elevators.

The situation poked at Kate's concern and heightened her curiosity. Now, she had nowhere else to turn except Scott. She'd been determined not to ask for his help again. Yet, no matter what she did, fate brought them together. A shiver coursed through her. Or was it fate?

Chapter Eight

Scott stopped at the red traffic light and organized his thoughts for the hundredth time. He'd spent a restless night thinking about Kate, and this evening, he was determined to get things out in the open.

From the day he met her, she'd brightened his drab life—black-and-white textbooks, white doctor's coat and traditional black bag. Now, Kate colored his world with the pink flush of her cheeks, the blond shoulder-length hair that glinted in the sun, the green flecks in her eyes and the soft coral of her lips.

He sounded lovesick, and maybe he was. A few years earlier, when he'd all but dismissed time for romance, he'd met Lana. She was bright, bubbly and worldly. Raised as a Christian, he'd never known Lana's wilder lifestyle. But he'd heard college days offered opportunities to spread his wings, and he did.

Taking his nose from the books, he'd puffed on a cigarette and tried liquor, then tossed those experiences aside. That wasn't for him. But Lana was soft, tempting, and willing. He'd longed to accept her offer and make love to her. But he couldn't. Not only his parents' voice rose in his head, but God's Word. And when Lana betrayed him—hurt him so deeply—he'd all but given up on women again. Until Kate.

And now that he'd loosened the fetters that bound his emotions, Kate had pulled away. But he wasn't a fool. Though she denied it, part of her cared about him. He was positive. But something inside her—fear or uncertainty—held her back. Tonight he wanted to offer her a solution to their problem.

Pulling into Kate's driveway, he turned off the ignition and sat without moving. On the spring day he first came to Kate's house, the sunshine filled the air with the scent of lilacs as he sat with Kate on the glider in the backyard.

Today, browned leaves had settled into dried, papery piles along the fences and on the ground. The autumn breeze smelled earthy—a blend of moist soil and decomposing foliage. Much had changed since that first day. Including himself.

Scott opened the car door and headed toward the house. Though only six o'clock, the sun had already lowered on the horizon, sending streaks of purple and gold against the graying clouds. He hoped Phyllis was out for the evening so he and Kate could talk privately. Maybe then, he could lift the weight from his chest.

Before he knocked, Kate opened the door. Though she smiled, he saw the hesitant look in her eyes.

"Why were you sitting in the car?" she asked.

"Daydreaming," he said, pushing the door closed. "I was thinking about the first time I came here. It was spring. Hard to believe, it's already the middle of October."

She looked at him curiously. "Time flies,"

An appetizing aroma drifted from the kitchen.

"What smells so good?" Scott asked.

"Beef stroganoff. Do you like it?"

"I'm sure I will. But I invited you to dinner."

"I felt like cooking."

Scott shrugged and quickly tucked his concerns away until later. No sense in messing up the meal if things didn't go well. His chest tightened with the possibility.

Kate beckoned him into the kitchen, speaking over her shoulder. "Phyllis is out with Darren, again. I think it's getting serious." She flashed him a smile.

"Sounds like it," he said, wondering if Phyllis would soon be walking down the church aisle. She and Darren had known each other a long time, and their romance had escalated in the past couple of months.

A fantasy fluttered through his thoughts. *Kate.* Would things smooth out for them? He'd prayed that the Lord would direct him, and he believed tonight he was following God's will.

Still, Scott wondered. In college he'd stepped beyond his books and medicine and was devastated by Lana's betrayal. Would Kate be any different? He prayed she was. If not, he prayed he would realize it before he was hurt again.

Scott leaned against the kitchen doorjamb, noticing the table had been set already. Kate motioned to a chair. When he sat, Kate placed a salad and a platter of rich, creamy stroganoff on noodles in front of him. Knowing that Kate had cooked for him gave him a comfortable, optimistic feeling. He hoped his intuition wasn't wrong.

After Kate asked the blessing, he dug into the meal. They ate in silence for a few moments, then Kate laid down her fork. "I went to the hospital today."

The words took a moment to settle into Scott's brain. "To see Amber's grandmother?"

She nodded. "Her arm and hand have burn scars just like Amber's."

Burns? The fact piqued his curiosity. "Did you talk? What did she say?"

"She's bad, Scott. She slept the whole time I was there. The nurse said she doesn't talk anyway."

"I was afraid of that," he said, watching the disappointment grow on her face.

"I don't know what to do, now," she said.

His spirits lifted, knowing he could help her. "Kate, it's not a rumor anymore. I know when I finish at the Haven, I'll be up on medical. I'll see what I can find out then."

"Her doctor's name is Khodijian. Do you know him?"

"Not yet, but I will. Give me a few weeks, and I'll see what I can do."

"I know you're trying to be helpful. But every day that passes without finding a way to help Amber kills me."

"A couple more weeks, Kate. That's all."

She didn't respond. Finally she picked up her fork and continued eating. Her sadness dampened Scott's appetite, and he nibbled the rest of his meal, hoping she didn't notice.

When they were finished and the dishes cleared away, Scott suggested they talk.

"About what?" Kate asked.

"Let's grab a soda and sit outside. In a couple of weeks, it'll be too cold."

"It's already cool."

"Grab a jacket," Scott suggested, his hand on the doorknob.

Kate hesitated, then shrugged and hurried away. She returned with a lightweight jacket.

As they walked across the grass, Scott wanted to hold her hand or wrap his arm around her, but she seemed so distracted again he thought better of it.

They settled on the swing and he rested his arm across the back of the seat, as close as he could get to having her in his arms.

"Look at the sunset," Kate said. "Like an artist's palette."

It was beautiful. The purple and gold streaks he'd seen earlier had run together in shades of red, orange and lilac. "Pretty," Scott agreed.

"So, what do you want to talk about?" She turned to face him. "I hope you're not going to lecture me about Amber's grandmother."

"No lectures," he said, catching her sweeping hand in his and holding it against his knee.

She didn't pull away.

"Then about what?" she asked.

He let her question lay unanswered while he calmed his galloping heart. Finally, he responded. "About us."

Her hand beneath his fingers tensed, and bewilderment settled on her face. "I don't understand."

"Let me explain. From the day I met you, I felt you were special. You made me feel good and look at things differently. You didn't squawk when you went with me to look for apartments, and later you offered to let me stay here longer."

"I'd do that for any friend."

"But you weren't my friend, Kate. You barely knew me then. I was just Phyllis's brother. But just like you are with all people, you opened your arms and let me come in...that is until something happened."

"What happened?" A deep scowl creased her forehead.

"I don't know."

She tilted her head, staring with confusion into his face.

"That's what I want to talk about," Scott said.

Kate pulled her hand away. "I don't understand what you're saying." She pushed a lock of hair behind her ear.

"I think you do, Kate. But if you really don't, then I'll try to explain."

She lowered her head, and he suspected she did know what he meant.

"I like you a lot, Kate. You've added so much to my life. For a while, we laughed and had good times together. Then things changed. Maybe, since I moved in with Cass. You grew distant."

He reached over and titled her chin, directing her eyes to his. "You must realize it. Sometimes it's as if a fear comes over you and you pull away...not physically, but mentally or emotionally."

She turned away and shook her head. "I guess I don't want to get too involved with anyone, Scott."

"Okay. But why?"

"I don't know. I'm thirty-four and have a life and career." She shrugged. "I suppose I'm set in my ways."

"Set in your ways? You're young, Kate. I'm thirty-two and I'm willing to go off the deep end and do something different once in a while."

"Maybe that's the problem. I'm older than you. I'm two—"

A deep laugh burst from his chest. "Don't tell me that you think two years makes a difference?"

"It's not funny. Two years can make a big difference. Ten minutes can make a difference."

"What..." *Ten minutes?* He'd laugh, but the situation wasn't funny. He caught her face in his hands. "Kate, can we back up? Let's go back to when we first met. I like you...a lot. But I'm not heading anywhere that you aren't ready to go." The words caught in his chest. "Do you understand?"

"I don't know, Scott. I like you, too. I spend too much time at my job and not a lot on myself. You're special, too...and maybe I'm afraid of that. I don't want to be hurt." She tugged her fingers through her hair.

Scott drew her to his chest. "Kate, I won't hurt you. I promise." He edged her back, looking into her misted eyes. "How could I hurt you? I want to be your friend. Your closest friend."

Tears rimmed her eyes, and Scott's heart twisted with the emotion he saw in her face.

"You're too good for me, Scott," she said.

"I'm what? No one is too good for you, Kate. No one. Look at you. You give your life for everyone, but yourself. I see the love you have for Amber. You're doing everything you can to help that little girl. You're so full of compassion and love for everyone." He hesitated, wondering how far he could go. "And you're a beautiful woman...inside and out."

Tears rolled down her cheeks, and without hesitation, Scott leaned down and kissed the moisture that ran in trails down her face. He pressed his lips to her cheek and kissed her eyes, then touched his lips to her mouth, tasting the salty droplets.

Her body trembled against him, and Scott longed to know what secret lay hidden so deeply in her heart that she couldn't release it—speak it so it would fly away on the evening breeze.

Resting his head against her soft hair, he breathed in the fruity scent of her shampoo. She felt small and fragile in his arms. And he didn't speak, letting the emotion wash away with the tender moment.

"I'm sorry," Kate whispered against his chest. "I guess I'm feeling sorry for myself."

"You shouldn't. You should feel sorry for me because I need a friend...and you're holding back." He lightened his tone, hoping she'd relax and find the humor in his words.

She tilted her head back and looked at him. "I need a friend, too."

"Then," Scott said, his voice lilting with mimicry, "won't you be my friend?"

"I will," she said, a grin pulling at her lips. "How can I say no to that?"

Finally, Scott did what he'd wanted to do all evening. He wrapped his arm around her shoulders and nestled her to his side. When Kate laid her head against his arm, the weight that had pressed against his chest lifted and spiraled toward heaven. He looked up at the darkened sky and followed the north star to the big dipper. His heart felt as full, and he smiled, thinking his cup runneth over.

Kate stood back, resting on the leaf rake, and watched Scott. HELP couldn't have had a nicer Saturday to do the seniors' lawns, and she couldn't have been happier when Scott said he had Saturday free.

The talk they'd had a week earlier sat haphazardly in her thoughts. She struggled continually with her deep fears, pushing them away, so she could be Scott's friend. That had been their deal. Friendship. Nothing more, nothing less. Still her own heart sensed more than friendship.

The talk and the actions that night didn't mesh. He talked friends, yet she could not forget his tenderness. His gentle kisses that washed away her tears. And she thanked God he didn't ask her why she cried. Instead, he offered her his shoulder. And he promised he would never hurt her. She could ask for no more.

Turning from her thoughts, Kate grinned, watching Scott tug at the rake. Since they'd arrived at the senior's home, Mr. Brooks had latched on to him, and now as Scott tried to rake, the elderly gentleman bent his ear, following him along with sage words and nostalgic tales.

The man's loneliness shivered through Kate's mind. So often, she had felt loneliness creep up her back and tie her in knots of solitude. But since their talk, Scott's warm smile loosened the tangles.

Lifting the rake, Kate dragged the leaves through the grass to the large pile along the street in front of the house. When she turned, Scott's despondent gaze told her he needed help with Mr. Brooks. Hiding her smile, she ambled across the grass. "How are you doing?" she asked, giving the older man a smile.

"He's doin' pretty good, missy," Mr. Brooks answered in Scott's stead. "I just told him you'd be a pretty good catch."

"You did?" Kate's curiosity awakened. "And what did he say?" She caught Scott's wry grin as he sidled away.

"He said you were too slippery to get caught. Is that right?" He grinned at her with bare gums.

"He's probably right," she said, unable to draw her eyes from his toothless smile.

The man edged toward Kate as Scott made his escape.

"He's a good-lookin' fella," Mr. Brooks said. "And a strong one, too. I wouldn't wait too long, missy. There's a lot of fish in the sea, but not too many like that young fella."

She laughed, but didn't respond. Instead, she clutched the rake and pulled away the leaves caught on the fence.

Finally Mr. Brooks wandered across the grass, but his words stayed with Kate. Scott was everything the man had said. What would she do if one day he introduced her to a lovely young nurse or an attractive woman that he'd met somewhere? Could she bear it? She yanked the rake through the leaves while the possibility tugged at her heart.

Chapter Nine

Scott marveled at the crowd filling the church's fellowship hall. The area was decorated with a harvest motif of pumpkins, bushels of apples, and bunches of cornstalks. The event was Pastor Ray's thank you to the HELP group for their efforts throughout the summer.

Scott grinned, recognizing the pastor's keen public relations know-how. Besides the church's volunteers, he'd also invited the senior citizens of the community. Scanning the hall's white-haired guests, Scott eyed the talkative Mr. Brooks and dodged him, fearing he'd be cornered for the night. But guilt marched into his conscience, and Scott knew he'd relent before the night was over. Something about the older man pulled Scott's compassion out of hiding.

The church's youth had been rallied to work at the celebration. Dressed like farmers in jeans, plaid shirts, and straw hats, the teen's chatter and good cheer raised the noise level. Looking for Kate, Scott finally caught sight of her beside a screen emblazoned with the sign, Go Fishing. Kate stood near the front of the line with a couple of elderly ladies that Scott recognized from the last Saturday of leaf raking.

Passing groups playing comical, devised games like Pin the Tail on the Plow Horse and Drop the Carrot in the Mason Jar, Scott ambled to Kate's side. "Good evening, ladies," he said, smiling at the three women.

"Want to fish?" Kate asked, gesturing to the six-foot screen decorated with colorful paper fish. "We'll give you cuts."

The ladies nodded, but he declined and grinned as Kate cast the bamboo pole, looping her line over the tall barricade. In a moment, her pole bent with a tug and she pulled in her catch. On the end of her hook was a cellophane bag of Gummi Worms. She laughed when she latched onto her prize.

"Not quite what you expected," Scott said, drawing her away from the game.

Kate opened the package and dangled a yellow-and-orange candy worm above his nose. He tilted backward and snapped at it until she let go.

A manly chuckle met Scott's ears, and he turned to face the young clergyman. The worm hung from between Scott's teeth.

Pastor Ray clasped a hand on Kate's shoulder. "If you caught this fishing," he said, gesturing to Scott, "you caught yourself a big one. Almost a six-footer, I'd guess."

Kate laughed and Scott sucked the sticky candy into his mouth with an embarrassed grin.

The pastor's face grew serious. "I'm glad I found the two

of you together," he said. "I heard from one of the church elders that Mrs. Finkell is doing okay, thanks to you." He looked at Scott. "She was diagnosed with diabetes as you suspected. A few more months without treatment could have been deadly."

"I'm so glad she's okay," Kate replied. "Scott bugged me about her for a couple of weeks before I called you."

The pastor extended his hand to Scott. "Thanks. Having a doctor on our HELP team is a godsend. Never hesitate when you're concerned. All I do is call one of the agencies and someone drops by to check things out. You saved the woman's life."

He patted Scott on the back and moved off to another group.

"I'm sorry I didn't listen to you," Kate said.

"When did you ever listen to me?" Scott countered and gave her a wink. Yet the blood coursed through his veins, thinking of saving a life. What could be more important than his career?

"I listen," Kate said. "But I'll listen more carefully next time. I promise." She gave him an innocent smile, then gestured toward the food counter. "Hungry?"

He eyed the chafing dish of steamed hot dogs, the boxes of doughnuts, and jugs of cider. "Let's wait awhile. Do you mind?" His stomach egged him to consider a steak and baked potato.

"Okay, but keep in mind I'm ready any time." She took his arm and urged him across the floor to where a few courageous souls were bobbing for apples.

"Let's take a turn," she said, pulling him toward the group gathered around the large metal tub.

"No way. But I'll be your cheerleader," Scott said.

Kate rolled her eyes and edged forward, joining the group of young and old around the container and laughing at the dripping teenager with a bright-red apple clutched in his teeth.

Scott lagged back, not wanting to douse himself. Concentrating on Kate, he jumped when a hand clamped over his shoulder. He pivoted and faced a toothed Mr. Brooks.

"Howdy there, young fella," the man said. "Looks like that pretty girl of yours is havin' fun."

Scott nodded, keeping the conversation to a minimum.

"You know, when I look at young couples like you and her, I wonder where my head was so many years back."

Couple? Scott looked at Kate. That's not exactly what they were...but then what were they? Dropping his question and curious about Brooks's statement, Scott focused on the man. "What do you mean?"

"Back when I was your age, I thought my work was more important than everything else—family, friends, wife, children."

"What did you do back then?"

"Engineering. I worked for the auto industry. Cars. Tanks during the war. Thought seein' those vehicles come off the line and knowin' I played a part made me feel good," the older man said. "I figured my life was full. Didn't need a doggone thing. But I was dead wrong."

Scott's spine stiffened. Maybe engineering wasn't a

worthy career, but being a physician was. If Scott had nothing else in life, he'd know that he'd helped families live healthier, happier existences.

"What do you do for a livin'?" Brooks asked.

"A physician. I'm a resident at County General."

"Now that's a career you can be proud of. But that's not all there is. I hope you know that."

"I'll begin my own practice...eventually," Scott added, defensiveness tightening his shoulders.

"Your own practice? Now that's good." The older man pulled the spectacles from his nose and drew out a handkerchief from his back pocket. As he cleaned the lenses, he pointed an elbow toward the group gathered around the apple bobbers. "Now, there's something worth hanging on to."

Scott spotted a gray-haired gentleman rising from the floor, water dripping from his face and an apple in his teeth. Then Kate knelt down and gathered her hair in her left hand, smiling at the cheering crowd around her.

"Her," Brooks said. "That's what's important. Not jobs, not money, not a mansion or a fancy car. A lovely young woman that commits to you." He turned and locked his eyes to Scott's. "Now, that's important. One that gives you a family, son."

A knot twisted in Scott's gut. "You have no family?"

"Never did. Like I said, I thought the sun rose and fell on my work. I fooled around a little, I hate to admit, but I didn't have time for marriage and children. And you know what I got to show for it?"

Scott's pulse skipped, watching that same sadness that tugged at his heart rise again in the elderly man's eyes. "I—I'm not sure, sir."

"Nothin'. Nothin' but loneliness. None of those things mean a tiddly wink to a loving family." He held his arms out shoulders height. "And look at me now. Too old for that. I have no children to leave all that money I invested. I have no wife to cuddle and share my memories on those long quiet nights. I have nothin', son."

A lump rose in Scott's throat as he watched the older man's eyes mist. "You have a point. When you're young it's easy to forget the later years." But Brooks's words cut through his blindness, like a sharp knife.

"Young people don't usually think that far. Oh, sure, they put a few bucks in some financial planner's hands. They think ahead that much. But not about things that count. Now, you on the other hand, you've got that lovely young lady there."

"Kate's a great friend," Scott said, not sure what else to say.

"I've seen her working with this church for the past few years, and you know what I see?" He didn't pause for an answer. "I see an honest, kind and beautiful woman."

He nudged Scott's ribs. "And these old eyes can see she loves you. If you don't grab her while the gettin's good, someone else will."

Honest, kind and beautiful. Yes, Kate had all those great attributes, but Scott lingered on only one phrase. *She loves you.* Was Brooks right? Scott sensed Kate cared for him. But love? Love so evident Brooks could see it?

Scott turned and watched Kate dry her dripping face with a terry towel. Her laughter drifted to his ears, and his body warmed at the sound. She looked at him, her smile opening like a dewy morning glory, her face radiating like the sun. Scott's heart tripped and tumbled.

Kate dropped the towel into a container and walked toward him with a wave.

"Here she comes," Brooks said, motioning back.

Kate put the apple between her lips, near enough for Scott to hear the snap of the skin and to see a fine mist of juice spray into the air. "Time to feed me," she said with a playful whimper, then chewed and swallowed the bite.

Brooks gave her a friendly wink and wrapped his arm around Kate's shoulder. "I was telling this young man that if he didn't take good care of you, someone else will. Makes me sorry I'm so old."

Kate slipped from his arm with an amiable pat on his shoulder. "I don't need to be taken care of, Mr. Brooks. I think it's you men who need looking after." She flashed a teasing grin.

Scott watched Brooks's smile sag. "You're more truthful than you know, young lady." He squeezed her arm and walked away.

Kate hesitated, then caught Scott's hand. "What was that all about?"

"Nothing," Scott said, knowing it was everything.

Chapter Ten

Kate stared at Amber's drawing lying on her office desk. Before today, she'd made no progress with the child, and despite Scott's offer to help when he moved to the medical unit, he had yet to be reassigned. She'd learned nothing new. Kate felt as if she were walking backward.

She'd used the stuffed animals, building blocks and telling stories, but Amber recalled nothing of her past—only a dog named Sparky. Today, out of frustration, Kate recalled something Scott had suggested months earlier about association. While searching through a bottom desk drawer, she stumbled across a box of colored markers and wondered what a drawing might accomplish.

When Amber arrived for her appointment, they had sat together drawing people, animals, landscapes. Not until Kate began drawing her house did things change.

Amber leaned nearer, resting her elbow beside Kate's and watched intently. After a few moments, she picked up a black marker and drew a building of her own. But instead of drawing a small bungalow, Amber's drawing was a tall rectangle, more like an apartment or office building. Then, she outlined a window in the lower portion, filling it in with black. The top square she colored in a bright red that spilled beyond her black marker boundaries.

Kate speculated its meaning: day and night, light and dark, happy and sad. When she asked Amber why she'd used those colors, the child replied, "I want it that way." Yet, the look on the child's face sent a shiver down Kate's back.

After Amber left, Kate stared at the picture, putting the pieces together, and added a new conjecture: smoke and flames. Could it be? Had Amber and her grandmother lived together back then and survived an apartment fire? She closed her eyes and bit her lower lip, grasping at fragments of the puzzle.

"Something wrong?"

Kate's eyes flew open, hearing Scott's voice. "Thinking," she said, then turned the picture around to face him. "Amber drew this today. What do you make of it?"

He ambled into the room, a hand tucked in his trouser pocket, his lab coat unbuttoned. He stood back and eyed the picture from a yard away. "Well, I'd say the windows don't look very happy." He leaned over it, looking more closely. "She didn't stay in the lines up there," he said, pointing to the upper window. "She got carried away with the red marker."

He gave Kate a grin, but she didn't smile. Instead she surveyed the drawing.

Scott scowled. "What do you think?" he asked, looking from the drawing to Kate's face.

Explaining her earlier deliberation, she added her resent speculation. "What about smoke and fire?" She punched her finger against the red color in the drawing.

He snatched the picture from the desk, studying it more carefully. "Looks like an apartment or office complex, maybe. It could be fire. What did Amber say?"

Kate repeated Amber's comment, then shrugged. "I don't know, but I hope I can get more from her. Whatever happened, she was young, I'd guess."

Scott sank into the chair that Amber usually occupied. "We should know soon."

Kate tilted her head. "Why?"

"Good news," he said with a faded grin. "Good and not so good."

"Tell me." Noting the shifting emotion in his face, Kate's breathing shallowed. "Is something wrong?"

"Barlow's coming back next week. That means I'll be full-time again at County General...at least for now. But I've been reassigned to the medical unit. Sixth floor."

"Annabel Yates is on the sixth floor." She lifted her eyes to his.

"I know. That was the good part. The not so good is I won't be here with you."

Though she would miss his pop-in visits, Kate clung to his first statement. *The sixth floor.* Kate sank into the chair near him, knowing she'd allowed an intervening stretch of silence. "I'll miss you," she said.

But Scott reacted as if she'd said this as an afterthought.

He leaned forward, elbows on knees. "Next Thursday's Thanksgiving," he said.

He'd caught Kate off guard. She had anticipated a comment about her delayed response. The topic shift confounded her and she weighed the meaning. *Thanksgiving?* "Are you working?"

"No, I'm off, by some miracle. I'd like you to come to my folks' house for dinner."

Maybe it shouldn't have, but the invitation rattled her. Her first question was why? She'd met his parents when she stopped there with Phyllis, but this invitation wasn't from Phyllis. It was from Scott. The ramifications bothered her. Struggling to find a response, she faltered.

"You've already made plans," Scott said, his disappointment apparent.

"No, it's not that." She averted his scrutiny.

"Then, what is it?"

"I just wonder...well, holidays are personal times for families." She inched her gaze upward and shrugged. "I—I don't think I'd be comfortable."

"I can fix that. I'll have my folks adopt you."

His attempt at humor bounced off her like a cement block. *Adopt.* The word whacked her between the eyes and her protective shield rose between them. Accepting his invitation was too... She couldn't find the word. "Your folks will assume we're, well, serious, maybe."

His jaw sagged.

"I mean," she continued, "they'll think we have a commitment. I don't want to mislead them."

He rose and stood over her. "Kate, what's wrong? My folks will think you're my friend...and Phyllis's friend. Nothing more." With his thumb and finger, he tilted her chin upward. "And would their wondering about us be so terrible?"

Yes shot into her mind. Yes, because she could never allow herself to love Scott...and she wanted to so badly. "It's not true, that's all."

He stepped backward, his face pinched and dark. "I've invited you, Kate. I hope you'll come." He shrugged, then dropped his shoulders with a weighted sigh. "We can talk about it later."

He spun on his heel and, without looking back, stepped through the office doorway.

A blast of air shot from Kate like a punctured balloon. Why had she acted so ungrateful? Now, she'd spend Thanksgiving alone. And really, she enjoyed his family. They had always been kind. So why was she afraid?

She wrestled with her reasoning. If Phyllis had invited her, she'd have accepted without a thought. But Scott made it different. Why? Because he was a threat. A threat to her secret. Her shame. Her guilt.

What would he do if he knew about her baby? Turn his back and walk away? She was positive he would. Any decent man would...or end up throwing it in her face eventually. And even if he didn't turn his back, his parents would certainly think she was an unfit woman for their son.

Their son? Adopted son. But that made no difference. Scott might be an adopted child, but he was loved as much as their birth daughter, Phyllis. She'd heard that from Phyllis, and she'd seen it in action. How could a fallen woman fit into the life of a man as moral and perfect as Scott?

She rose, grasped Amber's drawing from the edge of the desk, and dragged herself around the corner of her desk chair. Her back felt tense and her shoulders ached. She slid into the seat and scanned her office, remembering a time when the room gave her a sense of purpose and a feeling of success.

Lately things had changed. The colors seemed drab, the pale walls like a prison, the furniture worn and marred...like she felt. Would she ever feel whole again?

Pulling her gaze from the room, Kate refocused on the picture. Her thoughts bounced from Amber's plight to her own. If she had no other plans for Thanksgiving, what logical reason could she give Scott if she refused? He'd probe and question until she'd want to scream. She had to accept. But she'd make it very clear that they were only friends. Now and always. Only friends.

Scott gazed across his parents' dining room table at Kate. The woman amazed him. Confused him. Discouraged him. She was a jigsaw puzzle. So many pieces looked the same and each time he tried to make a match, the piece didn't fit no matter which way he turned it.

Earlier, when he picked her up at the house, she was distracted. She smiled, but he witnessed the tension in her jaw and the tight clamp of her even white teeth. Her smile was fabricated, painted on like a clown's.

With each new struggle, he questioned what it was he saw in Kate. Beautiful, she was. But lots of women were attractive, some even more beautiful than Kate. No, it wasn't beauty, but the woman herself.

His attraction was her tenderness and sincerity. And most of all, her vulnerability. Maybe it was his doctor's sensitivity to people's pain or the need to heal, but she had tangled around his heart. Each time he saw fear or regret fill her eyes, the emotion knotted in his chest until he could barely breathe.

He'd prayed, talked to God often about what he could do to make things better. But Kate gave him so little to go on. Only a bad relationship with her sister...and her parents, too. But why? When she let herself go, Kate was delightful—fun, compassionate, intelligent and determined. He saw that trait in her desire to help Amber. Why wasn't she as determined to help herself?

And today, he had to let her down again. His news wasn't good, and he'd tossed it around in his head like a fresh-from-the-oven baked potato. Too hot to hang on to, yet not the right time to lay it on the table. She'd counted on him for so long, and he had nothing to give her.

"Potatoes, Scott."

He lifted his eyes and caught his mother's strange expression.

"I asked you to please pass the potatoes," she repeated.

"I'm sorry." He lifted the dish and moved it across the table, pushing away his thoughts and latching onto the conversation.

"Scott tells us your parents live out of state," his mother said to Kate.

Kate's face shifted to a fleeting look of discomfort, then back to her strained smile. "Yes, Florida. My sister's in New York."

"Is your sister single, too?" his mother asked.

Kate flinched with the question. "I believe she is...now."

"Oh?" His mother lifted her brow in question.

"She's recently divorced, I think."

"What a pity!" his mother responded.

Listening to the dialogue, Scott ached, watching Kate's distress. Her qualified answers filled him with curiosity. Was Kate's family that estranged to make her so uncertain? His mind whirred at topics to pull his mother away from her kindly inquisition.

"I've told you about all the work we do at Phyllis and Kate's church, haven't I?" Scott said, knowing they knew, but hoping his ploy worked.

"Sounds like a wonderful congregation," his father said. "Since Phyllis got involved, I've been dropping a bee in our pastor's ear. This community could use a group like that. Now what was it called?"

"HELP," Phyllis, Scott and Kate rang out together. Their chuckle took the edge off the growing tension.

Kate continued, "'Helping the Elderly Live Proudly' is what it means."

Sitting in his parents' dining room, Scott's awareness drifted from Kate to his parents' elegant decor. Kate fit in with the rich, polished mahogany table and china cabinet filled with heirlooms and antique platters that his mother collected. Like the room, Kate seemed like a rare curio, more delicate and fragile than many of the modern, liberated women with whom he worked.

He wasn't against being liberated, and he believed women were as capable and worthy as men, but somewhere along the line, too often "liberated" had lost sight of tradition and old-fashioned values that Scott admired. Kate still embodied those traits.

As Kate chatted on relating her experiences and tales about the HELP group, she grew more animated and less tense. Scott relaxed, too, hoping he could steer the conversation back to neutral ground if his mother headed off into unsafe territory again.

But Scott's own mind was swamped with questions. He'd tried to press Phyllis for information, but she either covered up well or didn't seem to notice Kate's occasional tense withdrawal. Or maybe it was only Scott who triggered her negative reaction. Would Kate ever trust him enough to share her deep wound? And if not, should he let the relationship fly away before he was hurt again?

Thinking back to his limited experience, he seemed to have bad luck with females. A bookworm in high school, he'd dated a little, but the girls seemed to be looking for someone more adventuresome. In college, he'd buried his nose in his career, except for Lana.

And now he'd found Kate, and he'd thought she'd be different. Being a Christian, he assumed they would think alike, share the same morals and values, and flow together like two mountain streams. Instead, they seemed more like the St. Mary's River in Michigan's upper peninsula, dropping twenty-one feet from Lake Superior to Lake Huron in a tumult of white-water rapids.

But like the St. Mary's River, innovative people built locks to make passage down the river possible. What steps could he take to build a stronger, more trusting relationship with Kate? He'd prodded her once to trust him. She still didn't. But he had hopes. Maybe if she found their relationship a sure, safe haven, she'd open her heart. But he couldn't do it alone. Lately, he'd bent God's ear for direction.

When Scott tuned into the family conversation, it had shifted to Kate's work at Children's Haven. He eased against the chair, listening to his mother barrage Kate with questions about being a social worker. This time, Kate answered with confidence, filling in details and his mother's face was as animated as Kate's as she listened.

After the meal ended and the cleanup completed, they settled in the living room. His dad pulled out the family's favorite board game, and they gathered around. Between moves, they joked and chatted on safe, general topics of conversation. When the game ended, his mother protested a second game and suggested dessert.

Covering a relieved sigh, Kate watched the family's interaction, her tension lightened. Scott's mother had halted her friendly inquiry and his father kept the conversation headed in a variety of directions that didn't probe into her family. She was grateful.

They were warm and loving people. She understood why Phyllis and Scott behaved as they did, and why they cared so much for each other. They embodied what Kate thought was a true Christian family.

Yet, as the deliberation rippled through her mind, a longing slid over her...and the usual guilt. Why wasn't her family open and forgiving? They were Christians, too, but their faith was bound up in rules and self-pride. Somehow, the Lord's grace and forgiveness slipped away beneath their murky precepts.

"Okay, who wants pie?" Mrs. Ryan asked as she rose from the game table.

Hands rose, including both of Phyllis's, and they laughed.

"You want two pieces?" her mother asked.

Phyllis laughed. "Darren said he'd come by for dessert. He should be here any minute." She rose. "Let me help you, Mom."

Kate caught her arm. "No, please. You helped earlier. It's my turn."

Without a struggle, Phyllis returned to her seat, and Kate followed Scott's mother to the kitchen.

The room was as charming as the rest of the house, a

blend of modern conveniences and trusty antiques. Mrs. Ryan pulled out a tray and loaded plates and cups while Kate whipped the cream.

When she finished, the older woman rested her hand on Kate's arm and grinned. "I was hoping we'd have some time to talk privately."

Panic spilled down Kate's arms and stopped at her trembling knees. Her mouth dried and words clotted in her throat.

"Sit," Mrs. Ryan said, patting the wood of a sturdy ladder back chair.

Kate caved into the cane seat and searched for her voice.

Scott's mother sat beside her, a gentle smile on her face. Grasping the server, she sliced pie and slid portions onto the plates as she spoke. "I'm so happy Scott and you are such good friends. I've prayed so often for him to find a nice Christian woman." She lifted her focus from the pie to Kate.

A prickling sensation ran up Kate's spine. "Scott's wonderful...and a good friend. I treasure him and Phyllis, too." Kate hoped adding Phyllis would change the tone of the conversation.

"Yes, you two have been good companions. Phyllis says the nicest things about you. I suppose you don't want me to list all the attributes." She grinned and brushed a strand of her hair from her cheek with the back of her hand.

"I can do without the list," Kate said, forcing her voice to be lighthearted.

Mrs. Ryan chuckled. "I don't know how serious you two are. Scott and you, I mean, but I approve of your relationship. More than approve." Her eyes caught Kate's and held her there. "His father feels the same way."

Kate let go a nervous laugh—too loud and exuberant. "You don't really know me. I'm afraid you'd be disappointed, Mrs. Ryan."

"Please, call me Anne," she said.

Kate nodded.

An amiable smile spread across Mrs. Ryan's face, then she shook her head. "We'd never be disappointed. Scott has dropped little tidbits about you, now and then. I think he's very fond of you. Very fond."

Kate's hand shook as she slid the pie plates onto the tray. "I'm...fond of him, too."

"That's good." His mother said, patting Kate's hand. "Now, I think that's about it. I'll put the coffee in a carafe, and you can carry the tray for me."

Kate nodded and rose. She drew in a deep breath, hoping to steady her hands. The woman had said nothing, really, but the impetus of her words rattled Kate's thoughts. What had Scott said about her? And what would this kindly woman think if she knew the truth?

Chapter Eleven

Driving Kate home from Thanksgiving dinner, Scott's thoughts centered on his disappointing news. The evening had gone well. Although during dessert, he noticed Kate had tensed again. He wondered what his mother had said to her in the kitchen.

When they pulled into the driveway, Scott turned off the ignition, hoping that Kate would invite him in. He hopped from the driver's seat and headed for the passenger door.

But she swung it open before he arrived. "What's up, Sir Galahad? You're not trying to impress me at this late date, are you?" She gave him a toying look. "Would you like to come in?" Her question was accompanied by a knowing grin.

Praying Phyllis was still out with Darren, Scott followed her to the door. He had the news about Amber's situation, but more than that concerned him. Inside, he slipped off his jacket and hung it on the old-fashioned coatrack in the foyer.

"Tea, coffee, soda?" she offered.

"Any hot chocolate?" he asked.

She nodded and headed for the kitchen.

He trailed after her.

"I hope my folks didn't bore you to death," Scott said, wondering if she'd let slip what had troubled her. He slid into a kitchen chair, his hands folded on the table.

"They're great people," she said, glancing over her shoulder while she rummaged through the cabinet. "They weren't at all boring."

"I'm glad. They like you, too. I can tell." He studied her, wondering if she'd respond.

"I know."

Her reply jogged through his ear and bounced back a mental question. How did she know? From their behavior, maybe, but he guessed it was more than that. "My mom cornered you in the kitchen, right?"

With her back to him, Kate mixed the chocolate powder with milk and popped the mugs into the microwave. Finally, she turned. "I'm not sure *cornered* is the right word."

"But I hit the location." He shook his head, wishing he'd thought to go to the kitchen with them. Stupid, he guessed, but it hadn't entered his mind since Kate had seemed like her old self by the time they were through with dinner. "So what did she say?"

"Just what I expected," Kate said, turning to withdraw the hot chocolate. Concentrating on the mugs, she carried them to the table, then sat across from him. "She thinks we're serious about each other...or at least, she hopes we are."

His gaze sought hers. "And that's totally out of the question?" he asked. His heart sank when he saw stress pull at her face.

"Getting serious about anyone is out of the question," she said, averting her gaze from his. She studied her fingernails, rubbing her right thumb across the pale-pink polish of her left hand.

"But why, Kate? I'm sorry my mom made you uncomfortable, but I really don't understand."

"I'm too old to change. My life is settled. I have a career and...well, the church. I guess—"

The muscles knotted in Scott's neck and his shoulders felt as rigid as a private's facing a four-star general. He felt his jaw twitch as he unclamped his teeth to speak. He'd heard her "too old" comment months earlier, but he believed it was more than that. "A month ago I said the same thing about my career," he said.

Her face tilted as if he'd piqued her interest. But she crimped her fingers into a tight fist, her uneasiness remaining.

"Talking to Mr. Brooks at the harvest party made me think. And I mean, really think." He paused, organizing his thoughts. "He has no family. Did you know that?"

Kate shook her head, her face creased with tension.

"Brooks never married. Never had time for a family and children, he told me...that is until it was too late. He thought his career was all he needed. But look at him now, Kate." He slid his hand across the table and rested it on hers. "He's a lonely old man with no one to share his memories, his treasures or his time."

"People need hobbies," she said.

"Hobbies!" His voice rose, and he drew in a calming breath to soothe the emotional slap he felt from her words.

Kate's eyes were closed as if trying to block his anger by not seeing it.

But he continued, undaunted. "We're not talking hobbies, Kate. We're talking *love* and companionship. I don't know one crocheted doïly or one golf club that can take the place of love." He released her hand and fell back against the chair. Kate exasperated him. Why did he bother? Giving up on her fluttered through his thoughts. Was she worth the hurt and frustration?

The room remained silent until Kate opened her eyes. Only then did Scott see the dewy mist that clung to her lashes. His chest tightened, and he mentally answered the question without hesitation. Yes, she was worth it, because he loved her. Pure and simple.

"I'm sorry, Scott. My family isn't as close as yours. And not as love-filled as yours, either. I suppose that makes it more difficult for me to want love and companionship. No one in my life...no one to hurt me."

Those few words pushed a seed into Scott's thoughts. Was that Kate's problem? Loving meant opening herself to hurt. If he didn't ache so much, he'd laugh. For years, he'd done the same thing himself. He'd buried the desire for female companionship, uncomfortable to share his

Christian beliefs...and afraid of being rejected, again, because of them.

And despite his terrific childhood, he'd grown up with questions about rejection, wondering what his birth parents were like and wondering if he might have been more loved by them. But Kate? She was raised by birth parents. Didn't that make a difference?

"I'm sorry your childhood wasn't as happy as it should have been, Kate. Growing up, sometimes I wondered about my birth parents, but that doubt was fleeting. When I really thought about it, I knew that no one could love me more than the parents who kissed and bandaged my first scraped knee and nursed me through measles and whooping cough."

Unclasping her fingers, Kate leaned forward on her elbows and rested her chin on her hand. She listened with the intensity of a child, seeing a new, fascinating sight. But why? Scott still didn't understand.

"I'm grateful to my birth mother for having me, but I love my parents for raising me. I always thought that if a person had both birth parents to raise him the experience would be unbelievable."

"It depends on the parents," Kate said. "I don't mean to sound bitter. My parents did the best they could. They raised me to know about Jesus, but they dropped *golden* out of the golden rule. They had unbending standards, and unlike God, if you broke a law—God's or theirs—it was unforgivable."

He wanted to ask what law she had broken. What horrible thing had she done? Or had it been numerous petty things?

"Anyway," she said, "you'll meet them."

"I will?"

"I heard from my mother. She and Dad are coming here for Christmas this year. Kristin, too."

"I'd like to meet your parents. It's nice they're coming."

"I'm not sure it's nice. They're upset with Kristin...her divorce, I should say. They couldn't get her to fly to Florida for Christmas. She told them she wanted to come back here to visit some old friends...so they decided to fly in, too." She rolled her eyes, then offered a faint smile. "Lucky me."

"No matter how you look at it," Scott said, "they're your parents—for better or worse, I suppose...like marriage." He smiled with his mouth, but his heart felt sorrowful as Kate's fleeting grin wilted to sadness. He longed to take her in his arms and show her what real love felt like.

"Maybe it's time both of us trust the Lord's guidance," Scott said. "In the scheme of things, it seems God wanted the world in twos. I suppose that's why under all of our personal fears, people long for a partner. Like Mr. Brooks."

For the first time, Kate captured his gaze. "It's not that I don't feel emotion, Scott. Maybe, I'm afraid of it. I don't want to be carried away without using my reasoning. Did you ever let your desire win over your good sense? Maybe I'm afraid I can't control my emotions."

Her eyes filled with a mixture of emotions: fear, hurt, sorrow. Scott didn't know which.

Then, Kate lowered her head. "Maybe that's what I'm

afraid of...that I'm incapable of hearing God's will when I'm so tangled in my own."

Her words spun through Scott's puzzled mind. He speculated what she might have done in her childhood. Or maybe what she hadn't done that she should have.

The conversation sagged and he didn't know what else to say, fearing his words would only bog things down worse. Then Amber's plight nudged him again. Their present discussion hadn't gone well, and he knew the next wouldn't get any better, but he couldn't let it go any longer.

His pulse shifted into passing gear as he shuffled through words, trying to decide the best way to tell her what he'd done. Finally, he spit it out. "I didn't find anything in Mrs. Yates's records to help you."

Kate's body stiffened, and she pulled her back from the chair. "You checked?"

"I had a chance to look yesterday...but I didn't mention it earlier. I hated to put a damper on Thanksgiving dinner. I knew how much you hoped for something more definite."

"Nothing? Are you sure?"

"Positive. The records stated, 'Old burn scars on right hand and forearm.'"

Kate slumped against the chair and closed her eyes.

"I'm sorry, Kate."

She opened her eyes and stared into space. "I'm being foolish. What difference would it make if I knew what happened? I'm not sure it'll help Amber one way or the other." She raised her hand and pressed two fingers against her temple, rotating them in gentle circles. "But if I understood, I'd hope I might be able to—"

"I've been thinking," Scott said.

"Thinking?" She dropped her hand. "About what?"

"Newspapers."

Her disappointed face brightened, and she leaned forward.

"If a child was burned in a house or apartment fire, we should find it in the newspaper. The library keeps microfiche copies of all the periodicals. As long as it happened in the metro area, we should be able to find it."

"It would take forever, Scott." Her excitement dimmed.

"Maybe not. At least, we can try."

And even if it took forever, it would give him more time to prove to Kate that he loved her and that he wasn't like her parents. Scott would forgive her for anything.

Through her wide front window, Kate sat on the sofa and watched a few downy snowflakes drift and twirl on the winter wind. She checked her wristwatch. Scott should arrive any minute and she prayed the heavy snowfall waited until they selected her Christmas tree.

With her family coming for the holidays, Kate had taken a couple of days off at the Haven so she could shop and decorate the house. No matter how difficult their visit would be, she promised herself to focus on Christ's birth. That would cheer her, no matter what.

Then Scott was another story. Daily, she asked herself what she was doing. Why had she allowed him to get under her skin and into her heart? If she had any gumption, she'd end it now. Now, before more pain settled into her soul and eradicated the little joy and purpose she had found in her work.

In a way, she knew how it happened. They'd called a truce of friendship. If they'd been able to stick to that agreement, things may have worked...but even then, she knew better. With the smoothness of satin, her emotions had slipped away and tangled in Scott's heartstrings.

And Scott was right about one thing. She'd allowed her past to weigh too heavily on her life. No one could rid her of the feelings, but herself...and God. A wave of shame washed over her at her neglect. When would she accept the truth that with God all things are possible?

On her own, she'd struggled to develop a plan of action, like she would for one of her clients at the Haven. But working on someone else's problems was a million times easier than working on her own. She needed to open her heart and mind to the Lord's will.

Scott's sedan slowed and turned into the driveway, and Kate rose. She slipped on her jacket and wrapped a scarf around her throat. No matter what the day held, Kate prayed she could take each moment as it came, accepting whatever it may be. And deep inside she knew that something kept her from walking away. Sometimes, she liked to think it was really God's bidding...and not her own wishful dreams.

The doorbell sounded, and before she could move, the door opened.

"It's me," Scott called, as he stepped into the foyer. When their eyes met, a grin slid over his lips. "I'd say you're ready."

"Just need my boots," she said, sliding off her terry cloth slippers. "I'd like to get the tree before it snows any heavier." She stepped into her sturdy footwear, then bent down to tighten the laces.

"We're supposed to get three to four inches."

When Kate lifted her head, they stood face-to-face, only inches apart. Her pulse skipped as the scent of mint hovered on the air.

Scott captured her chin between his thumb and fingers. "Do I detect a smile on these lips?"

Unable to speak, she nodded, longing to have his full sweet mouth touch hers. Though her logic resisted, her heart cried out to be loved.

As if God answered her prayer, Scott lowered his cool lips and warmed them against her own. His peppermint mouth lingered tenderly while his arms drew her tightly against his icy jacket.

As if nothing mattered, Kate yielded to him. The wintery weather outside couldn't penetrate the inner warmth that rose from her knees to her heart. With amazing gentleness, Scott's lips caressed hers, and when he drew back, the radiance in his eyes melted her hidden fears.

"Now that's more like it," he said, brushing his fingers along her cheek.

Without another word, he opened the front door and

herded Kate outside. Scott continued down the steps while she locked the door.

Kate hated to break the spell that snuggled lovingly in her thoughts, but once on the way, their conversation switched to Christmas and, finally, to her latest idea that she'd tossed about. Not knowing how he'd respond, she held her breath.

"I've been doing a lot of thinking about Amber. But I need your help...one more time."

He glanced her way without a word, then shifted his concentration back to the road.

She studied his face, wondering if he was upset with her request, but the telltale twitch of his jaw remained unmoved so she continued. "I was thinking that all we need is the date of the fire...that is, if we're right about a fire."

"So how can I help?"

Noting the positive ring to his voice, Kate mustered courage and plowed ahead. "You can ask someone in the hospital records department if Amber Yates has ever been admitted to County General and if she has, then ask the date."

"Don't get your hopes up, Kate. What if Amber had been admitted for asthma or something else when she was a child—"

"I know it's a long shot, but could you try?"

He flashed her a tender grin. "Sure, but don't be disappointed, okay?"

Though she nodded, Kate had to face her inability to deal with disappointment. Her success rate was zilch.

The conversation shifted back to Christmas plans, and

soon, they pulled up to a large Christmas tree lot. Kate wrapped her scarf tightly around her throat and tugged on her gloves before exiting the car.

The wind had strengthened, and the snowflakes were blowing into mounds along the curbs and buildings. Scott moved beside her and caught her fingers in his as they stepped between the chain-link fence and trekked down the row of trees. With their hands united, Kate felt complete and nestled against his side as they trudged along.

The evergreens were now weighted with the snowy burden, and large snowflakes caught in Scott's hair and the crystalized patterns sprinkled his shoulders. He slowed, then halted and grasped a tree that leaned against the fence. After shaking its branches, Scott turned and displayed the full, but squatty Scotch pine. "What do you say?" His breath lingered as a smoky cloud on the air.

She shook her head. "I don't like pines that much. I want a *real* Christmas tree."

His cheeks glowed with a rosy tint, and deep smile lines dimpled his face. "A 'real' Christmas tree? And what might that be, Katie?" His voice lilted with humor.

"I'll know it when I see it. They're different."

His face twisted in bewilderment, then brightened. He grabbed her hand, and she ran beside him to keep up with his long strides. They scooted up one row and down the other while the snow fell in heavy sheets, piling on the branches and their lashes.

Finally, Scott slid to a halt. He released her hand, eyed a

pile of trees far back on the lot, lifted one, shook the branches, then faced her.

A smile pulled on her mouth as she eyed what she considered the ideal Christmas tree. "Perfect," she said, admiring the tall-reaching top spire waiting for her Victorian angel and the stair-stepped limbs with short needles, so much sparser than a pine. "Now, that's a real Christmas tree. See all of the places I can hang my special glass ornaments."

Scott drew her into his free arm, then eyed the tree. "For future reference," he said, giving her a wink, "this is a plain old balsam."

"Balsam," she repeated, feeling the prickly branches pressing against her cheek. "I like plain old things."

He let the tree drop back to the pile and nudged her around to face him. "Not me, Kate. I like charming, young things with glowing cheeks and sparkling eyes." He traced his gloved finger along her jawline, then cupped her chin in his hand. "Especially ones who like balsam Christmas trees."

Kate knew what was coming and tilted her eager mouth to meet his. No longer did Scott's sturdy physique drag out her old memories. Today, hidden from other customers by the row of evergreens and the fast-falling flakes, she clung to his broad frame. And when their icy lips touched, her entire being warmed with her hopes for Christmas and the sweetness of their growing relationship.

Chapter Twelve

Scott's brain was as tired as his body. The night shift was a killer, and the past four weeks hung on his memory like a bad dream. The only day that glowed in his mind recently was the afternoon he helped Kate buy the Christmas tree. But now, he groaned with the long nights and even longer days when he tried to sleep.

He drew in a grateful sigh, knowing that later that day he would hear if he was headed for the afternoon shift or if he'd miraculously be reassigned to days. Shift changing was the plight of doctors doing their residency.

Kate's spirit had brightened in the past weeks. Whether it was the excitement of Christmas or their talk, Scott didn't know. And he didn't care. He enjoyed every minute of her laughter, smiles and good cheer. They'd shared warm, tender moments, and Scott had no doubt where his heart was headed. Right into Kate's arms. His only concern now was assurance she felt the same way.

With Christmas only two weeks away, Scott had offered to help Kate put up her decorations, and he hoped to be the bearer of his own joyful tidings that day. But when he contacted the records clerk at County General, she found no reference to Amber in the hospital files. With that news, Scott felt as disappointed as he knew Kate would feel.

He hated to disappoint her again and had struggled with the problem of Amber's background. When the obvious resource slithered into his head, he wondered why Kate hadn't thought of it first.

During his hospital dinner break, he found an unused telephone and called his sister, praying she would be home...alone. Kate had mentioned she'd be out that evening doing some heavy-duty Christmas shopping.

When Phyllis answered, he explained the situation. "So I figured if anyone knew a way to access a child's records, you'd have some ideas."

Silence filled the line.

Knowing his sister, Scott waited, praying she'd offer him a possible solution.

"I'm thinking," Phyllis said. After a lengthy pause, she responded. "If Amber's drawing showed a high-rise apartment, my guess is that they lived in Detroit back then. So logic says, she'd have been treated at a city hospital."

"That's a lot of hospitals," Scott said, trying to keep the disappointment from his voice.

"Her birth record would list the hospital where she was

born, and if the fire occurred when she was two or three, the family may have lived in the same area and—"

"And she would have gone to the same hospital," Scott said.

"That's seems logical," Phyllis agreed.

Scott agreed. "So where can I get a copy of her birth records?"

"You can't. Not in Michigan."

Frustration plowed through him. "Why not?"

"Birth records are restricted to family and a few legal exceptions."

Though her words were discouraging, her voice hinted that she could offer some hope. Praying he was correct, Scott asked, "And the exceptions are?"

"Legal guardians."

A smile skipped to his face. "And right now, Children's Haven is Amber's legal guardian." If Phyllis could identify Amber's birth hospital, then Scott prayed he was only one telephone call away from learning the date of the fire.

On Friday night, Kate moved the storage boxes filled with her Christmas decorations into the living room. Working at the Haven all day and preparing for the holidays at night made her more than tired. She was grateful Scott had volunteered to help.

This year, Phyllis was spending more time with Darren, and Kate guessed her friend would be wearing an engagement ring after the holidays. Though she was happy for

Phyllis, Kate felt sorry for herself. Her life would be even lonelier without her housemate's presence.

Tugging open a large cardboard box, Kate pulled out a lengthy strand of evergreen roping. Though artificial, it looked festive draped down the staircase and tied with big red bows. Having the house look perfect was important this year for her family's visit. Though she tried not to feel as she did, Kate wanted to demonstrate how successful and happy she was...even if it wasn't totally true.

Thinking of Kristin, Kate's jealousy surfaced again. Perhaps this year, her parents' frustration would be aimed at her sister and her divorce, giving Kate a breather.

Divorce was one of her parents' unforgivable sins. Though God lovingly forgave those who repented their sins, Kate reveled in the knowledge that remaining single meant divorce was one sin she would not commit. But then Scott's image appeared, setting her nerves on edge.

When reality struck her, Kate knew inviting Scott over to meet her family was the last thing she wanted. But it was the only appropriate thing she could do. She'd wrestled with a million reasons and excuses. And that's exactly what they were—excuses. Scott wouldn't understand if she avoided an introduction and neither would her parents. So again, she prayed, hoping to hand her fears over to God.

Shrugging off her worries, Kate gathered up the strand of roping and lugged it to the bottom of the staircase. She dropped it in a pile, then returned to the box. More roping lay curled in the bottom, and she pulled it out and carried the shorter piece to the mantel. Once she twisted the roping with miniature lights and set out a display of holiday candles, she knew it would create a lovely effect.

As she untangled the roping, Kate heard the door open. She spun around and paused, seeing Scott standing in the doorway with packages tucked in his arm.

"I didn't wait long enough, did I?" he said, eyeing the boxes piled on the floor.

"You'd have to wait days," she said, giddily juggling two large candles. "What's in the bags?"

"Something to set a festive mood." He placed one package on the chair and pulled a carton of eggnog from the other. "Voilà."

"Eggnog?"

"It's tradition. This and Christmas music go along with decorating. That's how I grew up."

"You had a pretty special life," she said, wanting to make a joke, but none came to mind. Often, she wondered about her own baby's life. Baby? No, not any longer. Her daughter would be eighteen now. Almost nineteen. She prayed God had guided her child to a loving, Christian family like Scott's.

He scooted to Kate's side and slid his arm around her waist. "You don't like eggnog?"

She nearly laughed at his pensive expression. "Sure. Why?"

"Because you look so serious."

Hastily, she pushed away her melancholy and veiled the truth. "I was guessing what's in the other bag."

"Ah, so that's it." He shot across the room and grabbed up the second bag. When he returned, he slipped it into her hands. "It's a little gift."

"For me?"

He nodded.

Puzzled, she opened the sack and peeked inside. A six-inch cube-shaped box sat on the bottom. She opened it and caught her breath. "It's beautiful, Scott."

Undoing the protective covering, Kate pulled out a delicate glass ornament. Its iridescence reflected a myriad of pastel hues, and gold lettering spelled out My Special Friend. Tears pushed against the backs of her eyes and ran, unbidden, down her cheeks.

Scott caught her in his arms and pressed his cheek against her wet skin. "It's not nearly as beautiful as you are, Kate."

She faced him and reveled in the tenderness that glinted in his eyes. "I love it, Scott." The words she wanted to say stuck in her throat: And I love you, too.

"I remembered when you said you liked places to hang your special ornaments. So I'm adding one to your collection." He tilted her chin upward and gazed at her with heavy eyelids. "And I pray it's the first of many."

As his mouth lowered to hers, a tremor wavered through her limbs and quivered in her chest. She came too close to losing her senses in this man's arms.

Delighting in the sensation, she clasped the back of his neck, feeling his muscles tighten, then slid her hand to the flexing strength of his shoulders. His thick arms held her captive and she surrendered to the swirling emotions.

His body trembled against hers. Then, he drew back. "I don't think this is getting your house decorated. Not in a million years."

She wanted to tell him she didn't care about the ornaments and bows, but instead, she flagged her flailing emotions with a heady sigh, nestling her face against his jacket and smelling the musky scent that surrounded him.

They stood still, caught in each other's arms until Kate drew back. "How about some eggnog?" she said.

Scott's laugh broke the silence, and she joined him, knowing she needed the humor to bring her back from the uncontrollable feelings she had experienced.

"With ice. Lots of ice," Scott added with a sheepish grin. He stepped away and pulled off his jacket. "While you get the nog, I'll put on some music."

Kate carried the carton into the kitchen and filled two glasses with the thick holiday drink. She used the time to calm her emotions and rein her thoughts. If she truly loved Scott and he loved her, she had to tell him about her past...about her child. But how could she?

No matter how much Kate's feelings grew, Scott's words pressed against her thoughts. Chastity, a gift for a spouse. When they first met, Scott's athletic physique had triggered unwanted memories about Ron. But no more. Tonight, she clung to Scott's firm, strong frame with only thoughts of him.

Kate shook her head. She would lock her fears away. Forget her horrible concern for the time being and enjoy the holiday.

She refocused on the two tumblers and breathed a sigh. As Christmas music drifted into the kitchen, Scott's pleasant baritone voice rode along on the carol. After Christmas, maybe then she could deal with her dilemma and make a sensible decision. At the moment, she had no strength to fight her feelings. She would enjoy the holiday...and revel in Scott's attentiveness.

She grabbed the two glasses, and when she returned to the living room, Scott was plowing through the cardboard boxes, a Christmas table covering draped over his shoulder like a cloak.

"Practicing to be a Magi?"

"Something like that. I do believe in miracles."

The grin on his face caused her to halt, and she faltered, studying him for a moment. "Okay, I give. What's up?"

He tilted his head with the look of sheer innocence.

Kate marched toward him, pushing the glass of eggnog against his chest and moving him backward to the sofa. When the seat was behind him, she shoved the drink in his hand. "Now, sit, and tell me why you look like the cat who ate the canary."

She sat beside him on the edge of the cushion and rested the glass on her knee.

"What do you want to hear first?" he asked.

Anxiety sizzled along her nerve endings. "If it's something about Amber, that's what I want to hear."

He grinned and began his story, detailing the path that led him to Phyllis. "So she called the Wayne County birth records clerk and requested the birth hospital name. They gave it to her over the telephone."

Kate's heart beat so fast she felt as if she couldn't breathe. "So tell me," Kate said.

"She was born at Harper Hospital."

"Then we need to check there—"

"I already did."

Excitement reeled through Kate's body. "So stop with the suspense. What else?"

"She was admitted to Harper Hospital with burns three years ago in February, and was moved to Children's Hospital the next day."

Kate fell back against the seat cushion. "I can't believe it was that simple."

Scott chuckled. "Easy for you, maybe. You didn't do anything." He tousled her hair.

Kate retaliated, then threw her arms around his neck. "Thank you, Scott. And Phyl, too."

Scott brushed her hair from her cheek. "Remember, this is only the beginning. We still need to check the library."

"I know."

"Phyllis tried to pry a little more information out of the clerk, but the woman asked her to mail an official release of information slip, so she just thanked the clerk and hung up."

As reality shuffled through her, Kate shifted on the cushion. "If anything happens to Mrs. Yates, the Haven will need to investigate further anyway. Amber must have some family somewhere. What happened to her mother and father?"

Scott shrugged. "Hard to tell. Parents place kids for adoption. Who's to say they don't give them to relatives? Amber's parents might not want to be found. Or sadder, maybe, they died in the fire."

Kate closed her eyes, unable to face either of the possibilities. She cringed at the concept of parents not wanting their children. Though it had been best, years earlier she would have done anything to keep her baby, but the choice wasn't hers. At the age of fifteen, what kind of life could she have given the child?

"Hey, cheer up!" Scott said, jostling her back to the present. "All we need is some time in the library and you should have your answer."

"Right," she said, jumping up from the sofa and struggling to recapture her Christmas spirit.

Scott grabbed her hand. "I almost forgot. Here's some more good news. I'm back on days starting Monday."

"Great. How did that happen?" She loved Scott working days. He'd spoiled her with his attentiveness and spur-of-the-moment invitations. The past weeks with Scott on the night shift, he slept before going to work, and the evenings dragged for Kate like they had months earlier before she knew him. Worse than dragged. Then, she hadn't realized how lonely and empty her life had been. Now, the awareness seemed overwhelming.

Her thoughts had drifted again and she missed Scott's explanation. But when one horrible phrase struck her inner ear, her breath vanished and she choked. "What? Say that again," she said, trying to regain her voice.

"Madonna House. Have you heard of it?"

Had she heard of it! Her heart slid to her toes, and she nodded a feeble yes.

"I'm working there like I did at the Haven. Three days a week."

"But you're not a gynecol—"

"No, but we do regular checkups, deal with health issues, etc. Once a month a gynecologist comes in to check on the pregnancies."

"That's so different from—" Fear rose up her arms and pushed against her heart. What had she done? She'd almost confessed without realizing it.

Scott's puzzled eyes studied her. "Different from...?" he asked.

Her mind flew, searching for a response. Any answer than to admit that's where she had been eighteen years earlier. Gooseflesh prickled on her skin. "Different from many of those agencies. I figured they still used nurses. I knew a girl from high school who went to one of those homes."

"Ah," he said, his quizzical expression shifting to a grin. "I suppose that many years ago it was different. Times have changed. Attitudes have changed. I'd guess it's easier now."

Easier? Never. Not when you carry a child for nine months. Not when you feel the weight against your belly and feel the tiny limbs shift and kick inside you. Not when you lay on a hard table to be examined as if you were little more than a sheep...or worse. How could it be easy to never see the child who carried your blood through its tiny veins?

This time Kate caught herself drifting in thought and prayed the ache in her throbbing heart would calm. She pulled her gaze upward, unknotted her hands, and drew his attention with a sweeping gesture to the unadorned room. "If we're going to get some decorating done, we'd better get busy."

Scott captured her extended hand and drew her into an embrace. "How about slapping a bow on the banister and calling it a day. I'd rather sit on this sofa and cuddle you in my arms."

"Don't sweet-talk me, buster. Get busy." Playfully, she broke loose from his arms, but her teasing had been a ploy. She tucked her trembling hands into the pockets of her jeans, praying he hadn't felt the nerves quaking in her body...and in her soul.

Chapter Thirteen

Listening to Kate's family after dinner, Scott struggled to unlock his jaw and release the tension. From the moment he arrived, Kate's well-meaning parents chopped away at both their daughters' defenses. He tried to understand, assuming they only wanted the best for their girls. Scott sorted through their comments, and his heart lifted, praising God for the Lord's unfailing forgiveness. Mr. and Mrs. Davis did not know the meaning of the word.

Meeting Kate's sister offered Scott an in-depth view of their sibling relationship. Though Scott found greater beauty in Kate, Kristin's face and figure were perfection...and Kristin, obviously, knew it. She had swung her hips, flaunted everything below her neckline and pursed her lips in what she probably thought was a seductive pose.

But Scott turned lovingly toward Kate and, emotionally, caressed the natural charm of her near-round face, creamy skin, delicate button nose and eyes that took him on a journey to her heart.

Why couldn't Kate see that her loveliness was both inside and out? Nothing in Scott's opinion could replace sincerity, honesty and selflessness. Kate had it all.

Drawing himself from his thoughts, Scott had lost the family's conversation and sorted through the snippets he'd heard.

"Kate, I know you," her mother said. "You're much too involved with those pitiful children. I wish you'd look for a job that has a good income and gives you a sense of achievement."

Tension stiffened Kate's back while her eyes narrowed and sparked. "It's people's impression of these children that's pitiful, mother, not the kids. To me, they're precious. I wish you could understand that I love my career."

With a sidelong look at Kate, Scott's reserve crumbled. "You should see Kate at the Haven," he said, unable to control the defensiveness that rose to his shoulders. "She's respected by the staff and loved by the children. These kids are victims of circumstance."

"That might be," Mr. Davis said, "but the way I look at it, the circumstance is mainly unChristian women not using their God-given sense."

"Not using birth control," Mrs. Davis muttered.

"That's not true," Kate said, her voice fading with defeat, "but you'd have to be there to understand."

"It's difficult understanding stupidity," Mr. Davis said. "The Lord gave us *ten* commandments...not eleven or twelve.

Ten clear-cut commandments. Even my own girls can't seem to follow them." His narrowed eyes focused on Kristin.

Kate's face paled, and she shriveled into the cushion.

Scott heard her father's words, but their meaning was lost. What had Kate done that was so horrible that her father dredged it out today? Struck by a possibility, Scott balked. Divorce? No, Kate couldn't have been divorced, too.

"Sorry, Dad," Kristin snapped, "I guess my *husband* didn't learn the one about coveting his neighbor's wife."

Neither of Kate's parents commented. Instead, her father turned his attention to Scott. "Now, here's a young man that a parent could be proud of." He leaned forward, balancing his elbows on his knees, his hands folded in front of him. "And you've got what I call a career," he said. "One day, the money will be rolling in."

Scott leaned forward with a chuckle. "You might think I'm naive, but I didn't become a doctor for the money. I like helping people, pure and simple. Just like Kate."

"That's very benevolent, young man." He leaned back and pulled on the end of his thin mustache. "I read the Good Book. We should all show compassion like the Lord commands, but...a little green stuff never hurt anybody." His lip curled in a wily grin, and he rubbed his thumb against his upturned fingers.

Scott's stomach churned at Kate's parents' lack of discernment, and he wondered how Kate turned out so warm and caring. Many times, Kate had made references to her less-than-loving childhood. He'd witnessed Kate's fear to accept peoples' approval and to trust them. How many times had she backed away from him? The more determined he was to reveal his growing feelings, the more Kate scrambled out of reach.

With a long-awaited lull in the conversation, Kate suggested dessert and headed for the kitchen. Scott trailed after her, promising himself not to make reference to any of the tension that had transpired. Kate's misery struck him as if it were his own.

When Kate realized he'd followed, she turned around. "I can do this alone."

"I know, but I want to help."

She shrugged and pivoted to face the cabinets.

Scott stepped behind her and slid his arms around her shoulders, pressing his cheek to her sweet-scented hair. "I really wanted a minute alone...to hold you in my arms."

"Why would you want to do that?" she asked, pulling dessert plates from the cabinet.

Scott grasped the plates from her fingers and, with his free hand, turned her to face him. He eased the china onto the counter and wrapped his arms around her waist. "Because I love you, Kate."

Astonishment leaped to her face, and her mouth sagged. Grasping his words, she shook her head as a frown furrowed her brow. "No. No, Scott, you can't love me. We made a deal."

He froze in place. "A deal?" His mind whirled backward, seeking the moment they had made a deal. "I don't remember a *deal,* Kate."

She pressed her hands against his chest, pushing him away, but he held her fast.

Her eyes pleaded. "A couple of months ago...you said 'Let's back up and start over.'"

"And we did," he said, remembering the day that was so like this one.

Her face paled, and misty tears welled in her eyes.

"We started over," he continued, "and we ended up here...in each other's arms."

Her palms pushing against his chest belied his statement. But he couldn't release her. Kate had to see the reality and learn to accept it. Neither she nor Kristin were as awful as their parents inadvertently made them feel. The Davises were confused, not knowing how to teach God's laws without forgetting God's love.

But Scott knew both and would hang on to Kate as long as he could. "Don't be afraid of me, Kate. You're already a part of me, and I can't let you go. Please, let me help you. We can deal with the past. I promise."

Her drawn face tilted upward. "I'm not the wonderful person you seem to think, Scott. You deserve a good mate, a loving woman who's pure and comp—"

"Pure?" He lifted his hand to her trembling chin, cupped it, and pressed his fingers against her lips to silence her. "You're pure as the driven snow, Kate. You're as white and guiltless as God's promise."

Her eyes widened. "I know I'm sinless in God's eyes, but I'm not in my parents'...or in yours if you knew the—"

Addled with her determined condemnation, he did what his heart desired. He silenced her with his lips, tasting the salty tears and cherry flavor of her lip gloss. She trembled against his body, and he ran his hands across her back in soothing strokes, longing to cradle her in his arms.

"My, my."

Kristin's voice cut through the tender moment, and Scott peered at her without moving.

"I wondered what was taking so long," she said, arching an eyebrow. A mocking snicker left her throat.

With Kate's face buried against Scott's chest, she furtively brushed the tears from her eyes, then slid out of his embrace and pulled the cups from the cupboard.

"My fault," Scott said, making light of the moment, "I can't resist your sister. She's like a magnet." He drew his hand across Kate's unyielding shoulder, then turned to Kristin. "Did you come to help?"

Kate's sister chuckled, again. "Doesn't look like you need any help."

"We all need help," Scott said, piling the cups onto a tray.

"What can I do?" Kristin asked as she strode across the floor toward them.

Kate gave her quick instructions, and together, they filled the tray with the Christmas china and desserts. Scott lifted the tray while Kate carried the carafe.

Sidling to Scott's side, Kristin snatched a cookie from the plate with a wink. "Mommy and Daddy are such sweeties, aren't they?" Her eyes locked with Scott's.

"They're well-meaning," Scott said and slipped passed her heading for the living room, his mind twisting and turning, hoping to decipher Kate's puzzling world.

Kate stretched out on her bedspread, her mind reviewing the holiday. Phyllis had popped in and out, spending most of her time with Darren's family, and as Kate and Scott had suspected, Phyllis's finger now boasted a beautiful diamond.

With her parents away visiting friends for the New Year and Kristin staying with an old high school girlfriend, Kate had her first quiet moment since the holiday began.

Yet, her thoughts were less than peaceful. As if providence would not let go, Scott had asked her to attend a holiday party with him at Madonna House. Unable to find a valid reason to refuse, Kate agreed. Now, the weight of memories and fears pressed against her heart.

She trembled, wondering how she could return to the place where she'd stayed like a prisoner for nearly six months. The name alone, Madonna House, wrenched through her, tearing away the years that cushioned the miserable memories and shame of her stay there, hiding her growing truth from the world.

No doubt time had changed the facility and improved—if that was possible—a pregnant girl's stay. Never during her residency had there been a holiday or occasion celebrated with a party, especially one that included a doctor.

Her darkest recollections hinged on the faces of the unknown men in white coats who treated her with animosity and degradation. She never saw the same physician twice, and none of them had prepared her for the pain of childbirth or the sorrow of releasing her unseen baby for adoption.

The frightened occupants' main source of care was a few nurses who soothed them with good-meaning words that still tore at her very fiber. "You'll have another baby some day. Just wipe this whole thing from your thoughts," and "You don't want to shame your family, do you? We'll find your baby a good home."

Like opening a wound, other festering words oozed from her mind. "You're selfish, not thinking of your child." "You can't take care of a baby." Though their words bore the truth, they had pierced Kate's self-esteem just as her parents' shame had knifed through her guilt-filled conscience.

Tonight, she had to face both Madonna House and Scott. With her family's presence, he hadn't questioned her parents' numerous innuendos and inflexible thinking. Knowing Scott, Kate had no doubt he would ask eventually. And she was too weary to contrive an answer.

All this had happened on the heels of Kristin's visit. Her sister's presence had wedged its way into Kate's old insecurities. Kate viewed her sister's blatant flirtation with Scott and shriveled, feeling less appealing and less worthy. And why? Scott said nothing, no reference to Kristin's beauty or behavior. Zero.

With the time drawing nearer, she pulled herself up from the coverlet, and after studying the clothes in her closet, she tugged out a muted-green knit ensemble. Kate stepped into her skirt, then tugged the long tunic over her head. The garment discretely covered her slender frame, and best of all, the color and style allowed her to hide beneath its simple design.

The gold necklace Scott had given her for Christmas lay on the dresser, a series of golden beads interspersed with pearls. Though the chain was beautiful, her mother's adage marched through her thoughts. "For every pearl a woman wears, she will cry a hundred tears." Inspecting the lovely beads, Kate assessed that she had already cried her share for every pearl that adorned Scott's lovely gift.

At the bathroom mirror, she highlighted her cheeks with blush and her eyes with shadow, and she brightened her mouth with a lush coral shade. Looking at her straight hair, she caught it back in a gold hair clip and added pearl studs to her earlobes.

As she snapped off the light, Scott's voice sailed down the hallway. He met her halfway, and when he saw her, he stopped—and so did her heart. Tonight, his broad shoulders and chest were bound beneath a hunter-green mock-turtle-neck with a beige-flecked wool sport coat. His good looks amazed her, and as he drew her into his arms, she remembered to breathe.

"Is this new?" Scott asked. "You look great."

"No, it's been hanging in my closet. It's too dressy for work."

His finger traced the drape of the gold-and-pearl beads, then lifted his hand up to her shoulder. "The necklace looks nice. And your hair...you don't wear it up often. I like it."

His last words were a murmur as he bent down and pressed his lips to the unprotected curve of her neck.

An electric tingle shot down her arm and settled in her solar plexus. Protecting her sensitive skin to his touch, she pressed her ear to her shoulder.

He didn't linger, but wrapped his arm around her and walked beside her to the foyer closet. When she had slipped on her coat, Scott opened the door and a cold blast of air swirled around her ankles, sending chills down her arms. As she stepped to the porch, cold, anxious fear shivered down her spine like a criminal taking his last steps to the gas chamber.

Standing beside Kate at the table covered with a holiday paper cloth, Scott surveyed the dishes filled with simple appetizers and Christmas cookies. While they visited and munched on snacks, a few parents arrived and another physician from the hospital.

Scott took in the surroundings. Shy, plain-faced girls clustered in small groups at one end of the room, their bulging tummies pressed against lacy maternity tops while noisier teens, their eyes outlined with black kohl and lips highlighted with dark color, bounced to the cassette player's rhythmic beat. These girls were dressed in clinging T-shirts with phrases, like Baby emblazoned above a bright-yellow arrow pointing to the telltale protrusion.

Though Kate had hesitated accepting the invitation, she'd been a good sport. When he arrived, she had looked so lovely...and fragile.

Stepping into Madonna House, Scott had noticed Kate's curious expression as she scanned the large, unadorned living room and glimpsed into the open doorways. He suspected she was thinking of the needy children she worked with daily at the Haven. Kate's heart was undauntedly tender.

Speaking at length with the housemother and a nurse, Kate had learned about the facility, and Scott noticed her withdraw for a brief moment like she did with her parents. He hadn't spoken to Kate about them but wanted to grasp the reason for their strained relationship.

Now, Kate nibbled on cookies and spoke with her usual kindness to the girls who wandered by and stopped to talk.

After an appropriate amount of time, he nudged Kate's arm and whispered in her ear. "About ready?"

She nodded, a look of relief on her face, and he grinned, knowing she was probably hungry. "Tired of chips and dip, huh? And you want some 'real' food."

Though Kate grinned at Scott's comment, she felt nauseated. She'd struggled to maintain a sense of calm, then panicked, wondering if some ancient housemother might remember her face or recall her name. She'd been foolish. Most of the young staff wasn't much older than Kate's own daughter.

As they took leave, Kate waved goodbye, then stopped near a lone young lady. "Thanks for having us," Kate said to the quiet girl who reminded Kate of herself at that age.

"We're glad you came," she responded, her hand bracing the large swell of her belly.

Outside, Kate drew the refreshing, frigid air into her lungs. Unexpected, her frosty breath seemed warmer than the icy feelings that crept through her veins. Inside Madonna House, she'd forced herself to smile and make friendly conversation while her heart wanted to weep.

Kate assumed that nowadays facilities like Madonna House were uncommon. With the newer laws, most single, pregnant girls were allowed to attend their regular school and most kept their babies, but a few, tossed out by angry parents or hidden by well-meaning families much like her own, still found a haven at Madonna House.

"I hope that wasn't too unpleasant," Scott said, tucking her hand in his as they walked to the car.

"It was fine." She wished she could say something nicer, something more positive, but the words stuck in her throat.

Reaching the car, Scott pulled out the key and opened the door. His frozen breath hung on the air. "The whole world has changed, and it seems as if I haven't."

She heard it coming and slid into the car, hoping the darkness blocked the fear that rose to her face.

Scott closed the door, rounded the car, and climbed into the driver's seat. He turned the ignition key, then leaned over and kissed Kate's cheek. "I hope you don't mind spending time with an old-fashioned guy. I'm going to sound like your father, but I don't understand why kids get into these situations."

"They want to be popular," Kate murmured, peering through the passenger window, her face turned away from his, her mind tangled in the past.

"Popular? Really? I'd think they'd have more common sense."

"They don't," Kate said, fighting the tears that welled in her eyes. "They're desperate."

"I figure males think of promiscuity as a conquest—like St. George slaying the dragon or King Arthur seizing Excalibur. But females—"

"Want to be needed and loved. It boils down to that, Scott. Two little words and one big problem."

Scott grasped Kate's frigid hand and kissed her fingers. "And that's why I need you, Kate. You and I have the same convictions. Nothing could be better."

The winter moon slipped behind a cloud, and Kate's world turned as black as the night.

Chapter Fourteen

Scott added a log in the condo's fireplace. Glancing at Cass's computer now sitting in the niche of shelving, he chuckled to himself and couldn't wait to share his newest realization with Kate. Calling himself an old-fashioned guy was sadly appropriate. In a world of technology, why hadn't he or Kate thought about searching on a newspaper's Web site for information on the suspected apartment fire? After dinner, he planned to surprise her with surfing the Internet.

The aroma of tomatoes and spices drifted from the kitchen, and Scott returned to toss the salad. Though his culinary skills weren't exemplary, he could make a mean scampi, and he hoped steaming the rice wasn't beyond his talent. He'd never prepared dinner for Kate, though she had often surprised him with a home-cooked meal. Tonight, he'd promised her a taste of his gourmet skills.

In the dining alcove off the living room, Scott had

hauled out Cass's fine china dinnerware—white ringed with a black-and-gold band. With black place mats and napkins, he added black-handled silverware. He'd even thought to pick up a small bouquet of flowers for the onyx vase with matching candlesticks he placed in the center of the table. He stood back, admiring the setting. He had outdone himself.

His mind filled with a mixture of thoughts and questions, Scott hoped this night would be special. His confession of love hadn't sat well with Kate, but he prayed that the idea had grown on her. At times, he was confident that Kate felt the same, that only her wavering self-worth kept them apart.

Other times, he feared that Kate's problem lay deeper, that he might never uncoil the knots of her uncertainty. He'd prayed for God to intervene—that the Lord would give him the strength and assurance that he and Kate were meant for each other. He felt it in his heart. But was it only...

The flash of car lights stretching across the wall alerted him, and Scott strode to the front window and glanced outside. Kate climbed from the car and hurried up the walk. When she stepped inside, she brought along the scent of brisk January air and sweet melons.

"Hi," he said, brushing a kiss on her cheek.

"Smells good," Kate said.

"So do you."

She grinned. "I meant whatever you're cooking."

Scott hung her coat in the closet, then took her hand and guided her to the dining alcove. "Pretty fancy, huh?"

She nodded, but a look of apprehension rose in her face. "Almost like a special occasion," she said, searching his eyes.

"Only you. You're my special occasion." Though he smiled, a cold sinking sensation shivered through him. Was she fearing a proposal? Not tonight, but one day soon, he hoped to ask her to marry him. Would she respond with this same look of anxiety? He refused to worry about it tonight. He prayed God would direct him.

He sent her to the CD player to put on a disk, and Scott returned to the kitchen. Lifting the pot lid, he peeked at the rice, now fluffy and plump. Success! He pulled the salad from the refrigerator, dressed it, and carried it to the table. Then returned for the scampi and rice.

After the blessing, Scott handed the salad to Kate and dished up the entrée. With general chatter interspersed with compliments to the chef, they ate, but Scott's eyes were drawn to the computer, hoping that tonight Kate would get her answer.

After dinner, before Scott mentioned the child, Amber's name came into the conversation.

"I've been giving a lot of thought to Amber," Kate said. "I'm afraid Mrs. Yates isn't going to recover. Or if she does, she'll be unable to take care of Amber. You're the doctor. What do you think?"

"I agree. When I stopped by yesterday, the nurse told me she's had another stroke. Her status seems grave, and she's definitely comatose. No response at all."

Kate leaned forward and ran her fingers through the

length of her hair, then brushed the tresses behind her shoulder. "I'd like to be a foster parent to Amber. That's what I've been thinking. I want to take her home."

"Home? But Kate you work every day. How can you be a foster mother and spend your days at the Haven?"

"Mothers do it all the time, Scott. Having a child doesn't end a woman's career."

"But this is different. You'd be investigated. Scrutinized. Wouldn't they want to place a child in a home with two parents? Where the mother is home to be with the child?"

"Amber goes to school almost the same hours that I work. If I can offer her a good home, I don't think it should make a difference. You don't think I'd be a good parent?"

Scott shook his head. "Don't be silly. You'd make a wonderful mother. The best in the world...but it would be difficult."

"Life's difficult." A ragged sigh shuddered from her throat. "Anyway, once we can get to the library and find a way to locate Amber's parents, there'll be no need."

Remembering his plan, Scott's spirit lifted. "Speaking of that, I've had an interesting insight."

She snapped her head in his direction. "About what?"

"That I can bring the library to us."

A puzzled frown settled on her face. "What do you mean?"

Scott swung his hand toward the computer desk. "Technology, Kate. We're sitting here with a computer and a modem. We have access to the Internet and to the daily Detroit newspapers."

Kate's eyes widened and her frown vanished, replaced by an astonished grin. "I feel stupid. Why hadn't either of us thought of that before?"

"I'm not alone with that old-fashioned tag I mentioned. We were too caught up in the problem and didn't think."

Kate rose and took a step toward the computer. "So, can we?"

Scott rose to her side and wrapped his arms around her from behind, then scooted her along to the chair that faced the monitor. "Sit."

"No, you. I'm shaking so badly I can't even think."

Scott acquiesced and plopped into the desk chair. He hit the power button, and they waited silently as the computer booted up.

Kate's trembling hand rested on the chair arm, and Scott slid his palm over her icy fingers, praying the task was easy and productive.

When the desktop was ready, Scott clicked the mouse on the appropriate icons, listed his password, and typed the address into the key word slot. In another minute, the web site of a Detroit newspaper appeared.

"This is today's news," Kate said, the disappointment wilting her tone.

"Don't jump to conclusions," he said, scanning the choices. "I'm sure they have back issues." He moved the mouse and clicked Services, then Search.

"Archives," Kate yelled, poking the monitor where the word appeared.

In a heartbeat, Scott stared at another key word search. "Here goes." He typed in "Yates" and "fire," then filled in the date that the hospital had given. When he hit Search, Kate leaned over his back and gripped his shoulders. Finally, a headline appeared in the small box, Three Die in House Fire.

"Is that it?" she yelled, motioning to the sentence.

Scott scrolled down the incomplete article which ended abruptly. Red lettering followed the short blurb of information. "There's a 1.95 fee for the whole article," he said, reading the instructions. Using his credit card, he continued. Finally, the full article appeared.

The facts marched before him. Kate read in a whisper the reporter's words of the fire that destroyed an upper flat, killing Roland and Donna Yates, and their son James.

"Amber had a brother," Kate said, her voice hushed by the dire news. "Look." She pointed to the screen and read, "Also lost in the fire was the family's pet spaniel...Sparky."

Kate's ragged breath sounded behind him, then she whispered. "The day I handed Amber that toy puppy, she called it Sparky. She remembered the dog."

Emotionally touched by the article, Scott scanned the report, detailing the event. "Roland's mother and his youngest daughter Amber, who had spent the night with her grandmother in the lower flat, escaped with minor burns."

Scott fell back against the chair. "So it was a flat and not an apartment."

Kate shrugged. "Guess her drawing made us think apartment. Amber's father was an only child," she added, pointing to the final paragraph.

Scott scanned to the end and read the words himself.

"What about Donna Yates? There's no reference to her family." He twisted in the chair to face her.

Kate shrugged, her face filled with thought. In silence, she rested her crossed arms on the back of the desk chair and stared at the monitor.

Scott waited, knowing her mind was mulling through the information.

"I'm going to look into being a foster parent," Kate said. "If something happens to Amber's grandmother, I'll be able to..." Her voice halted and tears filled her eyes. "I'd take her now, Scott. I really love that little girl, but I'm only setting myself up for hurt if Mrs. Yates pulls through...and I sure don't want to pray for anything else."

"You can't let every kid at the Haven tear you up like this," Scott said, concern filling his thoughts.

"I don't. I never have before. There's just something about Amber. Something I can't explain." Disappointed at his attitude, she bit the corner of her lip, wishing he'd encourage her decision instead of listing all the problems. She searched his face for a flicker of understanding.

He closed the programs and rose from the chair, then captured her in his arms. "Okay, but I worry about you."

"It's a lot of things, Scott. It's not just for Amber or me. Jesus said, 'Whoever welcomes one of these little children welcomes me.' It's the Lord's will, too."

"I know, Kate."

Nestled beside him, Kate wished she could explain the truth, how Amber would fill her desire to be a mother and would release the guilt and love she'd bound inside her.

"Amber's special," Kate said. "And if I never..." She faltered. How could she say that if she never married, Amber could make amends for her adopted baby daughter? She could atone for her sin.

Scott eyed her. "Never what?"

"Well, if I never...try to be a foster parent, I'll never know." The cover-up tumbled out of her mouth.

"It's a big step. I don't know." He circled his hand gently across her shoulder blades. "Kate, have you thought about how your parents will react to this?"

She stiffened in his arms. Her parents? What did he mean?

"Please, don't get upset," he said, apparently sensing her tension. He guided her toward the sofa and sat down beside her.

"It doesn't really matter," Kate said. "You saw them in action. They have their opinions and not much will change them. My parents' interpretation of God's will is different from many people's."

"I saw that when we were together." He slid his arm around her shoulder. "Kate, I know why they're angry at Kristin. Christian parents don't accept divorce, especially their own child's, but why are they so uptight with you?"

She froze, unable to think. Unable to speak.

"I'm sorry. I shouldn't have asked. But whatever it was, Kate, you were probably just a kid. You made some kind of mistake." He eyed her. "You got in trouble with the law or...?" He paused as if waiting for her to fill in the blank. "It couldn't have been that bad."

Kate felt him tense.

He stepped back and peered into her face. Fear altered his compassionate face. "You aren't divorced, too, are you?" His face had paled.

"No," she said, finding her voice, "I was never married." But she should have been for all she'd done. The truth propelled through her like buckshot. "It was long ago. It's over."

"But it's not. You've suffered for some kind of infraction...for too long, I think. If this is why you're afraid to love me, Kate, please stop fighting it. Just love me."

"I can't love you, Scott. I can't love anyone. I'll never marry. Now, I've said it, and as soon as you understand, the better it will be for us both. I'm not worth the anguish. You deserve someone—"

She stopped not knowing what else to say. The expression on his face twisted her heart and sent an ache coursing through her body.

"You can toss me aside, Kate, but I'm not giving up on you."

She stared across the room at the computer monitor that had sent her hopes flying, and now she was spiraling downward in a fatal nosedive. Amber had been only one dream. Scott, the other. Together, they made her world whole. Could she trust Scott? Could she tell him that she wasn't the virgin he prized? That she was used goods. Not a rape. Not an accident. But a planned activity, tossing away all that was important in hopes that she would be popular like Kristin.

"Kate?"

Scott's sad voice touched her ear, and she lifted her head. "I'm okay. Give me time, Scott."

"You can have all the time you need, Kate. But please don't push me away. I have my own guilt...my own hurt."

Kate studied his face, wanting to ask him what he meant. But if she couldn't talk to him, how could she ask him to bear his heart? She needed to pray for God's help...for the Lord's will. If Scott loved her enough to put up with her constant turmoil, she needed to ask God for guidance. Yet, she feared that Scott deserved more than she could give.

Chapter Fifteen

When Kate opened the door just before dinner, the flower deliveryman surprised her. He held a lovely floral arrangement of white lilies, delicate pink tulips, and rose-hued carnations. She carried the flowers into the house and noted the gift card. Scott's message peeked out of the blossoms. "With the Lord, all things are possible."

Admiring the lovely flowers, Kate felt a tender longing flow through her. She plucked the card from the bouquet and ran her finger along Scott's familiar script—the long slash across the double *t,* the snake-curved *s.*

Always thoughtful, Scott had been gentle and persistent since their dinner at Cass's. That evening the moment the conversation reached its peak, Kate had expected to tell him goodbye, but the words bunched in her throat, and "I love you" filled her mind instead. And she truly did.

But the foreboding remained.

Many nights, she tossed and turned in her bed, trying to

create a dialogue—a way to explain herself, a way to break the news of her unchaste youth, a way to ask forgiveness before she spit out the horrible words.

Pretending she was Scott, Kate mentally recited and listened to her tale, then cringed when the words smacked her across the face—a story she already knew. The test run failed. How could she second-guess Scott's reaction? Yes, he loved her. He'd told her often, though she'd only uttered "I love you" once, afraid that saying it would make a commitment she couldn't handle.

Two years younger, handsome and chaste, Scott had much to offer a pure Christian woman. Sure, Kate was a Christian, but pure...? And no matter what she did, she could never bring back the chastity that she longed to give her husband.

Why hadn't she realized the truth of that terrible moment when she willingly slid down against the seat cushion in the back of Ron's car and watched the rain running in rivulets like the tears that rolled down her cheeks? Her knotted hands dug into her palms as his square, muscled frame arched above her, then the undefinable moment—the loss of her morals, her faith, her innocence. Why hadn't she realized that the deep piercing hurt would stab her heart and leave her feeling sorrowful and unworthy for the rest of her life?

Corralling her anguish, Kate pulled her thoughts back to the lovely bouquet. In the last dredges of winter, Scott had sent her a little taste of spring. The thought caught in her mind. Scott's love offered her the same, the promise of rebirth following the bitter years of dying. She buried her nose in the flowers and drew in the sweet, promising scent.

"How do you rate?"

Kate turned toward Phyllis's voice. "I didn't hear you come in."

"That's because I'm crawling." Phyllis grinned and crumbled into a chair. "Planning a wedding is too much work. I tried to convince Darren we should run away. Elope and send a telegram."

"You'd never do that," Kate said, shaking her head at her friend's foolish idea.

"I know, but it sounds good." She gestured toward the arrangement. "So, who sent the flowers?"

"Take a guess."

"Oh, him," Phyllis said, feigning surprise. "When are the two of you going to make the big announcement?"

Empty hope plodded through Kate's veins. "I don't know, Phyl. Maybe never."

"You're kidding. Why?"

"I'm too old to settle down. I'm set in—"

"Poor excuse, Kate. You've been sputtering around here for the past weeks filling out paperwork to become a foster parent. You don't think that will change your life and make you settle down?"

Kate shrugged, hoping to mute the sadness that sat like a rock against her heart. "I'm too old to manage that many changes."

"Don't hand me that." Phyllis leaned forward, peering

into Kate's face. "Don't you love Scott, Kate?" Her expression announced her disbelief. "I can't imagine that you don't. I know he loves you."

Kate skirted the issue, relating her upbringing again, her inability to love, her fear of commitment.

Phyllis listened quietly for a few minutes, then pressed her palm against the air like a traffic cop. "Stop, Kate. You're making excuses. What you say and do is contradictory. Upbringing, sure, that can be a problem, but I've seen you with Amber and Scott. You have love spilling out of you, and with foster care, you're promising a commitment to Amber. So why can't you do the same for Scott?"

Kate tried to respond, but Phyllis rose and shook her head. "Look, if you don't love Scott enough to marry him, that's one thing. But if you're handing me excuses for some other reason, please don't. You owe me nothing, Kate. I owe you."

"You don't owe me a thing. What do you mean?"

"I've lived here in your home, I've taken advantage of your friendship, I've burdened you with my ups and downs. You've put up with my idiosyncrasies, my antics—"

"Now, you stop," Kate said, rising and putting her arms around Phyllis. "I love Scott. I love him with all my heart." She lifted her teary eyes to Phyllis's tense, confused face. "I have some personal problems to resolve. I can't do anything until I deal with those issues. That's the long and short of it."

"Can I help?" Phyllis asked, moisture pooling on her lashes.

"No. I have to do it alone."

"But—"

Kate pressed her forehead against Phyllis's. "Don't ask, Phyl. I'll tell you when it's time. Please understand?"

She felt her friend's head nod against her own. When she calmed, she stepped back and forced a smile to her tearstained face. "Now, tell me about the wedding plans. I can't wait."

Looking over her shoulder, Kate chuckled at Scott, paint-splattered from head to toe. "Did I ever mention you look good in pink?"

His mouth drooped, and he peered at his spotted jeans and T-shirt. "Did I ever mention I'm not a painter?"

Seeing his silly expression, Kate sputtered a laugh. "I'll agree you're no Rembrandt. But I hope you can wallpaper."

He shook his head and bent down to add paint to the roller.

Kate returned to her task and picked up the paintbrush. She loved the shade she'd chosen for the upstairs bedroom—as delicate as a cherry blossom. Amber would love it...if things went as planned.

Kate sighed. Her application for the foster parent license had been accepted, her finances verified, her mental and physical health scrutinized. She'd provided three character references. They'd even checked her for a criminal record. So far, she'd passed all the requirements. Now, she expected a home visit in the next couple weeks. Having the room ready was at the top of her list.

Amber. With wavering emotion, Kate struggled, facing the paradoxical reality. If Mrs. Yates improved, Amber would returned to live with her grandmother. Kate would be joyful for Amber, her own sorrow salved by the child's reunion. Until she faced that day, the room would be a little girl's dream: ribbons, lace and ruffles.

Scott had even let her drag him to the Birmingham Decorating Shop and waited while she poured through books of wallpaper samples. Cartoons, clowns, ballerinas, fairy tales, pandas—nothing seemed to fit until she noticed a dainty print paper, posies tied with lengths of pink ribbon on a white background, as delicate and ethereal as Amber.

Kate peeked at Scott, busy behind her, and grinned. He put down the roller, blew a stream of air from his lungs, and perched on top of the four-rung wooden ladder. "I hope all this work isn't going to waste."

"I'm thinking positive. So far, they've approved my application. The agency only has a few more things to check."

"Look at it this way, if something goes wrong, you've decorated your guest room."

Kate gaped at the pastel walls. "Pink? I hope dear old Uncle Albert doesn't come for a visit."

Laughing, Scott rose from the stool and walked to her side, nuzzling his head against hers, but keeping his smeared hands out of reach. "Things'll be fine, I'm sure."

With a peck on the cheek, he turned back to the wall and his roller. Kate dipped the brush into the paint can, adding a glossy coat to the moldings and windowsills.

The room hummed with their efforts, and when Kate finished the trim, she stepped back and admired the effect. She checked Scott's progress. With even strokes, Scott rolled the second coat of color on the final wall. Tomorrow, all she had left was the wallpaper. An easy job, she hoped—one single, unbroken wall.

Admiring the dainty colored walls, she faced her fears. No matter how she tried to convince herself, she'd feel devastated if, for some reason, Amber were placed in another foster home.

"Done," Scott said, stepping back and dropping the roller onto the pan. "Looks good, if I do say so."

"It does. And the wallpaper will make it even better."

"I'm on staff that day," he said, halting her inquiry. He chuckled at his wily excuse. "Listen, I'll clean up this mess if you'll order a pizza...or two. I'm starving."

His offer sounded like a good deal, and she scurried off to clean up and make the call.

Scott lugged the paint and supplies to the basement and stood over the laundry tub, scouring the brushes and roller.

Worried about Kate, he imagined her disappointment if things didn't go as she had planned. Foster parenting wasn't easy, especially for someone unmarried and holding down a full-time job. Like an arrow, the word *unmarried* pierced his emotions. If Scott had anything to say, Kate would be married in a minute.

Grasping the fingernail brush, he attacked his paint-spattered hands. Even when he first met Kate, he recalled his hesitation to get romantically involved. Though he found her interesting and attractive, he wanted no part of the ups and downs of romance. He'd lost faith in women and himself. And he'd felt shame for his religious convictions.

That was the brunt of his problem with Lana. She'd made him ashamed to be a Christian—embarrassed to stand up for his moral values, his belief that chastity wasn't only important, but was God's directive.

In the past months as he'd drawn closer to Kate, he'd let those old fears slide into his locked trunk of unwanted memories. Now he was falling all over himself, trying to convince Kate to love him. Maybe, the real issue was to trust him. But how could she?

Kate knew he had old hurts and regrets. He'd hinted at them enough times. Could that be what she was waiting for? Would she think that if he trusted her enough to open his old wounds, then she'd be willing to reveal hers?

Though a sense of relief marched through him, anxiety rattled the key to the truth deep in his mind. Maybe he'd talk today. But he'd wait for the right moment. Definitely not before the pizza.

Spreading the brushes and roller out to dry, Scott soaped, rinsed his hands and arms, dried them, then checked his face in the lavatory mirror. He scraped off a few telltale splatters and rinsed. Pulling a comb from his back pocket, he dragged it through his hair and deemed himself ready.

As he climbed the basement stairs, he heard Kate in the kitchen. When he stepped into the room, he saw she had set the table with paper plates and salad bowls.

Kate smiled over her shoulder. Her face gleamed from the scrubbing, and he imagined what she might look like in the morning, fresh from a shower.

At the counter, she was tossing salad greens into a bowl. "Giorgio's doesn't have salads so I thought I'd make one."

"Great," he said, slipping behind her and snatching a piece of cucumber from the greens.

"How do you expect me to do this with you hanging on me?"

"I don't," he said, sweeping her around into his arms.

He popped a kiss on her nose, then grinned when he spotted the paring knife clutched in her hand. He cautiously pivoted her back to the counter with her laughter ringing in his ears.

Along with her laugh, the doorbell jingled, and Scott hurried off to answer, hoping it was the pizza delivery. With his wish fulfilled, he hoisted the two containers over his head, chuckling that she'd taken him literally. In the kitchen, they settled down to tall glasses of soda, the garden salad and the thick, hot squares of deep-dish pizza.

When he pushed back from the table, Kate arched an eyebrow and jiggled the cardboard box containing the eight slices. "I thought you said order two."

"I didn't mean large." Though he gave her a wink, his earlier thoughts sat on his mind, and he wished he could chow down a couple more pieces to delay the inevitable.

He rose and helped Kate clear the table, then wandered back into the living room, tempted to snap on the TV or do anything to avoid the nettled thoughts that prodded him.

In a moment, Kate joined him, carrying their refreshed tumblers of ice and soda. He grasped his and slid it on the nearby table. Kate chose an adjacent chair and sat. "I hope that paint smell doesn't hang around too long."

"It won't," he said, wishing the same for the words that lodged in his throat. He pulled his T-shirt away from his Adam's apple and swallowed.

"Kate, you know how I feel about you, and please, don't stop me. I have some things I really want to get off my back."

"What things?" Her face tensed, and she knotted her arms against her chest. "Did I do something?"

"No, nothing like that."

Her face relaxed.

If he were honest, he'd tell her she *had* done something—not love him in return. But in his heart, he believed Kate did love him. She just didn't know it, yet.

"This is about me, Kate."

He sensed he'd piqued her interest. She rested her elbow on the chair arm nearest him and balanced her chin in her hand. "What is it?"

"I told you a long time ago that I had something that bothered me. Things I'd done that made me ashamed."

"Please, Scott, no, it's not necessary—"

"It is Kate. I want to be completely honest with you, and it's not so much what I did, but how I reacted. That's the part that bothers me most."

She didn't respond, but she didn't try to stop him, either. He continued. "I've always been a bookworm of sorts. I suppose part of me has tried to pay my folks back for loving me. Just a quirk of being an adopted kid, I guess. They never gave me cause to question their love. But somewhere in me I felt different from others, not as loveable maybe."

He grasped the strands of his rambling concepts and quickly tried to tie them together. "Getting to the point, when I was in college, I met an attractive girl. Lana. She was wilder than me. More adventurous. She'd smoke sometimes and have a drink. I knew I shouldn't get involved with her, but she was enticing...and to be honest, one of the first girls that captured my interest."

As if puzzled, Kate shifted in the seat, sipped her soda, and leaned against the cushion, her face intent. He could almost see her counseling wheels turning.

"Anyway, besides the other things Lana tried, she was eager to learn about passion. Sometimes when kids leave home, they want to try all the things that their parents forbid. I have to admit I was tempted. Lana made herself available, but I avoided getting involved. The more I made excuses the more she chided and manipulated. Finally, I got up the nerve to admit I believed in chastity."

Kate's face paled and a look of concern washed over her. Scott pushed himself forward, wanting to finish his confession.

"She laughed, Kate. 'You're a virgin,' she said, as if I were some kind of freak. I groveled in self-pity. She tempted me, pushed me as far as I let her, and then she told me to take her home."

His voice caught, and shame filled him again, recalling that day. "I should've stood up for myself and my faith, Kate. I let her attitude make me embarrassed that I believed in God's Word. I should've told her to leave, instead of letting her make me the fool."

Kate leaned forward. "But the sin was hers, not yours, Scott. You stood your ground. You didn't let her push you to do something you thought was wrong. You were better than she was."

Her defense touched him, and he wished she'd do the same, tell him her past pain so he could stand up for her.

"I'm not telling you for your social work skills, Kate. I just wanted you to know that we all have things that we hate remembering, shameful memories that hang on in the back of our minds like leeches."

Kate straightened herself in the chair. "I didn't mean to sound like a social worker. I'm sure that was an awful time for you, Scott. You're a great guy and it's obvious you didn't let it destroy you or weaken your faith. Maybe it strengthened you. Made you more sure of your beliefs."

It felt easy to tell her now, and he decided to add the last chapter of the story, hoping she would see the depth of his scar and encourage her to talk with him.

"She tried to humiliate me a few months later," he said. "On my way to class, she stopped me. She was latched on to some big strapping dude that she left standing alone while she strode across the grass.

"She had an arrogant smile plastered on her face and a stack of books propped on her belly. It took only a minute for me to realize she was pregnant. She told me she was getting married. As she left, she hollered over her shoulder that it was a shame I wasn't a real man."

Kate released a gasp. "You are a real man," Kate said.

"More than that, you're perfect. You listen to God and do what He asks. That's why you deserve the best."

Scott faltered hearing her voice. He sensed that a distance had stretched between them, as if a drawbridge had lifted and a moat separated them. And he didn't know why.

Chapter Sixteen

Kate shifted the paperwork on her office desk, unable to concentrate. She couldn't get Scott's confession out of her mind. Like a social worker, she'd listened with concern, analyzing the situation and helping him face the truth. Then like a snake slithering out of the tall grass, his words chilled her to the bone.

As if a wedge had been hammered between them, Kate faced her own truth. No matter how much she loved him, a relationship was impossible. Even if Scott said he had forgiven her sinful behavior, she'd know he never could. He stood up for himself against Lana, despite how he felt. Rather than making a sexual conquest—using her willingness for a new experience—he lived by his faith, like David against Goliath. But Kate had embraced sin and, like Bathsheba, had hurt her family and lost her child.

A tap on the door roused her from the dark thoughts, and she looked toward the door.

Phyllis stepped into the office. "Got a minute?"

"Sure."

"I just want to remind you we're shopping after work for bridesmaid dresses."

"How could I forget? You all but tattooed it on my forehead."

Laughing, Phyllis caved onto a chair. "I'm a little preoccupied I guess. I've been meaning to ask you about Amber. I saw her in the hallway earlier. How's she doing?"

"Good. I think we're making some strides. Besides remembering Sparky, she now remembers the fire...vaguely, mainly how her grandmother carried her outside."

"I'd say that's good progress. How about the bad dreams?"

"Better. She has them once in a while, but they don't affect her like they did. That's the best thing that's happened."

Phyllis yawned and rubbed her eyes. "How about her parents? Any memories?"

Kate shook her head. "Nothing really, and I don't want to push. Anyway, I wonder if she spent most of her time with her grandma."

Phyllis shrugged. "Maybe her parents both worked. Speaking of which," she said, standing up, "I'd better get back. I'm so lazy today." She headed toward the door, then stopped. "Think about colors."

"Colors?" Kate asked.

"For the gowns."

Kate laughed. "Do you think of anything else?"

"Not until May 26. Two and half months."

"I can't wait," Kate said, realizing how much time went into planning even a small wedding.

Phyllis hurried from the room, and Kate flipped open a file, staring at the page. How would she feel if this were her wedding? A flutter of jealousy shivered into her thoughts and out again.

She glanced through the window, seeing the tiny nubs of green poking from the trees. In spring a young man's fancy turns to thoughts of love. The old saying jogged through her head, and she gave it a twist. Not only man's, but woman's. She blamed it on Noah...and God, animals marching two by two.

Her telephone rang, sending Noah and his animals running for cover. She snatched up the receiver and said hello. When she heard Scott's voice, a ripple of longing waved through her. "What's up?" she asked.

"My procrastination got the best of me today."

She lifted her eyebrows. Always, she had to sort through his puzzling words. "What's that mean?"

"It means I called Pastor Ray to check on Mrs. Finkell."

"Ah, guilt with a capital *G*. I thought she was in a nursing home."

"That was only for a short time while she recuperated and learned to give herself insulin shots."

"So, she's back home?" Kate asked.

"Uh-huh, I thought we could go and visit her after work. What do you say?"

"I say I'm going to the bridal shop to look at bridesmaid gowns with Phyllis."

"Oh."

She heard the disappointment in his voice. "Sorry. Do you want to postpone?"

"No, I called her. She's expecting me."

"Well, have fun and give her my best." Kate said, picturing poor Scott trying to conjure up conversation to interest the elderly woman.

"Will I see you later?" he asked.

"Sounds good," Kate said.

A lengthy pause dragged through the line. "Could you do me a favor?"

She hesitated, curious as to what he had in mind. "Sure, what?"

"Check out those wedding dresses while you're there, okay?"

After she hung up, she sat frozen in place. Though she knew she'd responded with a witty comment, she had no recollection of what she said.

Pulling dollar bills from his pocket, Scott paid for the small spray of carnations and fern. He wished he had stock in a florist shop for all the flowers he'd purchased lately. He'd been persistent, doing everything to show Kate how much he loved her.

But this bouquet wasn't for Kate. They were for Mrs. Finkell. He was disappointed that Kate couldn't come along. Besides enjoying her company, he'd thought she'd take him off the hook of finding things to talk about. But he'd come up with something.

He knew he'd erred when he teased Kate about checking out the wedding dresses. A deafening silence had filled the line before she sputtered back a short response. He should have thought before opening his mouth.

His sister's wedding was approaching with the speed of a comet, and with that thought, a wave of frustration washed over him. He'd hoped to be engaged to Kate by Phyllis's wedding date, but Kate's acceptance was as slow as a child waiting for Christmas. He wasn't sure his efforts had made a second's worth of headway.

Outside, he headed for his car, and after placing the flowers on the passenger seat, he pulled into traffic and headed toward Mrs. Finkell's home.

Scott parked in the driveway of the familiar house, and the door opened before he reached the porch steps. The older woman eyed the bouquet with a growing smile.

"For me?" she asked, her arm extended toward the flowers.

"None other." Scott handed her the carnations and stepped inside.

"Thank you," she said, burying her nose in the bouquet. "No one brings me flowers anymore. My daughter sends an arrangement on Mother's Day, sometimes."

Scott followed her into the tiny kitchen where she pulled a vase from under the sink and filled it with water.

"Need some help?" Scott asked, watching her shaking fingers try to undo the florist's packaging.

She stepped aside, and Scott went to work. "You look better than the last time I saw you," he said, removing the wrapping.

"I'm much better, thanks to you. I've thought of you so often, wanting to tell you how grateful I am. I could be dead, you know." She lifted her wrinkled face to his and grinned.

"I know," he said, "but you're fit as a fiddle, as they say."

"Sure am." She plopped the flowers into the vase and tucked the ferns around the blossoms. "There now. Real pretty." She turned from the sink. "So, could I get you a drink?"

"No, I'm fine."

She nodded, grasped the flowers, and headed back to the living room, her voice sailing over her shoulder as Scott followed. "You're fine, huh? I've been wondering about that young lady and you."

She set the vase on a table and motioned toward an easy chair. "Have a seat."

"Kate, you mean?" Scott asked, sinking into the cushion.

Mrs. Finkell settled on the sofa. "I think that's her name. Pretty girl with blond hair and a smile as bright as sunshine."

"That's her," Scott said as Kate's image rose in his mind.

"So, you two getting married?"

"I wish."

"What's that mean? Did you ask her?"

"Not exactly, but—"

The woman tossed her head backward with a chuckle. "Do you need an old lady to tell you how to court a girl? They never say they'll marry you unless you ask."

Her words tickled him, but she'd hit upon the truth. He'd thought his intention was clear. But maybe not. Or was Kate waiting for something else? Had he missed a clue? Had he done something wrong to discourage her? "She knows how I feel, but Kate says she needs time. I'm thinking she—"

"Time, you say?"

He nodded.

"I suppose women say that. Might've myself. But time means there's hope."

Her puzzling words were lost to him. "What?"

"If she didn't care, she'd say so. A woman knows when it's no. It's the yes that's harder to say."

Looking at her creased face and white hair, Scott wondered if she meant Victorian women or today's.

"You think I'm too old to know what I'm talking about?"

Scott laughed out loud, positive she was a mind reader. "I'm thinking that might not hold true for modern women."

"Women are women. It's not playing hard to get. It's wanting to know their hearts." She pressed her gnarled fingers against her chest. "Everything happens right here," she said, tapping two fingers against her cotton print dress. "Lifetime commitments don't come easy."

"You're right about that." Scott thought of his own struggles, and how he'd finally faced them.

"Now, the big question. Do you *really* court her?"

"You mean send flowers and say 'I love you'?"

"That, too, but I mean let your actions do the work. I've seen many a bouquet and endearments that held empty promises. Actions count."

Actions count. The thought rumbled through his mind.

He'd asked himself what he'd done wrong. Maybe the question was what hadn't he done. Amber came to mind. He'd definitely discouraged Kate's idea of being a foster parent...except for helping her paint. His words weren't encouraging. But he was protecting Kate, that was all. Then, another "hadn't done" came to him. He hadn't trusted that, in time, she'd tell him what pressed so heavily on her heart.

"I hit a sore spot, I see," Mrs. Finkell said.

"You've given me things to think about. I can tell you all the things I've done to let Kate know how much I care, but you've made me think of things I *haven't* done."

Mrs. Finkell nodded, her pale eyes misting. "Love is give and take. But it's lots more give. That's a hard lesson to learn. I remember when I was a young bride, I tried being thoughtful, but I did it for the wrong reason."

"What's the wrong reason?" Scott asked, amazed that this white-haired lady had become a biblical Mrs. King Solomon.

"The wrong reason is wanting something back. Never give to get. Give because you love the lady so much that if she gave you nothing back, you wouldn't give a hoot."

Her words spiraled through him, and he grabbed at the dangling strings of thought, trying to weave them together into a solid understanding. First thing he needed was prayer. The Bible taught to give and you'd be rewarded, but the Bible didn't say give *so* you are rewarded. There's a difference. Mrs. Finkell put her finger on it.

* * *

As soon as Scott entered the house, tears rushed down Kate's cheeks.

"What's wrong?" Scott blurted, rushing to her side and taking her in his arms.

"Mrs. Yates died this morning, and I had to tell—"

"Amber," he finished, as her sobs overtook her. She buried her face against his chest.

He held her in his arms, letting the tension wash away. When Kate lifted her face, her puffy eyes were rimmed with moisture and damp rivulets clung to her cheeks.

"I'm sorry," she said. "I don't mean to be so emotional. Telling Amber was unbelievably difficult, and then, I know the Haven has to arrange placement for her...and my approval hasn't been finalized yet. I don't know what to do."

Without responding, Scott guided her to the sofa and sat beside her, resting her head on his shoulder.

"I'd think the Haven could be reasonable, Kate. They know you and they know Amber. Why can't they—"

"State regulations, Scott. If it were up to my director, she'd let me bring her home." She raised her head. "I've been thinking...and I—I want to adopt Amber."

"Adopt her? But—" He stopped, remembering his talk with Mrs. Finkell two weeks earlier about giving without expecting anything in return.

Kate continued, "I know you don't like the idea. You don't even like—"

"That's not true, Kate. Amber's a wonderful kid who deserves a loving parent. You're the most loving woman I know. It's a perfect match. She even looks a little like you. It's *you* I've worried about. You being hurt or disappointed if Amber was returned to her grandmother."

"I worried about it, too, but now...things are different."

"They sure are." Still, a new thought poked his fading concerns. "Will they look for more family now?"

She drew the back of her hand across her misty eyes. "Yes, but I think they'll learn what we already know. Even if they find someone, I doubt they'll take her, especially if they know someone wants to adopt."

Conviction planted itself firmly in Scott's mind. He loved Kate, and he wanted to marry her no matter what. And today was as good as any to tell her.

"Why sit in here?" he asked, grappling for a few more minutes to organize his words. "Let's go outside. What do you say?"

Kate nodded, grabbing a sweater from the closet, but when they stepped off the back porch, she faltered, raising her hands into the air. "It's like spring."

"Told you," he said, slipping his arm around her shoulders and heading for the glider. "Look at the flowers popping up. Remember when we first met? We sat out here, and all I could smell was lilacs...and you."

She nudged him. "Liar."

"You're sweeter than any lilac, Kate."

She grasped the arm of the glider and sat, ignoring his comment. "I like spring," she said. "Everything's new and fresh. Wish we could do that to our minds."

"You can. Gardens don't grow without effort. It just takes work. If you let the weeds take over, they kill the flowers. Cleaning out the mind's the same thing." He lifted his arm and rested it across the seat back."

"I've been praying a lot," Kate said. "Praying that I can give things to God and not hang on to them. I guess I like weeds. Those problems sprout in my mind and cover all the good things."

"That's what I mean." His heart galloped, wondering if today was the day she'd finally open up.

Kate straightened and faced him. "Oh, well, enough of that. Let's talk about something more pleasant."

The gallop halted, and his heart mired in disappointment. Still, Scott refused to stop now. He had something more pleasant to suggest—much more pleasant.

He swiveled on the seat and captured her chin in his hand. His chest swelled with the surprise in Kate's eyes, and he lowered his lips, enjoying the gentle feel of her mouth against his. She did love him. He was positive.

When he drew back, her eyes searched his.

"What brought that on?" she asked.

"Do I need a reason to kiss you, other than the obvious?"

She lowered her head. "I'm scared, Scott. My life is about to change and I'm praying I'm making the right decision—that what I'm doing for Amber isn't motivated by my own agenda."

"What agenda?" Her comment left him puzzled.

"You know what I mean. Doing it for the wrong reason."

Wrong reason. Mrs. Finkell's words shot through him like

an arrow. Often he'd done things for the wrong reason, but today was different. He drew in a deep breath, garnering the courage he'd need to see him through.

"And that leads me to another idea," Scott said, sending up a silent, speedy prayer. "Since you're in the change mode, I have an additional one for you."

Her head jerked toward him, a look of bewilderment and dread inching across her face. "What?"

"Marry me, Kate. I've wanted this for a long time, and—"

"Oh Scott, this isn't a good time to—"

"It's never been a good time. But for once, I'm doing something without expecting anything in return, Kate. You love Amber, and having a husband will make adoption easier. It might even speed up the foster parent decision, who knows?"

She opened her mouth to speak, but Scott pressed his index finger on her lips to stifle her words. "Don't talk. Let me finish. I know you have fears and problems. I expect nothing from you, Kate. Be my wife, and we can pray that God makes things right for us. There are no strings. I mean this from my heart."

He pulled his finger away from her lips, watching tears well in her eyes, and like a dam that collapsed, a torrent of emotions spilled over her like a waterfall.

"Kate, please, don't cry. I didn't want you to cry."

"It's not you, Scott. It's me," she said, her words mingled with her sobs.

"But I love you the way you are. All the surprises, the laughs, the tears, everything. I want you, Kate."

"I've dreamed of this day," she whispered. "In the back of my mind, I pictured this moment...but I never completed the dream. I never sensed how I'd answer." She brushed the tears from her hands knotted in her lap. "I need to think. I need to pray, Scott." She lifted her eyes. "Can you give me a little time?"

Mrs. Finkell's shaky voice sailed into Scott's mind. *But time means there's hope.* "You can have all the time you need, Kate." He repeated the phrase over and over in his head. Time means hope.

Chapter Seventeen

Peering through the window into the backyard, Kate felt her heart lift as she watched Amber playing with a neighborhood child. Somewhere in her moments of panic, she stopped and prayed, prayed from the depths of her heart, and God had heard the prayer. Letting God handle problems was the wisest decision, yet the hardest task a person had to face.

Kate remembered how often she'd wrestled with her fears, pinning them to the floor, only to have them rise again and capture her in a stronghold for the count of ten. Why hadn't she learned that God moved mountains, yet carried the lambs in his bosom. For so long, she'd needed mountains moved and God's shepherding. Kate still needed the Lord.

With Scott's proposal pinioned in her thoughts, Kate's eyes filled with tears. His compassion and kindness, with the offer of marriage, touched her heart, but she didn't want his pity or self-sacrifice to make her dream come true. He was the best man she knew—the best she would ever know.

Now, God had blessed her with Amber, and the adoption papers were filed. Scott hadn't mentioned his kind offer again, but continued being part of her life—and Amber's.

Each day the proposal rattled in her conscience, pushing her to give him a kind and tender refusal. Avoidance didn't sit well with Kate.

Her reluctance was Phyllis's wedding. She and Scott were part of the bridal party. If tension happened between them, their attitudes could set the wedding on edge. She'd wait until after.

Kate turned away from the window and filled a glass with tap water. She took a long drink, analyzing her thoughts. If she were honest, her hesitation had to do with more than the wedding.

She'd talked to God and read her Bible, seeking a way to make her sinful confession. She owed that to Scott. Why? Because she loved him. But he deserved more than she could give. She was used goods, damaged merchandise. Scott merited the purest of all that was good.

Setting the glass on the counter, Kate floundered for a sense of serenity. If not a husband, God had given her a child—a child to nurture and to love, a chance to redeem herself. She'd opened her arms to Amber, just as God had opened His loving arms to her.

Kate flung open the back door and wandered outside. The new play set had been installed in the back of the yard, and she headed toward the glider, breathing in the sweet lilac-filled air. Amber's and her friend's giggles rose on the warm breeze, and the sun kissed Kate's arms, helping her feel nearly whole again. Nearly.

She sat on the glider, stretching her legs in front of her. Happiness shuffled along her spine, hearing Amber's content voice. When she lowered her head for a moment, her focus shifted to an army of ants, marching up the hill and another trooping down. Kate recalled a similar incident a year earlier. Gooseflesh rose on her arms. So much had happened since then.

As if it were yesterday, she remembered that special afternoon when she announced to no one in particular that she needed to take hold of her life. And moments later, she was wielding a flowered umbrella in Scott's face. The memory tugged a hearty chuckle from her chest.

"What's so funny?"

Kate lurched upward.

Scott stood a few feet away, his arms burdened with the largest stuffed bear Kate had ever seen.

"Scott," Amber yelled from the jungle gym and rushed to his side.

"Here you are, sunshine," he said, plopping the bear into her outstretched arms.

"That thing is as big as she is," Kate called, smiling at the mammoth stuffed animal.

Amber clutched the bear against her chest and waddled to Kate's side. "Look at my present."

"I can't miss it, sweetie. It's almost bigger than you are."

"But I love it," Amber said, plopping the toy on the glider beside Kate, then running with a leap into Scott's arms.

He wrapped her in a giant hug, and Amber pecked his cheek.

"Thank you," she said, her voice piping with excitement.

Amber's friend, Carrie, joined them, and the poor bear was dragged across the grass by the two girls, chattering about taking the toy down the slide and on the swing.

Scott grinned and dropped beside Kate. "You're almost as cute as Amber, Katie," he said, lifting her hand and kissing her fingers.

"You shouldn't have bought her that bear. It cost a fortune," Kate said.

"She's worth it. All the women I love are worth more than rubies."

"You sound biblical."

He gave her a wink. "That...and more."

The past months during their time together, Kate had finally learned to decode many of Scott's vague comments. She knew what he meant. The "more" he referred to was his love for her. The idea rattled her. Not wanting to deal with it, she shifted gears.

"Did you pick up the tux?"

"Sure did. Are you getting nervous?"

"Me?" Kate asked. "Tonight's only the rehearsal."

"I know, but I'm nervous. Best man has to remember, well, the ring and—"

"And the ring," she said with a chuckled. "I have to lift her veil, hold the bouquet and crawl around on the floor a million times to straighten Phyllis's gown. They should retitle the job Chambermaid of Honor."

"Very original," Scott said, sliding his arm around her and nestling her to his side.

"You smell sweet," he said.

"It's the lilacs," she said. "You seem to get us confused."

He laughed.

Kate rested her head against his shoulder, watching the children and the giant bear, but thinking about Scott. She didn't question whether Scott cared about her, but she wondered if he'd mentally rescinded his proposal since Amber arrived.

Whether he had or not, Kate had to give him an answer. Marrying Scott would be a dream, a wonderful dream. But she couldn't marry without laying her life out in front of him. Marriage was based on honesty. But she wasn't sure she would have the courage to be honest. Then she wasn't sure how he'd react. She halted in midthought. Pastor Ray's kindly face rose in her mind. Could she find the courage to talk with him?

With the swell of the pipe organ, Kate bent down for the fifth time to adjust Phyllis's sweeping lace veil as she and Darren prepared for their triumphant recessional. Arm in arm, they headed down the aisle. Next in line, Kate stepped forward to follow, capturing Scott's arm. Her pulse raced.

Though she'd always considered Scott a handsome man, her heart somersaulted when she saw him in the afternoon, dressed in the black tuxedo that accentuated his broad shoulders and trim waist. He wore a lavender cummerbund and tie in a shade to match the attendants' dresses, and the pastel purple filled Kate's thoughts with spring—lilacs, creeping myrtle, grape hyacinth, and wild violets.

Clasping Scott's reassuring arm, Kate moved down the aisle, a smile on her face, her eyes seeking Amber. When she saw the girl's happy face, Kate gave a small wave, and the child lifted her hand and wiggled her fingers in greeting, wrenching Kate's love-filled heart. Scott and Amber. Together her life would be complete.

When she and Scott reached the foyer, they followed the bride and groom into the fellowship hall. Forming a receiving line, they greeted the guests, and when Amber arrived with Cass, Kate knelt and gave her a giant hug.

"You look pretty," Amber said, her eyes wide with excitement.

"Thanks. You look beautiful," Kate said in return, running her finger along the delicate trim of Amber's neckline.

With this being Amber's first wedding, Kate and she had shopped for hours to find the perfect party dress almost the same shade as Kate's. Today, Kate had combed back the sides of Amber's hair and held it with a purple scrunch, the curls hanging like a ponytail of ringlets. Kate was a proud mother.

Amber stepped away and encircled Scott's neck with a giant squeeze, then skipped along with Cass, like a little lady. Kate's heart melted at the sight.

When the receiving line ended, Scott carried a stack of wedding cards across the room to Darren, and Kate hurried away to find Amber. The child was sipping a cup of frothy punch beside Cass at one of the round tables.

"Where's Scott?" Amber asked, as soon as Kate neared.

"Talking with Darren." Kate pointed a finger in their direction.

"Can I go?" Amber asked.

Kate gave her an agreeing nod, and she skipped off, her full-skirted tulle dress bouncing as she ran.

"Have a seat," Cass said, patting Amber's vacated chair.

Painfully aware of her tired feet, Kate thought the idea sounded good. She sat beside him with a relieved sigh.

"Punch?" he asked.

"Sure."

He rose and returned in a moment, bearing a glass filled with the fruity drink.

"Thanks." She took a sip. "Tastes good."

Cass leaned back in the chair, twirling his cup with an index finger. "You two surprise me."

"Amber and me?"

"No, you and Scott. He's crazy about you."

Crazy about you. "I know. But we're just good friends."

"Maybe, that's what *you* think, Kate, but that guy loves you. I thought you'd be engaged by now. I would have bet on it."

An uncomfortable flush edged up her neck. "Well, you're wrong."

Cass hesitated. "Don't tell me he hasn't asked you? I can't believe that." He arched a brow, as if waiting for an answer.

"He has, but—"

"Here you are," Scott said, halting her response.

Relieved, Kate rose. "Just giving my tired feet a break." She squeezed his arm. "I want to talk with Phyllis a minute, do you mind?"

"No, go ahead," Scott said. "I'll be right here when you get back."

Kate hurried off, thanking God Scott had interrupted the questions before Cass gave her the third degree. How could she explain?

Heading across the room, she noticed Pastor Ray talking with some wedding guests. *Pastor Ray.* An earlier thought struck her. While she struggled for courage, she couldn't stop now.

As he stepped away from the group, Kate nabbed his arm.

"Kate." He smiled.

"Could I ask you a favor?" Her voice sounded strained in her ears.

"Certainly." A puzzled expression leaped to his face. "Is something wrong?"

"No, well, yes, I suppose there is."

"Something here...today?" he asked.

"Oh, no, everything's lovely. It's a personal problem."

His face relaxed.

"I'd like to talk with you. That is, if you have time."

"Kate, I always have time for you. Did you mean now?"

"No, not today. Sunday? I know that's a bad day, but I've finally gotten courage, and I—" Tears pressed behind her eyes, and she struggled to gain control.

He touched her arm, his eyes insightful. "After service, Kate. If you're anxious to talk, I'm available." With the lump knotting in her throat, Kate only nodded.

"I'll see you tomorrow, then." He gave her arm a reassuring pat and moved away.

Kate hurried toward the rest room, her heart weighted with anguish, her mind clotted with fear.

With Amber tucked in bed, Kate slipped into a pair of slacks and a top, then joined Scott in the living room.

Stretched out on the sofa, he'd stripped the tie and cummerbund down to an open-necked shirt and trousers, his rented patent leather shoes tossed to the floor.

"You look comfy," Kate said.

"I am." He propped himself up on an elbow. "Tired?"

"A little, but my mind's still whirling. So don't worry about keeping me up, I need to unwind."

He patted the sofa beside him. "Come over here."

"Can't. You're hogging all the space."

He chuckled and slid his legs over the sofa and sat up. "No excuse now."

She rose and sat beside him. "Happy?"

"Sort of," he said.

Anticipating the direction of conversation, her heart hit a speed bump. She sent up a prayer that he not ask her anything serious tonight.

"You'd look beautiful in a white wedding dress, Kate."

White. She lowered her head without response.

"I'm sorry," he said. "I don't mean to push, but—"

"I know, Scott, you've waited a long time for an answer. I thought once my license came and Amber moved in that you'd be relieved."

He drew back, his face contorted with question. "Relieved?"

"I know you felt sorry for me that day when I was so stressed."

"I've never felt sorry for you, Kate. I've felt sorry for me."

"You?"

"Yes, because I love you so much...and you don't believe me."

Her stomach twisted into a tight knot, nausea rising to her throat. She swallowed, closing her eyes to subdue her emotions. "I don't feel very lovable."

"You've told me, Kate. I just don't understand why."

"Tomorrow." The word sailed off her tongue before she could halt it.

"What do you mean...tomorrow?"

The commitment was made...and maybe for the best. "We'll talk tomorrow." Her throat constricted. "I promise."

His eyes searched hers, a blend of relief and confusion filling his face. He nodded, then slipped his arms around her and pressed his cheek to hers.

Clinging to him, Kate felt the thud of his heart against her own. She loved Scott, and if God was willing, she would deal with her sin, then accept Scott's proposal. She wanted to be his wife with every fiber of her being.

As if God presented her a gift, the weight lifted from her heart. Tomorrow—the day she would say goodbye or embrace the love he offered.

Chapter Eighteen

Filled with nervous energy, Kate paced the living room, waiting for Scott to arrive from work.

The house seemed strange with Phyllis married and gone, but Amber's presence added a new challenge to her days. What had once been simple was now complex, like getting herself ready for work while getting Amber ready for school.

For Amber, the transition had presented its ups and downs. Though she had grown close to Kate during counseling, the child now faced a new school, a new home, and a new way of life. The loss of her grandmother and the dramatic change had dragged her nightmares out of hiding. But with prayer and love, they had faded to an occasional night of waking, before drifting back to sleep.

As Kate waited, she felt grateful and relieved that Amber was occupied for the evening. The occasion was her first sleep-over with her neighbor friend, Carrie. Now, in the impending silence, Kate heard every creak and groan of the rafters, every sound of traffic on the street.

She sank to the sofa and leaned her head against the cushion. Her mind reeled with her conversation earlier that day with Pastor Ray.

After they had prayed, Kate sat inside his office, the door closed, and wept uncontrollably admitting her sin and shame, revealing the presence of a daughter that she would never know, and telling him of Scott's love for her...and his belief in chastity.

Watching the pastor's face, Kate had feared seeing him blanch with her confession or hearing him mumble some patronizing words of forgiveness, then sending her out with a pat on the back.

Instead, his eyes were filled with compassion and his words were not his, but the Lord's. He reminded Kate of the biblical woman, deemed a sinner by the Pharisees, who had kissed and oiled Jesus' feet. Looking into her eyes, Pastor Ray spoke Jesus' words. "Your sins are forgiven."

In her heart, Kate knew God had forgiven her. The problem was she hadn't forgiven herself, and as the Lord's prayer reminded her, if she wanted to feel God's forgiveness fully, she had to forgive others, including herself.

The pastor's words washed over her. He had assured her that her sins were forgiven, the same as the woman in the Bible. "You've worshiped in the Lord's house each Sunday," Pastor Ray had told her, "you've given your time to HELP, you've taken a needy child into your home, and you've repented. In your own way, Kate, you've kissed Jesus' feet."

But Kate wondered. Had she really kissed Jesus' feet or were her actions an impossible attempt to buy forgiveness? She questioned herself. Could her deeds truly have been a reflection of her repentance?

When the conversation with Pastor Ray turned to Scott, Kate's heart had lifted. Trusting in the Lord's promise, her concern wasn't God's forgiveness, but Scott's. Then, the pastor reminded her that Scott demonstrated Christian virtues—compassion, kindness, humility, gentleness and patience—all the qualities that God commanded of His children. And if that were so...then Scott would also hear her confession and forgive her.

Thinking of the verse in Colossians, Kate was struck with the last sentence. "And over all these virtues put on love, which binds them all together in perfect unity." How could she deny that Scott had shown her love? He'd stuck by her side even though she pushed him away; he'd joined her search for answers about Amber's past, then embraced the girl as if she were his own; and he'd demonstrated his love for Kate in every thoughtful way.

"Forgive and put on love binding them as one." Kate wrapped the words around her heart. Was God directing her to bind herself to Scott in marriage? Did the words give her assurance of Scott's acceptance and pardon?

Recalling her past behavior, Kate realized she needed to ask Scott to forgive her for more than her sinful past. She needed forgiveness for her lack of trust and her unwillingness to accept his love.

With heightened anxiety, Kate rose and looked out the front window. She eyed her wristwatch. Six o'clock. Scott should be there any minute. Her head pounded, and she massaged her temples, hoping to ease the thunder in her ears.

Instead, she heard the slam of a car door, and her heart rose to her throat.

In a flash, Scott flung open the front door and called out a greeting.

Grasping her courage, Kate met him in the foyer.

He carried a small grocery bag in his arm. After giving her a fleeting kiss, Scott looked over her shoulder. "Where's the noisemaker?"

"Amber's spending the night with Carrie."

"On a school night?"

Though rattled by anxiety, she grinned. "You sound like her parent."

A ripple of good humor cured his lips, and he shrugged. "No school tomorrow?"

"Yes, there's school, but don't worry," she said, amazed at his concern. "Her class has a field trip early in the morning, so Carrie's mom offered to drive the girls to school.

"Where are they going?" Scott asked.

"The zoo. They're taking the first and second graders."

Scott glanced at the bag under his arm. "Then I guess she'll have to wait for her ice cream. I bought her favorite. Double chocolate."

"I'll put it in the freezer," Kate said, reaching for the bag. She struggled to remain calm and amiable, but their talk hung before her like a black curtain. They'd delayed it long enough. "She'll enjoy it tomorrow." He placed the bag in her hand, then turned toward the kitchen.

Scott stopped her. "Don't put the other flavors in. I'm ready for mine now."

Her heart sank. "Others?" she asked.

"I bought your favorite. That goofy kind with the peanuts, marshmallow and cherries."

He shot her a dazzling grin, and her heart melted as quickly as ice cream in the summer heat.

Mentally dealing with their delayed talk, Kate headed for the kitchen and Scott followed, watching while she dished up the dessert. Before she handed him the bowl, Scott slipped his arm around her waist and drew her to his side.

"I just want you to know that I think you're more luscious than that ice cream," he said.

Amazed, she stared at him. Had he totally forgotten her promise to talk with him? She tensed, and she knew he sensed it by the expression that shot across his face. She wanted to pull away, to escape the confines of his arms, to run outside so she could inhale the fresh air.

"Are you all right?" he asked.

"Not really," she said, "but it can wait."

His quizzical expression changed to dismay, and the look punctured her heart.

"We should eat this before it melts," she said, hoping to veil her sharp words. "It looks good. Thanks."

"You're welcome," he mumbled.

Kate chastised herself. If she'd kept her emotions in check, the situation wouldn't have fallen apart. Now, Scott looked on edge and her anxiety heightened. "Let's go outside?"

Without answering, Scott stepped aside.

Kate moved ahead of him and hurried to the back door, then outside to a refreshing breeze.

He followed, and in unison, they crossed the lawn in silence and sank into the shaded glider.

Though the late spring flowers brightened the yard, Kate's thoughts faded the colors to blurry drab. Why didn't she trust God to guide her words and trust Scott to forgive her? Her weak faith frustrated her.

She ate the ice cream in half spoonfuls. The flavor was her favorite, and if she hadn't been so preoccupied, she would've hugged Scott for his thoughtfulness, much like Amber did with every gift she received.

But Kate's mind was nailed to her distress. She gave Scott a sidelong glance. As if he were alone, he kept his attention riveted to the dish of ice cream. The way she'd reacted, he might have been better off alone.

"I'm sorry, Scott. Very sorry. You brought the ice cream as a treat, and I acted terribly."

He didn't respond, but she knew he listened.

She continued. "It's not a good excuse, but my mind was

tied up with our conversation last night. I'd promised to talk with you today, and—"

"That's why I brought the ice cream. A celebration."

Like cold, spiny fingers, regret worked up her spine. Unaware of the ensuing conversation, he'd planned a party. Her chest constricted around her hammering heart, and with shallowed gasps, she struggled to breathe. "I'm sorry," she said, the only words she could wrestled from her lips. "Maybe, I was wrong, Kate. I've been so certain that you'd trust me and tell me what's bothering you, then tell me that you love me. I was wrong."

"No, you're not wrong, Scott. I love you with all my heart. But I owe you an explanation."

A look of surprise jumped to his face. "Kate," he said, relief evident in his voice, "I've wanted you to trust me for so long." He captured her hand in his.

The confinement frightened her, and she slowly pulled her hand away, pressing it into her lap. "I talked with Pastor Ray this morning about us."

"About us? What about?" Scott asked, his voice constricted.

"About everything. Your proposal and my fears. He gave me a lot to think about and—"

Scott straightened, shifted to the edge of the glider, and faced her. "Kate, get on with it, please. I'm dangling over a cliff and I can't hang on much longer."

She had wanted to explain—lead up to her confession, but his complaint rankled her. "You want a bald-faced confession." She turned on him. "I'm not a virgin, Scott. I haven't been since I was fifteen."

His head jolted backward as if she'd slapped his face. Though his jaw dropped and moved like the gills of a fish out of water gasping for life, no words fell from his lips, no sound, only silence.

"I'm sorry. I've told you so often you deserve someone better than me. An untarnished Christian woman who'll love you the way you deserve."

"Kate..." Her name fell from his mouth in a breath.

"I know I've disappointed you. I've more than disappointed myself. I was young and stupid. That's not an excuse...it's a fact. I knew what I was doing, but I wanted to be popular and loved so badly that I didn't care. All my Christian upbringing went down the drain, along with my self-worth and hope."

Her voice trembled with each declaration, and tears pooled in her eyes and rolled unbidden down her face.

"Kate, please—"

"Don't stop me," she said and rattled on the hurt and shame she'd felt after she'd ruined her life.

"It's okay, Kate. I'm shocked but—"

"And that's not all, I had a baby daughter given for adoption when I was fifteen. She was born at...Madonna House." The last word faded into her sobs. She continued, "I'm unfit for a decent Christian man like you."

Scott reached out to hold her, but she pushed him away, sensing his shock, knowing he was repulsed.

Before she could stop herself, before she could catch her

breath and realize what she'd done, Scott rose and stumbled away from her.

"I can't fight you any longer," he said. "This is the last thing I thought would happen tonight. I'm sorry, but I can't handle this." He spun on his heel and tore across the grass out of sight.

Kate curled into a ball on the glider, her body reeling with spasms of guilt, her sorrow knotted within her like a hangman's noose. She'd taken every measure of her inner bitterness and flung it at Scott as if he were the sinner, instead of her.

Forcing her tearstained eyes to open, Kate peered into the darkening heavens. The sunset bled across the sky in orange and scarlet, like fire and flames—like damnation.

Chapter Nineteen

During the night shift at County General, Scott's distraction concerned him. He struggled to concentrate on the patients and push his own desperation aside. He'd spent a couple of sleepless nights plodding through the horrible memory of Kate's disclosure, overwhelmed by the outcome.

Yet, her confession was the least devastating. What hurt him to the core was her lack of faith in him. After knowing him for a year, sharing untold hours together, why hadn't she told him sooner? He'd done everything under heaven to let her know that his life was empty without her, and still, she didn't trust him to share her doleful secret.

He thought back to her family's Christmas visit. The puzzling pieces fell into place, and the cheerless picture rose in his mind. Her Christian parents, so devastated by their daughter's offense, so fearful of gossip and disdain, shut her away in Madonna House, trying to do what they thought was right.

Scott's heart ached, envisioning the fifteen-year-old Kate, her slender frame bearing the swelling of her sin, alone and frightened. And he was sure she was as naive and vulnerable then as is a child. Scott imagined her parents' pain, wanting to be proud of their lovely young daughter, yet confronted by her disgrace. A family caught in the middle.

And...Kate's daughter. His chest tightened with the reality. A little girl, perhaps as lovely as Kate, was growing up somewhere in the vast United States, never knowing her birth mother. Thinking of his own situation, a mother he would never know, his personal longing yanked his emotions, and the old melancholy shrouded him.

Amber. Kate's tremendous longing took shape as he understood her desire to take the girl into her home. Though she could never atone for her own child, Scott saw how Kate might sense God was giving her a second chance.

The perplexing fragments of his relationship with Kate puddled in his mind. Scott moved from bed to bed, patient to patient, nailing his mind to their complaints and pushing his own aside until the shift ended and he drove home in a blur of bright sunlight and exhaustion.

With Cass on day shift, Scott had the condo to himself. He slipped off his shoes and made a cup of decaf. Bits of the past tumbled into his awareness and icy slivers of reality shredded his conscience. Sitting right here in this room, he recalled a discussion with Cass and his prideful declaration. "Chastity is a precious gift between husband and wife."

Those were his very words, and Kate was sitting in the room listening, her heart, most likely, aching with her own sorrow.

Scott flinched, remembering a day with Kate when he'd disclosed the situation with Lana. Again, he stressed his belief in chastity—how he'd stood up for his faith. And Kate sat beside him, defending him, telling him he was a real man. "Perfect" she'd said. And then, her final comment. "You listen to God and do what he asks. That's why you deserve the best."

Unbidden, tears flooded Scott's eyes, and his stomach cramped, holding back the deluge of emotion that washed over him. He never cried, not even over his humiliation with Lana, but today the misery poured from his heart and rolled down his cheeks. Kate meant more to him than a million Lanas. He hammered his fist against the sofa cushion, appalled that he'd been so stupid. So blind, not to understand sooner.

Kate, with her distorted perception, viewed herself as the worst, not the best for Scott. In her eyes, she was used goods, marred by her past. Yet, Scott perceived a different Kate—a lovely, ideal woman inside and out. A woman who cared about needy children, who gave her time to help others, who made him laugh...and made him cry, a woman who loved the Lord.

Somehow he had to show Kate she was wrong. Though he despised sin, he loved the sinner—a young girl who gave too much to be loved—so much that she no longer loved herself.

No one was without sin. Each person on earth allowed pride or money, career or lust, greed or gluttony—things that satisfy the flesh—destroy the spirit. Scott was a sinner.

A flash of memory cut through him the day Kate had told him her secret, and he'd let his pride respond, instead of compassion. Hurt that she'd pushed him away, irate that she'd kept her shame to herself for so long, he'd turned his back on her and walked away. That had been his gravest sin.

Why couldn't Kate see the truth? He cherished her. Determination rallied in him. He wouldn't give up, and in time, Kate would listen. She had to, because in Scott's eyes she was perfect. He loved her more than life and wanted her to know she was forgiven.

With Amber dancing around her legs, Kate put the last few items into the picnic basket.

"Are we ready, yet?" Amber asked for the hundredth time.

"When Phyllis and Darren get here. We're going with them."

Amber scurried out of the room, and Kate knew she was heading for the living room to press her nose against the picture window, to wait.

Her heart constricted. She had taken this little girl into her life and heart, not realizing how few experiences she'd had. Living with her grandmother, a woman who probably struggled to make ends meet and whose energy level was different from a young mother's, certainly put a different spin on Amber's life. Picnics, amusement parks and travel were all unknowns in Amber's world.

Kate carried the basket to the living room and chuckled when Amber turned from the window to ask, "Is it time, yet?"

Repeating the same message that they were waiting for Phyllis and Darren, Kate kissed the girl's head and returned to the bedroom for just-in-case sweatshirts.

In her own room, she sat on the edge of the bed, clutching her shirt and overcome with loneliness. Scott had phoned three times during the past week, but she'd let the answering machine take the calls. She'd never been that unkind before, not even to salespeople, but she couldn't bear to be patronized or to hear another apology.

Yesterday, she received a bouquet of flowers, saying he loved her and asking to see her. She'd withdrawn the card and clutched it in her hand, her fingers trembling, wanting to call him so badly, but feeling that theirs was a love that could never be.

Only a week had passed since she saw him. It seemed like years. Kate had adjusted to her solitary life before Scott came along, but once she knew him, his absence left a hole as deep and wide as the Grand Canyon.

Even Amber questioned her. "Where's Scott?" she had asked. Not once a day, but numerous times, Amber's question stabbed through her. "Why doesn't Scott come to see us?"

Kate had used every excuse, except the truth. He's working, he's busy, he's away. The truth hurt more than the lies.

"They're here!" Amber's piping voice sailed into the bedroom.

Clutching the two sweatshirts, Kate rose and hurried to the living room. She hadn't seen Phyllis since she returned two days earlier from the honeymoon, and she was eager to hear about their romantic Caribbean cruise.

Kate pulled open the screen door and waved to Darren, standing by the trunk.

"Ready?" he asked.

She nodded and laughed as Amber darted through the doorway and scurried to the car with a Frisbee and ball clutched in her hands.

Kate grabbed the shirts, basket and her shoulder bag, then locked the door.

"Are we ready?" she echoed as she reached the car. "We've been ready since you called." She tilted her head indicating Amber, who'd already climbed into the car.

With their gear packed, Darren pulled out of the driveway, and from the moment Kate asked the question, the conversation was filled with the sights and sounds of their five-day cruise.

At the park, trying to keep her emotions in check, Kate plastered a smile on her face, and whether playing Frisbee with an exuberant Amber or forcing herself to eat the picnic lunch, her heart wasn't in it.

After clearing away the paper dishes and storing the leftovers, Kate conceded to play blindman's bluff. When it was Kate's turn, Amber giggled so loudly that Kate could have found her in a flash. Instead, she held her hands in front of her, feeling the air, until she touched a muscled arm and, moving her hand upward, a man's jaw.

"Darren," she said laughing and pulling off her blindfold.

Kate's heart stopped. Scott stood in front of her, his face tired, his eyes serious.

"We need to talk, Kate. And you can't make a fuss."

Before Kate could respond, Amber was wrapped around his legs, bubbling with questions and nagging him to play.

He knelt down and gave her a bear hug. "I need to talk with Kate for a few minutes, okay? Then I promise I'll play whatever you want."

Though disappointed, Amber released his neck and stood aside while Scott captured Kate's arm.

"We'll only be a minute, Amber," Kate said, looking toward Phyllis and Darren and wondering if this picnic was part of a plot.

"We'll keep on eye on her," Phyllis called.

With Scott's arm linked to hers, Kate stretched her legs in long strides to keep up with him. He didn't speak, but she sensed his determination and knew that her protest wouldn't make a difference.

When they were out of sight of the others, Scott slowed. The sound of water floated on the air, and he guided her down a path to the stream. A large rock, like a granite bench, stood between the trees, and Scott stopped.

"Let's sit," he said, motioning to the huge stone.

"Phyllis told you we were coming here," Kate said, knowing the answer.

He nodded. "But Stoney Creek's a big park. I've been driving around for an hour looking for Darren's car."

"But why did—"

"I didn't know how else to corner you, Kate. I wasn't going to come to your house and stand outside while you refused to see me. That would confuse Amber and—"

"I understand," she said. "I haven't made it easy." Kate hesitated. But why had he dragged Phyllis into it? "What did you tell your sister, Scott? She acted the same as always, so she doesn't know about me. What did you tell her?"

He lowered his eyes. "I told her everything, Kate. I had to, so she'd understand what happened."

"But she's treated me—" Her senses spun with the awareness.

"Kate, the difficulty is yours. Yours alone. Phyllis felt only sorrow for what you went through all these years. She loves you like I do."

"You can't love me, Scott. That's why I didn't answer the telephone. You might try to forgive my past, but you won't forget."

"There's nothing to forgive, Kate...and nothing to remember."

"But you walked out," she said, her heart rising to her throat. "When I told you, you said you couldn't handle it."

"I couldn't handle the fact that you didn't trust me enough to tell me sooner—that you pushed me away no matter what I did. That's what I couldn't handle, Kate. But I had time to think. I remembered so many things I said about chastity that must have torn you to the core."

The memory jolted her.

"I finally realized what I'd done. We can believe in something," he said. "We can know what God wants and try to do it, but we can't sit in judgment of others. We can't flaunt our Christianity as if our faith makes us better than someone else. That's being prideful—and that's what I did."

"No, you were standing up for your faith," Kate said, fighting the tears that pooled behind her eyes.

"You're being a social worker. From your gut, Kate, admit it. I hurt you so many times. I'm so sorry."

He slid his arms around her as moist droplets ran from his eyes and clung to his lashes. "Forgive me, please."

Her mind swirled with longing and fear. Could he ever forget? Then as if guided by God her mind filled with scripture. "Forgive as the Lord forgives you. And over all these virtues put on love, which binds them all together in perfect unity."

"There's nothing to forgive," she said, her heart and arms yielding to his outpouring of love.

Scott stood and drew her from her rocky perch. With dewy eyes, he searched her face, and his voice nestled against her ear. "I love you, Kate. I have and always will."

His lips neared hers, and without hesitation, Kate tilted her face upward, meeting his mouth.

Happiness and completeness rolled over her in waves of emotion. The strength of his arms, the masculine scent of his skin mingled with a spicy aftershave, the gentle touch of his powerful hands against her face, each enveloped her in a warm, safe comfort. The secrets of her heart were laid open and bare...and still, she was loved.

Scott drew back, his eyes glinting with the sunlight that filtered through the trees. “Let’s do this right,” he said, edging her backward toward the rock.

The granite pressed against her legs, and she sank to the hard seat. Scott clasped her hands with one of his and knelt against the sun-speckled earth. With the other hand, he reached into his pocket and withdrew a black velvet box.

Kate’s heart soared. A nervous smile spread across her face.

“I’ve waited a long time to say this the right way.” He looked into her eyes. “Will you be my wife, Kate? I want...” He faltered. “Even more... I need you and Amber to make my life complete.”

Kate’s heart swelled, pushing the joyful words from her lips. “Yes, yes, yes. I love you with all my heart.” With tear-blurred vision, she gazed into his eyes. “I don’t have to speak for Amber. You know she loves you.”

He slipped the jeweler’s box into her hand. When she lifted the lid, the sunshine reflected in the diamond and sent prisms of sparkling colors into the air, but not nearly so beautiful as the love glinting in Scott’s eyes.

Chapter Twenty

Eleven Months Later

The stiff ruffled shirt pressed against Scott's Adam's apple, and he swallowed to control the engulfing emotion that pounded in his temples.

He looked down the aisle to the end of the white runner where Amber, in measured steps, concentrated on plucking pale-peach rose petals from a basket and dropping them along her path.

Her blond hair was swept into a cap of curls spilling over her crown where small white blossoms were tucked around the ringlets. Her pretty apricot-colored dress bounced below her knees as she headed toward him, an occasional shy smile flashing his way.

Filled with familial love, he looked at his parents dressed in their formal attire, their faces filled with pleasure and pride. Even Kate's parents had made the trip for the occasion, and across from his own folks, Kate's mother sat looking equally content.

At the front of the sanctuary, the bridal party waited, focusing on the end of the long runner. Phyllis and Darren standing nearby gave him a sidelong glance. Amazed, yet grateful, Scott looked at Kristin, Kate's matron of honor, a demure smile on her face. He thanked God that Kate's acceptance of his love had moved her to pardon her sister's flaws and to make amends in her own heart.

With the swell of the organ, the guests rose and turned toward the door. Scott caught his breath, seeing Kate on her father's arm walking toward him. Her ivory gown shimmered with sequins and beads, and a cascade of the same peach roses clustered with ivy and lace trailed down the folds of her gown.

Scott turned his eyes toward Amber, and seeing her loving grin riveted to Kate, he knew his world was complete.

Kate stared straight ahead down the long aisle. With trembling hands, she clung to her father's arm, washed in a sense of grateful forgiveness. Nothing was said, but her parent's arrival didn't knot her in fear as in the past. She welcomed them, bubbling with her own happiness, and she saw the change flow over into them.

With slow steps, they neared Scott who stood like a Titan, tall, strong and handsome. How many years would she have lived tangled in her own prison if Scott hadn't given her the key to open the door of her heart?

Scott stepped forward, taking her arm, and Amber nestled

at her side. Somewhere another young woman might be preparing to be a bride, a daughter Kate would never know, but today, with deeper understanding and familiarity with Scott's family, Kate was assured that God had guided her child to a loving home.

As they moved forward, Scott clasped her trembling hand in his. Feeling whole and cherished, Kate looked into Scott's love-filled eyes and listened as Pastor Ray read the joyful words, "Dearly beloved, we are gathered here in the presence of God and these witnesses to join this man and this woman in holy matrimony...."

* * * * *

Dear Reader,

Children's Haven is patterned after a real children's home in Oakland County. For many years I worked in the educational system as a licensed counselor, listening to individuals' heartaches, secret hurts and shames. As I wrote this story, I reflected on how we so often wish we could "rewind and erase" portions of our lives that cause us pain—incidents we wish we could hide and forget. But we cannot do that. Instead, like Kate, we bear the burden alone and allow our lives to be affected by the weight of our shame that depletes our trust, hope and spirit when we have a simple solution: give our sins and troubles to God.

I hope you enjoyed visiting with Kate and Scott, who with the Lord's help released their burdens and let Jesus carry their sorrow and shame. Then, following Jesus' command to "let the little children come," they opened their arms and hearts to little Amber. May God bless each of you as you trust and love one another during life's difficult moments, remembering that hope is an assurance when you trust in the Lord.

I appreciate and look forward to your comments and letters. Please look for my next Love Inspired novel.

Gail Gaymer Martin

Love Inspired
CLASSICS